BUILDING

BLOCKS

J.A. Armstrong

CHAPTER ONE

Governor Candace Reid sat behind her large maple desk attempting to massage away the throbbing in her temples. She looked over at the mountain of folders that stood stacked on the corner of her desk and closed her eyes. Defeat was never an option for Candace, not in any facet of life. Lately, she felt as if she needed forty-eight hour days to complete everything. And, at the moment, one thing was weighing on her mind above all others. Road repairs, bridge construction, community revitalization projects and budget initiatives all took a back seat to a little boy named Cooper. Candace lifted her glasses from the bridge of her nose and placed them in the drawer of her desk. She closed her eyes for a brief second, took a deep breath and lifted the phone receiver inches away.

"Hello?" a familiar voice came on the line.

"Hi."

"Candace?" Jameson asked. "Bad day? You sound beat."

"No, and yes, I am."

Jameson chuckled. "He's fine," she told her wife. "He's taking a nap."

"Fever gone?" Candace asked.

"Yeah. He really is okay. I promise," Jameson assured her wife.

"Maybe I should send my regrets to Senator Stevens."

Jameson sat down on the couch and shook her head. "No, you should not. He's okay. I think he is kind of looking forward to spending some time with Spencer and Marianne, to be honest," Jameson told Candace.

"I don't know."

Jameson smiled. Cooper had come into their lives unexpectedly and changed everything in an instant. Candace had met him on what was supposed to be a routine community stop to visit a shelter for women and children. Routine was not a word that ever equated to life for Candace and Jameson. Cooper had immediately and simultaneously stolen and broken both Candace and Jameson's hearts. He had already endured a lifetime of upheaval at the tender age of four. Moving from place to place, at times homeless with a mother who Candace was certain loved him, but had been unable to care for herself much less a child. Cooper's mother's sudden death had placed him into a cavernous system laden with millions of cracks—cracks that without someone's intervention he likely would have fallen into. That was not a scenario that either Candace or Jameson could live with. And so, again the Fletcher-Reid family grew by one.

For the last month, Candace and Jameson had endeavored to be certain that one of them was home every night at bedtime and every morning when Cooper would wake up. It was a commitment to make their son feel secure—to assure him that for more than a million sleeps and a million wakes he would find that home was with them. Tonight was supposed to be the first time that Cooper would fall asleep in someone else's care. It seemed ill-timed. Earlier in the week, Cooper had fallen prey to a nasty ear infection. Candace had made the decision to stay at the farmhouse for the first two days until she could no longer avoid the need for her presence in Albany. She had left late the previous night albeit reluctantly. Tonight, she and Jameson were expected to make an appearance at a benefit for the Democratic Party honoring Senator Martin Stevens.

"Candace," Jameson called over the line to her wife compassionately. "It will be okay."

Jameson heard the heavy sigh that escaped her wife and smiled again. She had not thought it would be possible to fall more deeply in love with her wife—she had. Candace had always been devoted to her family. Her devotion to Cooper did not surprise Jameson, but watching Candace with their son moved Jameson in ways she could not have expected. In truth, Jameson would have preferred to stay home with her family. She did feel it was time that Cooper experience the reality of life in their family. That reality would dictate that there would be times he would fall asleep and perhaps even wake up in a different house or with a familiar face other than his parents' making him breakfast.

"Are you worried more about Coop or Marianne dealing with all three of the kids?" Jameson wondered.

"Maybe a little of both. I can't help it, Jameson. I felt horrible leaving last night when he was still sick."

"I know," Jameson said. "He slept all night and he is much better today."

"I can send our regrets."

"You could, but you are not going to."

"Oh?"

"No, you are not. I bought a dress for this shindig of yours, you know?" Jameson told Candace.

"Shindig? How much time have you been spending with Pearl anyway?"

Jameson laughed. She was relieved to hear a bit of levity in Candace's voice. Candace always had a million people clamoring for even a moment of her time. Jameson continually marveled at the way Candace managed to juggle all of it and give attention to people's needs and opinions. At the end of any day, Jameson knew that Candace's top priority would forever be her family. She also was aware that Senator Martin Stevens had a unique ability to annoy the hell out of her wife.

"If you want, I can make a play toward the senator and spill a drink on him when he starts talking too much," Jameson offered knowingly.

Candace laughed. "You might need to keep a bottle at the ready in that case," she said.

"Ha! I knew it! Coop is your 'Get out of Jail Free' card!"

"You are a lunatic. And, I would never use our son as an excuse."

"Yeah, right," Jameson teased. She could tell that Candace was still apprehensive, but she could also hear Candace's light chuckling. "Come on; I haven't gotten to dance with you in a long time."

Candace smiled. "You liked that Inaugural Ball, admit it."

Jameson had enjoyed Candace's inauguration. She always loved to watch Candace at work. She loved the way people looked at her wife with admiration, and Jameson had enjoyed every moment of standing beside Candace. Jameson often recalled that evening. Her heart had soared at the sparkle in Candace's eyes as she had reached for Jameson's hand and led Jameson to the dance floor.

"I just wish I knew why they have to call them balls," Jameson deadpanned. "Don't they know by now that we are lesbians?"

Candace laughed again. "You are nuts."

"Feel better?" Jameson asked.

"I do," Candace said.

"I'll have him call you before I leave, okay?"

"When are you headed this way?' Candace asked.

"Marianne took Spence and Maddie to the store with her. She should be back in about an hour. I'll leave once she gets settled in."

"What kind of dress did you buy?" Candace asked.

"What kind of dress did *you* buy?" Jameson returned.

"Something you'll approve of," Candace said.

Jameson grinned. "Low cut, huh?"

Candace laughed again. "I'll talk to you in a bit."

"Is it?"

"Goodbye, Jameson."

"It is."

Candace kept laughing. "I'll talk to you."

Jameson hung up their call with a smile. "It is."

✂✂✂

"Jay?" a small voice called from the bottom of the stairs.

"Hey, Coop," Jameson greeted the little boy. Cooper rubbed his ear and yawned. "How's the ear?"

"It's okay," he said as he made her way to her.

"Itchy?" she asked.

Cooper shrugged and yawned again. "I'm firsty."

"And, still a little sleepy," Jameson observed. She scooped him up, and he wrapped his arms and legs around her gratefully. "Juice?" she asked him. He nodded.

"Jay?" he asked as she sat him at the table.

"Yeah, Coop?"

"Is Miss C. at work?"

"Yes, Cooper. Candace is at work. And, remember I told you that we have to go somewhere tonight for a while. You are going to stay here with Marianne and Spence, okay?" she said as she placed a cup of juice in front of him. Cooper nodded and gulped down the juice. "Whoa," Jameson laughed. "Slow down, buddy."

"Sorry," he said softly.

Jameson smiled at Cooper. He had a tendency to apologize for everything no matter how much she and Candace sought to reassure him. She kissed his forehead. "You don't have to be sorry, buddy. I just don't want you to choke. Okay?" Cooper nodded. Jameson winked at him. "Want some more?" she asked knowingly. Cooper nodded again. "A man of few words today, huh?"

Cooper giggled. "Jay?"

"Yeah, buddy?"

"Me and Spen can watch a video?" he asked.

"I'm sure if you ask Marianne politely, she will let you two watch a video, yes."

"Addlin!"

"Aladdin," Jameson corrected him with a smile. "How come you like that one so much?" she asked him curiously.

"Genie is funny," Cooper explained. "He's blue!"

Jameson laughed. "He is blue. I wonder why he is blue?"

"He's a genie, Jay."

"Oh, of course," Jameson said. "Are all genies blue?"

"I don't know. He's da only one I know," Cooper said before taking another sip from his juice.

"Well, that makes sense."

"Jay?"

"Hum?"

"When will Miss C. be home?"

Jameson smiled. Cooper adored her, and she knew that, but he had a unique bond with Candace. And, Jameson could not deny that she sensed he still held his share of insecurity that one day Candace might leave too. Candace also sensed it. Jameson sat down beside Cooper again.

"Candace is at the big red house, buddy. And, tonight we both have to go to a big dinner. We will both be home late when you are already asleep. But, we'll be here when you wake up tomorrow, okay?" Jameson watched as Cooper considered her answer. "Would you like to call her?" Jameson asked. Cooper nodded a bit sheepishly. "We can call her, Coop. She loves when you call her."

Cooper brightened measurably. He watched Jameson as she retrieved her phone and pressed the screen a few times. "Hey, Susan. Yeah. I promised to have Coop call."

Cooper smiled when Jameson handed him her phone. "Say hello when she answers, so she knows it's you," Jameson whispered. Cooper sat up in his chair and waited.

✕✕✕

"No, that is not going to be adequate, Bill."

"Candace, be reasonable," Bill DeGrasso implored his boss.

"I hate that word, Bill."

"We don't have enough support in the legislature for broader measures," he said. "It's too costly for their taste. You know they do not want to cut to spend."

"Governing is all about where to cut so that you can spend where it's needed," Candace said.

"I'm telling you that the votes are not there."

"And, I'm telling you to get me the votes to pass it," Candace said flatly just as the phone on her desk beeped.

"Yes, Susan?" Candace answered. She smiled. "Excuse me for a minute," she told the group gathered in her office. "Put it through…. Hello?"

"Hi, Miss C.," Cooper's voice came across the line.

"Well, if it's not my favorite caller," Candace said. She heard Cooper giggle. "How are you feeling?"

"Itchy."

"Itchy?" Candace asked. "Your ear is itchy?"

"A little," Cooper answered. "Jay let me call."

"I'm glad she did."

"Jay gave me juice," Cooper told Candace.

"She's good like that."

"Yep. Me and Spen are gonna watch Addlin tonight."

"Aladdin again?" Candace chuckled. "You like that genie."

"Yep," Cooper agreed. "He's funny like Jay. Only Jay's not blue."

Candace laughed. "No, she's not."

"'Cause she's not a Genie, else she'd have to live in a bottle too."

Candace shook her head in amusement. She could only imagine the expression on Jameson's face as she listened to Cooper. "You are feeling better."

"Yep. Are you at work?"

"Yes, sweetheart, I am," Candace said. She waited but Cooper said nothing.

"I miss you," Cooper whispered.

Candace closed her eyes. "I miss you too, Cooper. I will see you tomorrow, though…. Cooper?"

Cooper handed Jameson the phone and ran out of the kitchen.

"Candace?"

"Jameson? What happened?"

"I don't know," Jameson confessed with a sigh. "Hold on, okay?"

Candace took a deep breath and waited.

"Coop?" Jameson called up the stairs.

Cooper came running back with his stuffed frog and handed it to Jameson. He stretched out his hand for the phone. Jameson handed him the phone with a puzzled expression.

"Jameson?" Candace called over the line.

"It's okay, Miss C.," Cooper answered.

"Cooper?"

"I gave Jay Fwoggie. He knows da way," Cooper told Candace.

Candace choked back a wave of tears. Spencer had given Cooper his stuffed frog months earlier before Cooper had moved in with Candace and Jameson. Cooper had gotten upset at the end of one of their visits, and Candace's grandson had given him the frog to cheer him up. Spencer had told Cooper that Froggie knew the way back home. It had not escaped Candace's notice that the stuffed frog went everywhere with Cooper. The knowledge that Cooper had thought to give Jameson the frog now told Candace two things—Cooper loved them, and Cooper was afraid they might not find their way back.

"That was very sweet, Cooper," Candace praised him. Cooper smiled. "We'll take good care of him, I promise."

"If you get lost, he can find me," Cooper said.

Candace closed her eyes. "Cooper, we will always find you. I promise, sweetheart."

Cooper kept smiling. "Okay," he said happily. "I love you."

"I love you too, Cooper," Candace said. "Let me talk to Jay, okay?"

"Okay!" he said. He handed Jameson the phone. "Can I draw?"

"Yes, Coop, you can go to your room draw," Jameson told him. She watched him scurry back up the stairs.

"That's it," Candace said. "I'm canceling."

"No, you are not."

"Jameson..."

"No," Jameson said firmly. "You know I am right."

Candace did know that Jameson was right. "I don't have to like it."

Jameson chuckled. "I don't like it either. We have to do this. You know it, and I know it."

"I hate that he is still so afraid."

"So do I, but I think I have an idea."

"Oh?" Candace inquired.

"Yeah, but I need you to trust me."

"Why do I not like the sound of that?"

"Do you trust me?" Jameson asked.

"You know that I do."

"Then trust me!" Jameson said.

Candace sighed. "I do."

"Good. I will see you in a couple of hours."

"Yes, you will," Candace agreed.

"Go do governor things," Jameson instructed her wife.

Candace chuckled. "I'll try."

"There is no try, Candace. You've seen the movie."

Candace rolled her eyes. "Goodbye, Genie."

"You love me in blue," Jameson said.

"Guilty as charged. But, please stay out of the bottle."

Jameson laughed. "I'll try. Please try not to worry, okay? I've got this."

"It would help if you would grant me three wishes," Candace joked.

"We'll see just how low that dress is."

Candace laughed. "Lunatic. See you in a bit," she said as she set the receiver down.

"I am positive that I don't want to know," Shell told her mother.

Candace grinned. "Cooper has an infatuation with genies."

"Uh-huh," Shell said.

"Now, about this bill," Candace shifted gears.

✖✖✖

Jameson took a step into the bedroom that she and Candace shared at the Executive Mansion and froze. Candace had her back turned to Jameson. Her head was forward slightly as she attempted to fasten the clasp of her necklace. Jameson closed the short distance between them and let her hands fall onto Candace's shoulders. "Let me," she whispered.

Candace looked into the full-length mirror to capture Jameson's gaze. She smiled at the gleam in Jameson's eyes.

"It is low," Jameson whispered.

"Not that low," Candace replied.

"You look stunning," Jameson said in awe.

"You are biased."

"Not so," Jameson said.

Jameson often wondered what Candace saw when she looked in the mirror. One thing that Jameson did know; she was hardly the only person who looked at Candace in awe. As confident as Candace was in the political arena, she could be incredibly self-effacing when it came to comments or compliments on her appearance. Candace may have possessed confidence; she also possessed humility. For Jameson, that made Candace infinitely more attractive. Jameson fastened the clasp on the string of pearls and leaned into Candace's ear again. Candace closed her eyes as Jameson's warm breath caressed her neck.

"You take my breath away," Jameson said emotionally. "Every time I look at you."

"Jameson."

Jameson turned Candace to face her. She leaned in and kissed Candace lovingly. "You always have and you always will," Jameson said.

Candace smiled and cupped Jameson's face in her hands. "I love you."

Jameson returned Candace's affectionate gaze. "Good thing since you are stuck with me."

"Happily," Candace replied.

"Still worried, huh?" Jameson guessed. Candace pursed her lips and shrugged. "Did you worry this much with The Stooges?" Jameson asked curiously.

"Sometimes," Candace answered honestly. "They did not have Cooper's past."

"I know," Jameson said.

"You still didn't tell me your secret plan."

Jameson took a deep breath. "I gave Froggie to Marianne to put in his bed after he falls asleep."

"Jameson, if he wakes up he will..."

"He will realize that we don't need any help to find him."

Candace groaned. "I know you are right. I just...Jameson, things do happen."

Jameson smiled reassuringly. "And, a stuffed frog can't change that. Trust me."

"I do," Candace said with a kiss. "You know; you are an amazing mom already."

"I have good teachers," Jameson responded.

"And a little magic," Candace winked at her wife, noting Jameson's navy blue dress. "Maybe you really are a genie."

Jameson shrugged playfully. "I've been known to grant a few wishes."

Candace laughed and kissed Jameson on the cheek. "You truly are a bit touched, you know?"

Jameson smiled. "Are you ready for this..."

"Shindig?" Candace finished the thought. "I would rather be home watching Aladdin with the boys if you want to know the truth."

"Ah, but then I wouldn't get my wish."

"Genies get wishes too?" Candace teased.

"Why not? We work hard."

"Uh-huh. So, what's this wish, Genie?"

"I would like to dance with the most beautiful woman at the ball."

"That could prove difficult," Candace said seriously.

"Why?"

"Well, I am married to her, and I don't particularly care for watching anyone else in her arms."

Jameson grinned. "Who's touched?"

"God willing Coop will be asleep when we get home."

"Ah, I see your agenda now, Governor."

"Well? Are you open to negotiations?" Candace flirted.

"I look forward to your presentation," Jameson replied.

"Nut," Candace chuckled.

Jameson held out her hand. "Come on, Governor, take me to the ball."

CHAPTER TWO

"**G**enie is funny," Cooper giggled. "Like Jay."

"Jay Jay is silly," Spencer agreed.

"Jay is your Nana too?" Cooper asked innocently.

Spencer shrugged. "Yeah."

"How come you don't call her Nana?"

"Dunno. She's Jay Jay. Nana is Nana."

Cooper considered the answer and then shrugged too.

"Okay, you two," Marianne's voice carried through the room. "It is past time for bed."

"One more time?" Spencer asked his mother.

Marianne raised an eyebrow at her son. "It was one more time last time," she reminded him. "Now, come on. Cooper is still getting over his ear infection." Marianne smiled at the boys. "Spencer, say goodnight to Cooper, so I can give him his medicine and get him to bed too."

"Five more?" Spencer pleaded.

"No more," Marianne put her foot down gently.

Marianne held back her laughter. Spencer and Cooper were joined at the hip whenever her mother and Jameson were able to stay at the farmhouse. They were less than a year apart in age and reveled in their friendship. Marianne had noticed that things often went more smoothly when Cooper visited while Candace and Jameson were at work. Spencer was used to having his Nana and his Jay Jay's undivided attention. Cooper's entrance into their family had changed that dynamic a bit. For Marianne, it had proved an unexpected Godsend.

Marianne had been struggling since her husband Rick's death. Life as a single parent had never been in her plans nor on her radar. They were supposed to do this to-gether. They were supposed to grow old together and chase Spencer and Maddie's children. In an instant, everything had changed. Some days Marianne still struggled to get out of bed. She had found herself pondering lately how much Cooper had helped with that struggle. Suddenly, Spencer began to seek out his mother more frequently for both companionship and comfort. In some ways, Marianne understood that her son had no intention of sharing her the way he now had to share his Nana and his Jay Jay. Beyond that, Candace and Jameson were spending more time in Albany, and Spencer naturally began to gravitate closer to his mother.

Cooper and Spencer were different children. Spencer was playful, talkative and often silly. Cooper was quiet, thoughtful and generally followed Spencer's lead, even though Cooper was five months older. Marianne often noticed the way people looked at Spencer and Cooper, who didn't know them. They seemed to puzzle over the pair of boys. Spencer was fair-skinned with blue eyes and almost a full head shorter than his best friend. Cooper's bronze skin and light brown eyes stood in stark contrast to Spencer's appear-ance. Normally, Spencer would be chatting, and Cooper would be listening. Without warning, the two would break into a bout of laughter. They fit. It was not lost on Marianne the kin-ship that the two boys shared. Spencer had lost his father suddenly, and Cooper had lost his mother. In both cases, the boys had found solace and safety in the loving care of her mother and Jameson. Marianne pondered that reality often since Cooper's arrival.

Spencer looked at his mother with a doe-like expression and Marianne rolled her eyes. "That might work on Jay Jay," she said. "I know it doesn't work on Nana, and it does not work on me either. Come on, brush your teeth and into bed."

Spencer groaned and pulled himself up dramatically. "You and Nana are stickwers."

Marianne chuckled. "Sticklers and yes, I am. Thank you."

Spencer marched out of the room and Cooper looked up at Marianne curiously.

Marianne smiled. "Well, Coop, seems you and me have a date with some crackers and pink goo."

"Ick," Cooper whispered.

"How about if I sweeten the deal with a cookie instead?" Marianne suggested. Cooper brightened. "Okay, you go down and wait for me in the kitchen. I promise I will be right there once Spencer is in bed."

"Okay," Cooper agreed.

Marianne watched him walk out of the room. She heard her son talking through a mouthful of toothpaste a few seconds later. "I be wake, Coop," Spencer told his friend.

Marianne shook her head. "No, you will not," Marianne called down the hallway. "If you are going to plot you might want to spit out your toothpaste so you can whisper." She heard Cooper giggle and his footsteps hit the stairs. Marianne made her way to the bathroom and leaned on the doorframe. She raised an eyebrow at Spencer, who grinned. Marianne shook her head. "Well, at least, he isn't hiding in the cabinet," she thought.

✗ ✗ ✗

"Martin," Candace greeted Senator Stevens.

"Governor. I hear congratulations are in order," he said. "Can't say I imagined a stork in your future."

Candace smiled. "Neither did I," she confessed.

"J.D.," the senator greeted Jameson. "How is life with hi-ho here?"

Jameson liked Martin Stevens. She had never quite understood what it was about the man that irritated Candace so much. He had always seemed genuinely friendly and he had always made a point to engage Jameson. Even as she smiled at the senator, she could feel Candace's aggravation growing.

"Hello, Senator," Jameson said. "Life is good, thank you."

"And, parenthood?" he asked.

"Less stressful than this," Jameson joked. She heard Candace mutter. "It's an adventure," Jameson answered the senator politely. She looked at Candace. "If you will excuse us, the governor promised me a dance," Jameson said.

Senator Stevens tipped his head in acknowledgment. "Of course, who wouldn't want Governor Reid on his dance card?"

Candace's contrived smile almost made Jameson laugh.

"Nice to see you, Martin," Candace said politely as Jameson led her off. Candace muttered something under her breath again and Jameson chuckled.

Jameson guided Candace onto the dance floor and put her hand around Candace's waist. "Want to tell me why you hate the senator so much?"

"I don't hate him," Candace said. Jameson's bemused look made Candace chuckle. "I don't particularly care for his company."

"Yes, I know. What I don't know is why."

"Jameson, you know how you love to look at those Where's Waldo books with the boys?"

"Yeah?"

"That's Waldo."

Jameson started laughing as she swayed with Candace. "I didn't see a striped anything. And anyway, what do you have against Waldo?"

Candace chuckled. "I mean that he is a lurker."

"Waldo?"

"No, Senator Stevens, you nut."

"What do you mean—lurker?" Jameson asked cautiously, beginning to see the light. "Candace? Did he make a play for you?"

Candace smiled. "Would it matter if he did? You know that no one's overtures will ever work, no matter what they pretend to offer."

Jameson's jaw tightened. "Can I drop that drink on him now?"

"No," Candace chuckled.

"He's the reason they still call these things balls," Jameson muttered.

Candace laughed and brought their lips together for a brief kiss. "Thank you."

"What are you thanking me for?"

"I think you know."

Jameson placed her cheek against Candace's. She did know. Candace needed to get away for a night. She needed a night outside of her office and away from sniffling toddlers, children seeking advice and impromptu phone calls about everything from the weather to worker strikes. This may not have been the ideal setting, but it was a world that Candace enjoyed, even when it sometimes frustrated her. And, Candace needed a dose of playfulness and laughter. She needed to take a breath.

"Just so you know, your dance card is full this evening," Jameson whispered.

Candace tightened her hold on Jameson and closed her eyes. "Good to know."

Marianne walked into the living room with a small cup of juice for Cooper. Cooper was studying her thoughtfully and she wondered what was going through his mind.

"Are you feeling okay, Coop?" she asked.

Cooper nodded and accepted his juice. "Thank you."

"You're welcome," Marianne replied, taking a seat next to him. Cooper looked up at her again. "What is it, Coop? Are you worried about something?"

Cooper shook his head. "Miss C. is Spen's Nana."

"Yes," Marianne said.

"And you're Spen's Mommy."

"Yes," Marianne said. "And, Spencer's Nana is my mommy."

Cooper seemed to consider Marianne's answer almost as if he were trying to solve a riddle. "Jay is his Nana, but she's still Jay."

Marianne was beginning to follow Cooper's line of questioning. She smiled at him compassionately. "Yes, J.D. is Spencer's Nana too because she is married to my mom."

Cooper took another sip from his cup. "Jay is your mommy?"

"Well, I guess she is in a way, but because she's not too much bigger than me, she's more like my friend. Like you and Spencer."

"Miss C. is my Nana?" Cooper tried to put the pieces together.

Marianne smiled at him. "No, Coop," she began. Cooper frowned sadly. "Cooper," Marianne gently took his hand. "Do you know what it means to be adopted?"

"I get my sleeps here."

"Yes," Marianne agreed. "You do get your sleeps here. You get your sleeps anywhere my mom and J.D. are. Do you know why?" she asked. He shook his head.

Marianne nodded. She was aware that both her mother and Jameson had tried to explain things to Cooper. Cooper was only four. It was not an easy concept for him. And, Marianne could understand why. The Fletcher-Reid family was a unique blend of personalities and relationships. If Marianne had tried to label everyone, she was certain that she would have gotten lost in the process. For Marianne, like her siblings, labels were not all that important. They had all been given the privilege of growing up with both of their parents in their lives even if they had divorced. The Fletcher children had always accepted Pearl as their grandmother just as they had their biological grandparents. They had never needed to ask questions. Things were as they were. Cooper was different. He was old enough to understand many things, but still too young to put the pieces of a complicated puzzle together by himself. And, he needed to know where he fit in that puzzle even if he couldn't completely make sense of all of its pieces.

"Coop," Marianne began again. "You know that this is your family now, don't you?" she asked.

Cooper nodded. "I get dis as home. Jay says. Miss C. says I get ta stay fo-eva."

Marianne smiled. "That's right, Cooper. That's what being adopted means. It means that someone wants you to be part of their family. You get to be a part of this one," she said. Cooper nodded. "It means that Mom and J.D. wanted you to be just like me and Shell and Jonah."

"Old?" he asked.

Marianne laughed. "No, sweetheart, not old. They want you to be their son, just like I am their daughter." Cooper wrinkled his brow and concentrated for a minute.

"It means, Cooper that Miss C. is your mom, just like she is mine."

"My mommy's dead."

Marianne took a deep breath. "I know, sweetie."

"She was sick."

"Yes, she was," Marianne said. "But, remember you asked me if J.D. was my mom and I said that in a way she is?" Cooper nodded. "Sometimes, Cooper we get a second chance. You don't have to call J.D. or Mom, Mommy if you don't want to. They will understand. Just like I don't call J.D. Mom either," Marianne tried to explain.

Cooper pursed his lips. He stayed quiet for a minute. "I can have two mommies?"

"You can," Marianne promised.

"But dat's fwee," Spencer counted on his fingers. "Fwee is too many."

"No, sweetie. Three is not too many," Marianne told Spencer. "You have one mommy in heaven to watch over you, just like Spencer's daddy watches over him. And, you can have two mommies who are right here."

"Does Spen get two daddies?"

Marianne smiled genuinely. "Someday, he might get another daddy. I don't know."

"You're Spen's Mommy."

Marianne nodded again. "That's right. And, Miss C. is my mommy."

"And Miss C. is my mommy?"

"Yes, Cooper. I think she would like that."

"And Jay is my mommy?"

"And J.D. can be your mommy too, yes," Marianne said. Cooper sighed. Marianne pulled him into her lap. "And, do you know what that means, Cooper?" she asked. He shook his head. "That means you are my little brother," she told him. Cooper's eyes grew wide. Marianne chuckled. "Yeah, pretty cool, huh?"

"Like Mads and Spen?"

"Yes, just like Maddie and Spencer. Only, I still have to be old," she said as she tickled his stomach. Cooper laughed. Marianne pulled him closer and kissed him on the head. "I love you, Cooper," she said.

"I love you too," he said as he snuggled into Marianne.

"What do you say we spend a little brother-sister time and have another cookie while Mom is still out," she whispered conspiratorially. Cooper grinned and nodded. "Okay,"

Marianne said lifting Cooper up with her. "Now, this is our secret, okay?" Cooper nodded.

"Mawianne?"

"Yes, Coop?"

"I get two sisters?"

"Yes, you do—me and Shell, but I am cooler," Marianne said. Cooper giggled. "And, you get a brother too. But, I am still cooler. I have better cookies," she told him. Cooper's smile brought tears to Marianne's eyes. "Come on, little brother. I need one of Grandma Pearl's chocolate chip cookies."

�;✕✕

Jameson opened the front door and held it for Candace. Candace took a couple of steps forward and stopped cold.

"What is it?" Jameson asked.

Candace shook her head and Jameson followed her gaze ahead in the faint light. Marianne and Cooper were snuggled against each other on the sofa, both sound asleep. A plate with cookie crumbs sat beside two cups on the coffee table. Jameson wrapped her arms around Candace and laughed.

"Kids," Jameson joked.

Candace inhaled a deep breath, overcome by the sight a short distance away. Cooper was smiling in his sleep and she could not recall the last time she saw such a relaxed expression on her daughter's face. Candace couldn't help but be curious about the scene. She clasped Jameson's hands for a moment and then pulled away.

Jameson watched as Candace made her way to the sofa and brushed the hair out of Marianne's eyes. She didn't need to see Candace's face to know the expression it carried—love—that was the expression.

Candace reached for the afghan that was draped over the back of the sofa and began to cover up the sleeping pair. Marianne moved slightly but did not wake. Candace bent down and kissed Cooper on the head. She started to walk away and was stopped by a small voice. Candace turned back. She could not make out what Cooper had said.

"Hi, sweetheart. Did you fall asleep with Marianne?" Candace asked him.

Cooper rubbed his eyes and nodded. He caught a glimpse of the plate and looked at Candace guiltily. Candace followed Cooper's line of sight and then looked back at him.

"Cookies, huh?" she asked. Cooper nodded. "I see. Did you have a bad dream?" she asked.

Cooper shook his head. He looked past her to Jameson, who was slowly approaching. "Hi," he said.

"Hi, Coop," Jameson replied. "Tired?" she wanted to know. He nodded. "Do you want to stay here with Marianne or go upstairs?" Jameson asked him.

Cooper looked at Marianne and smiled then he looked back at Candace sheepishly. Candace raised her eyebrow. "Are we in twouble?" Cooper wanted to know.

Candace tried not to laugh. "Why would you be in trouble, Cooper?"

"It's 'asposed to be a bwofer, sister secwet," he whispered.

Candace became slightly unsteady and Jameson placed her hands firmly on Candace's hips to anchor her.

"A secret, huh?" Jameson intervened.

"Yep. Cause Mawianne is da cool sister."

Jameson started laughing. She could only begin to imagine what had led to that statement. Whatever it was, it had left the two people on the sofa feeling happy and contented. That was obvious.

"Shhh...Coop, she'll tell Shell," Marianne mumbled.

"Tell Shell what?" Jameson wanted to know.

Marianne pried one eye open and looked at her mother and Jameson. She pulled Cooper to her. "That I am the cool sister," Cooper grinned ear to ear. "Right, Coop?" Marianne said.

Cooper giggled. "I get two sisters too."

Jameson held Candace tighter. "Yes, you do," Jameson said, sensing that Candace could not speak.

"And, I can have fwee, Mawianne said."

"Three?" Jameson inquired.

"Mommies."

Jameson felt Candace's body jerk and held her close as Candace covered her mouth to try and stifle her tears. Marianne looked at her mother and smiled.

"Why's you cwing?" Cooper asked. "Are you sad, Mommy?"

Candace shook her head. Jameson answered. "No, Coop. No one is sad at all, I promise. We just missed you."

"Fwoggie knows the way, Mommy," he said to Jameson.

Jameson felt her heart lurch in her chest. She looked at Marianne.

"Yes, Froggie knows the way," Marianne said. She pulled herself up and Cooper clung to her. "I think, Coop now that your Moms are home, maybe we should all head to bed, huh?"

"Dey're your mommies too."

Marianne hugged Cooper. "Yes, they are. So, why don't you go say hello to them? I'll bet they missed you."

Cooper sprang up and into Candace's arms. Candace looked at Marianne and smiled gratefully. "Gosh, you are getting heavy," Candace said. "How many cookies did you eat?" she teased him, mostly to rouse herself from the emotional tide sweeping her under.

Cooper giggled. "Only two."

Jameson smiled. "Well, I don't think Mommy is carrying you up the stairs in those heels, buddy. How about if I give you a piggy back?"

"In that dress?" Candace asked.

"Yeah, why not?" Jameson countered.

"Jameson, you are worse than the kids."

Cooper giggled again.

"Honestly," Marianne said. "Come on, Coop. I'll take you up. Then Mom and J.D. can hobble their way after us. They are older."

"Hey!" Jameson chimed. "Six years, Marianne. Six years."

"Yeah, Momma. I know," Marianne laughed. Cooper could not stop laughing. "We'll see you upstairs in a minute," Marianne said.

Jameson looked back at Candace. "You all right?"

"What on earth happened tonight?" Candace wondered.

"Sounds like your daughter had a heart to heart with Cooper," Jameson said.

"Jameson, I've tried explaining…"

"Well, Governor, maybe he needed that to come from someone else. Maybe from his sister and not his mom."

Candace closed her eyes. "He called you Mommy."

"He called you Mommy too," Jameson said.

Candace smiled. "I wasn't sure he would ever…"

"Neither was I."

"Are you okay?" Candace asked.

"Yeah, I just didn't expect it to feel like that, I guess," Jameson said.

"Like what?"

"Like the first time I kissed you. That's the only thing I can compare it to. Like, I don't know…Like…"

"Like coming home," Candace murmured.

"Yeah, like that."

Candace nodded. "Jameson…"

"I know. I'll get him," Jameson promised with a smile. Candace nodded her thanks. Jameson leaned in and kissed her gently.

"I'm just going to clean this up," Candace said.

Jameson nodded her understanding. Candace needed a minute to compose herself. "Don't take too long, okay?"

"I won't," Candace promised.

✂ ✂ ✂

Jameson hit the top stair, stopped and took a deep breath.

"He's waiting for you. He found Froggie," Marianne said. Jameson nodded and closed her eyes. "J.D., are you all right?" Marianne asked, reaching out for Jameson's arm. Jameson nodded again. "It's a bit overwhelming the first time you hear it," Marianne said knowingly.

Jameson opened her eyes and let out her breath slowly. "Honestly, I never imagined anyone would ever call me that, not even Cooper."

"Thought you'd get away with being Jay Jay forever, huh?"

"Actually, yes."

Marianne smiled. "Can I say something?" she asked carefully. Jameson nodded. "He needs to say it. He needs you to be that, J.D.—both you and Mom. And, truthfully, I think you both needed to hear that too."

Jameson looked up at the ceiling and blew her breath out forcefully. "I'm so afraid I will screw it up."

"Welcome to the club," Marianne said.

"Seems to me you did a pretty good job tonight."

"Easier being a big sister than Mom. He goes back to you."

"Yeah, I know," Jameson said. She looked down toward Cooper's room. "Can you..."

"I'll go and check on Mom."

"You know, Marianne," Jameson started. "I don't know how everything happened tonight. I do know how much seeing you two together meant to her."

"I know," Marianne said. "We'll trade for a few. You take care of Coop. I'll take care of Mom."

Jameson chuckled. "Good luck."

"Why? Think I'm in trouble for the cookies?" Marianne cracked.

"Not unless you raided her stash of fortune cookies."

"I don't have a death wish, J.D.," Marianne replied as she made her way to the stairs.

Jameson took another deep breath before entering Cooper's room. She looked around and smiled. Cooper loved trains and dinosaurs. Neither Jameson nor Candace had yet to discover what started his fascination, but Cooper loved anything and everything that had to do with trains or dinosaurs. He still struggled to pronounce basic letter sounds at times. But, ask Cooper about a dinosaur and he would take his time to sound out the most complex names and he knew them all. His bedroom was a reflection of his four-year-old passions.

The walls of Cooper's bedroom were painted a light green highlighted by a border of marching dinosaurs—not the cartoon ones. Those would not do. When Jameson and Candace had taken him to pick things out for his room, Jameson had suggested a cartoon dinosaur wallpaper. Cooper had shaken his head and pointed to the border that depicted life-like dinosaurs roaming in a forest. He had a large wooden train set that ran the length of the far wall and two shelves filled with toy trains. In this case, cartoonish passed his inspection. As long as it was a train, it was welcome in Cooper's room.

"Hi, Coop."

Cooper looked at Jameson and frowned. "You fo-got Fwoogie."

Jameson nodded and took a seat next to Cooper on his bed. "Froggie wanted to stay with you, I think. And, see? We're home now. We'll always find you, Coop."

Cooper looked at Jameson again. "Can I have fwee?"

"Three?"

"Mommies."

Jameson smiled. "Yes, Cooper, you can," she said. Jameson watched as Cooper studied her. "Why do you look sad?"

"Can you be?"

"Can I be what?" Jameson asked.

"My mommy."

Jameson pulled Cooper to her and held him. "I would love to be if that's okay with you."

"Miss C. too?"

"Yes, Coop. Does that make you happy?" Jameson asked.

Cooper nodded. "It means I can keep you."

"Aw, Cooper, yes, you can keep us and we will always be here for you."

"For all my sleeps.... til I'm old."

Jameson chuckled. "You got it. How about if you come and sleep with us tonight? Would you like that?" Cooper nodded. "Do you want to bring Froggie?"

"No, I don't need him."

Jameson smiled. "Okay. Come on, let's go hog all the covers before your Mommy comes up," Jameson suggested playfully. Cooper giggled and took Jameson's hand. "Make sure you get the squishy pillow," Jameson whispered.

Marianne reached the bottom of the stairs and was surprised to find Candace sitting on the sofa. "Mom?"

Candace looked up and smiled. She looked back at her lap and Marianne noticed that Candace was thumbing through an old photo album. "Come sit," Candace said.

Marianne took a seat next to her mother. It was obvious that Candace had been crying. "Mom?"

"Do you know that I remember the very first time you tried to say Mommy?" Candace began.

"Still?" Marianne teased. "That was a long time ago."

"That's something you never forget."

"I know. I sometimes wonder if I will remember things with Maddie the way I do with Spencer. The way things have been, I…"

Candace reached over and put a comforting hand on Marianne's leg. "You will. I thought the same thing after Lucas—when Shell came. God, I was so afraid that I would forget something important."

"I don't know if I could have survived that," Marianne admitted. "Losing Rick has been, well, there are still days I want to crawl back under the covers. If that had been Spencer or Maddie…How did you…"

"I had you," Candace said honestly. "Honestly? The first month, I felt this stab of guilt every time I held you, almost like I was betraying him somehow. But, then you would look up at me and I would fall in love with you all over again. It kept me sane. You kept me sane," Candace told her daughter. "Shell was a surprise. I was terrified the day she came. She was this faint blue color. I thought for a moment," Candace stopped herself and gathered her emotions. "But, she was healthy and she was lively."

"Even then," Marianne joked.

"Even then," Candace agreed.

"Do you ever stop missing them?" Marianne asked.

"No, you don't, not ever, but you learn how to live and how to love again," Candace told her daughter. She was curious about what had transpired with Cooper. "Marianne.... Cooper..."

"He asked if you were his Nana too," Marianne explained. Candace nodded. "I think he just was trying to put the puzzle together; you know? Who we all are and where he fits."

"I do know. What did you say?"

"I explained that you are Spencer's Nana because you are my mom."

"That led him to..."

"No, not that so much as me explaining that you and J.D. wanted him to be just like me and Shell and Jonah—your son. I think when I told him that meant he was my little brother, that's when he sort of understood, at least, a little."

Candace smiled softly. "You know, you are an amazing woman, Marianne. You don't see it, but I do."

Marianne pushed back her tears. "I haven't felt very amazing lately."

"Grief is a bitch," Candace said bluntly surprising Marianne. "It is," Candace said. "It makes you question a lot of things, even yourself."

"I wouldn't have made it this far without you and J.D."

"You would have," Candace disagreed. "Because you would have had no choice for Spencer and Maddie but to do it alone. And, Marianne, you are much stronger than you think. You don't have to do it alone just like they will never have to do it alone."

"Neither does Cooper," Marianne reminded her mother.

"Not anymore, but he still feels that," Candace said knowingly. "He's done it alone in so many ways for his whole life," she said.

"Mom, he is a lucky kid to have you and J.D."

"He's a lucky kid to have you and your inferior brother and sister," Candace quipped.

Marianne snickered. "Hey, I just told him the truth. I've had more time to gain cool sister status," she said. Candace smiled. "I envy him a bit," she admitted quietly.

"Why?"

"I love dad; you know that."

"I do know that," Candace said. "You two have always been close."

"Yeah, but more because I never gave him that choice and I know that, Mom. I smothered him, not the other way around."

"Your father adores you, Marianne. He may not show it the same way, but he adores all of you. He may never have adored me, but he loves you. Don't ever doubt that."

"I know that, but he's...Well, even with me..."

"He has a hard time expressing his love and his pride. Yes, I know."

"You know, Mom, not many kids get what Coop has now."

"What's that?" Candace asked.

"Two parents who love each other as much as they love their kids," Marianne said. Candace smiled. She knew that Marianne was right. "I know that I was not very supportive when you and Jameson were first..."

"Marianne, that was a long time ago."

"Yeah, well, I feel the need to say this so just let me, okay?" Marianne said. Candace nodded. "I'm glad that you decided to adopt Cooper. It's helped me too—with the kids, I mean."

"I know."

"And, you know, I think you and J.D. would have missed out on a lot if you hadn't, so would Cooper," Marianne said. Candace sighed. "Mom? What is bothering you?"

"Nothing is bothering me," Candace assured her daughter. "I never imagined being called Mommy again, Marianne. I know Jameson has never envisioned that. It's just a little…"

"Overwhelming?"

"You could say that, yes," Candace said. "In a way, it is more so with Cooper."

"How so?" Marianne asked curiously.

"Well, you got me as your mother. You didn't choose me."

"I would choose you again and again," Marianne said emotionally.

Candace pulled Marianne into her arms. "And, I would choose you."

"But, I think I understand what you are saying."

"You do?" Candace asked.

"Yeah. When Coop was asking me questions—when I told him I was his sister and his eyes lit up? It was like I had given him a sleigh full of presents all at once. I chose him. I think he understood that on some level. And, he chose me. I had to get the cookies or I would have lost it completely," Marianne told Candace.

Candace kissed Marianne's head and placed her head on her daughter's. "Thank you."

"You're welcome," Marianne said. "But, I think it's me who should be thanking you, Mom—you and J.D. I owe you both."

"You don't owe us a thing. You might not realize it, but Jameson loves you too."

"I realize it," Marianne said. "I'm glad you found her."

"Me too, sweetheart. Me too."

CHAPTER THREE

"You look tired. You okay?" Dana asked Candace.

"I'm fine," Candace promised.

"No offense, Candy, but I'm not buying it."

Candace smiled half-heartedly. She had been feeling less than energetic for a couple of days. Until the last hour or so she had chalked it up to fatigue. Candace was beginning to wonder if she was coming down with something. Other than the occasional head cold, Candace had not been sick in years. She imagined that she had built up some type of immunity to common germs from interacting with so many people all the time. The pace of the life dictated that she learn to cope with the occasional ache and pain, upset stomach and all too often headache. She took care of herself, but Candace had always seemed to possess a natural defense against sickness—save morning sickness.

Candace groaned. "Just not feeling a hundred percent."

"No offense again, but not looking it either," Dana observed. "Maybe we should table this meeting until you are feeling better."

"No," Candace replied firmly. "Some pain reliever and a steady supply of water and I will be fine. This has waited too long already."

"Look, I know that this infrastructure plan is your passion..."

"It's not my passion, Dana. It's a long overdue necessity. You know that as well as anyone. Don't start sounding Bill's warning bells. We may not get everything, but we damn well are going to get most of it. We can't afford not to."

"Candy..."

"Don't you Candy me," Candace said. "We are behind the curve and you know it. Not to mention that this state has been playing Russian Roulette with everything from bridge and rail repair to water safety. There are more ticking time bombs in this state than I can count. And, do you know what will happen when one of them detonates?"

"Yes," Dana said. "But, Candy, you are facing a Republican majority legislature this year. They do not want to spend—least of all on anything *you* suggest."

"That's the media talking, Dana. None of these people want to be hung out to dry when something happens, and trust me on this—it will. The public supports the initiatives. That's why they elected me. I still have friends on the other side here."

"Yes, you do. But, Candy no one wants to give you more power than you already have in this party."

"Fairytales again? Dana, I am governor. I've been governor for less than six months. I'm not running for office."

"Yet."

"Dana," Candace warned. "I did not seek this office as a stepping stone and you know it."

"I may know it, but that doesn't mean other people believe it, Candy. I love you, but sometimes you put entirely too much faith in people."

"What is that supposed to mean?"

"It means that not everyone possesses your conscience. That's what it means."

Candace nodded. "I'm no saint, Dana."

"No, but you do care."

"And, so do most of the people that serve this state. Now, let's change this topic before I lose my patience."

"Okay. CNN called. They want to do a piece on the adoption."

"No."

"Candy..."

"No."

"It's a human interest story."

"I said no," Candace repeated.

"People are curious."

"Cooper is not a curiosity."

"You had to realize that this would stir up interest. Come on, Candy be..."

"Don't say that word," Candace held up a finger. "I hate that word. I am perfectly reasonable and the answer is no."

"You are impossible!" Dana said in exasperation. Candace was always firm, but the last few days Dana had found the governor to be downright disagreeable at times which was completely out of her character.

Candace raised her brow. "Are you through?"

"No, I am not. What has gotten into you?'

Candace took a deep breath to calm her rising anger. "Dana, I am not parading my son in front of the press. Cooper is just starting to adjust."

"You can't avoid this forever."

"Maybe not, but I can avoid it for now, and I intend to."

"You know; it might help with..."

"Stop," Candace warned. Her blood pressure was rising fast.

"Mom?" Shell called into the office. "Bill's outside waiting for you to head to the Capitol."

"I'll be right there," Candace told Michelle.

Michelle nodded and headed back out the door. Candace grabbed the suit jacket hanging behind her desk and stretched. She stopped and covered her eyes for a moment and grabbed the corner of her desk to steady herself.

"Candy?"

"I'm all right, Dana. Let's get this done."

Dana followed Candace out of the office, watching her closely. Candace was not acting like herself and Dana wanted to know why. "Maybe it's time to call J.D.," she thought.

✕ ✕ ✕

"Hey, Mom. Thanks for coming up," Jameson greeted her mother.

"You think I would miss a chance to spend time with my grandson? No way. I'm glad you had to work," Maureen Reid replied. "J.D.? Is something wrong?"

"I'm worried about Candace."

"Why? Stress at work?"

Jameson shook her head. "No, it's not that. She always has stress at work. I know that she's worried about this new infrastructure plan. She's been up at all hours on calls. But, that's not new."

"Yes, but she hasn't had to do that in a long time with a toddler vying for her attention," Maureen pointed out.

"True, but it's something else. She was tossing and turning all night last night."

"It's probably just everything."

Jameson forced an unconvincing smile. "I don't think she was feeling well last night."

"You think Candace is sick?"

"I'm not sure, but I think it's possible. And, you know her, she won't slow down. Being sick is the one thing she probably would not tell me," Jameson said.

"J.D., if you are that concerned, talk to her."

"I tried this morning. I almost lost my head."

"That doesn't sound like her."

"Exactly."

Maureen sighed. "Well, you said she didn't sleep and doesn't she have that big meeting today? She was probably just over-tired and focused."

Jameson wasn't buying it, but she decided a change of topic was in order. "Where's Coop?"

"Laura stopped by to drop off some pictures for you and Candace. He wanted to show her his new train."

Jameson laughed. "She'll never get out of that room once he starts show and tell."

"It's good practice for her," Maureen laughed. "Besides, once J.J. wakes up she'll have an excuse to leave."

"That's one way to look at it. I'll bet you got a lesson in trains too," Jameson chuckled.

"Yes, I did and I learned a great deal," Maureen said. "He's very bright, J.D."

"Yes, I know," Jameson replied proudly. "It's hard for him, I think, going between the two houses."

"Well, I think as long as you two are here, he will be fine."

"Yeah, well...I think we are going to be *here* most of the time now," Jameson said.

"Oh? Is this your idea or Candace's?"

"It's too much for all of us—the back and forth," Jameson said.

"Uh-huh."

"It is."

"You think it's too much for Candace," Maureen surmised. "Be careful, J.D., she knows what she can handle."

"No, she doesn't always know what she can handle, Mom. She will try to handle everything. That's Candace."

"Jameson...."

Jameson shook her head. "I know what you are going to say. We'll spend some weekends there, holidays, part of the summer. This is what is best for all of us right now. Cooper needs a place to land. We've talked about it. It's just..."

"You both miss Spencer and Maddie."

Jameson nodded. "And home. That will always feel like home."

"Well, I can understand that. Maybe you just need to find a way to make this feel more like home to you."

"Thing is, Mom when we are here it is harder for her to relax. I just..."

"J.D., you are all adjusting—to more than one thing. Give it a little time. Trust me on this. It's something I know a little about."

Jameson smiled at her mother. This was a topic her mother understood intimately. Maureen Reid had grown up in Brooklyn, the daughter of a New York City beat cop. She had met Jameson's father, Duncan when he had been working on a neighbor's house with his uncle's company. Maureen had fallen for the charming construction worker overnight. She had often told Jameson that she had no idea how swiftly her life would change.

Duncan and Maureen came from different worlds. Maureen was in her first year teaching at a local elementary school at the time. Duncan lived in Ithaca, and when the job his uncle had hired him for had ended, the couple had struggled to find adequate time to spend together. Weekend visits were taxing and infrequent. Six months into their courtship everything changed. Maureen discovered she was pregnant. Two months later, she and Duncan were married and Maureen found herself living in what at times seemed to be a different world.

"How did you do it?" Jameson asked.

"What?"

"You missed the city."

Maureen nodded. "That I did. I missed your Gran and your Grampa. I missed your uncles and my cousins. I missed home," she said. Jameson listened. "Then, one day I realized that home was with your father and Toby. You know, he offered to move us to Brooklyn and take a job with his uncle's company."

"You never told me that," Jameson replied.

"Well, he did."

"You didn't want to go?" Jameson was surprised.

"I did, but the fact was I could teach anywhere when I decided to go back. He was just starting to build his own business. I wasn't going to take that away from him. And, what I wanted was changing daily."

"You mean Toby."

"Yes, and you and Doug—as it turns out," Maureen said. "Never thought I'd have three kids."

Jameson laughed. "Never thought I'd have any."

"See what I mean?" Maureen said. "Things change. It's just a house, J.D."

"Not really, Mom."

Maureen smiled. "I know. It's memories. That's what makes it home. You'll make memories no matter where you are, and you will have stress no matter where you go. A lot has changed. Take a breath."

"Sage advice," Jameson said.

"Oh, no, sage implies old. I am not old."

"No, Mom, you are definitely not old," she commented with a wink.

"I love your wife, you know. She gives you the proper perspective."

Jameson laughed. Candace and her mother had become close friends over the last few years. They shared a great deal in common. Both had raised three children, both loved being grandmothers, both women had a passion for politics and both loved Jameson deeply.

"You can't have her," Jameson joked.

Maureen picked up a throw pillow and put it to good use. Jameson caught it and threw it back. She was about to continue their banter when her phone rang. She answered it still in the midst of laughter. "Dana? What? Where..."

Maureen watched as Jameson's face fell and swiftly drained of all color. She made her way to her daughter's side and grabbed Jameson's arm. "J.D.? What is it?"

"Candace..."

⚒ ⚒ ⚒

Candace sat at a long wooden table in a conference room at the State Capitol. She listened to the Senate President and Majority Leader talk over each other from across the room. Candace understood passionate debate better than most people. She had learned early on in her political career how to listen. Over the years, she had heard many pundits analyze her demeanor and style. Often, people asserted that her unwillingness to raise her voice corresponded to her gender. Candace would not have denied that being a woman in politics required a unique savvy. Women who became heated in public discourse were typically regarded as emotional whereas their male counterparts were described as forthright. That was a fact that anyone in politics and media understood. Candace's calm exterior, however, was rooted in something else.

As a child, Candace had followed her grandfather everywhere. Governor Stratton had been Candace's hero. She observed him up close and at a distance for many years, mentally taking notes. He had been an affable and jovial man. She had seen him more than a few times engaged in a battle of wills. She'd listened outside his office door at raised, frantic voices. Seldom had she ever heard him join in that frenzy. He would wait if he could until the shouting dwindled and then he would speak. Candace could only recall a few times she had ever seen him lose his patience. When debate became nothing more than yelling or discourse took a personal turn, Governor Stratton would intervene with a forceful "enough!" That would effectively end all discussion, and the governor would begin his summation of the meeting. The first time Candace had run for office, she had asked her grandfather if he ever felt compelled to shout back.

"Every day," he had laughed. *"Sometimes, Candy, I'd like to strangle those SOBs."*

Most days, Candace just wished she could put the windbags that permeated her professional life in time-out. At times, some of her peers and even her staff behaved worse than her children ever had. And, every once in a while, even Candace Reid felt the pull to choke the sense into someone. When those moments arose, she always recalled what her grandfather told her.

"Let them yell as loud and as long as you can. Sooner or later they forget what they were screaming about in the first place. When someone is screaming, Candy it's because they want to be right. When someone is listening, it's because they want to do right. Listen until you can't listen anymore. People have a hard time arguing with a listener."

Candace scratched her brow as Senator David Conlon chastised Majority Leader Gordon Ellis. She cleared her throat and instantly both men turned their attention to her. Candace closed the portfolio in front of her, removed her glasses slowly and looked back across the table at the two men.

"Are you finished with your playground antics now?" she asked calmly. Before either man could protest she continued. "So, from what I was able to discern in the last ten minutes, you are concerned about the cap on budget spending with these increased infrastructure measures."

"Governor Reid, there is no feasible way to cap the budget with the plan your office provided," Senator Conlon said flatly.

Candace pursed her lips and nodded as if she were considering his statement seriously. "David," she began evenly, "Did you read the proposal?"

"Everyone heard the proposal for months before you took office," he snapped at her.

Candace cocked her eyebrow and tipped her head. "So, in other words, and you correct me if I am wrong, your familiarity with this proposal comes from two-minute soundbites in a stump speech from my campaign. Is that right?" she challenged him.

He bristled slightly. "That is not what I am saying. You committed to a cap on the budget increase..."

"I also committed to addressing a sagging infrastructure."

"We have a comprehensive plan that your predecessor..." Conlon began.

"We must have different definitions of the word comprehensive. Twenty-six percent of our bridges are functionally obsolete, David," she said.

"They are structurally sound. You know that rating has nothing to do with safety..."

"I do know. It has to do with productivity and, David...Let's just put it all out there. While we may not be looking at structural compromise in terms of a collapse, we have several of the most traveled bridges in this country that do not have adequate safety features for drivers. We either compromise capacity or we compromise their safety. Functionally obsolete—there is a reason for the term. I did serve as the ranking member of the Environment and Public Works Subcommittee for eight years," she reminded him. "I might have a handle on the terminology. Let's not even begin to address our water issues—contamination risk, delivery problems. You want to explain to your constituents why their children end up with lead or arsenic in their water? How about when we compromise critical rail lines? Would you like to address why people cannot get to work? We cannot afford not to do this. It's not political, gentlemen, it is a necessity."

"All due respect, Governor Reid," Gordon Ellis said. "But, where are we going to get the funds for this? To say it is ambitious..."

Candace offered the men a taut smile. "First, I would suggest that you *read* the proposal, not give it to an intern to interpret for you," she advised. "Then I would suggest you review the addendum with the surveys of the sites that the proposal targets over the next six years. Do that and we will have a starting point. I suspect most of your questions will be answered. And, I will expect that at our next meeting you have a better command of the facts," Candace said as she rose from her seat with everyone following quickly.

"I am sitting here because the majority—the vast majority of your constituents saw fit to put me here," Candace said before continuing forward. "Largely, I might remind you because of these issues. If you would like to take this down a partisan road, I am all too happy to oblige. I would caution you on that path. It doesn't generally end well for anyone," she said. She extended her hand to both men. "Have a good weekend, gentlemen."

Candace walked through the solid oak doors that Bill DeGrasso held open for her.

"Jesus, Bill she didn't flinch once," Ellis commented.

Bill DeGrasso smirked. "Did you actually expect her too?"

Michelle brushed past her boss and picked up her pace to catch up with her mother who was walking beside Dana. "Mom..."

Candace shook her head as they entered the elevator. "If there is one thing I hate more than ignorance it is arrogance. Ignorance you can cure, arrogance...."

Dana snickered at Candace's perturbed and frank observation.

"Mom, do you think maybe we should have tried to leverage..."

"Your mother is right," Dana said flatly.

Candace exited the elevator and headed toward the main foyer of the Capitol.

"Mom, where are you going?"

"For a walk," Candace said. "I need some air."

"Governor," Sergeant Evans, Candace's police escort stopped her. "At least, let me check out the front if that is your plan."

Candace nodded her understanding and smiled at the young officer genuinely. Drew Evans was one of her favorites on her security detail. He was young and she could tell that he saw the assignment as an honor and not an inconvenience. He attempted to be stoic, but Candace often caught him chuckling at her and Jameson and he was extremely personable with Cooper and Spencer. She trusted him implicitly.

Michelle took a deep breath as a school tour group headed toward their location. "Mom, maybe…"

"It's fine, Shell. Get Drew back here. He will not be happy if I start shaking hands without him."

Candace spent the next fifteen minutes talking with everyone in the tour group, taking pictures and thanking them for taking the time to visit the capitol. This was the part of her chosen career that Candace thrived on—pressing the flesh. It was something people had always questioned her about throughout her career. Many politicians preferred to stand behind a podium and expound their worth and wisdom. Candace's preference had always been to speak with the people she sought to represent—any age, any place, anywhere.

"Thank you so much for talking to all of them," a young teacher said to Candace.

Candace smiled at the young woman. "Thank you for stopping and letting me speak with them. And, thank you for what you do," Candace said sincerely. The young woman blushed and Candace's smile broadened. "My daughter was a teacher until she decided to follow me on this crazy ride to Albany," Candace explained. "And, my mother-in-law taught history for thirty years. I have an affinity for teachers."

"Well, thanks for saying that," the teacher replied. "The kids will really have something to make this trip memorable for a long time."

"Trust me when I tell you that they will forget all about meeting me long before they forget about you," Candace said honestly.

"Governor," Officer Evans called to Candace.

"You take care," Candace said as she grasped the young woman's hand. "It seems I am being herded again," she whispered good-naturedly. She allowed Officer Evans to lead her toward the front door.

"Governor," he whispered in her ear. "Are you all right, ma'am?"

Candace kept pace with the young man as he placed a protective arm around her. She smiled at him as best she could. "Just tired."

Officer Evans moved to the front door and nodded to a security guard who held the door open for Candace. Candace stepped out of the door toward the sunlight and stumbled uncharacteristically.

"Governor Reid," Officer Evans caught Candace and urged her gently. "Please..."

Candace looked at him and closed her eyes. The pain in her chest and shoulder were making it increasingly difficult for her to stand on her own power. Michelle picked up her pace and reached out for her mother as Candace wavered again.

"Mom?"

Candace closed her eyes and took a ragged breath. The color had drained from her face.

"Mom?" Michelle called to Candace nervously. She looked helplessly at Officer Evans just as Dana caught up with them.

"Let's get you inside. I'll get EMS," Officer Evans said to Candace quietly.

"No. Get me to the car," Candace ordered.

"Mom!"

"Call for the car to meet us out front, Drew," Candace repeated. "That is not a request," Candace said as her hand instinctively found its way to her chest. Michelle's fear was palpable. "I'll be all right, Shell."

"Mom, please.... Let Drew call an ambulance."

"No."

"Candy," Dana pleaded.

"Dana, just help me to the car—please. The last thing we need is a press nightmare over nothing."

"Candy," Dana lowered her voice as she and Officer Evans helped Candace as discreetly as possible down the Capitol steps. Candace's breathing was labored and Dana noticed that Candace grimaced with each breath. She leaned into Candace's ear as they reached the car. "You are going to the emergency room—now."

Candace climbed into the back seat and nodded her agreement.

"Drew," Dana grabbed the officer's hand. "Call it in. I think she might be having a heart attack."

"Already done," he assured her as he climbed into the front seat with the officer driving them.

"Dammit, Candy," Dana scolded her friend.

Michelle crawled into the seat next to her mother. She took one look at her mother's face and felt a wave of fear course through her, unlike anything she had ever known. Candace could barely speak. She squeezed Michelle's hand and closed her eyes.

"Call Jameson," Candace murmured. Michelle took a shaky breath.

"I'll call her," Dana said.

CHAPTER FOUR

Jameson ran into the emergency room and straight into the back of Officer Drew Evans.

"Ms. Reid," he took hold of her arms gently.

"Where is she?"

"They're with her right now," he said calmly.

"Drew?" Jameson pleaded.

"I don't know. Michelle went in with her," he explained. "Let's get you in there," he said leading Jameson to the desk.

Jameson heard the conversation a few inches away, but it sounded to her as if it were being spoken in some alien language. Her heart was pounding with such enormous power that she thought she might fall over. Never in her life had Jameson Reid been so utterly terrified.

"J.D.," Dana's voice called for Jameson's attention. Jameson looked at Dana. Dana smiled. "She'll be okay," Dana tried to reassure Jameson.

"Dana, what happened?"

"I don't know. You know her, she will stretch herself until she's ready to snap."

Jameson's jaw tightened. "Heart attack? Dana, what..." Before Jameson could finish her thought, she felt Officer Evans guiding her away.

Time slowed down for Jameson as she followed Officer Evans blindly through a long corridor. She had the fleeting wonder if this was at all how Candace had felt when she had come home to find Jameson in the hospital over three years ago. Jameson's stomach was churning violently. She needed to get her emotions under control. The last thing she wanted was to show Candace her fear. Jameson concentrated on her breathing, attempting to steady her nerves as they approached the room Candace was in. She closed her eyes for less than a second. When she opened them, she saw Michelle standing in the corner of the small room. Two doctors were standing over Candace's bed. Jameson felt a gentle nudge into the room. Michelle caught sight of her and smiled weakly.

"J.D...."

One of the doctors turned and Jameson captured Candace's gaze. Candace held out her hand to Jameson and Jameson moved to accept it.

"I'm all right," Candace assured Jameson.

"What happened? Is it," Jameson began.

"We don't know yet," one of the doctor's answered the obvious question. "The good news is that it is not her heart."

Jameson heard her breath escape in a dramatic rush. Candace tightened her grip on Jameson's hand.

"Dr. Everett," the man introduced himself by extending his hand. "This is Dr. Brewer," he explained. Jameson nodded dumbly. Dr. Everett smiled compassionately. "It could be any number of things. Given the degree of pain, gall bladder seems the most likely culprit."

"Gall bladder?" Jameson asked.

"Well, we need to do a few more tests. Let's get those done and then we will go from there, okay?" he suggested.

"Thank you, Dr. Everett," Candace said.

Dr. Everett winked at the governor. "I'll be back shortly. The pain medication should help."

"The pain is much better anyway," Candace told him.

"That's good. Let's just find out why you've been in pain at all, shall we?" he suggested. "See you in a bit," he repeated. He made his way out of the room with Dr. Brewer following on his heels.

"I'm going to go and let Dana know you are not dying," Michelle told her mother.

"Good idea," Candace agreed. She tugged on Jameson's hand. "Hey…"

Jameson looked at Candace. Her eyes were brimming with tears. "Dana thought you were having a heart attack. I thought you were…"

Candace sighed. "So did I," she confessed.

"Candace…"

Candace pulled Jameson down to her and kissed her lips softly. "I'm okay."

"If I lost you, I…"

"I'm right here," Candace promised.

"You weren't feeling well last night or this morning," Jameson stated the obvious.

"I thought it would pass."

"Candace," Jameson's voice dropped to a whisper. She took a deep breath and looked at her wife. "How are you feeling now? No bullshit either."

Candace chuckled. "Better. Not great, Jameson. Better."

Jameson nodded. "I need to call my mother and let her know," she said absently.

"How's Cooper?" Candace asked.

"He was having Show and Tell time with Laura."

Candace smiled. "What did you say to him?"

"Nothing," Jameson said. "I wasn't about to scare him unnecessarily."

"Jameson?" Candace called gently. Jameson was trembling.

"I walked upstairs. He didn't know I was there. He was smiling so proudly, showing Laura everything. All I could think was if you…"

Candace directed Jameson to look at her. "I understand. You should call your mother and let her know that I am fine."

"Um, you are not *fine*. You are lying in a hospital bed. That is not fine."

Candace grinned. "Jameson, are you mad at me?" she teased in an attempt to relieve Jameson's tension.

"Mad?" Jameson responded without thinking. "I'm scared shitless!"

Candace sighed. She remembered the call to inform her that Jameson had been rushed to the hospital. For nearly thirty minutes, Candace had run through every possible scenario in her mind. No matter what possibility she considered, her thoughts inevitably had turned to one reality—she did not want to imagine her life without Jameson in it. Her concern had lingered for longer than Candace had ever intended to share with Jameson. She could see that same fear plainly now in Jameson's eyes.

"I'm sorry," Candace apologized.

"No," Jameson shook her head. "I'm sorry."

"For what?"

"For not seeing how much you needed to slow down or, at least, for not making you see it."

"As I recall, you tried," Candace admitted. She jostled herself slightly in the bed and winced in pain.

Jameson leaned in and kissed Candace on the forehead allowing her lips to linger. "I love you so much."

Candace reached out and pulled Jameson down to her, tenderly holding Jameson's face in her hands. "I'm sorry that I scared you," she said. "I love you too, Jameson. More than I think you will ever realize," Candace promised. Jameson let out a relieved sigh and placed her forehead against Candace's.

"Sorry," Michelle poked her head in the room.

Jameson closed her eyes. Candace's hands held Jameson in place, her thumbs tenderly stroking Jameson's cheeks to comfort her.

"It's all right, Shell," Candace said without allowing Jameson to move. "You are not getting rid of me that easily," Candace whispered to Jameson. "We have too much to do." Jameson chuckled and bit her lip. "Do you hear me?" Candace asked. Jameson nodded against Candace. "Good."

Jameson reluctantly pulled away. Candace wiped an errant tear from Jameson's cheek and smiled at her. Jameson cleared her throat. "I'll let you talk to Shell for a minute while I call Mom. I'll try to catch Pearl. I'll be back in a few minutes," she promised. With one last kiss to Candace's lips, Jameson took her leave.

"I'll be here," Candace joked.

"Yes, you will be," Jameson agreed as she left.

"Mom," Michelle made her way to Candace's bedside.

Candace sighed regretfully and embraced her daughter as Michelle broke into tears. "It's okay," Candace reassured her. Candace attempted to comfort her daughter. It took longer than Candace would have expected for Michelle's tears to subside enough that she could speak.

"I thought you were going to die," Michelle choked on the words.

"Not today, sweetheart."

"Not ever," Michelle continued to cry.

Candace held Michelle close. "Shell…"

"Mom, you didn't see you."

Candace laughed. "No, but trust me I was pretty scared there for a few minutes."

"It's not funny," Michelle snapped.

"Shell…"

"Mom, why didn't you say something?"

"I honestly thought that it would pass," Candace said. "I don't have time to be sick."

"Well, I don't have time for you to be dead," Michelle returned. Candace raised an eyebrow. Michelle chuckled. "Okay, I get it. You're not dying. But Mom, I saw J.D.'s face just now. I know how she feels. I still can't stop shaking."

Candace smiled. "I'm sorry, sweetie."

"Right now, I don't care about bridges or schools or the state," Michelle said. "I'm sorry, but I don't."

Candace closed her eyes and rubbed them gently. "Shell, you don't mean that."

"Yes, Mom—I do. I do mean that."

Candace opened her eyes just as Jameson walked back into the room.

"She does mean it," Jameson said. "I know exactly what she means." Jameson walked up beside Michelle and put her arm around her. "I know that you think you have to be everything to everyone all of the time," Jameson continued. "I don't mind sharing you with the world. That is part of who you are. I won't risk you because of them. Please don't ask me to."

Candace nodded. "Message received," she murmured.

Michelle leaned in and hugged her mother. "I want you here when I get married. When I have kids."

Candace saw the opening and took it. "Is this your way of telling me I need to save for another wedding?"

Michelle laughed. "Not yet," she promised. "I don't want to do it without you."

Jameson looked at the floor. Michelle was incredibly sensitive, but she was positive she had never seen her step-daughter so shaken up. Jameson wondered if Candace truly understood how much their family loved and needed her. She hoped that this scare might be enough to remind Candace that as strong as Candace might be, no one was invincible. Jameson also knew that it was in Candace's DNA to try and handle everything without burdening anyone else. Pearl had told Jameson that Candace had always been that way. Being a mom, being a daughter, being governor—being caretaker was as much a part of Candace as her blue eyes or her laughter. Jameson would never seek to change that. She loved Candace for the woman that Candace was. Jameson, however, hoped that Candace might begin to realize that there were people who needed to care for Candace as well. Love was about giving. And, sometimes Candace got so caught up in that reality that she lost sight of the fact that there were people who needed to give to her as well.

Jameson squeezed Michelle's shoulder. "Do me a favor, Shell?"

"If I can," Michelle said as Candace wiped a few tears from Michelle's cheeks.

"Go and wait for Grandma. She'll feel better if she hears that the governor here will survive to torment her another day from you rather than from a stranger or even Dana."

"Grandma Pearl doesn't know Mom's okay?" Michelle's eyes widened.

"I tried to call her. She's probably playing Mario Andretti on the way here," Jameson said.

"What did you tell her?" Candace wanted to know.

"Only that you were on your way to the hospital," Jameson said. "That was enough."

Candace groaned. "She's going to kill me."

"When she finds out that you are not dying and also not slowing down? Yep, I would count on it," Jameson agreed.

"Maybe they will take me for tests before she gets here," Candace said.

Jameson and Michelle both laughed. It was a needed moment of levity that was laced by honesty.

"I'll catch her before she blows the place up," Michelle promised. She leaned in and kissed Candace on the forehead. "I love you, Mom," she whispered.

"I love you too," Candace said, giving Michelle a reassuring wink.

"I saw Dr. Everett in the hallway. He says they are sending you for an ultrasound to see if anything is hanging out in there that shouldn't be," Jameson told Candace. She grinned evilly. "You're not pregnant, are you?"

Candace's jaw fell open and then swiftly closed again. She swatted Jameson, glad to see Jameson in better humor. "Lunatic."

"Mmm...Relieved," Jameson said. "I'm just relieved."

"Me too."

"He did say that you might need surgery," Jameson commented.

"Yes, I know. He mentioned that before you came in the room," Candace said. She watched as Jameson's complexion grew slightly paler. "If it is what he thinks, it's routine. I'll be fine."

"Yeah, well, I don't have to like it," Jameson said.

"No, you don't. Trust me; I don't like it either. Did you get your mother?"

"Yeah. Listen…I asked her to let Coop know I was going to bring him down."

"Jameson, is that such a good idea? This place can be…"

"Well, you are the governor. I have it on good authority that they are moving you to a private room in a few minutes," Jameson said. "Drew and Dana have apparently been pretty vocal about it," she snickered.

"And, the press?" Candace asked wearily.

"Oh, no…No, you don't even think about any of that," Jameson warned.

"Jameson, it's a reality that…"

"That you are not to give a single thought to. I mean it, Candace. Right now, I don't give a shit about you being governor or what anyone thinks," Jameson said sternly. "I care about my wife and that is it. Shell and I are on the same page. The rest of the world can go to hell as far as I am concerned."

"Jameson…"

"Don't you dare Jameson me," Jameson warned Candace gently. "No worrying about anything but whatever the doctor says you need to do."

"What about Cooper? I don't want him to be frightened."

"Neither do I. I think we both know that not seeing you will unsettle him more than seeing you here. He expected you to be home tonight."

"I know," Candace agreed. "I must look lovely right about now."

Jameson chuckled. "Afraid that hair of yours will scare our son?" she teased.

"Funny."

"I thought so," Jameson replied. "I'll wait to see what the doctors have to say. Then we can decide what to tell Cooper. Okay?" Jameson offered. Candace nodded and closed her eyes. "Not feeling so great, huh?" Jameson guessed. Candace shook her head. Jameson kissed her on the cheek. "Maybe I should let you get some rest before they start prodding you again," she said. She felt Candace grab her hand.

"Just sit with me," Candace asked.

Jameson felt her heart rate rise dramatically. Candace was a master at painting on a strong face. Banter aside, this incident had clearly shaken Candace. Jameson was sure that only two people would be able to see the evidence of Candace's unease—Jameson and Pearl. Jameson slid a chair over next to Candace and stroked Candace's hand as she held it.

"You know, it's okay to let it out," Jameson offered knowingly.

"Not now," Candace said.

"Okay."

"Jameson?"

"Yeah?"

"Thank you."

"You never have to thank me. Just do me a favor and don't leave me if you can help it, okay?" Jameson said. Candace nodded.

Jameson watched as Candace began to drift off to sleep. She took a deep, cleansing breath and released it slowly. Emotional exhaustion was threatening to pull Jameson under. As much as she wanted to close her eyes, she could not divert them from Candace's sleeping form. Part of her feared that if she did, somehow Candace would be gone. She had heard the doctors. She could tell that while cautious, they felt confident that whatever had caused this episode could be handled without any major long term effects. Jameson knew that no matter how much reassurance anyone granted, she would not be able to rest easy until Candace was home safely. She lifted Candace's hand to her lips and kissed it lovingly. "There's too much ahead of us," she said. "Too many things we still have to do." Candace squeezed Jameson's hand. Jameson wondered if Candace had heard her.

"Close your eyes, Jameson," Candace directed her wife. "I'm not going anywhere. I promise."

Jameson obliged Candace's request and let her eyes fall shut. "I'll hold you to that."

"I never make promises I don't intend to keep," Candace said. "Never."

✂ ✂ ✂

"Shell?" Pearl spoke into the phone

"Grandma..."

"I just found a place to park this damn car," Pearl griped.

"Grandma, where are you? Jameson tried to call you."

"What happened?"

"Nothing. Mom is fine."

"Your mother is *fine*? Your mother is most certainly not fine, Michelle. Your mother has gone to the hospital four times in her life—all for the same reason, and I am positive that is not what drove her here."

"I mean, it's not her heart. She's in a private room now. Where are you?"

"Where do I need to be?" Pearl responded.

Michelle couldn't help but chuckle. She could hear the worry and the irritation in Pearl's voice.

"Shell?"

"Meet me in the lobby. I will go up with you."

"I'm almost there. Michelle..."

"I'll tell you everything on the way up. I promise."

Dana sat in a small conference room at the hospital trying unsuccessfully to beat a throbbing headache into submission. She had waited to make a statement until Candace had definitive news. The New York press sometimes reminded Dana of a rabid pack of wolves. Candace was always a curiosity. She had been the first openly lesbian senator. She was the first lesbian governor, who happened to be the granddaughter of a legendary New York lawmaker. Candace was a woman with a wife twenty years her junior who had just adopted a child almost the same age as her grandson—a biracial child at that. And, she was a woman thought to be headed on a direct course for a run for The White House in three years. Candace's life was under a microscope. The slightest blip on the radar about the popular yet often controversial governor put Dana's job into overdrive.

"Dana?" Michelle opened the door. "She wants to talk to you before you make the statement."

Dana nodded and blew out a frustrated breath.

"You okay?" Michelle asked.

"Not really."

Michelle stepped into the room and shut the door. "What is it?"

"Lawson Klein," Dana made her reply.

"Marianne and Jonah are on their way here," Jameson walked into Candace's room.

"They don't need to come here, Jameson."

Pearl lifted both eyebrows at Candace.

"What?" Candace asked.

"You know perfectly well what," Pearl replied. Candace rolled her eyes. "Candace Stratton!"

Candace jumped slightly. Jameson chuckled at the wounded look on Candace's face. Jameson had never heard Pearl reprimand Candace by her maiden name. She was sure by the expression on Candace's face that it had not happened in a long time.

"I'm perfectly fine," Candace said.

"You are perfectly delusional is what you are," Pearl said flatly. "Don't you look at me like that. They don't need to come here? They're your children. Of course, they need to come here. You're perfectly *fine*? Perfectly fine people are not in a hospital awaiting surgery."

"You know what I meant," Candace bit back sharply.

"Yes, and you know exactly what I am about to say."

"Pearl..."

Pearl help up her hand. She turned to Jameson. "Jameson, would you give me a moment with Candy. Please?"

Jameson smiled and nodded. "I'm actually going to step out for a bit and go pick up Cooper."

"If Marianne is coming here, who is going to watch the kids? Your mom doesn't need to..." Candace began.

"Stop worrying," Jameson said. "Believe it or not, we can figure it all out on our own," she told Candace. "I'll see you in an hour or so," she said. Jameson looked at Pearl. "Make her behave."

Pearl smiled as Jameson left the room and then turned back to Candace. "Did you hear your wife?"

"Pearl..."

"Did you? Because, honestly, Candy you need to listen to what she just said."

"How exactly am I not behaving? I'm glued to a bed!"

"No, you're not, but that can be arranged," Pearl told Candace. Candace grumbled. Pearl sat down on the edge of the bed and shook her head. "You are not used to being kept down."

"No, I am not."

"Well, sometimes life will slow you down if you don't realize that you need to slow it down first."

"Pearl, this is not…"

"It's a bump in your road that you could not anticipate. It means that someone has to take care of you for a change," Pearl said. "And, you need to let her."

"You mean Jameson."

"Yes, I do."

"Jameson always takes care of me," Candace said lovingly. "More than anyone realizes."

"Um-hum."

"She has enough on her plate without this."

"Without what? She has enough on her plate without you making it harder for her to take care of you. You remember that time Jameson was in that big old tree?"

"Which time?" Candace quipped.

"You know what I am talking about, Candy."

"I suppose, I do."

"You still hate it when she climbs on the roof of that barn or up on a ladder."

"Yes, but I don't stop her," Candace pointed out.

"No, but imagine that your roles were reversed. This is a wake-up call. I suggest you wake up."

"Oh, for heaven's sake it's gallstones. It's not as if I am dying."

"And also an infection, which unless Jameson suddenly developed a flair for the dramatic, the doctor told you can be life-threatening if they do not intervene now," Pearl reminded Candace.

Candace sighed. "Pearl…"

"Not working, Candy. I'm serious. You gave us all a good scare—me included," Pearl said honestly. Candace nodded. "You are right about one thing."

"What's that?" Candace wondered.

"We all need you. Most of all Jameson and Cooper," Pearl said. Candace's eyes twinkled at the mention of both names and Pearl smiled. "Everything else will wait. You know that as well, maybe even better than anyone, Candy."

"There's just so…"

"So much to do?" Pearl guessed. "There always is. Take my advice on this one. Let Jameson lead for a few days. Let the kids dote on you for a change. It's good for them."

"Speaking from experience?" Candace asked rhetorically. Pearl winked. "I promise," Candace said. "I will behave."

"No, you won't," Pearl laughed. Candace narrowed her gaze for a moment and then laughed along with her. "Just do me a favor and try?"

"Promise."

"You really did scare me. If it hadn't been for the fact that I thought Jameson was about to keel over on the phone, I would have panicked myself," Pearl told Candace. "She was a wreck."

"I'm sorry. To tell you the truth, I'm glad you're here."

Pearl kissed Candace on the forehead. "A little nervous, huh?" Pearl guessed. Candace smiled weakly. "Well, take a lesson from this little scare, will you? You know, I don't want to outlive you. That's just not in my plan."

"I know," Candace replied.

"I know you know," Pearl said. "No mother wants to outlive her children. So, do me a favor and just remember that includes me."

"Jameson," Maureen Reid greeted her daughter as soon as Jameson walked through the door. "How's Candace?"

"Grumpy," Jameson replied with a chuckle.

"I'll bet."

"And, if I am not mistaken a little shaken up," Jameson said. "She seriously thought she was having a heart attack. It scared her more than she's willing to let on. Where's Coop?"

"He's in the other room watching Aladdin."

"Again?"

Maureen laughed. "Again."

Jameson nodded her understanding and headed down the short hallway toward the room that Cooper was in. She stopped in the doorway and watched as Cooper stood in front of the television acting out the characters on the screen.

"Fwee wishes ta be exact!" Cooper pointed at the television.

Jameson smiled as Cooper continued his dramatic reenactment. As she watched Cooper, she found herself wishing that Candace could be home to see his theatrics. That singular thought flooded Jameson's veins with a stream of powerful emotions. Only a few hours earlier, Jameson had feared she might never hold Candace again, talk to her or be able to say "I love you." She inhaled a deep breath to settle her still-frayed nerves and called to Cooper.

"Hey, buddy," Jameson called over. Cooper turned around and ran directly into Jameson's arms. "Hey, what is this about?" she asked as Cooper clung to her. Jameson picked Cooper up. His legs wound themselves around her hips. "What's wrong, buddy?"

"Mommy's sick. Gwandma said."

Jameson smiled at her son. "Well, yes, she is, buddy," Jameson said. She carried Cooper over to a reclining chair and sat down, placing him on her lap. "She's okay."

"Mommy was sick," Cooper whispered.

Jameson steadied her breathing. Candace had expressed her concern over Cooper visiting the hospital. He had been at the shelter when the ambulance had rushed his bio-logical mother to the hospital. Everyone had explained to Cooper that his mother had been sick. She had never made it home. Candace feared that if Cooper saw her in the hospital, it might set him back. Jameson disagreed.

It surprised Jameson a bit—the level of sensitivity Candace had concerning Cooper's fears. They had both fallen in love with Cooper. Jameson had expected that Candace would be the parent who would push Cooper gently past his anxieties while Jameson struggled with worry. Jameson had watched how Candace continued to navigate the minefields of grief with Marianne and Spencer. With Cooper, somehow things were different for Candace. Jameson suspected it had to do with Candace's regrets. And, Candace did have regrets. Candace had shared with Jameson more than once how painful it had been for her to watch her children go through her divorce and her split from Jessica Stearns. Candace had tried to be present for her children. At times, she had told Jameson, she felt that she had slipped in that endeavor. Jameson knew that none of Candace's children felt that way. However, after only a couple of months with Cooper in her life, Jameson could understand Candace's feelings. Jameson often found herself worrying that she was not dedicating enough time to Cooper.

Jameson smiled at Cooper and set out to address his fear. "Well, that's true, Coop. But, Mommy – Mommy Candace is going to be all right. You know how your ear hurt for a few days?" she asked him.

"It was yucky."

"Yeah, I know. And, you know what? Mommy feels kind of yucky right now too."

"Is her ear itchy?" Cooper asked innocently.

"No, but her tummy is kind of achy. So...The doctors are going to make that better. Kind of like they did with the pink goo you drank."

Cooper studied Jameson for a moment. "When's Mommy coming home?"

"Well, Coop, she has to stay where she is for a couple of days. And, then? When she comes home? You and I are going to have to take care of her for a few more days." Jameson said. Cooper nodded sadly. Jameson smiled. "Would you like to go see her?" Cooper looked up hopefully. "That's what I thought. She misses you," Jameson said.

"Can we go now?"

"Yes, Cooper, we can go right now."

"Momma?" Cooper looked at Jameson thoughtfully.

"Yeah, buddy?"

"Can we stay with Mommy?" he asked.

"No, we can't," Jameson told Cooper. She watched his face drop slightly. "But, I will tell you what—both of us will be home for a whole week when Mommy comes home."

"Here?"

"No, Mommy wants to go to the big white house," Jameson explained.

Cooper grinned. "With Spen and Mawianne?"

Jameson tried not to laugh. "Yep," she said. Cooper hugged Jameson and hopped off of her lap. "Where are you going?"

"Get my jacket."

Jameson watched Cooper sprint off and chuckled.

"He's in a hurry," Maureen observed as she entered the room. Jameson looked at her mother. Maureen wasn't sure what she saw in Jameson's eyes. "What?" Maureen asked.

Jameson shook her head. "Will it ever get old?"

"What's that?" Maureen wanted to know.

"Hearing him call us Mom?"

"Nope. Well, until the whining phase starts."

"There's a whining phase?" Jameson asked.

"Usually."

"When?"

"Well, with your brothers it was at about eight. With you, it was at about six."

"I never whined!" Jameson argued.

"Oh, J.D. if you only knew."

"Weady, Momma!" Cooper skidded into the room in his socks.

Jameson looked at Cooper's feet and smirked. "I think you might have forgotten something," she said. Cooper was puzzled. Jameson tried to keep a straight face. "I think Mommy might appreciate it if you wore those sneakers she bought you."

"Wight!" Cooper said before sliding off again.

Jameson shook her head and smiled. "Thanks for staying, Mom."

"Trying to tell me to pack up?"

"What? No!"

"Good, because your father is bringing me some things," Maureen said.

"Mom, you don't..."

"J.D., I know you. You will be at the hospital most of the day tomorrow. Marianne will be here tonight with the kids and Pearl. I can help for a couple of days until you are ready to take Candace home."

"Mom, I don't expect..."

"Jameson," Maureen said firmly. Jameson looked at her mother expectantly. "You asked me if it will ever get old. The answer is: only if you stop being Cooper's mom. And, that never stops. You never stop wanting to take care of your kids, even when they have kids of their own."

"I know," Jameson said. Being married to Candace had taught Jameson that lesson firsthand. "I just don't want you to feel..."

"What I feel is grateful that Candace is going to be all right. Spending time with Cooper is not an obligation," she said. "He's my grandson."

"Yeah. Weird, huh?" Jameson joked.

"Not really. I always knew you'd be a great mother. Just took you a while to realize I was right—as usual."

Jameson rolled her eyes.

"Momma!"

"I'm coming, Coop."

"Tell Candace I said hello," Maureen said. "If Marianne feels comfortable, tell her I am happy to watch Spencer and Maddie so she can have time with Candace."

Jameson leaned in and kissed her mother's cheek surprising Maureen. "Thanks, Mom—for everything."

"Go on. I wouldn't keep those two waiting if I were you."

"Momma!"

"Truer words, Mom...Truer words," Jameson laughed.

CHAPTER FIVE

"**N**o. No, I'll make the statement. No," Dana told Lieutenant Governor Dan Moore.

"Candy is going to pop when she finds out you kept this from her. Does J.D. know?" he asked.

"Not yet. I'll talk to her when she gets here," Dana said.

"What exactly does Lawson Klein hope to accomplish?" Moore wondered.

"I imagine he wants to hurt Candy."

"Politically? The only people who will buy his bullshit are the ones who already do," Moore observed candidly.

"Maybe. Maybe not. You know as well as I do that Candy is either incredibly popular or massively controversial. It's always a crapshoot."

"Exploiting their adoption?" Moore mused. "That seems low even for a bottom-feeder like Klein."

Dana agreed, but she had dealt with Lawson Klein for years. Nothing the man did or said surprised her anymore. "If he hits her popularity rating that will only be a bonus."

"You think this is about his daughter?"

"I think he hates Candy. He always has. Laura being with Jonah? Laura being close to the person he despises most in the universe? Yeah, I think that is a massive blow to his over-inflated, bigoted ego. He wants to hurt Candy—personally. And, I don't believe he cares at all who the casualties in that crusade might be—Cooper or Laura."

Dan Moore groaned. "I'm not sure I want to be around when you tell J.D.," he said.

"Yeah, me neither," Dana said.

"Mom?" Marianne opened the door to Candace's room to find Jonah sitting beside Candace's bed.

"Hey you," Candace greeted Marianne.

"Hey, sis. Where are the gremlins?" Jonah asked.

"Where's yours?" Marianne returned.

"With his mom," Jonah replied.

"With J.D.'s mom," Marianne gave her answer. "I figure if she survived J.D. and Toby, she can survive Spencer for a couple of hours."

"Good bet," Candace agreed.

"How are you feeling?" Marianne asked Candace.

"I'm okay," Candace promised.

"Yeah, right. You in a hospital bed?" Marianne chuckled. "No way are you okay."

Candace shrugged. "If I don't stay, Pearl and Jameson will glue me to it."

"They aren't the only ones," Jonah said.

Candace smiled at her children. "You all forming some kind of coalition or something?" she teased.

"Yes," Jonah said. "The Mom Squad."

"The Mom Squad?" Candace laughed.

"Yeah," Jonah said again. "Don't think we all don't know that the minute one of us leaves, you'll be up to your tricks."

"I am not sure I want to know what that means," Candace raised her brow.

"Well, let's just say that we all think you should table Bible Study for a while," Marianne smirked. She laughed at the expression on Candace's face. "Mom? Did you just blush?"

"It's warm in here," Candace said. Jonah and Marianne both laughed. "You are spending too much time with your sister," Candace told Marianne.

Marianne smiled at her mother warmly and took a seat on the edge of Candace's bed.

Jonah hopped to his feet and leaned in to kiss Candace's cheek. "I'm going to let you two visit. Laura's still at your house."

"You mean at the Executive Mansion," Candace said.

"Well, yeah. You do live there, Mom," Jonah reminded her. "I should give her a break," he said. "I will see you tomorrow."

"Jonah, you don't need to come in here."

Jonah shook his head and looked at Marianne. "Did you hear something?" he asked his sister.

"Nope," Marianne replied.

Candace rolled her eyes. "I'm just saying that…"

Jonah grinned and kissed Candace's cheek again. "Get some rest, Mom. I'll see you tomorrow."

Candace let out an exasperated sigh as Jonah left the room. Marianne lifted an eyebrow at her mother.

"You know the Mom Squad is a real thing," she told Candace.

"Marianne, you all have things that you need to take care of."

"Yes, and one of them is you," Marianne said. "So? How does one get stones in one's body exactly?" she asked Candace.

Candace finally laughed. "Well, if you were to ask some of my detractors, I am sure they would have a few ideas on that subject."

"So? How are you really doing?"

"I'm okay. I would much rather be home."

"I can imagine," Marianne said. "Maureen said J.D. was on her way here with Cooper. Surprised she isn't here yet."

Candace shrugged. "She's probably letting him run off some energy first."

"He'll be okay, Mom."

Candace sighed. "I hate him coming here to see me like this."

"He'll just be happy to see you."

"I hope so."

"I know so," Marianne said. "Listen, if you want, I can take the kids to Dad's when you come home. That, or I can stay with Grandma Pearl for a few days."

"Why would you do that?"

"Two toddlers and a baby while you need to rest?"

Candace waved off Marianne's concern. "Marianne, it is a minor surgery. Honestly. I will be home the day after and that is only because they are being overly cautious. I think Pearl and Jameson might have paid off the hospital."

Marianne giggled. "Distinct possibility."

"And, why do I think my wife might have something to do with this Mom Squad you have going?"

"You'll have to talk to your son about that one," Marianne said. She pulled out her phone and opened up a text message. "And, I quote, 'This calls for action. We need a Mom Squad. Otherwise, J.D. and Pearl will either kill her for real or end up in the hospital in her place. You with me?'"

Candace's jaw fell open and then she swiftly burst into laughter with Marianne. Jameson opened the door with Cooper holding her hand. He looked up at Jameson curiously and Jameson shrugged at him.

"I think your Mommy is a little loopy," she said.

Candace heard Jameson's voice and looked directly at Cooper. "Hi, sweetheart," she called to him. "I am not loopy, although I think my older son may be," she said.

Cooper looked at Candace tentatively and tugged on Jameson's hand. Jameson squatted to his height and he whispered in her ear.

"Yes, you can, buddy. Come on," she told him.

Candace watched as Marianne stood and Jameson walked Cooper over. Cooper looked up at Candace with pleading eyes. She smiled at him reassuringly. "Can I have a hug?" she asked him.

Cooper nodded and Jameson placed him on the bed next to Candace. He looked at the tube in her arm. Candace kept smiling at him, giving him a moment to study her situation. "Come here," she said as she reached out for him. Cooper practically threw himself into Candace's arms. "It's okay," she told him. "I missed you, you know?" Cooper remained silent and snuggled into Candace's embrace.

Marianne looked at Jameson, trying to discern what might be frightening Cooper so much.

"Hey, Coop," Jameson called over. She reached into a small backpack. "Why don't you stay here with Mommy for a while? I'll leave your pad and your crayons next to her bed, okay? Marianne and I will go and get you some juice. Sound good?" she asked him as she placed the items on the tray next to Candace's bed. Cooper nodded. Jameson leaned in and whispered in Candace's ear. "It's the IV," she explained. Candace nodded her understanding. "Okay, Coop. Take care of Mommy for a few minutes," Jameson said placing a kiss on his cheek and then on Candace's. "Be back," Jameson whispered.

Candace wrapped her arm around Cooper and waited for Jameson and Marianne to leave. She looked down as he studied her arm. "That's kind of scary looking, huh?" Candace guessed. He nodded. "Mmm...It doesn't hurt, honey. You know that medicine you had to take?" he nodded. "That's all this is," she told him. "And, when I come home this will be all gone." He looked up at her. "Promise," she said.

"Mommy?"

Candace smiled and jostled Cooper's curls with her fingertips. "What, sweetie?"

"I stay with you?"

"Well, you stay with me here for a while until Momma takes you home for bed."

"You be alone," he said sadly. "I didn't bwing Fwoggie."

Candace kissed Cooper's head. "I won't be alone, honey. There are lots of people here to take care of me. I promise. Okay?" Cooper nodded. "Tell me, did you have fun with Grandma today?" Cooper smiled and nodded again. "Yeah? Did you show her your trains?"

Copper's grin grew. "Yep," he said. Then he looked at Candace's arm again.

Candace seldom found herself at a loss. "Cooper? Are you scared of the tube?" she asked him. He nodded.

"How about you come sit on the other side of me?" she suggested, directing him to climb over her. Cooper complied and Candace watched as he started to relax a bit.

"Can I draw?"

"Of course, you can draw," Candace said. She reached over and grabbed the pad and crayons Jameson had brought and gave them to Cooper. "Mommy?"

"Yes, Cooper?"

"I love you."

"I love you, Cooper—all the way to the moon and back," she told him.

Cooper giggled. "I love you to da sun."

"Oh? I love you to all the stars," Candace returned.

"I love you bigger dan Genie!"

Candace laughed. "Well, how do I compete with that?" she asked. Cooper's grin warmed her heart. She kissed him on the head as he began coloring on his pad. "Are you going to draw a train to take me home?" Candace wondered.

"Nope."

"No? I know! A Brachiosaurus."

"He has a big neck, Mommy. He eats weaves on twees."

"He does?"

"Yep. Not like da Rex. He eats ofver dinosaurs."

"I see. So, are you going to draw a Rex?"

"Nope."

"No? What are you going to draw?"

"Genie," Cooper told her.

"Ahh…. With Aladdin?" she wondered.

"Nope. With you."

"With me?"

"Yep. Den Genie can stay here. He's magic."

Candace smiled and stroked Cooper's back. "Thank you, Cooper."

"It's okay, Mommy. Genie will pwotect you."

"You know something, Cooper?" she asked. He looked up at her. "I am very glad that you are my son."

Cooper beamed. He nodded and turned back to his paper. Candace watched his tongue pop through his tight lips as he concentrated on his masterpiece. She smiled as she watched her son work intently on his picture. She bit her lip to keep from laughing when he tapped his crayon against his forehead in thought. Often, when Jameson was working on a sketch, she did the same thing. Spencer did it when he sat drawing as well. She shook her head. Both the boys sought to emulate Jameson. It made Candace's heart sing with gratitude. She kissed the top of Cooper's head. "Oh, Jameson, if you only knew how much these kids love you. How much we all do," she thought.

❌❌❌

"Hey, Dana," Jameson greeted her friend with a smile. "I thought you would have headed home by now." Dana's discomfort was evident, and Jameson narrowed her gaze. "I don't want to know, do I?" Jameson guessed.

"I'm glad I caught you, actually. Hi, Marianne," Dana greeted Candace's daughter.

"I'll leave you two to talk," Marianne offered.

"No," Dana said. "It would be good if I could speak to both of you."

"What the hell is going on?" Jameson asked.

Dana cringed as she spoke. "Lawson Klein," she said. Jameson lifted her hands in questioning. "J.D..."

"What's his 9-1-1 this time? I suppose Candace is responsible for the storm last week somehow. God is striking down the State of New York for electing a heathen."

Dana shook her head. "I wish it was that."

"What is it?" Jameson asked.

"J.D..."

"Dana, for Christ's sake! I have had a shitty day already, just tell me."

"He's got a piece coming up tomorrow on a news show about Cooper."

"Excuse me?" Jameson snapped.

"Apparently, he found Cooper's grandmother. He's asserting that you and Candace stole Cooper right out from under her to bolster Candace's popularity rating."

Dana was positive she could see steam rising off of Jameson. And, she was certain she had never seen her friend so angry—never.

"I need to call Jessica," Jameson said.

"I already did," Dana said. "She's expecting you to call later. Listen, she says there is nothing to worry about legally. He can parade the story all that he wants. You don't have anything to worry about as far as the adoption. Jessica covered every base, J.D. None of us can stop him from hitting the press, unfortunately."

"I'm going to kill that fucking son of a bitch," Jameson said harshly.

Marianne took hold of Jameson's arm. It may have been an empty threat, but Marianne understood the honest emotion it held. She could feel bile rising in her throat. The truth didn't matter. The mere idea that anyone would implicate an innocent child in such an offensive scheme was detestable. She'd seen Jameson irritated but Jameson rarely swore nor did Jameson make threats. Marianne could not blame Jameson. She felt compelled to say the same thing.

"J.D.," Marianne said gently. "How are we going to keep this from Mom?"

Jameson rubbed her eyes and groaned. "Son of a…"

"Look, just keep the television off in her room," Dana suggested.

Jameson looked at Dana in disbelief. "Dana, that's all well and good. This hospital employs how many people? Am I supposed to sequester her from the nurses too? People talk," Jameson pointed out the obvious.

"Let me talk to Dr. Everett," Dana said. "I'm sure that we can contain this until she's ready to go home. It's only a day, J.D. She will be in recovery when it airs."

"Yeah, she's going to kill me when she finds out that we all knew and didn't tell her."

"It's your call," Dana said. "If you think we should tell her, I will support that."

"No, I don't believe we should tell her until after the surgery. I'd prefer not at all," Jameson admitted. Her thoughts traveled to Laura. Jonah's girlfriend had been put through emotional hell by Lawson Klein, her own father. It was inconceivable to Jameson that any parent could be so hurtful. "Damn that asshole. Laura's going to…"

"J.D.," Marianne tried to calm Jameson. "I will talk to Jonah and Laura, okay? I'll stop there before I go home. Okay?"

Jameson offered a tiny smile of appreciation to Marianne. "Your mother is going to want to…"

"I know," Marianne said. "Hey, you've got The Mom Squad to back you. Don't worry; we'll keep her in line."

Jameson chuckled in spite of her frustration "The Mom Squad?"

"Jonah's idea. Sometimes it takes a village—to coin a phrase," Marianne explained.

Jameson groaned. "Dana, how big could this get?"

"I'll do my best to contain it, J.D., but we both know Lawson Klein. Whatever he hopes to gain, he will push it as far as he can."

"Just so you know, Dana, if he does anything to hurt Cooper the gloves are off," Jameson declared.

Dana nodded. She had no doubt of the sincerity of Jameson's statement, and she fully expected that Candace would be prepared for battle as well. Dana had worked with Candace for years. Candace tended to take the high road with people like Lawson Klein. She spoke with civility about him when she was forced to comment and she ignored his rhetoric as much as possible. Implicating or compromising her children, any of them, would change the playing field and Dana knew it. People often underestimated Candace's power. Reality was that Candace Reid possessed connections in every realm of society. She had influential friends who sat on the bench of the nation's highest court. She possessed allies in The White House, in foreign embassies and in foreign administrations. She enjoyed the support of leaders in business, banking, and the non-profit sector. And, what many people chose to ignore—Candace had close, personal friends in powerful positions on both sides of the political aisle. She kept her alliances close to the vest and she only deployed her resources when she needed to. Compromise her family? Dana could only imagine what Candace might pull out of her hat on Lawson Klein. Candace Reid might be a woman who loathed dirty politics, but Dana could foresee this situation taking more than a few nasty turns.

Jameson massaged her face with her hand and shook her head in disgust. "Marianne, can you bring Cooper his juice. Tell your mother I ran into Dana and I will be right there?"

Marianne smiled at Jameson. "No problem, take as long as you need."

Jameson handed Marianne Cooper's juice and nodded her thanks before turning her attention back to Dana. "Dana?"

"J.D., I really don't know. I'm pulling all the strings I can to get a look at this piece before it airs. We'll handle it."

"Yeah, I know. That doesn't mean no one gets hurt. I know that too. You know, he's put Laura through hell this last year. That's taken a toll on both Jonah and Candace. She feels responsible."

"I do know," Dana said. "I'm sorry. I didn't see this coming."

Jameson sighed. "Nah, it's not your fault," she told Dana. "I'm just tired and...And, I really hate that guy. That's the last thing any of us needs right now. Cooper's been through enough and so has Laura. What kind of person does this stuff? For what, Dana? Because Candace is married to me? That's batshit crazy."

Dana snickered. "That might be the best assessment I have heard yet. Look, J.D., this isn't just about Candy being a lesbian if I had to guess."

"Then what is it about?" Jameson asked pointedly.

"Candace is a powerful woman, J.D.—more so than many people realize."

"And?"

"Some people don't like powerful women. Being a lesbian was just the icing on his cake—another weapon against her in his flimsy arsenal. She stands for everything he hates. I mean everything. That would be okay if she were at home in her kitchen discussing it with her friends. She's vocal. You know that."

"She's respectful, Dana. She has more than one friend that doesn't even support our right to be married. Sometimes it pisses me off."

Dana smiled. "You don't say? Ever tell her that?"

"No," Jameson finally laughed. "And you know why so don't even ask. The point is..."

"The point is that Lawson Klein is an asshole bent on power," Dana said. "He wants what Candace has—power. He wants people to sit on the pedestal he thinks she commands. And, he's trying to knock her off it."

"She's not on a pedestal," Jameson said.

"Not in her eyes, no. In his? Yes, J.D., in his eyes she has been given a higher place than she deserves, one he deserves. He'll tell you it's about morality. It's not. It's about power. Candy knows that. Morality is not what drives people to this."

"How do you stop him?"

"You won't like my answer."

"Dana? I'm asking."

"I think we'll have to wait for the person who might know that answer or at least, have some ideas about it."

Jameson tugged on her ponytail and groaned. "You think Candace will know what to do? What do you think she will do?"

Dana shrugged. "I don't know. I think she'll do whatever she needs to do on this one. That's what worries me."

"You think she'll go for the jugular? I..."

"I think he finally put the final nail in his coffin," Dana said flatly.

"You think this could hurt Candace's future?"

"I think Candace will forget all about her potential future politically when she hears he has invoked Cooper."

Jameson sighed. "You are right about that."

"J.D., I'm not worried about Candy's career right now. I'm worried about Candy."

"She'll be okay, Dana," Jameson said assuredly. Dana's skepticism remained. "She will. That much I do know," Jameson smiled. "Don't worry about Candace. Worry about Lawson Klein."

"No. He's not worth that energy."

Jameson agreed. "No, but Cooper and Laura are," she said. "Find out what you can. The more I have to tell her when I do, the better it will be."

"I promise."

Jameson squeezed Dana's arm. "I need to get back. Call me if you find out anything. I mean anything, Dana."

"I will."

Jameson hugged Dana goodbye and started back to Candace's room. "Careful, Klein. You just opened the genie's bottle and that can be unpredictable," Jameson whispered as she left.

�֍ ✖ ✖

"Hey?" Jameson called into the room quietly. "Is he asleep?"

Candace nodded with a smile. Jameson watched as Candace closed her eyes in contentment. It made Jameson's heart swell and sink simultaneously. She hated keeping anything from Candace—ever. That was not how they existed. Their relationship had always been founded on openness and honesty. Jameson was an open book to Candace most of the time and she knew it. She didn't have any desire to hide her emotions from her wife. The same was true for Candace. Jameson knew that as well. Jameson closed her eyes and sighed in frustration.

"Want to talk about it?" Candace asked without opening her eyes.

"I'm fine."

Candace opened her eyes, lifted her brow and smirked. "You may be a lunatic, honey. You are not a liar. What's wrong?"

Jameson made her decision instantly. "I don't want to upset you."

"Well, now that we know my heart is healthy, I think you can rest easy about that. What is it that you don't want to tell me? Dana was walking on eggshells the entire time she was in here and Marianne kept spinning her wedding ring. What is going on?" Candace asked. Jameson hesitated. "Jameson, if you don't tell me I will be worried."

"When I do, you will be livid."

Candace smiled. "I gathered that already. Otherwise, you would have told me. She motioned to Jameson to come closer. "I am going to be fine tomorrow, Jameson," she said assuredly. Candace kissed Cooper's head and took Jameson's hand. "Don't do this to yourself," she said knowingly. "We've never kept anything from each other. Don't let a routine procedure change that."

"It's surgery, Candace. I don't find that routine."

"I know. I know you're scared. I can see it in your eyes. You know that I will be okay. Whatever it is, just tell me."

Jameson sucked in a nervous breath. "Lawson Klein apparently found Coop's grandmother in Ohio. I don't know how or why…"

"I know why," Candace said flatly. "To hurt me. And?"

"There's a television segment running tomorrow. Dana's sources say it suggests that we basically stole Cooper to help…"

"My career?" Candace guessed. She took a deep breath and released it slowly. "I need to call Jessica."

"Dana already spoke with her. So did I—just before I came in here. There's nothing to fear legally."

"No, I didn't imagine there would be. Jessica is thorough. That's why I called her."

"She cares about you," Jameson muttered.

"Yes, she does," Candace conceded. "We had some good years, Jameson. You know that."

"I know," Jameson said. "I like Jessica. I wish I didn't sometimes."

"She's not the love of my life," Candace reminded Jameson gently.

"I know that too. You're taking this better than I imagined."

"I'm furious. Right now, I can't do much about it. Jessica will have the agreement that Ms. Cosgrove signed when she made the choice to forego any place in Cooper's life."

Jameson nodded. "I didn't want you thinking about this."

"Jameson," Candace said, offering Jameson a sympathetic smile of understanding. "I'm glad that you did."

"I can see the stress in your eyes, Candace."

Jameson watched as Candace kissed Cooper's head. Candace took another deep breath. Jameson understood each action as a necessary part of Candace's effort to gather her thoughts and control her emotion. Jameson smiled when Candace looked down at Cooper as only a mother could. She hated herself for causing Candace any additional stress. Withholding the truth for even a day or two felt like a deception to Jameson. One look in Candace's eyes and Jameson knew that she could not keep the news from her. She could plainly see concern and anger in Candace's eyes. One thing Jameson was certain of; those two elements would ultimately result in Candace's steady resolve; a resolve that few people possessed in earnest.

At the moment, Jameson almost felt sorry for Lawson Klein—almost. Candace was passionate about politics and policy. The politician in Candace was willing to fight for what she believed in no matter how many insults were leveled at her or roadblocks were thrown in her way. One thing eclipsed that passion—family. Candace's children were her greatest love. Jameson adored that about the woman who shared her life. She had learned from loving Candace that children added a dimension to life. Cooper had become a light in their life together. At times, he added some challenges. They were no longer a pair; they were parents of a toddler. But, more than Jameson could have imagined, having Cooper in their life had made Jameson fall more deeply in love with Candace. Klein had decided to step onto Holy ground. She pitied him for that miscalculation.

"Candace?"

Candace smiled again at Jameson. "I would like to talk to Jessica, Jameson."

Jameson nodded. "Do me one favor? Just wait until you are home? Please? Like you said, there is nothing you can do right now. You know, the kids are going to think I was crazy for telling you."

"None of you can lie to save your lives," Candace laughed. "You least of all," she repeated. "It's one of the things I love so much about you."

"Do you want me to take him so you can get some rest?" Jameson asked. Candace shook her head and patted the bed. "I don't think three of us are going to fit in that little bed," Jameson chuckled.

"Are you suggesting that I am getting fat?"

"What? No! But, with all those fortune cookies you have stashed..."

"Come here, you lunatic," Candace said.

Jameson jostled herself into the bed on her side and put her arm over Candace. "I just want to take you home."

"I know," Candace said. "It's only a couple of nights."

"I hate it."

Candace laughed. "I promise; I will handle Lawson Klein."

Jameson groaned slightly. "I can't tell you what I'd like to do to him."

"I think I can imagine."

"What are you going to do?" Jameson wondered.

Candace gripped Jameson's hand. "That depends entirely on him. Forget about him right now. Just stay for a while."

"How about until they kick me out?" Jameson suggested.

"I guess you'll be here in the morning then."

Jameson laughed. No one was likely to fight Candace when she put her foot down. Jameson kissed Candace's temple. "Get some rest."

Candace closed her eyes. She was completely drained. Jameson's news had not surprised her. It had rattled her more than she intended to let on to Jameson. She tightened her grasp on Cooper as Jameson held her. "You have no idea who you are dealing with," she thought silently. "No idea."

CHAPTER SIX

Jameson was sitting with her face in her hands, trying to calm her nerves.

"J.D.?" Jameson turned to find Michelle and Melanie entering the small family waiting room she was in. "Any word?"

"Not yet," Jameson told the pair. "I would imagine soon. He said it would probably take about two hours, maybe less. It's only been an hour."

Michelle nodded. "What time did you leave last night?"

"Late, why?"

"No offense, J.D., but you look like shit."

"Thanks, Shell. I love you too."

Michelle chuckled. "I'm serious. I'm worried about you. I don't need both of you in here."

Jameson smiled. "I didn't sleep much. She knows, Shell, about the interview today and Klein's involvement."

"You told her?" Michelle asked.

Jameson nodded a bit regretfully. Michelle sat down beside Jameson and regarded her thoughtfully for a moment. She'd never seen Jameson look so tired before. Jameson had dark circles under her eyes. Michelle studied Jameson, determining that not only had Jameson failed to get much rest, but she had also likely cried for an extended period of time.

"Probably better for everyone that you did tell her," Michelle said.

"What about for her?" Jameson asked rhetorically.

"For Mom too. You know her; she's better when she has the information. Stop beating yourself up," Michelle told Jameson. "How was she this morning?"

"Actually, she seemed pretty good," Jameson admitted. "I'm not sure how much of her cheeriness was for my benefit."

"One look at you and she probably was worried you'd end up in the bed beside her," Michelle commented. Jameson snickered. "Oh, God. Only you two would conduct Bible Study in a hospital bed."

Jameson rolled her eyes. "Very funny, Shell. No one was quoting scriptures."

"There's a first," Michelle returned.

Melanie chuckled listening to her boss and her girl-friend. "I'm going to go so that Jonah can come over here, okay?" she asked Michelle

Michelle leaned in and kissed Melanie softly. "Thank you."

"Anytime," Melanie replied. "J.D.? You two want Jonah to bring you anything?"

Jameson shook her head.

"Coffee, Mel. Tell my little brother to bring the zombie we call our step-mother a coffee. Me too, if he wouldn't mind."

Melanie nodded. She looked at Michelle with concern. She had also noticed Jameson's demeanor. Jameson was quiet, almost withdrawn. It didn't surprise Melanie that Jameson appeared to be both exhausted and worried. Michelle had filled Melanie in on the major points of the prior day. Melanie didn't need to see Jameson to know that all of Michelle's news would have taken its toll on her friend. Melanie had known Jameson before Jameson had met Candace. She remembered vividly what it had been like to watch the change in Jameson after Senator Candace Fletcher had come into Jameson's life. None of Candace's children had that benefit. They had always known Jameson as the woman their mother had fallen in love with. Melanie's perspective differed. She knew Jameson as the woman who had fallen in love with Senator Candace Fletcher.

Michelle noted the concern in Melanie's eyes and offered her a wink. "Coffee, Mel. Tell him the biggest one they have for her," Michelle joked.

Michelle waited for Melanie to leave and then turned to Jameson. "What gives, J.D.?"

"What?"

"I know you are tired. That's not all."

"I'm worried, Shell. I can't help it."

"About Mom or about Lawson Klein?"

"Both."

"Mom will be okay, J.D., and she can handle Klein."

"Maybe, but she shouldn't have to. I hate this."

"What?" Michelle asked.

"Being helpless."

"You're not," Michelle said.

"Shell, Jesus! My son's past is about to be splashed across the national news, completely vilifying my wife, who is currently in surgery. I can't do one thing to protect either of them. Do you know how much that pisses me off? What about Laura? She needs this now? I'm supposed to protect my family, Shell."

"J.D., none of this is because of you."

"Maybe not, but I can't even stop any of it."

Michelle released a heavy sigh. "I understand."

"I'm sorry, Shell. I hate this. I don't like to hate people. Right now? Right now, I hate Lawson Klein."

"Well, you have a lot of company in that club."

Jameson laughed. "I am sorry."

"Don't be. I talked to Marianne on my way here. She spent over an hour talking Jonah off the ledge last night. I think he's close to confronting that asshole. Maybe more like knocking him out with one punch."

"It won't help," Jameson said.

"No, I know. He knows that. The thing is, J.D., you and mom are worried about everyone else. Cooper is our little brother; you know? You don't do that. We might have our moments. We do have each other's back no matter what. And, to be honest, none of us like anyone messing with our parents."

The protectiveness in Michelle's voice made Jameson smile. "I know."

"You'd like to deck him too," Michelle grinned.

"I'd like to kick his sorry ass into next Tuesday," Jameson confessed. "Your mother would kick mine if I did."

"That's for sure."

"How are Jonah and Laura?" Jameson asked. "I haven't talked to him yet."

"Pissed, like I said. I don't understand how an asshole like Lawson Klein can have such a great kid. I mean, seriously. Laura is nothing like him."

"No, she's not. It's still got to hurt her."

Michelle decided to turn the conversation. "How is Coop? Marianne said he was a little scared last night?"

"He's okay. Worried about his mom, I think. He fell asleep with her last night. He barely groaned when I picked him up to leave. He's got Spence there today. That should take his mind off of it. He drew your mom like ten pictures of Genie to keep her safe."

"Man, he loves that Genie."

"He sure does," Jameson said. "I think it's the magic thing."

"What do you mean?"

"I think he sees Genie as someone who can be a friend and protect him."

"From what?"

"From being alone," Jameson said sadly. "He's lost everyone he ever cared about, Shell. He might be little, but that much he understands."

Michelle sighed. "People suck sometimes."

"Only a few," Jameson said. "It's like Froggie. He just needs something to help him believe we won't leave him—any of us."

"I'd like to pummel Laura's father."

"Stand in line," Jameson said.

"Are you going to watch it?" Michelle wanted to know. "The interview?"

"Nope. I'll leave that to Dana."

"You know Mom will want..."

"She promised me that she would let it go until we were home."

Michelle snickered. "You do know that the car will constitute home, right? The minute she's out of this place, she's going to want to jump in."

Jameson nodded. "Yeah. Still ready to pull the emergency Mom Squad together?"

"At your service," Michelle promised.

"Good. I have a feeling I will be calling 9-1-1 for your help sooner than I'd like."

Michelle broke into laughter. "We should get T-shirts made now."

Jameson began to chuckle. "Thanks, Shell."

"No problem. You really do need that coffee, though. Otherwise, someone's apt to try and send you to the morgue."

Jameson rolled her eyes. "And, your mother calls me a lunatic."

✂✂✂

"Tell us, Ms. Cosgrove, your daughter ran away from home?"

"At fifteen. She didn't like the rules, ya' know? Wanted to be with those friends of hers."

"Friends you didn't approve of I am guessing?"

"Running with a wild bunch. She came back once. Started again right off, ya' know? Ended up, well, she ended up in a bad way."

"A bad way?" Dana spat at the television screen.

Jessica chuckled caustically. "Not the words she used to me," Jessica offered.

"And, she ran away again?"

"Sure did. Didn't like the rules. Never knew where she was. Didn't call. At some point, what do you do? She was almost eighteen by then. She had the right to go."

"And, when did you learn about Cooper?"

"Never met the boy," Cooper's grandmother answered. *"Sad. Only family I got left."*

Jessica laughed. "Can't imagine how many times they rehearsed that sob story."

"You're laughing?" Dana looked at Jessica as if Jessica had lost her mind.

"What do you want me to do? Break the screen?" Jessica returned.

Dana's gaze grew harsh. Dana was not Jessica Stearns' biggest fan. Jessica had created a massive upheaval for Candace's career. Her infidelity was splashed across the news media which made life for Candace more than difficult for nearly six months. Worse, her affair had broken Candace's spirit in a way that only those closest to the then-senator understood.

Jessica sighed. "Still haven't forgiven me."

"What I think doesn't matter," Dana said flatly.

"Dana, I fucked up with Candy. I know that. She knows that. We all know that, okay? You think that because I am laughing, I don't want to eviscerate Lawson Klein and this woman? I do. Trust me on that. I do. That's not going to help Candy. You and I both know she's donning her battle gear now."

Dana huffed. "I've got some counter-press lined up. Most people will see through this. It's still going to leave an impression, though. It always does."

"You think Candy wants to run for higher office?" Jessica asked.

"After this? I really don't know," Dana said. "When I talked to J.D. this morning.... Well, Candy is still Candy. She loves this. She'll say she doesn't aspire to more. She always has. It's in her DNA."

"Yes, I know."

Dana nodded. "Yeah, but Candy is also different now."

"So I noticed," Jessica replied.

"You still love her," Dana surmised.

"I still care about her, Dana. Seven years is a long time. Longer than some might think. I might know her better than even you might want to admit. She's not thinking about future elections, Dana—not now."

"I know," Dana admitted. "That's why I have to."

"I agree. She needs us to be steady, not reactionary. That won't help."

"You have something on Klein?" Dana asked.

Jessica grinned. "I have something on everyone, Dana. It's up to Candy what we use and how we use it."

"Anything I can use now?" Dana asked.

"Tidbits, yes," Jessica said. "Who do you have lined up to spin this debacle?"

"Kendra Lawrence and John Donaldson."

Jessica took in the information and let it roll in her mind. Kendra Lawrence was considered a middle of the road journalist and news anchor—politically speaking. Her evening news show was touted as balanced by both sides of the aisle. Jessica was confident that Lawrence had little use, however, for the antics of Lawson Klein and his group Family Values International. FVI, as it was called, did not enjoy the support of the majority of mainstream media. That had never changed the fact that the group continued to enjoy immense financial assistance and connections within all halls of power. When FVI made statements, they often left lingering impressions regardless of fact. A fair assessment of fact versus fiction in the media always mattered in public life. Lawrence would be an excellent ally in ensuring that.

John Donaldson, on the other hand, was viewed as a liberal-leaning pundit. His morning show on a major cable news network had done little to change that perception. His coverage would bolster Candace further with those that already tended to be her staunch supporters. The danger in Donaldson's piece might be its ability to insight more blowback from the right wing. Nevertheless, Jessica understood Dana's course of action. Jessica had traveled this road with Candy for years. One thing she did know, Dana was a master.

"Logical choices," Jessica commented. "Lawrence is a good grab, Dana."

Dana nodded. "I've known Kendra for years. She's fair-minded. She has no love of FVI that much I can tell you."

"What do you need from me?" Jessica asked.

"Facts. Ms. Cosgrove did, in fact, willingly let go of any possible rights to seek custody of Cooper."

"That's an understatement," Jessica said.

"Understatement?" Dana inquired.

Jessica groaned. "She didn't tell you what Laureen Cosgrove said about her grandson; I take it?"

"Candy? No. You know her. She shares what she needs to when it comes to family, even with me. Not because of trust, it's just..."

"I know," Jessica said. She took a deep breath and released it forcefully. "Ms. Cosgrove and I quote, said, 'I told that girl no nigger was growing up in my house. That's all she ran with, ya' know? I ain't having it. Told her that long ago. There's rules, you know? Ain't supposed to be mixin' that way,' end quote—as I recall it."

"Candy knows that?" Dana asked.

"She knows, J.D. too. It's in Cosgrove's statement. What she doesn't know is that I had her give a video statement as well."

"She said this on video?"

Jessica nodded. "And, a lot more. Laureen Cosgrove didn't have much use for her daughter, Dana. She has less for that little boy. I'm sure Lawson Klein has set her up nicely for a while. I'd also bet she made no mention of our conversation to his cronies."

Dana's fury simmered just below the surface. "Jessica, that tape could..."

"Oh, no—no way, Dana. I am not giving any of that up without Candy's consent."

"Candy will never consent."

"Probably not. No way. Even if I do think it might be best for her interests, I will not go against her wishes. This is up to her and J.D., not you and certainly not me," Jessica said flatly.

"What about the statement Cosgrove gave on paper?" Dana asked.

"No. I will give you the end of the statement, and you can feel free to let Lawrence and Donaldson know that Laureen Cosgrove had some choice words to describe her progeny."

"We could ask J.D."

Jessica shook her head. "Dana," she cautioned.

"Jessica! I'm tired of Candy falling on the sword. This is ridiculous. J.D. might just..."

"No, and you know I am right."

"Yeah, well...I don't like it. I want to put the screws to him, Jessica. I'm over it. This time, he has gone too far. Eventually, Cooper will see this. I don't care when. That's going to hurt. And, don't even get me started on Laura. What kind of person is that cold-hearted? What the hell is his deal with Candy anyway? It can't just be the fact that she is a lesbian," Dana mused.

"It isn't," Jessica replied.

"What do you know that no one has told me?" Dana asked pointedly.

"A lot," Jessica said. "But, that is for Candy to share, not me."

"Personal vendetta?"

Jessica shrugged. "Dana, I never told you this. There is a long history between the Klein family and the Stratton family. Most would call it ancient history. Unless something is sensational or can be sensationalized, no one revisits ancient history these days. It's not a secret, but it's not my story to tell."

"That's your way of telling me to go and do some digging."

Jessica smiled. "It's my way of telling you that there is always a little more to a story than anyone likes to admit. You learn that in a courtroom quickly. Klein is rude, pompous and selfish. He inherited those traits. You love history, Dana. Take a little time and review it."

"I don't know where to start," Dana said.

"Well, the beginning is a good place. Once upon a time, a different governor was living down the street."

"Jessica, I know we haven't...."

"Candy isn't just your boss, Dana. She's always been your best friend. You love her. I hurt her. I get it. Whatever you think, I never meant to," Jessica said. Dana nodded. "She ended up where she was supposed to be," Jessica continued honestly. "Believe it or not, that makes me happy."

"Me too."

Jessica smiled. "I'll be in touch."

"I imagine the governor already requested an audience with you," Dana lightened their conversation.

"Sure did. J.D. made her wait until she gets home. We agreed on tomorrow afternoon."

"J.D. must have loved that," Dana said sarcastically.

"She knows which battles to fight," Jessica observed. "Keep me in the loop, Dana."

"I will. Jessica?"

"Yes?"

"For whatever it's worth, I know it means a lot to Candy that you are handling so much of this."

Jessica smiled, grabbed her briefcase and opened the door to exit Dana's office. "Don't worry too much about Candy," Jessica said honestly. "Worry about how you will dispose of the pieces that were Lawson Klein when she's done with him. She's fair, Dana. Don't mess with a mother bear's cubs, especially hers."

Dana nodded. She watched as the door to her office closed and she flopped into her chair. "So, Governor Stratton has a history with the Klein clan. Just what haven't you told me, Candy?"

✗✗✗

Marianne kept a close eye on Laura as Laura fed little Jameson. Laura had been nearly silent since arriving at The Executive Mansion that morning. Other than suggesting that Marianne go ahead and go to the hospital, Laura had not spoken. Marianne stole a quick glance down the hallway, listening to Spencer and Cooper as they giggled. She was relieved that Spencer's presence seemed to have bolstered Cooper's spirits. Laura, however, looked sullen.

"You know," Marianne began to speak as she crossed the room to sit across from Laura. "You haven't gotten a chance to see Mom yet. She's awake. J.D. says she's doing well and in good enough spirits that she's already insisting she could be home," Marianne chuckled. "J.D. was planning to come get Coop in about an hour. Why don't you take him in my car instead? It'll give you a chance to see Jonah and Mom at the same time," Marianne suggested.

Laura shook her head. "No, it's okay. You take him. I'll stay here with the kids and Maureen. She's your mom."

Marianne pursed her lips. "You do know that she considers you a daughter, don't you? Just like she considered Rick her son."

"Not really the same thing."

"Why is that?" Marianne asked. Laura shrugged. "I see," Marianne said. "You know, Rick acquired that place long before we were married and had Spencer."

"Your mom is great."

"Mom loves you, Laura."

"I don't know why."

"Well, for starters, maybe because you are a caring person who has made her son happy," Marianne said.

Laura offered Marianne a faint smile. "I can't believe he is doing this to them—to Cooper."

"You know what Mom would say, don't you?" Marianne challenged Laura. Laura nodded. "I get it, Laura. I actually do get it. But, don't avoid Mom and J.D. because of him. They love you, you know? They're pretty upset about how much this will affect you."

"I just can't right now," Laura muttered. "When she's home, okay?"

Marianne nodded. She had come to adore Jonah's girlfriend. Laura was soft-spoken and kind. She was constantly doing little things for everyone in the family, Jonah most of all. And, it was no secret to Marianne that Laura Klein practically worshiped her mother. Laura looked up at Candace. Candace had taken the young woman under her protective wing. What Marianne was sure Laura did not fully comprehend, was the reality that Candace indeed considered the young woman part of her fold. That granted Laura all the same protections as any of her children and grandchildren.

"Okay," Marianne conceded. "If you want to talk, I'm always here."

Laura looked across the room at Marianne and smiled genuinely. Marianne had softened dramatically since Laura had first met Jonah's oldest sister. Much of it had occurred after Rick's death. But, Laura had seen the hard edges that Marianne had often sported beginning to smooth before that. It was strange to Laura that Jonah and Michelle had not recognized it as clearly. Laura guessed that motherhood had a great deal to do with the shift in Marianne. She suspected that something else also drove the change, something she knew only Candace would have considered—Jameson.

J.D. and Candace enjoyed a relationship that Laura envied, everyone around them envied their marriage. Candace had once told Laura that she and Jameson worked because they both loved and respected one another. She also had shared with Laura that every marriage had its moments of questioning, even hers to J.D. They were different people, different backgrounds, different ages and different ideas on everything from when to take a vacation to politics at times. Laura recalled that conversation often. It had occurred as many did, sitting at the kitchen table in Candace's old Georgian colonial over a cup of tea. Jonah and Laura had just endured of their first true arguments. Jonah wanted to buy a house. Laura thought they should wait another year. Laura had been nervous that she had somehow offended Jonah.

"Just out of curiosity, and you can tell me to mind my own business, why not buy a house now?" Candace wondered.

Laura shrugged and sipped her tea. "He's just starting at the firm. J.D. is great, but it's still just a beginning. I don't know. We don't need a house now. It's just the three of us. And, I'm not contributing anything."

Candace smiled. "I would say that raising your son is contributing quite a bit," she observed.

"Yes, but financially I have nothing. The money in my trust that I should have gotten after graduation...Well, you

know. The little I had saved myself, we've used. It's all on him. I never intended that."

"Laura, do you want to go to work somewhere?" Candace asked.

"Eventually, yes. Jonah and I agreed to wait a year. We do agree on some things," she said with a slight chuckle. "I just don't see why we can't hold on a year and then decide about a house. We're not even married. To me, I don't know...I think I'd like to put at least one horse before the cart. He thinks that's ridiculous."

"Sometimes, it's hard for us to see the other side when we want something," Candace said honestly.

"I guess. Look at you and J.D."

"What about me and Jameson?"

"You don't seem to have a problem seeing the other side."

Candace roared with laughter. She tried to stifle another round, but the expression on Laura's face threw her into another fit. "I'm sorry," Candace wiped a tear from her eyes. "You kids make me laugh sometimes," she said. "You sound like Shell. You think Jameson and I agree on everything? Hardly."

"Well, you don't fight."

Candace raised an eyebrow and smirked. "Sure we do. We just don't do it in front of any of you. And, we have our own parents to run to when we do," Candace said.

"You two seem like you're so in sync."

"Most of the time we are," Candace admitted. "Not always. I know where she will be at the end of the day, and she knows that too. It's not always easy for Jameson," Candace told Laura. "People don't think that age matters. It doesn't when you are talking about love. Practically? There are times it does. Jameson inherited three grown children when she married me. It's not simple sometimes."

"Yeah, but she's close to all of them even Marianne."

Candace nodded. "Now—yes, she is. But, Laura...That has not always been an easy road. You know, sometimes as *much as I love my kids they can make me crazy and that brings out her protective streak. She's in the middle sometimes, you know? It's not easy. I have to remind my kids that Jameson is my wife, not just their friend. And, I have to remind Jameson that as much as I love my children, she is my partner. Balancing families is never easy."*

"Well, we don't even have to worry about that yet and look at us."

"It's a typical disagreement," Candace said. "I hedged on running this campaign, you know? Huge fight between Jameson and I."

"Why? J.D. didn't want you to?"

"No, I was concerned about putting Jameson through that. Jameson is a relatively private person, Laura. She felt I was protecting her like one of my kids. Maybe, maybe I was a bit."

"You worked it out."

"Of course, somehow we always manage to. I was glad we did after she spent a night in Jonah's old room," Candace chuckled. "Sleeping without her when I am in Washington is bad enough. Under the same roof?" she laughed. "We both have opinions that we can be passionate about. Most of the time, we find the humor in it. It's work, even for us. It's worth it, though."

"I hope he feels that way."

"Jonah? Jonah loves you. Anyone with eyes can see that," Candace assured Laura. "He can be a bit like me at times. He wants to take care of everything, not because he doesn't think you are capable, but because he doesn't want you to have to. It's well-intentioned, but it gets us both in trouble every so often."

Laura laughed. "J.D.?"

"Mmm....It's hard when you've always been the caretaker to let someone take care of you. You're independent and giving, so is Jonah. So am I. So is Jameson. Learn to let the rope go a little and stop tugging for control. You both want the same thing. Just learn to loosen your grip a bit, and so will he. You'll find the middle ground. Learn to take care of each other. When you can do that? You know you've found the right person."

Laura looked at Marianne again. "Can I ask you something?"

"Sure."

"Is it weird for you? I mean, J.D. only being a little bit older than you and now having a four-year-old brother?"

Marianne sat quietly for a moment, pondering Laura's question. It was not at all what she had expected. "Oddly, no."

"Really?"

"Well, for a while it was a bit strange with J.D., not anymore. She loves Mom. I mean, she really loves Mom. Rick saw it the moment he had met her. He loved J.D. as much as he did Mom. She was like his sister; you know? It was different for him. It took me a while. Mostly because I didn't want Mom hurt again. And, maybe because we didn't have to compete for Mom's attention for so long."

Laura listened intently. Marianne's candor surprised her. It was evident that in some way, Marianne had thought about this subject privately. Laura wondered if Jonah's sister had ever shared any of her thoughts with Candace or J.D.

"The truth is, all three of us always competed for Mom's attention. Not that we didn't come first, we did. We competed with each other, and she was always busy, so we competed for her time. After Jessica had left, that was one less person, one less thing to compete with. She's a lot to live up to, my mom. She doesn't realize how much all three of us want to—live up to her, I mean."

"I think I can understand that a little."

Marianne smiled. "I don't know; then there was J.D. Now? The thing is, Mom is different now. The same, but more relaxed—happier, I guess would be the right word. That's because of J.D. I know that. And, Cooper? I didn't really see that coming, but when it did, somehow it didn't surprise me. You've seen them with Spencer and Maddie and J.J. I don't know, Laura. I think they were meant to be parents, not just grandparents. I can't really explain that. I just feel it," Marianne explained. She took a moment, sighed and continued. "I love my dad. We all do. He's not exactly the most emotional person if you know what I mean."

"Yes, I do."

Marianne nodded. "Cooper gets two parents who want him partly because they love each other so much. I'd like to think that was true of me and Rick. I wish Spencer and Maddie could have that. I wish Jonah, Shell and I had been able to have that. Our parents love us. They never really loved each other. Know what I mean? I think we exist mainly because Mom wanted us so badly and that was Dad's role to fill."

"Yeah."

"I'm sorry, I know things with your family have been rough."

"It's okay."

"No, it's not," Marianne said flatly. "Maybe it is not the same, but you have us, as dysfunctional as we may be."

Laura laughed. "I think I might have cornered the market on that."

"Nah. We are Dysfunction Junction," Marianne quipped. "But, it works."

"You're lucky."

Marianne nodded. "I know."

CHAPTER SEVEN

"Initial reaction?" Lawson Klein asked.

"What is it that you hope to gain here?" Michael Weller asked his boss.

Klein gloated. "Just stoking the embers, keeping it warm for the future, Mike."

"You think Reid is going to make a run for The White House; I get it. So what? You know this could blow up in our faces."

"I doubt that. Laureen Cosgrove did a fine job today. It will raise eyebrows. That's all you need. Put them on the defensive."

"Lawson, have you had any contact with Laura?"

"Why would I do that?" Klein scoffed at the question.

"Maybe because she is your daughter. You want influence as a family values advocate, you need to consider that she is your family."

"Not anymore, Mike. She chose."

Michael Weller shook his head. "Make an overture, Lawson. Let her rebuff it. Make it. It's good for your image. Some people will see this thing with Cosgrove as petty."

"You worry too much. Reid has never come after me directly," Klein said.

"What about FVI? You need to think..."

"I am. I've been at this a long time. Reid is soft. If she plays, we win. If she ignores, we win. She won't push, Mike. She won't bite. She never has. She's savvy, but she's no shark. Ask anyone. Plant the seed. No matter what she does, it will grow."

"I really hope you are right.

✖✖✖

"I think maybe we need to give you a bedtime," Pearl said when she saw Jameson in the kitchen. Jameson offered her a weary smile. "I know; it's been a long couple of days. How was Candy when you left?"

"Ready to jump in the car with me," Jameson said.

"I imagine."

"She is impossible at times," Jameson said. "It's one night."

"Candy is not used to being kept down, Jameson, not by anything."

"I know that. I'm just tired."

"No, you're annoyed. What did she do? Let me guess; she's got the whole crew coming to update her tomorrow."

Jameson rolled her eyes. "No, thank God. Just Jessica."

Pearl nodded and took a seat at the table with Jameson. "You don't like Jessica much."

"No, I like her just fine."

"Jameson, are you jealous?"

"No," Jameson said honestly. "It's not that. It's…"

"What is it then?"

Jameson shook her head ruefully. "She can help. It pissed me off a little, I guess. My wife's ex runs in to save the day while I sit in a corner watching."

"Is that what you think?" Pearl asked pointedly.

"It's not what I think, Pearl. It's the truth."

"I see."

"No, you don't," Jameson replied. She seldom challenged Pearl, but at the moment, Jameson was not certain anyone could understand how she felt. "Jessica is the cavalry.

The kids have formed this Mom Squad to help keep Candace quiet for a few days. Candace is already plotting her next move; I can see it. Dana is handling the press. Cooper? God, what would I have done without my Mom and Marianne? What the hell am I doing? Jesus, Pearl, I can't even drive my wife home. I get to push the wheelchair to the car, what?"

Pearl stayed silent for a moment. She could feel the frustration pouring off of Jameson. And, when she took a moment to think about it, she could hardly fault the younger woman. Everything that Jameson had proclaimed rang true. What Jameson failed to see, was that she had been handling everything. That is what had prompted Jonah's call to action to his siblings. It was what had led Maureen to insist on staying a few days to help with Cooper. Even where Jessica was concerned, Pearl had seen evidence of the empathy Jessica had for Jameson. Candace was a force to be reckoned with, reasonable when it came to dealing with issues, but when it came to herself, Candace could define stubborn. Everyone understood that. Everyone understood the uphill battle Jameson would have to get Candace to comply and recuperate in quiet for even a few days. Everyone also could see Jameson's dedication to the family.

Jameson had made a point to run in between the hospital and home so that Cooper would feel secure. She had taken a few hours earlier in the day to come home while Michelle stayed with Candace and Cooper at the hospital. She had decided to take Spencer out for McDonald's and a walk in the park. Spencer was having a hard time understanding why Cooper could go see Candace, and he could not see his Nana. Jameson had told Candace and Pearl that she thought a little one on one time with the toddler was in order. Jameson had been up at the crack of dawn to get to the hospital before Candace went into surgery. She had made a point to corner Laura and make the young woman promise that she would come to the house the next day to spend some time with Candace. The fact was, Jameson was exhausted. She was attempting to handle everything. And yet, she felt helpless. To Jameson, these were everyday things, and they were. What Pearl wanted Jameson to understand was that the everyday things were the most important to everyone at times like this.

"Jameson," Pearl began softly. Jameson looked up and shook her head. "I think you underestimate yourself," Pearl said. Jameson shook her head again. "You and Candy are a lot alike in some ways," she observed.

"I don't know about that."

"I do. You want to take care of everyone."

"I want to take care of my wife and my family."

"You do—you listen, now. You do. You have been running yourself ragged the last two days trying to make sure everyone is taken care of. You don't think Candy can see that? The kids? All of them? Even Cooper? They can, Jameson. So what if Jessica has the legal brain and Dana has the connections to deal with this idiot? You wouldn't expect to be the one to do surgery on Candy. Why should you be the one to deal with this? That's not your role."

"Oh? What is my role?"

"Maybe it's just to love them, Jameson. Taking Spencer for his chicken nuggets when I am sure you would have rather been at the hospital. Taking time to talk to Laura. Making sure Cooper has things to keep his mind off of Candy in the hospital."

Jameson sighed. "That's just little stuff, Pearl."

"Nope. No, sir, it is not. That's the most important stuff. When all the crap hits the fan, Jameson that is the *stuff*, as you call it that matters. That's what taking care of your family is all about. And, before you start trying to argue with me, remember that I have had a lot more years dealing with this family than you have, and I have a big paddle on that wall over there that I will add your name to if you are not careful."

Jameson snickered. "Threats of violence?"

"Whatever it takes, young lady."

"I just hate feeling helpless."

"Who doesn't? Give yourself a break," Pearl said.

"Or I get the paddle?"

"Like I said, whatever it takes."

"Pearl? Can I ask you something?"

"If I said no, would it stop you?" Pearl chided.

"Probably not," Jameson laughed. "I know there's history with the Klein family. Candace told me a little bit. That was over fifty years ago, though. I don't understand why Lawson Klein hates her so much."

Pearl sighed. "She told you about her granddaddy and Jeremiah Klein."

"A little. I know that he was going to run against her grandfather once. Candace said that had ended abruptly. And, she also said that at one time they were friends. When I asked what had happened, she just shrugged it off. You know Candace; she said everything was a rumor, and she doesn't deal in rumors."

"Mmm. Well, that might be true. But, then again just because something is a rumor it doesn't mean it isn't true," Pearl told Jameson. "Well, I don't know how much Candy told you. I do know that she's avoided digging into the story too deeply even though Jessica wanted her to," Pearl said. "Jessica is not one to be bullied, you know," Pearl laughed. "Lawson Klein came at Candy and her pretty hard. That prompted Jessica to do some digging. That much I do know. Candy put a stop to that—digging up old skeletons. I imagine some of that had to do with me. Not wanting anyone to find out her granddaddy's secret. Not wanting me to have to face the press about who my father was. She's smart enough to know that her granddad had his flaws," Pearl said. She let out a heavy breath. "You know, I loved my father even if I never got to call him that."

Jameson smiled. "I'm sorry, Pearl. If this is too…"

"No, no, it's fine, Jameson. I did love him. Candy's great-grandma, my grandma, she was my rock until she died, you know? She told me many things, and I learned a lot just by watching. Local politics is sometimes the dirtiest. People don't realize that. In small towns, small talk often influences small minds," Pearl said. "You drop a little tidbit, true or not true and it catches like wildfire. Ramblings or not, I'll tell you, word of mouth is powerful. From what Candy's grandma said to me that's really how it started," Pearl began.

"What kind of rumor could linger for over fifty years?" Jameson wanted to know.

Pearl sighed. "Jeremiah Klein was a nice enough man, Jameson," she said. She saw surprise light Jameson's eyes and laughed. "That surprises you? I guess I can understand why."

"Laura's grandfather?"

"No, no. Jeremiah would have been Laura's great-granddaddy, just like my father. No, Jeremiah had a son and a daughter, Hawthorne, and Maribel. Hawthorne was Lawson's daddy," Pearl explained. "Hawthorne was quite a bit younger than Candy's father. They moved from the area suddenly—all of the Kleins."

"Why?"

Pearl sighed again. "Well, Jeremiah's father, Ezra—he was about as ambitious a man as I ever saw," she explained.

"He was in politics?" Jameson wondered.

"Goodness, no," Pearl chuckled. "He was a minister at the Pentecostal Church of New Scotland. But, I heard my Grandma say more than once that Reverend Klein was sure his son would be president one day," Pearl rolled her eyes with the words. "Truth be told, Jameson—Jeremiah? Well, maybe he could have been. He was a natural. My father genuinely liked him. I think that was mutual."

"You think he would have beaten Governor Stratton?" Jameson wondered.

"Maybe," Pearl said honestly.

"You sound like you liked him? Jeremiah Klein?"

"Well, I was living with my Grandma at the time—Candy's great-grandmother. So, I only met him a few times, but yes, I liked him. He was genuinely friendly. And, truth be told, Jameson my father and Candy have one major thing in common—they are excellent judges of character. My father would never have entertained a friendship with a vicious person like Lawson Klein. He'd have been civil, just like Candy. He would not have dined with the man."

"I don't get it," Jameson confessed. "What happened?"

"Well, every family gets one, you know?" Pearl chuckled.

"One what?"

"One maverick," Pearl explained. "One person who just needs to go his or her own way. You know, a bit like Jonah."

"You think Jonah is a maverick?"

"In a sense. He's always gone his own way. Thing is, in this family that's allowed. That's not the case for everyone. Some might say Candy was the maverick, making the decision to live in the open," Pearl raised her brow.

Jameson was beginning to catch on. "Pearl? Are you telling me that Jeremiah Klein was gay?"

"Can't really say," Pearl replied honestly. "I can tell you that not long after he said he was going to run against Candy's granddaddy, word broke that he was having an affair."

"And?"

"Not with a lady, Jameson."

"You're kidding?"

"Nope, I am not. A young man named Thomas Brinker," Pearl said before shaking her head sadly.

"Thomas Brinker?" Jameson asked.

Jameson recalled the name. The story of Thomas Brinker was not national news; it was a well-known local story even many years later. Brinker was a twenty-two-year-old fresh out of college. He had been beaten in a field by a group of young men, allegedly for being homosexual. Two of the boys went to jail for the assault. The others were never even charged, and none with the young man's death which followed only two days later from his injuries. In modern times it was unthinkable. In 1961, in rural New York, it had been swept under the rug.

"Not the Thomas Brinker that was beaten to death," Jameson asked sheepishly.

"That'd be the one," Pearl said.

"Jesus. Don't tell me that Jeremiah Klein…"

"No, I'm sure he had nothing to do with that," Pearl dismissed the thought.

"But?"

"But, lots of folks thought Ezra did. One of the boys supposedly said Ezra paid them to beat that kid. A warning to keep him quiet, you know? Went too far. It wasn't more than a month after that the entire family left. Ezra moved to lead a congregation in Ohio. Jeremiah followed with his family."

"Even if that's true, what does that have to do with Candy?"

Pearl shrugged. "Well, from what I do know, Ezra maintained that my father started that rumor and the rumor about Hawthorne in the first place."

"Let me guess? He also tried to pin the beating on Governor Stratton?" Jameson guessed.

"Oh, I am absolutely certain that he did. Never stuck, though. The truth is, Jameson, lots of people knew about Jeremiah's relationships. They just kept it quiet. They liked him. That's what you did. You kept quiet. What no one knew didn't hurt anyone."

"And, Candace?"

"I don't know, Jameson. People can be strange. Jeremiah, he was in law—that I know. He stayed out of the political fray after that. Hawthorne, Laura's grandfather, he went into preaching like his granddaddy. Who knows why Lawson Klein hates Candy so much? My guess would be he learned that from someone other than his daddy, though," Pearl said honestly.

"His grandfather?"

"Probably," Pearl replied.

"You sound sad," Jameson observed.

"Maybe I am just a bit. Seems like a waste to me—all of it. Amazing what things can linger. Lawson is no more his father than Candy is her mother. But, you know, sometimes kids look to please. They do that in strange ways. Candy followed her granddaddy; maybe Lawson is following his."

Jameson shook her head. "Why wouldn't Candace tell me this?"

"Oh, I think you know that answer," Pearl said. "But, if you need to hear her say it, ask her yourself."

"Pearl, do you think it was true? Any of it?"

"I think Jeremiah Klein was a victim of the family and the times he lived in, Jameson. Do I think his granddaddy paid to have that boy beaten?" Pearl took a deep breath. "I wish I could tell you I believe that it was just a rumor. I don't. Some people will do anything to keep a secret and anything to get where they think they deserve to be."

Jameson put her face in her hands. "Cooper has nothing to do with this."

"No, he doesn't."

"Pearl, do you think Candace..."

"I think Candy has been reserved for all the right reasons when it comes to Klein over all of these years. I'm not sure she will have as many reservations after this if that is what you were going to ask," Pearl said honestly.

"That's why she wants to talk to Jessica."

"Oh, I would be willing to bet that Jessica has more that ancient history on Lawson Klein. I'd be willing to bet so does Candy. She may not like to get in the mud. Candy learned a lot from watching too. She will have done her share of poking into who Lawson Klein is, and what he deals in."

Jameson nodded. "Stupid," she mumbled. "It's ancient history."

"Only for people with sense, Jameson. And, you will learn the longer you live with Candy, not everyone has that—sense, I mean. Greed and power...The desire for power makes people do unthinkable things. It taints everything. Candy gets that. That is why she's handled Lawson Klein the way she has all these years." Pearl smiled at Jameson. "Trust her, Jameson."

"I do."

"I know you think that you are not pulling your weight. Trust Candy to handle this part of it. She knows what she's doing."

"I do, Pearl. I just..."

"She needs you to keep her steady, Jameson," Pearl said. She witnessed the evident skepticism in Jameson's eyes. "Don't believe me? Who pushed to get Cooper to leave that stuffed frog at home, Candy or you?" Pearl asked.

"That's not..."

"Ummm. She needs you to keep this family steady right now. And, you do. Trust me on this, Jameson. Let her handle what she can handle. She needs to do that right now."

"What aren't you saying?" Jameson asked.

"Candy never imagined being Mom again."

"I know that."

"Mmm. This little hospital stay scared her."

"I know that too," Jameson replied.

"So, then trust me. Let her handle what she can control for a bit."

"I think I get it," Jameson said.

"You do. The kids need you. I don't mean just Cooper, Jameson. I mean all of Candy's children. I think maybe they are just realizing how much that is true. She knew that long ago. But, this brought it home."

"Is that a bad thing?" Jameson wondered.

"No, but it is a big thing. Trust me; she will handle Klein, and she needs to. Jameson, when Candy lost Lucas...."

"I know, she told me."

"I'm sure she did," Pearl replied. "I tried to support her. Thought I understood what she was going through. The truth is, until you called me to tell me Candy was being rushed to the hospital, I had no idea."

Jameson watched as Pearl's eyes fell shut and the older woman deliberately steadied her breathing. Candace's health scare shook the entire family, far more than Candace realized. Jameson could see the toll it had taken on Pearl. She hadn't expected Pearl to be so open about that fact.

"I've never felt fear like that, Jameson not even when my husband died. Not when I lost my father or Candy's grandmother—never. Driving to that hospital was the most helpless I have ever felt in my life. You are supposed to protect your children. I understood at that moment what it had been like for Candy, at least, more than I ever had before," Pearl confided. Jameson nodded. "Laura's daddy has decided to tread on sacred ground. Cooper...Well...I see it with both of you. He's your baby. He's her baby, Jameson. And, Jonah..."

It was true. Candace had lost two sons already. Now, Lawson Klein's actions stood to cause pain for her two younger children. Candace would not stand for that if she could help it. Jameson was beginning to understand Pearl's advice. Both she and Candace would play a protective role in their sons' lives. It just would be a different role. Jameson smiled.

Pearl nodded. "See what I am talking about?"

"Yeah, I do," Jameson admitted. "But, Pearl? If Klein isn't careful, he will meet with more than Candace's wrath. And, believe me, I never expected to be anyone's mom. Now that I am? No one messes with my kids."

Pearl laughed.

"Is that funny?"

"No," Pearl said. "I just think it would have delighted Jonah to hear that, not to mention your wife."

Jameson blushed. "It's strange, I know...I..."

"No, it's not," Pearl said. "Not even a little bit," she said. "That's like saying it's strange that Candy is my daughter or Cooper is your son. Not strange in the least. Don't overthink it, Jameson. That's not how it works."

"Pearl? I don't want..."

Pearl waved off Jameson's next thought. "You don't worry about me. You tell Candy whatever you feel you should. I didn't tell you anything that wasn't my right to."

Jameson nodded her thanks. She stood up, stretched and kissed Pearl on the cheek. "I love you, Pearl. I guess I really don't say that very often."

Pearl's eyes twinkled. "Sure you do, just in your own unique way," Pearl said. "And, I love you too. Even if you do make me crazy sometimes."

"Hey! I got you, Jinx!"

"Oh, yes, I'm sure I was your motivation in that scheme," Pearl laughed. "And, anyway, the only time that cat even notices my presence is when you are all gone away. If it isn't Candy he's rubbing up against; it's Spencer and Cooper. Cat has absolutely no allegiance."

Jameson laughed. "Slip him some chicken fingers," she whispered before heading out of the room.

Pearl laughed and took a sip of her tea. "Candy's right; this family is certifiable."

✗✗✗

"Mom?" Candace turned to the sound of Michelle's voice. "Wow, you look like you," Michelle commented.

Candace lifted her brow and chuckled. "I look better in clothes, huh?"

"Depends on who you ask," Jameson mumbled. Candace whacked Jameson playfully.

"So, where is Drew? Am I ready to be sprung or what?" Candace asked impatiently.

Jameson shook her head just as the nurse walked in rolling a wheelchair. She snickered when Candace's brow raised again.

"What is that?" Candace asked.

"Your chariot, I would guess," Jameson said.

"My what?"

Jameson gloated. "I think it's hospital policy that you get rolled out."

"I've been up walking since last night. Why on earth do I need a wheelchair now?" Candace challenged.

"Mom," Michelle said. "Just take the ride." She pointed to Jameson. "Geez, that twenty years oughtta be good for something."

"Cute, Shell," Jameson replied. She looked at Candace and smiled. "Suck it up, Governor. You know all about rules."

Candace rolled her eyes and sat down in the chair. "Not in front of the press," she said.

"Mom..."

"No, way. The hospital can sue me. I know some good attorneys."

Jameson laughed. "Through the door and you can stand."

"That's not actually the policy," the nurse began.

Jameson smirked. "Trust me; it is now."

✂ ✂ ✂

"Mawianne?" Cooper looked up at his big sister.

"Yes, Coop?"

"Is Mommy coming home now?"

"Soon, Coop," Marianne promised. "Both your moms will be home soon."

"Mawianne?"

"Yes?"

Cooper hung his head slightly and shuffled his foot nervously.

"Cooper?"

Cooper looked up at Marianne sadly. "Spen don't like me?"

"What?" Marianne asked. She let out a small sigh and held out her hand to Cooper. "Why do you think that?" she asked him. Copper shrugged. "Did Spencer say something to make you sad?" Cooper nodded. "Cooper?"

"I didn't steal Jay."

Marianne fought the urge to sigh again. She smiled at Cooper reassuringly. "No, you didn't steal J.D."

"Spen says."

Marianne scratched her forehead and considered how to reply.

"I didn't steal," Cooper murmured. "I can't have fwee."

Marianne pulled Cooper into her lap. "Yes, Cooper you can. Mom and J.D. love you, and they love Spencer too, just like they love me. They are your moms, I promise. I think Spencer just misses them a little bit," she told him. She kissed Cooper's head. "Where is Spencer?"

Cooper shrugged. "In da big room."

Marianne nodded and placed Cooper on the floor. "Come on," she held out her hand to him as she stood. Cooper looked up at her skeptically. Marianne smiled. "It's okay, Cooper. We're going to find Spencer and have a talk."

"Am I in twouble?"

"No one is in trouble," Marianne promised. "Come on."

Marianne wasn't sure what she was going to say when she reached Spencer. Pearl had stepped out to take Maddie for a walk in her stroller before Jameson was due back with Candace. Jameson was not due home with Candace for at least another hour. Marianne had seen the evidence of Spencer's jealously growing. She had hoped that Jameson spending a few hours with him the previous day would have alleviated his hurt feelings a bit. Right now, she wished Pearl or her mother were available to impart some motherly wisdom. Jameson was Spencer's hero and Spencer adored his Nana.

Both Candace and Jameson had made an effort to spend one on one time with Spencer. In fact, Marianne was sure that her son had spent more time with Jameson and her mother individually than before Cooper's arrival. The problem was that Spencer was used to being with his grandparents as a pair, and he was also accustomed to being the center of their attention. Spencer was not only clearly intelligent, but Spencer was also articulate beyond his age. Marianne had to credit her mother and Jameson for that. They engaged Spencer in conversation regularly. No matter his intellect or ability to communicate, Spencer was only three. He missed his Jay Jay and his Nana, and he saw Cooper as the reason for that. His ability to articulate those feelings had deeply hurt Cooper.

"Spencer?" Marianne called to her son.

Spencer turned and frowned at his mother who was standing with Cooper slightly behind her legs. He looked at Cooper and turned back to the video on the television. Marianne took a deep breath and squatted down to Cooper. She had hoped that she could address the boys together. That seemed unlikely at the moment.

"Coop," she said with a smile. "Why don't you go up to your room and get your new train ready for when Mom gets home," she suggested. Cooper nodded sadly. Marianne kissed his cheek and whispered in his ear. "It's okay," she promised. "Spen is still your best friend. I just need to talk to him for a minute, all right?" she said. Cooper nodded again and headed off.

Marianne made her way to the television and clicked it off. Spencer looked at her with obvious displeasure.

"Spencer..."

"He steals."

"Spencer, Cooper did not steal anything from you."

"Did. Nana and Jay Jay."

Marianne shook her head and directed Spencer to sit in her lap on one of the large, leather chairs in the room. She smiled at her son and shook her head affectionately. "Spencer," Marianne began. "Nana and Jay Jay love you very much."

"They love him more."

"No, Spencer. That is not true," Marianne said firmly. "You know, you have a lot of people who love you," she told him. "I know sometimes you miss Daddy, but you still have me and you have your Jay Jay and Nana. You have always had all of us. Cooper is your best friend. Don't you think he should get to have those things too?" she asked. Spencer frowned. "Didn't Jay Jay take you out yesterday?"

"Yeah, but Coop stayed with Nana."

"Mm. Well, Nana was in the hospital, Spencer. She was kind of sick; you know?" Marianne said. Spencer looked up at his mother fearfully. "She was," she repeated. "Jay Jay was very tired, but she came home special to see you because she missed you. And, Nana misses you too, sweetheart. She'll be here later today."

"He sleeps there," Spencer whispered.

Marianne nodded and decided to try a different tactic. "Spencer," she began. "You know that Nana and Jay Jay adopted Cooper, don't you?"

"Yeah. He stays with them."

"Yes, but do you know what that means?" Marianne asked. Spencer shrugged. Marianne smiled. She hoped her explanation might help her son as much as it had Cooper. "Well, it means that Cooper gets to live there because Nana and Jay Jay are his mommies. Some little boys and girls don't have any mommy or daddy to take care of them. Sometimes, they don't have a Nana or anyone like Jay Jay either. Nana and Jay Jay wanted Cooper to have a family just like you do," she explained.

"They love Coop," he said sadly.

"Yes, they do, Spencer. They also love you. When Cooper came to live here that meant he also became my little brother," Marianne said. Spencer looked at his mother curiously. "Um-hm. And, that means that you aren't just Coop's best friend, you really are his nephew just like Uncle Jonah is your uncle and your Uncle Jonah's nephew. That means that Coop is really your uncle and Maddie and J.J.'s too."

Spencer's eyes widened. "Uncle is old."

Spencer's reaction mirrored Cooper's so closely that Marianne struggled not to laugh. "Well, you don't have to be old to be someone's uncle," she said. "But, just like being a big brother it does mean that you should look out for your nephew," she said seriously. "It's kind of an important thing to be. You know all about being a big brother. Cooper needs to learn what it means to be in a family, Spencer. You know how to do that. So, maybe you could help Cooper with that."

Spencer considered his mother's statement for a moment and shook his head. "Coop cried."

"Cooper cried when you told him he stole Nana and Jay Jay?" she asked. Spencer nodded. "Well, that's because Cooper loves you, Spencer. He looks up to you."

"He's bigger. And, he's the uncle. You said."

Marianne suppressed a snicker. "Well, yes I did. And, Cooper is taller, yes and a little older too, but that doesn't mean he can't want to be more like you. Sometimes, Spencer I look up to Uncle Jonah a little."

"You do?"

"Yes, I do because Uncle is very good with people just like Nana and just like you. He never quits. When he was little like you are now?" she mused. "He had a hard time walking. He never quit until he could run, even when he would fall and look silly, he got right back up. And, he is funny. Uncle Jonah can have fun anywhere. Sometimes I wish I could be a little more like him," she confessed.

Spencer hugged his mother. "You be funny too, Mommy," he assured her.

"You think so?" she asked. Spencer nodded his affirmation. "You know; you do an excellent job of sharing Maddie."

"Mads is wittle."

"Yes, she is. That's true. Maddie can't tell us what she needs sometimes. We have to guess."

"Cause Mads don't talk."

"Maddie can't talk yet, no. But, Spencer sometimes it is hard for Cooper to say what he needs too."

"Coop talks."

"Yes, but Cooper is scared sometimes to tell us things."

"Why?"

"I think because he is afraid we will get mad or not like him. He's scared that maybe we will send him away, I think."

Spencer pursed his lips. "But, Nana's his mommy."

"Yes, she is," Marianne agreed. "But you know, when Cooper's mommy left him he was alone with strangers for a while. That's scary." Spencer hung his head. "So, maybe sometimes Cooper needs Nana and Jay Jay a little more than you do, just like Maddie needs me."

"Coop is scared?"

"I think so, Spencer. Sometimes I think Cooper is still scared. Right now, I think he is scared that you don't like him."

Spencer looked at Marianne for a split second and then hopped off of her lap. He started out of the room and Marianne smiled, knowing exactly where he was headed.

"Coop!" Spencer called loudly through the house.

Marianne let out a relieved breath. "Maybe I can do this after all."

CHAPTER EIGHT

Jameson kept her hand gently on the small of Candace's back when Candace stepped up to the small group of journalists outside the hospital to answer a few questions. Jameson was positive no one else would have noticed the slight waver in Candace's gait. Candace had been up and around since the previous afternoon for short periods. She had not complained of any pain, although Jameson could tell that Candace was not comfortable. And, it was evident to Jameson that Candace was tired. Obvious enough that Jameson had stepped out of Candace's room that morning and had called Jessica to postpone any visits until the following day. Jameson expected that Candace would be irritated, and likely accuse her of over-protectiveness. Jameson didn't care. Candace's Lt. Governor Dan Moore and Bill DeGrasso had spent an hour briefing the governor that morning. Jameson had made no attempt to stop that. Candace was well enough to be kept in the loop on state affairs. And, Jameson would not interfere in that endeavor. While Jameson was furious about Lawson Klein's actions and worried about the potential fall-out, she did not see any need to address it immediately with Jessica.

Candace still needed rest. Cooper was still uneasy about his mommy's hospital stay. Jameson had noted a hint of sadness in Spencer the day before. She was sure that Spencer was missing Candace. And, Jameson wanted to have the rest of the day at home with family—just family. She had been running herself ragged for three days. She not only desired some quiet time at home, but Jameson also needed it. She had not slept more than a few sporadic hours since Candace had been admitted to the hospital. Jameson seldom went against Candace's wishes. She had no intention of discussing stressful topics at home once they arrived. The family needed to be together, and Jameson needed to be home with her family—Candace most of all. She smiled at the press as Candace spoke.

"How are you feeling, Governor?"

"Much better than the other day," Candace confessed with a wink. "Next time I will just ask for a personal day," she joked.

"You met with your staff already?" another woman asked.

"Well, many of them visited yesterday," she said. "But, yes, Lt. Governor Moore and I spent about an hour together this morning."

"When do you expect to be back in Albany?"

Candace nodded. "Jameson is forcing me to behave for the week," she quipped lightly. "So, I will be working from our home in Schoharie until next Monday. I will be at the Capitol late that afternoon for meetings as planned."

"Governor Reid," a man toward the back of the small group called out. Candace smiled at him. "I assume that you saw the piece with Laureen Cosgrove."

"No, actually I have not," Candace answered evenly.

"Do you have any response to the allegations?"

Candace offered the press a taught smile. Jameson pressed the palm of her hand firmly into Candace's back as reassurance.

"I would think that by now everyone would know that I don't respond to unfounded sentiments of any kind," Candace said. She took a deliberate breath and continued. "Jameson and I are thrilled to have Cooper as an addition to our family. He has certainly added a whole new dimension to our lives."

"What about you, Ms. Reid? Any thoughts on the accusation that you and the governor adopted this little boy to help bolster popular opinion?" a voice called over to Jameson.

Jameson smiled genuinely. "Our son could definitely win over the harshest critics," she said honestly. Candace smiled.

"No worries then?"

Jameson shrugged and fielded the question before Candace had a chance. "Oh, I worry all the time. I worry about anyone hurting him. I guess that goes with the territory of being a mom," she said.

Candace leaned into Jameson as Jameson gently guided her away. "Nicely done," Candace whispered to Jameson.

"What? I just told the truth," Jameson said as she held the car door for Candace.

"And, that is exactly why I love you," Candace replied.

Jameson closed the door and sighed. "Yeah, we'll see how you feel when you find out Jessica's not visiting until tomorrow."

"You ready?" Jonah asked Laura. Laura balked. "You can't avoid Mom forever," he said.

"Jonah," Laura spoke softly.

"What's wrong?" he asked. Laura lifted her eyes to his and began to cry. "Hey, why are you crying?"

Laura shook her head. "There's something I need to tell you."

Jonah nodded. "You can tell me anything."

"I really hope so."

Jameson looked at Candace and kissed her gently. "Ready?"

"Why is something going to pop out at me when you open our door?"

"Maybe," Jameson laughed. She put her hand on the door and pushed it open gently. The moment Candace stepped across the threshold two toddlers made a beeline for her.

Candace laughed at Spencer and Cooper as both collapsed into her sides. "Well, look who is home," she said.

"You!" Spencer laughed.

"Looks like it," Candace agreed. She kissed each boy on the head. "What have you two been up to?" she asked with the signature raise of her brow.

"Spen still likes me," Cooper told her with a smile.

Candace looked over at Marianne curiously. Marianne mouthed the word, "later."

"I should hope so," Candace said to Cooper.

"Okay, let Mommy in," Jameson said.

Jameson noted that Spencer held tight to Candace's hand and took the opportunity to lift Cooper onto her hip. She led the group into the living room. Cooper settled on Jameson's lap in a large chair. Spencer crawled up beside Candace on the sofa. Jameson smiled at Pearl when she entered carrying a tray full of snacks.

"Sorry, Candy no cardboard containers today," Pearl said.

Candace laughed. She looked at Spencer and smiled. His eyes held a timid expression that she immediately understood. She winked at him and gestured for him to crawl into her lap. "I'm okay," she whispered into Spencer's ear. "I missed you, Spencer."

"You still sick, Nana?" Spencer asked.

"No, sweetheart, just a little sore," Candace answered honestly. "Kind of like when you fell and cut your knee that time in the driveway. Remember?" she explained. "It will just take a few days to heal. Just like your cut."

"Do you have a cut?" he asked with wide eyes.

"Very tiny, Spencer. I'm all right."

Spencer surprised Candace by hopping off of her lap and running out of the room as fast as his legs would carry him. She looked at Jameson, who shrugged.

"Coop!" Spencer called from upstairs.

Cooper immediately jumped off of Jameson's lap and ran to find Spencer.

"What on earth?" Candace looked back at Jameson again.

Jameson shrugged again. "I'll go see."

Candace nodded. Marianne took a seat beside her mother.

"So?" Candace asked. "What happened while I was gone?"

Marianne smiled. "Oh, the typical. The boys just missed you."

"Why do I think there is more to it than that?" Candace challenged gently.

Marianne was about to answer when Spencer and Cooper came running back into the room with a giggling Jameson following behind.

"Here, Nana," Spencer said.

Candace looked at him curiously and accepted what he was handing her. She smiled broadly at the pair of toddlers.

"Coop's taller. He can reach," Spencer explained.

Candace looked at the Thomas the Train bandages in her hand and nodded her understanding. "Thank you," she said.

"I was gonna get Spiderman, but Coop likes Thomas," Spencer continued.

"Thomas'll take care of you like Genie, Mommy," Cooper said innocently.

"I know he will, sweetheart," Candace answered. Spencer looked at her, and she patted the couch for him to sit beside her. Marianne scooted aside to make room for her son.

"Come on, Coop," Spencer told Cooper. "You sit with me and Nana."

Cooper smiled but seemed to hesitate for a moment. Candace was beginning to put the pieces together regarding Cooper's earlier statement that Spencer still liked him. She patted the other side of the couch and Cooper crawled up beside her.

"So, Grandma Pearl says no chicken fingers for us today," Candace whispered to the boys.

"No, Nana. No chicken fingers for *you*," Spencer corrected her.

Candace's eyes flew open.

"Yeah, Mommy. Dat's bad for sore tummies. Grandma says."

Candace bit her lip and looked up at Pearl.

"That didn't work on me when you were a kid. It sure won't now," Pearl said. "You're lucky I even made you those cookies."

Candace looked at the tray of tiny cookies. She was certain the size had been deliberate. The truth was that Candace did not have much of an appetite yet. She'd had broth and then some oatmeal that morning. But, she had no intention of allowing Pearl and Jameson to baby her. "I don't have any restrictions," Candace said with strained politeness.

"Says who?" Pearl replied.

"Says my doctor."

Pearl looked at Jameson. "Please tell me you don't plan on any activity that..."

Jameson held up her hand. "No. No strenuous activity," Jameson said flatly. "Uh, and as I recall, the advice was solid foods gradually. And, he did say that you need to eat healthier," Jameson reminded Candace.

Candace arched her eyebrow at Jameson and grinned. "Since when is chicken unhealthy?" she asked playfully.

"I'll pretend I did not hear that," Jameson said.

Dr. Everett had warned Candace about fatty foods, fried foods, and cautioned her that she would likely have difficulty digesting some of what she was accustomed to. Candace looked at Jameson indignantly, and Jameson shook her head just as her cell phone buzzed.

"Hey, Jonah," Jameson answered. She cautioned Candace with a glance and left the room to take Jonah's call.

Pearl folded her arms across her chest. "Behave or I'll get rid of *those* cookies too."

Marianne broke out into laughter at the expression on her mother's face. Pearl meant business. Only Pearl could survive a threat to throw out Candace's fortune cookies. Only Pearl would have had the guts to admit she'd found them. Marianne thought her mother looked exactly like Spencer when Marianne had to reprimand him for something.

"What is going on in here?" Michelle asked as she entered the room holding Melanie's hand.

"Grandma threatened to throw out Mom's fortune cookies," Marianne told her sister.

"What fortune cookies?" Michelle asked. Marianne kept laughing. "Oh, my God, you have a stash, don't you?" Michelle asked her mother. "You do! What else are you hiding in this old house?" she asked Candace.

Candace's only reply was to grin and hand both Spencer and Cooper one of Pearl's chocolate chip cookies.

Michelle looked at her older sister. "Where are they? You know. I know you do, just like you knew where Grandma stashed the batteries all those years and wouldn't tell Jonah or me," Michelle accused Marianne pointedly.

Candace grabbed two more cookies, handed one to Marianne and took a bite of the other.

"What is this?" Michelle asked. "Some secret society?" Melanie started to laugh, and Michelle turned to her. "Watch it or I'll take that ring back," she said without thinking.

Candace coughed, and Marianne's mouth dropped open, a piece of cookie falling to the floor. The display instantly spurred Cooper and Spencer into a fit of the giggles.

"What did you just say?" Candace asked Michelle.

Melanie smiled and shook her head at Michelle. "Think you just gave up the goods, babe."

Michelle looked at the ceiling and groaned audibly. She nodded at Melanie and turned back to face the rest of the room's occupants who were waiting impatiently for clarification.

"Hey," Jameson's voice sounded from the hallway. "J.J.'s not feeling so great. Jonah and Laura will stop by tomorrow," she was finishing her thought when she walked into the room. Jameson looked at the display unfolding. She was partly puzzled and slightly amused. Cooper and Spencer were both giggling uncontrollably. Candace, Marianne, and Pearl appeared to be in some type of face-off with Michelle. "What did I miss?" Jameson wanted to know.

"Aww, hell," Michelle complained. "Jonah and Laura already know anyway."

"Know what?" Jameson asked.

Michelle blew out a frustrated breath. "Not how I envisioned this."

"What is going on?" Jameson asked again. She looked at Candace whose gaze was fixed on Michelle.

"Okay, it's like this. I asked Mel to marry me last night."

"*You* asked Mel?" Jameson replied in disbelief.

"Yeah? Why is that so weird?" Michelle retorted.

"She said yes?" Marianne teased, containing her laughter.

"Yes, she said yes!" Michelle snapped back.

Candace smiled at Michelle and gently made her way to her feet. She looked at Melanie and then hugged them both. "I'm happy for both of you," she told them.

"Thanks, Mom," Michelle replied. She looked at Jameson.

Jameson was surprised to see what she was certain equated to worry in Michelle's eyes. She decided against her inclination to tease the pair. "That's great, Shell."

"Really?" Michelle asked.

"Hey, I need as much company in this asylum as I can get," Jameson deadpanned. Candace whacked Jameson gently. "What?" Jameson feigned innocence.

"Well, I guess that calls for a toast," Pearl said. "I will get the wine." She looked at Candace, who had a gleam in her eyes. "Oh no," she wagged a finger. "You and the boys can enjoy a nice glass of juice."

"I," Candace began.

"Don't bother," Pearl said as she headed from the room. "Or, I'll give up where that stash of cookies really is."

"You wouldn't dare," Candace mumbled.

"One cardboard container or go near that wine rack and I most certainly will."

"What are you smirking about?" Candace asked her wife.

"Nothing," Jameson promised with a kiss on Candace's cheek. "I'll even drink juice with you to prove it."

Candace finally laughed. "This family is insane."

Candace looked at Jameson and raised her brow as Jameson shut the door behind Michelle and Melanie. "You need to go to bed," Candace told Jameson.

"What do you mean?"

"Jameson," Candace sighed. "You are exhausted. I can see it."

"I'm fine. I will go up once the boys settle down."

Candace shook her head. "You go on. Marianne and I will get the boys."

"Candace, you just got home from having surgery."

"And, I have been sitting around all day with all of you fawning over me like I was a lost puppy you had tied up," Candace said.

"That's not true."

"Yes, it is and believe it or not I love you all for it, but you need to trust me on this—I feel fine."

"No pain?"

Candace smiled. "It's uncomfortable," she said honestly. "I've felt much worse, believe me."

"You need..."

"Jameson, please."

Jameson sighed heavily and studied Candace thoughtfully for a moment. "You need a break from me, huh?"

"No. You need a break from everything," Candace observed candidly. She did not need anyone to tell her how much Jameson had been juggling. She had noticed the worry in Jameson most of the day after Jonah's call. "J.J. wasn't sick, was he?" Candace guessed.

"No," Jameson admitted. "Jonah didn't tell me everything," she said. "They want to see us tomorrow without all of the fanfare."

Candace nodded. She traced Jameson's jaw with her fingertips and then let them wander over Jameson's forehead. Candace watched as Jameson closed her eyes and her breathing deepened. "You are exhausted. Please, Jameson, please go and lie down. Marianne won't let me get too far out of line. Please?" Candace requested again. Jameson finally nodded. "I'll be there shortly. No offense, I hope you are asleep."

Jameson chuckled. "I look that bad, huh?" she asked. Candace tipped her head playfully. "That bad?" Jameson asked more seriously.

Candace laughed. "Go on, you lunatic."

Jameson leaned in and kissed Candace's lips sweetly. "Don't try and…"

"Go," Candace directed Jameson. She watched Jameson as Jameson walked down the hallway and sighed.

"Made her go up, huh?" Marianne guessed.

"I don't think I've ever seen her look that tired," Candace said.

"I don't think she's slept much," Marianne said. Candace turned to her. "I shouldn't tell you this."

"Yes, you should," Candace said. "I'll make some tea while the boys finish their movie, and you can catch me up."

"Okay, but I will make the tea."

Candace rolled her eyes but dutifully followed her daughter into the kitchen. She took a seat at the table and watched as Marianne set about the task of filling the tea kettle with water. Candace smiled softly as she watched. Marianne appeared relaxed. Candace was curious to hear about the last few days.

"So, what haven't you told me? And, why shouldn't you tell me?" Candace asked.

Marianne leaned against the kitchen counter. "I think she's still a little scared, to tell you the truth."

"Who?"

"J.D.," Marianne said. Candace sighed. "She hides it pretty well," Marianne admitted. "The night they admitted you? I think the only reason she went to bed was Cooper. She was downstairs at three in the morning drinking coffee. Yesterday, after she dropped off Spencer? I went to go see if she wanted me to wait and bring Coop back here last night with me and the kids. She…"

"What?"

Marianne sighed. "She was in your bed at the mansion holding your pillow. I know she was crying, Mom. I just walked back out. I know she's tired, but...Mom, we were all scared, don't get me wrong. Shell cried. I cried. Even Pearl cried in front of me. J.D.? She held it together for everyone."

Candace nodded. "I know," she said. "It's what she needed to do, though. Not for me," Candace clarified. "What she needed to do because that's who she is, Marianne."

"I tried to help."

"You did," Candace assured her daughter.

"You're worried about her," Marianne said.

Candace smiled. "I know her," she said. "Not worried," she corrected Marianne. "Aware."

Marianne nodded. She turned to retrieve the kettle from the stove just as it began to whistle.

"What happen with Spencer and Cooper?" Candace asked.

Marianne set their tea down and sat across from her mother. "He just misses you," she said. "Spencer, I mean."

Candace sighed and nodded. She had been surprised that Spencer had not shown more evidence of jealousy before her hospital visit. "Green Monster finally reared its ugly head, huh?"

"And then some," Marianne confessed. She noticed her mother was smiling. "Not surprised, I take it."

"No. I went through it with you and Shell both. Believe it or not, I remember when Jeffrey was born," Candace laughed. "I loved him, and I hated him."

Jeffrey was Pearl's eldest son and nearly fourteen years Candace's junior. Marianne chuckled. "Bet you loved those diapers."

Candace rolled her eyes. "Jeffrey broke me in for all the thousands I would change later," she laughed. "I'm not surprised. Curious as to how you got them to work it out."

"After I cursed you and Pearl for leaving me without anyone to call on?" Marianne began. Candace laughed again.

"I don't know, Mom. I basically told Spencer what I told Cooper when he asked if you were his Nana."

"You told Spencer that he's your brother?" Candace teased Marianne.

"Ha-ha. Glad to see they didn't remove your sense of humor with your gallbladder."

"Nope, they seem to have left that intact, at least, for now."

Marianne understood her mother's reply. She was grateful that Jameson had put her foot down regarding a visit from Jessica, and not just because Marianne still harbored a degree of resentment toward her mother's former partner. Marianne and Candace had gradually become close in new and unexpected ways since Rick's death. Living back at home had altered the way Marianne perceived many things including her family. She had grown comfortable confiding in both her mother and Jameson. And, if she were to be honest, it was not just Spencer who missed them. While Marianne was grateful for the effect Candace and Jameson's longer absences had on her relationship with Spencer, she missed her mother more than ever before. Marianne had come to cherish sitting at the kitchen table with Candace. She had become accustomed to and was entertained by the affectionate banter her mother and Jameson engaged in. It lightened Marianne's spirits and it gave her hope.

Candace's unexpected hospital stay had shaken Marianne as much as it had everyone in the family. She was glad that the day had been spent with only immediate family. No calls from Candace's staff, no visits from friends or colleagues, and no meetings with Jessica Stearns personal in nature or otherwise. She had come to understand her mother more than ever before and Marianne was positive that under her calm exterior, Candace was seething over the story about Cooper's adoption. As a mother, she could relate. One day, Cooper would inevitably be exposed to all of it. No matter how much Candace and Jameson nurtured and loved him and no matter how they endeavored to protect him, he would hear the ugly things that people had said about his mothers and his family. And, as Jameson had shared with Marianne two nights ago, it now seemed likely that Cooper would hear the ugly things his biological grandmother had said about him. No one deserved that.

"Marianne? Candace reached across the table. It was clear that Marianne had drifted away in thought for a moment. "You all right?"

Marianne snapped from her private thoughts and smiled. "I was thinking that I'm glad we had today without any visitors."

Candace nodded. "You mean Jessica," she surmised.

"I do," Marianne replied honestly. "But, not just Jessica," she said. Candace sighed and shook her head. "Mom...I mean anyone. I know you need to talk to her, and I know why. At least, I know partly why. Jameson told me about what Laureen Cosgrove had to say about Coop."

"She did?"

"Yeah, she did," Marianne said. "The other night when I found her up drinking coffee at three in the morning. I sort of gathered that maybe she needed to talk."

"What did she say?" Candace asked.

Marianne took a sip of her tea in order to gather her thoughts. She met Candace's expectant gaze and smiled. "She was angry," Marianne said. "Furious, actually. Not just about the name calling, but the fact that this woman had the audacity to speak about you so harshly. Not her, Mom—you. I think she was feeling.... Well, helpless if you want to know the truth. I think if she thought she could get away with it, she would have beat the shit out of Lawson Klein and Laureen Cosgrove. And, I'm not kidding."

Candace took a moment. She licked her lips and then bit down gently on the lower one in thought. "Did she say that?"

"Yes, actually."

Candace nodded.

"But, she said she would never do that to Cooper or to you. She was frustrated and angry, Mom."

"I know. That's part of the reason she was running so much the last few days. Jameson is used to being able to fix things," Candace explained with a smile. "Whether that's the leaky roof or my mood," she laughed. "This one requires more than her tool belt or some Chinese take-out, I'm afraid."

"Do you think that you can shield him from it?"

Candace shook her head. "Not forever. For now. And, I'm thankful he is too little to understand the words he might hear. But, someday he will hear them. I think for both Jameson and me, we realize that now more than ever before."

"What do you mean?"

Candace sighed. "The truth is, Marianne if it were not Lawson Klein, it would eventually be someone else. It will be someone else. If it is not about me or about Jameson and me, eventually it will be about who Cooper is or rather what some people will see him as."

"You mean his color."

"I do," Candace said bluntly. "I knew that. Jameson knew that when we adopted him. Hearing it? It's vile." Candace closed her eyes. "He's our son, Marianne. I know how Jameson feels—helpless as you put it. I can't stop it. I can only try and guide him through it."

Marianne felt frustration, anger, and pain rolling off her mother. She took Candace's hand. "Mom, we will all be there for him—all of us. After today? Well, if Spencer turns out as much like you and Rick as I suspect he will? I pity the idiot who messes with his uncle."

Candace smiled broadly. "Ah, so that was the answer to the Green Monster—make him the protector."

"Not exactly. He assumed that role all by himself," Marianne explained. "When I think about it, he has been doing that all along. He's a leader like his Nana."

Candace's pride was evident in the sparkle in her eyes. "He's confident because he has always felt secure," Candace said. "That's why, Marianne. You have as much if not more to do with that than Jameson or me or anyone else for that matter. You're his mother."

"I've been lost for a while. We both needed you," Marianne admitted hoarsely.

"I know. That's what moms are for," Candace told Marianne. "Some time or another, probably more than a few times, Maddie or Spencer will lose their way for a moment and you will step in to support them and guide them. You did that today with Spencer and Cooper."

"Not the same thing."

"Isn't it?" Candace challenged her daughter. "Sure it is. Those boys love each other. I swear, sometimes they remind me of twins they are so in sync. They need each other. Spencer, he needs to lead," Candace said. "It's part of who he is. It's also how he emulates Rick, Marianne. It's part of coping with a loss he feels but is too young to understand. And, Cooper? He needs a friend that will be his protector. Someone who is a peer but who will stand up for him. He doesn't have that confidence yet. They need each other. I'm sure that whatever happened between them hurt them both, not just Cooper."

Marianne found herself listening to her mother in rapt fascination. She had told Spencer the truth earlier in the day. Marianne often wished that she possessed her mother's gift for understanding and relating to people. Shell was affable and an excellent communicator, but it was Jonah who had inherited Candace's natural ability with people the most. He was less boisterous than Shell and less direct than their mother. Sometimes that prevented people from seeing Jonah as he truly was. Marianne chuckled as it occurred to her for the first time why Jameson and Jonah shared such a unique connection.

"Was something I said funny?" Candace was a bit bewildered by Marianne's laughter.

"No," Marianne said. "I was just thinking about Jonah."

"Jonah?"

"Yeah, and J.D."

"I confess, I am lost."

Marianne smiled. "When I was talking to Spencer earlier I told him that Cooper looks up to him. He didn't understand at first. Cooper is older and taller," Marianne explained. Candace giggled at the raw innocence of her grandson. It was incredibly endearing. "So, I explained that it's a bit like how I look up to Jonah," Marianne told Candace. The statement piqued Candace's curiosity. "Surprised by that?" Marianne asked.

"Curious," Candace corrected her.

"I was just listening to you talking about the boys. You have this way of seeing people, Mom that most people never can—of understanding them somehow."

"I've lived a while," Candace winked.

"No, it's not that. It's just part of you, I think. Shell is great with people too, but not in the same way. Jonah? Jonah got that gift," Marianne said affectionately. "He's always had it, even when he was little. I think people don't notice sometimes because he is quiet. He does, though."

"And, that made you think of Jameson?"

"Of Jonah and Jameson. You know, Jonah thinks of you two as his parents. I mean, he loves Dad, but he doesn't call Dad—ever. To him, you are his parents. Jameson loves us all; I know that, but Jonah is special, I think—because he is actually the most like you. It sort of makes sense."

Candace smiled softly. She had never taken the time to analyze Jameson and Jonah's relationship. She was sure that neither Jonah nor Jameson had either, but Marianne's observation was astute. Candace looked at her daughter proudly and shook her head. "I wish you could have heard yourself just now."

"Why?" Marianne wondered.

"I'd say that you have a wonderful sense about people," Candace complimented her daughter. "Sometimes it's easier to see those traits in someone else than in yourself."

Candace picked up her tea cup and brought it to the sink. Marianne reached her feet, and Candace pulled her into an embrace. Marianne held onto her mother tightly. Not for the first time in that last few days, Candace felt the fear her family had endured and the relief that followed. She heard Marianne sniffle and held her more tightly. Candace had realized one thing since arriving home, if Jameson had been the one running around trying to take care of everyone else, it had been Marianne who had focused on trying to alleviate the stress for Jameson. A few years ago, Candace would never have imagined that scenario.

"Thank you," Candace whispered.

"I didn't do anything," Marianne said.

"Yes, sweetheart, you did," Candace disagreed.

Candace pulled back and smiled. Marianne had turned an important corner. As much as Candace enjoyed nurturing her children, she found herself feeling an immense sense of pride in the woman standing before her. Marianne had been through hell. She hadn't simply survived; she had grown. Candace pressed her palm to Marianne's cheek, musing that no matter how old her children grew to be, she still saw the same pair of eyes looking at her as the first time they had each been placed in her arms.

"You, my love, have done far more than you know," Candace said. She kissed Marianne on the forehead. "What do you say we round up those boys and get some rest?"

Marianne nodded and began to follow her mother from the room. "Mom?"

"Hum?"

Marianne choked a bit on her words. "I love you."

Candace smiled. "I know. I love you too, sweetheart."

"Is it weird that sometimes I wish I could be Cooper and crawl into your lap?"

Candace laughed. "Not one bit. You'd have me committed if you knew how many times I still wish I could crawl into Pearl's."

"Never changes, huh?" Marianne asked as they headed to find the boys.

"Nope, thank God."

CHAPTER NINE

Candace closed the door to the bedroom quietly, replaced her sweater with an oversized T-shirt and climbed into the bed beside Jameson. She inhaled a deep breath, feeling her body begin to relax for the first time in days. Jameson was lying on her side and Candace scooted closer. She draped her arm over Jameson's middle and pressed her lips to Jameson's shoulder lightly. Jameson sighed and turned slowly to face her wife.

"Did I wake you?" Candace asked. Jameson shook her head. "You haven't slept at all?" Candace asked with concern. Jameson shook her head again. "Jameson."

"I didn't want to fall asleep without you. What took you so long?"

"I was talking to Marianne," Candace explained. "And, then the boys wanted to camp out in Spencer's room," she chuckled. "So, we helped them pitch a make-shift fort."

"Are you okay?" Jameson asked.

"I'm fine. I promise, the most strenuous thing I did all day was walk up the stairs." Candace watched as Jameson closed her eyes and let out the hint of a sigh. "You need some rest," Candace said.

Jameson opened her eyes and shook her head again.

"Jameson, I'm right here. Did you sleep at all the last two nights?" Candace asked directly.

"Not really," Jameson answered truthfully. "I don't know; my mind was spinning. I kept thinking about you there. I just..."

Candace placed two fingers to Jameson's lips. "I under-stand," she said. She leaned in and replaced her fingertips with the softness of her lips, kissing Jameson gently but deeply.

"I missed you," Jameson whispered. "Not like when we are usually apart. It felt different. I didn't like it."

Candace took Jameson's face in her hands. "I'm okay."

"I know you are, but…I can't explain it to you."

"You don't need to," Candace said before leaning in and kissing Jameson again.

Jameson held onto Candace's hands as their kiss deep-ened. She felt the rising tide of arousal begin to heat her skin and pulled back. "No strenuous activity."

Candace smiled. "Jameson, are you feeling strained?" she teased.

Jameson pursed her lips. "You know exactly what I mean. You are not up to that kind of physical activity, and we both know it."

Candace snickered and kissed Jameson's lips softly. She let her hand drift sensually down Jameson's body and lifted her eyebrow playfully. "What makes you think I am go-ing to strain myself?" she asked flirtatiously. "I don't find touching my wife particularly strenuous. In fact, I find it ra-ther enjoyable."

Jameson's eyelids fluttered and closed when Candace's hands wandered up her shirt and over her breasts. "Can-dace…This is…"

"Shh," Candace whispered in Jameson's ear before nip-ping it gently. "You just stay in my arms and let me remind you that I am here."

"Candace," Jameson gently protested.

"I'm right here," Candace repeated. Candace's lips met Jameson's tentatively, teasing Jameson deliberately until Jameson was helpless to do anything but invite Candace to ex-plore further.

Jameson attempted to resist Candace's gentle assault, but she had lost her resolve to fight. Candace's touch was tender and searching. It conveyed passion, but Jameson knew that Candace meant to communicate something far deeper than lust. Candace had sensed Jameson's lingering fear. Everything about Candace's touch told Jameson that Candace understood what Jameson needed most. She needed to be reminded that Candace was safe. Jameson turned her head and lost her breath the moment Candace's lips strayed to her neck.

Candace sucked gently on Jameson's pulse point as her fingertips softly brushed over Jameson's nipples. She sighed at the sound of Jameson's quiet moan of pleasure. Tender, loving, soft and slow—that is how Candace intended to make love to Jameson—so softly that Jameson would fall into Candace without warning and in complete surrender. She mapped out the flesh of Jameson's stomach and traced patterns downward to Jameson's thighs. Candace felt Jameson's body begin to tense. She coaxed Jameson to look at her just as her fingers began to explore lower.

"Look at me," Candace said. "I'm right here. I'm not going anywhere, Jameson. Just feel me right now."

"I don't want to hurt you," Jameson said.

Candace smiled at Jameson's honest concern. "Loving you could never hurt me," she promised.

Candace kissed Jameson softly and continued to tease Jameson gently with her fingers. Jameson clung to her and Candace was sure that Jameson was close to overload. She kissed Jameson passionately and pulled back when Jameson's body began to tremble slightly.

"Let go," Candace told Jameson. "I'm right here. Feel me, Jameson. Just feel me and let go."

Jameson opened her eyes and looked at Candace. Candace smiled lovingly at her, speaking a truth that no words could ever hope to explain. The connection between them had always astonished Jameson. She felt it acutely in the simplest moments, in the gentle grasp of Candace's hand, in an exchanged smile from across a crowded room, even in the tone of Candace's voice when she answered one of Jameson's impromptu calls.

"Candace," Jameson reached for Candace's face and held it as she felt herself begin to fall away from reality and into the woman that she loved.

Candace gentled her touch and Jameson's body immediately began to quake beneath her. "I'm right here," Candace repeated her promise.

Jameson let go completely. Her hands moved to Candace's back and held onto Candace firmly as Candace's touch lifted her again and promptly sent her body spiraling downward in blissful surrender.

"Don't leave me," Jameson nearly cried.

Candace pulled Jameson closer as the quaking in Jameson's body subsided into gentle tremors. She kissed Jameson's forehead and let her lips linger. "I'm not leaving you anytime soon if I can help it."

Jameson opened her eyes. "I love you, Candace. I don't know what I would do without you."

Candace smiled. "I love you. I don't want to think about life without you either, believe me," she professed.

Jameson pulled Candace down and into her protective embrace. "When you are feeling better, I am taking you away for a couple of days," Jameson said.

"Oh?"

"Coop can stay with my mom for some Grandma time."

"And, where are you taking me?" Candace asked. She breathed in Jameson's scent and traced delicate patterns over Jameson's skin as Jameson held her.

"Don't know. It won't be anywhere in New York or Washington. That much I can promise you."

Candace grinned. "Why is that?"

"Because...I'm selfish and I want you without people clamoring to share you. Just for a couple of days."

Candace propped herself up and looked at Jameson. "Do you miss it? Just being us?"

Jameson shook her head. "No. It was never just us," she laughed. "I would like to make time for just us every now and then. I think we both deserve that once in a while."

"I agree," Candace said.

"You do?"

"Why does that surprise you?"

"I don't know. You're used to having everyone around, I guess. I mean..."

"Jameson, you are the most important person in the world to me. You know that, don't you? I love the kids. I love Pearl. I love what I do, but I will tell you something. When Drew helped me in that car the other day, the first thought I had was you. I wanted you at that moment more than I have ever wanted anyone with me in my life."

"You really were scared."

"Yes, I was," Candace confessed. "I worry about losing you too, Jameson."

"Me? I'm not going anywhere."

"Well good, neither am I," Candace declared as she fell back into Jameson's arms.

"So.... Shell and Mel are finally gonna take the plunge," Jameson chuckled.

"I'm glad Shell figured it out."

"Did she tell you? What prompted it?" Jameson asked.

"No, she didn't have to. She's wanted to marry Melanie for months. She's just afraid of failing at it somehow. Sometimes, a little wake-up call that forever can come to an end on its own is what you need," Candace said. Jameson sighed. "Is that sigh about what I just said or something else?" Candace wondered.

"A little of both. I've been worried about you. Now, I'm worried about Laura and I'm worried about Coop."

"Well, you can rest easy about me. As for Cooper and Laura, so am I," Candace replied. "What did Jonah say today when he called?"

"Not much. Enough that I know Laura told him something about her father...Candace," Jameson began cautiously.

"Hum?"

"Do you think that the Klein family had something to do with that young boy's beating all those years ago?"

"Pearl told you."

"I asked," Jameson replied.

"The truth is that I don't know," Candace said. "My gut tells me, yes."

"Your gut is usually right," Jameson pointed out.

"Oh, I don't know about that. Seems it was pretty full of rocks for a while."

Jameson chuckled. "You call me a lunatic?"

"Must be contagious."

"Mm-hm," Jameson mumbled and then yawned.

Candace kissed Jameson's chest. "Go to sleep, honey."

"I don't want to miss sleeping with you."

Candace laughed. "You won't actually be sleeping with me if you don't actually go to sleep."

"Cute."

"No, just pointing out the truth," Candace said. Jameson yawned again. "Get some rest," Candace said as she settled against Jameson comfortably and closed her eyes. She felt Jameson's breathing even out and had just started to drift off when Jameson mumbled.

"Mm..."

"What did you say?" Candace asked quietly.

"I love my wife; you know?"

"Jameson?" Candace looked up and stifled a laugh. Jameson had fallen asleep with a stupid grin on her face. Candace had only once heard Jameson talk in her sleep. She decided to run with the opportunity. "You love your wife, huh?"

"Mm...She's the governor," Jameson declared proudly without opening her eyes.

"Really?"

"Mm...And, she's hot."

Candace's body shook with silent laughter. "She is?"

"Mm-hm. Totally. She's sleeping now...With me. I love her."

Candace stretched up and kissed Jameson's cheek. "Yes, she is, and she loves you too, you lunatic."

✖✖✖

"Jessica," Marianne greeted the woman at the door while carrying Maddie on her hip.

Jessica smiled warmly at Marianne in spite of the tension that lingered between them. "How are you, Marianne?"

"Better than I have been in a long time, to be honest," Marianne replied.

"How's your mom?"

Marianne took a deep breath. She had seen Jessica briefly during the adoption process but had managed to maintain a comfortable distance from the woman. That was not possible now. Jameson had stepped out with Spencer to go pick up Pearl at her house after Pearl's car unexpectedly died in the driveway. Candace was upstairs giving Cooper a bath after Cooper had managed to paint himself blue while working on an art project that morning. Marianne had just finished feeding Maddie when Jessica's knock fell on the door.

"Mom's doing remarkably well," Marianne said. "She'll be down in a minute. Cooper painted himself this morning," Marianne laughed affectionately. She gestured toward Jessica to indicate that Jessica should follow her to the kitchen.

"Sorry," she said. "You are stuck with me for a few. Pearl's car died. J.D. took Spencer to go pick her up."

"Sounds like a busy morning," Jessica commented.

Marianne laughed good-naturedly. "More like typical in this family. Coffee?'

"Sure."

Marianne put Maddie in her highchair and moved to pour Jessica a cup of coffee. "Still like it light and sweet?" she asked a bit playfully.

Jessica laughed. "I do, actually."

Marianne nodded and handed Jessica the cup. She poured herself one, put a few Cheerios on Maddie's tray and sat down. "I wanted to thank you," Marianne said.

"Thank me?" Jessica was confused.

"Yeah, for helping Mom and J.D. with Cooper's adoption."

Jessica nodded and sipped her coffee. "I was happy to."

Marianne regarded Jessica for a moment and sighed. "You still care about Mom, don't you?" she asked. It was a direct question, but it held no malice.

"You may not believe this, but I have always cared about your mother. That didn't change when we split."

Marianne nodded.

"You're still angry with me."

Marianne shook her head. "No, Jessica, I'm not," Marianne said honestly. She smiled. "The truth is that it hurt Shell and me too when you left."

"I know."

"But, it hurt Mom more, and that was hard to watch."

"Marianne..."

"Let me finish, okay? Because I think it's been long enough. The fact is, you are part of both Mom and Shell's lives in some way. I won't pretend to understand it completely, but I don't see that changing. So, let me just say what I need to so we can move forward."

"Go on."

Marianne took a deep breath. "Mom is happier than I have ever seen her," she said. Jessica nodded. "She trusts you. Which, if I am to be honest, I cannot really understand. Seems to me like J.D. does too. I trust them. I also love them, both of them," Marianne said firmly.

"Marianne, your mom and I are friends. That's all it is, and that's all it will ever be. I know that."

"Yeah, but I know you," Marianne said flatly. "Mom would never betray J.D. I hope you know that."

"Marianne, I have no designs on your mom. That ship sailed a long time ago," Jessica said. "I'm sorry that it did. I won't lie to you either. I regret a lot of things, but I am happy for your mother."

"I believe you," Marianne said.

"Pretty protective of J.D.," Jessica observed candidly.

"I guess, I am. J.D.'s more than just my friend, Jessica. I'm not saying this to be hurtful. She's not just Mom's wife either. She cares about all of us."

"You don't think that I cared about you and Shell and Jonah?"

"No, I know you did in your own way. But, I also think we were in your way a lot. Looking back I can see that more clearly."

Jessica sighed. "I wasn't a very good parent, was I?"

Marianne shrugged. "You were a good friend," she said honestly.

"And, J.D. is different..."

"She's a good friend too," Marianne told Jessica. "She's an even better parent, and I don't just mean to Cooper."

Jessica nodded. "Must be strange."

"What's that?"

"J.D. isn't that much older than you are," Jessica observed candidly.

Marianne shrugged. "It was for a while—strange, I mean—for both of us. I think that's because we both were thinking about it. Me more than her," Marianne chuckled. "I don't really think about it now. J.D. is who she is, and I am who I am. I don't analyze it anymore. We've had our moments and we have always gotten through them. No matter what, she is always there for me, for all of us. Truth be told even more so than our father."

Jessica smiled. "You've changed."

Marianne shrugged again. "Not really, I just have learned to let go, I think. I've had to."

"I'm sorry about Rick."

Marianne smiled genuinely. "I know you are. I am too. We all are," she said honestly. "I was lucky to have him," she said. "That's what I have to hold on to. I have Spencer and Maddie. I have my family. Some days, it's still impossible for me to believe that he is gone. He is. I'm not."

"You remind me a bit of your mom, you know?"

Marianne chuckled. "That's the highest compliment you could pay me," she said.

"Mawianne!" Cooper came running into the room full tilt.

"Hey, you aren't blue anymore," Marianne teased him.

"Nope," he said. He smiled at Jessica. "Mommy says I not a Genie," he giggled.

"Well, you might be magic, but you don't live in a bottle," Candace joked as she entered the room. She looked at Jessica and Marianne curiously.

"I not magic, Mommy," Cooper laughed.

"No?" Candace asked him.

"No!" Cooper laughed harder. "Genie is magic!"

"Oh…" Candace replied.

"You silly like Momma," Cooper kept giggling as he ran back to Candace.

"Really? And, what are little boys who paint themselves blue?" she asked with an arched brow.

"Silly!" he replied, looking up at her.

Candace laughed. She ruffled his hair. "Yes, you are," she agreed.

"Mommy?"

"Hum?"

"Can I watch Addlin now?" he asked.

Candace pretended to consider the request seriously. "I don't know," she said. "Are you going to try and paint yourself like Genie again if I let you?"

"No," he shook his head.

Candace smiled. "You can go watch Aladdin, sweetheart. Just remember that Momma will be home with Spencer and Grandma soon."

"And, me and Spen get to go with Grandma for pizza and da train!"

"Yes, you do."

"Okay," Cooper said. He hugged Candace's middle and she winced slightly but smiled.

"Do you need help with the T.V.?" Candace asked him.

"Nope! By myself," he declared as he ran out of the room.

Candace laughed and rubbed her side.

"You okay, Mom?" Marianne asked.

"Fine," Candace promised. "He is strong, though," she chuckled.

"You want some coffee?" Marianne asked. Candace shook her head. "Herbal tea?" Candace nodded her appreciation. Marianne got up and smiled at her mother, squeezing Candace's shoulder in gentle reassurance. Candace reached up and squeezed back.

"How are you feeling?" Jessica asked Candace with concern.

"Pretty well, actually. Relieved to find neither of you is bleeding in my kitchen," she joked. "I already spent the better part of an hour scrubbing blue paint from my son. I'm not sure that I am up to cleaning blood from my floors."

Jessica laughed.

"Mom, I would have taken care of Coop," Marianne said. She could tell that Candace had exerted herself a bit more than she had intended.

"I know you would have, but…"

Marianne held up her hand. "I know, you missed him. I get it. You okay? And, it's me and Jessica here. Truth before J.D. gets back."

Candace laughed. "Sore," she confessed. "But, okay."

"I won't tell on you," Marianne teased.

"Tell on who?" Pearl's voice asked. Candace looked at the table. "What did you do that you are not supposed to do?" Pearl asked Candace. Candace smiled sheepishly, and Pearl looked at Jessica and Marianne for an explanation. "You two have anything to do with this?" Pearl asked them.

"Nice to see you too, Pearl," Jessica replied humorously.

"Nice try, Jessica," Pearl said. "That lawyerese never worked on me, just ask Candy."

"Laywerese?" Jessica laughed.

"Yes. Deflect the question. Nonsense. Now, what did Candy do that you are keeping secret?" Pearl asked again.

"Where's Jameson?" Candace tried to change the subject.

"Why? Worried I got lost?" Jameson asked as she entered the kitchen. She made her way directly to Candace and kissed Candace on the cheek.

"Did you? Get lost?" Candace asked.

"Not this time," Jameson replied. "Hi, Jessica."

"Hi, J.D."

"So? What's going on?" Jameson asked.

Pearl looked at Jameson. "Candy was misbehaving."

Jameson looked at Candace to explain.

"No, I was not," Candace defended herself. Pearl raised her brow in silent challenge. "I'm fine," Candace said just as Marianne placed a cup of tea in front of her.

Jameson studied her wife for a moment. Candace seemed to be exactly as she said—fine. But, Jameson did notice that Candace was a tad pale. She leaned into Candace's ear. "Candace?"

Candace sighed dramatically. "I'm fine, I promise. Cooper's bath required a little more bending than I had planned. He was blue in some hard to reach places," she snickered.

Jameson smirked. She put her hands on Candace's shoulders and kissed Candace on the head. Candace took Jameson's hands gratefully. It was Jameson's silent way of ending the teasing. Candace did know her limits. There would likely be times that Candace would push them, but she would not push them in any way that endangered her recovery. Jameson also knew that.

"Sorry, I missed that," Jameson joked, effectively ending any more discussion as she took a seat next to Candace at the table.

"I know you have things to discuss," Marianne began.

"Sit down, Marianne," Candace directed her daughter. "You too," she told Pearl. "You might as well be part of this conversation too."

"Mom, I don't want to..."

Candace shook her head. "When it comes to what has been said about Cooper and what we need to do or will not do about Lawson Klein and FVI, Jameson and I will make the decisions. With that said, we will need your support. This is a family matter."

Jessica smiled at the group. "What do you want from me, Candy?"

"The truth. Obviously, Jameson and I have read Laureen Cosgrove's sworn statement and all the legal documents. I know there is more. I know you," Candace said with a smile.

Jessica nodded. "There is more. I have her on tape as well."

Candace was not surprised. Jessica didn't just cover all the bases; she covered the entire playing field whenever she presented a case. "You recorded her statement," Candace guessed.

"Video," Jessica replied.

"I want to see it," Jameson said.

Jessica sighed. "Some of it is not pretty, J.D."

"I want to see it," Jameson repeated firmly.

Jessica shook her head. "I figured that you would."

"Do you have it?" Candace asked.

"I said, I figured you would," Jessica replied.

"Jameson, get my laptop," Candace said. Jameson nodded and went to retrieve the computer.

The room remained silent until Jameson reappeared and set the laptop in front of Candace. Jessica reached into the bag beside her chair and retrieved the DVD. "I'm telling you that…"

Candace smiled at her former lover. "We need to see it, Jess."

Jessica nodded her understanding. She had not known Jameson long but she was positive that the architect was going to be sent reeling from Laureen Cosgrove's video. The woman had been abrasive and completely dismissive of her grandson. Unfortunately, Jessica Stearns had learned over the years not to take people's statements for granted. She'd spent seven years with Candace, and Jessica had witnessed firsthand the lengths that some people would go through to discredit the senator. While she had not anticipated this exact scenario, the fact that Lawson Klein had moved to find Ms. Cosgrove and spin a fictitious tale did not surprise her. Reading a transcript or a sworn statement would always pale in comparison to hearing it, seeing it and watching it unfold before your eyes.

Candace noted the apprehension in Jessica. She gently placed her arm on Jessica's and smiled again. "Jess, trust me, Jameson and I will be all right."

"I know you need to see it," Jessica said. She looked directly at Jameson. "It's just..."

"It's okay," Jameson said. "Go on."

Jessica handed Candace the DVD and Candace placed it into her computer. She took a deep breath and felt Jameson's hand reach for hers and squeeze gently. The first minute of the video was a black screen with Jessica's voice setting up the clip formally. Candace steadied her breathing, expecting a much different Laureen Cosgrove than had been gracing the airwaves the last few days.

"Ms. Cosgrove, you understand that this is for the purpose of documentation regarding a pending adoption case for your grandson, Cooper?"

"That's what you said. Don't know about no kid."

"But, Jackie Cosgrove was your daughter?" Jessica asked for clarification.

"Was."

"And, Cooper is Jackie's son, is he not?" Jessica asked.

"That's what you said. Know she had one. Never met it."

"You never met your grandson?"

"She was a runner. Not runnin' with her own kind neither. Told her if she kept on like that, she wasn't stayin here. No time for that in my house."

"You mean that Jackie ran away?" Jessica asked the woman.

"She was always running. Away? Yeah, she ran away a couple of times. She was always running with the boys. Some boy, lots of boys. Who knows? Bound to get in that way."

Jameson felt Candace's grip tighten on her hand.

"The girl never had a chance," Candace whispered.

Pearl shook her head and Marianne followed suit.

"What is wrong with people?" Marianne muttered.

"By in that way, I will assume you mean your daughter's pregnancy."

"Knocked up—kicked out. I ain't raising no nigger."

Jameson exploded. "Fucking bitch!"

All eyes turned to Jameson except Candace's. Candace stroked the back of Jameson's hand with her thumb. She understood the outburst, and she did not blame Jameson at all for the colorful language. Jameson's eyes never moved from the screen set in front of them.

"Do you know who Cooper's father is?" Jessica asked calmly.

"You must be kiddin'! Who knows? Why do I care? I told her and I told you—that ain't no way to live. And, that ain't the way nobody is living in my house. She was a runner. I told you."

"I understand that. Cooper is just a little boy." Jessica said calmly. *"Who just lost his mother."*

"Mother?" Laureen Cosgrove let out a caustic chuckle. *"You callin' Jackie a mother? Runnin' around with all kinds, no job—no respect. He belongs with his own kind."*

Candace felt Jameson's palms beginning to sweat. She briefly looked at Jameson in an attempt to calm her but her attention was pulled back to the screen by Jessica's voice on the DVD.

"Ms. Cosgrove, there is someone interested in giving Cooper a home. Are you saying that you would not be opposed to that? You have no desire to raise your grandson?" Jessica asked.

"I told you, I ain't got no grandson. Sure not one like that. I did my piece. Gave her a roof."

"Ms. Cosgrove, you do understand that your daughter is dead?"

"So, they said. So you say. Ain't seen her in over four years; why's that matter to me?"

"Well, because you have a grandson, Ms. Cosgrove."

"Ain't mine, I told you. She wasn't fit to be here. Told her to change her ways, else she wasn't staying under my roof. That ain't my way. And, that ain't my problem.

"Jesus Christ!" Jameson bellowed.

Candace took a deep breath and closed her eyes for a moment. No matter how many years she had lived on the earth, regardless of what she had witnessed, felt, and the atrocities she was often confronted with in her work, Candace would never become numb to the pain of a child—not any-one's—and certainly not hers. How any mother could dismiss her child as if that child was a thing confounded Candace. She'd seen and heard enough to know that whatever was coming would only be more of the same. Quietly she shut the laptop, bringing the brief, albeit telling, Laureen Cosgrove Show to a close.

"I've heard enough," Candace said calmly. She turned her attention to Jameson and softened her gaze. "Jameson," she called for her wife's attention compassionately. Jameson's body was quaking with anger. Candace reached out and stroked Jameson's cheek. "Go check on the boys, sweetheart," she suggested.

Jameson looked at Candace, her eyes brimming with tears. "What kind of person is she?"

Candace smiled. "It doesn't matter," she said softly. "Cooper is our son. Remember what you told me when we first talked about adopting him?" Candace asked. Jameson shook her head. At the moment, Jameson could scarcely breathe, much less process any memories. Candace smiled again. "You said that maybe we needed him as much as he needed us," she reminded Jameson.

Jameson exhaled her anger, closed her eyes and nod-ded. "I remember."

"Go check on *our* son," Candace repeated her sugges-tion. "Help Pearl get them ready for their afternoon of trains and pizza."

Jameson smiled weakly. She leaned in and kissed Can-dace's cheek before addressing the room. "Sorry for my language."

"Sorry?" Marianne asked. "Please, J.D., you just said what everyone else wanted to."

Jameson's smile grew in earnest. "Good to know," she said before making her way out of the room.

"Mom?" Marianne spoke first.

Candace's eyes were still riveted to the doorway Jameson had just passed through.

"Candy?" Jessica began.

Candace took a deep breath.

"It's her loss," Marianne said.

Candace smiled at her daughter. "It is, but it is also Jackie's and Cooper's. I don't take any joy in that," she said honestly. Candace shook her head despairingly. "I can't pretend to understand. Where Cooper is concerned, I don't want to try," she confessed. "But, I have to try. Someday, he will have all of those questions. Someday, no matter what, he will confront the truth and no matter how much we love him, no matter how much he loves us—that truth will cause him pain. I know that too."

"Candy, this could set the record straight," Jessica began.

Candace shook her head again. "No," she said flatly. "We are not using this. We are not getting in the media mud with Lawson Klein."

"Candy," Jessica implored the governor.

"No, Jess."

"Sometimes, I don't understand you," Jessica admitted.

Candace smiled. "I know you don't. This is not about me. If it goes out there, it becomes public. It's one thing to have to tell Cooper; it's another for him to ever have to see or hear that. I won't have that and neither will Jameson," she said. "This is not all you have, is it?" Candace asked.

Jessica's lips became taught and Candace raised a knowing brow. "It's all I have regarding Laureen Cosgrove and her family."

"But?" Candace urged.

"Candy, there is plenty of dirt Lawson Klein's family. Plenty on FVI too," Jessica said. "For a 'family values' group they certainly have some interesting values," Jessica replied.

"Beyond the rumors, Jess," Candace said.

"I'm not talking about history, Candy. At least, not ancient history."

"Enlighten me," Candace said.

"Why do I have a feeling that you already know about most of what I can offer?" Jessica asked with a smirk. "You did your homework," she observed. "You called me off the case and kept digging yourself."

Candace sighed. Marianne cleared her throat.

"I'm going to check on Maddie," Marianne chimed.

"I'm behind you. I'm sure Jameson has her hands full. I'd like to have lunch before dinner," Pearl said. She smiled at Candace and Jessica. "It was nice to see you, Jess," she told Jessica honestly. Pearl turned to Candy. "Don't you two go conjuring up old hurts and old arguments," she advised as she left.

Candace chuckled and turned her attention back to Jessica. "Jess..."

"I don't understand you. It's not like this is new. Lawson Klein had a vendetta against you. You know it. He attacked us, and you ordered me to let it go while you stayed hot on his heels. Tell me I am wrong," Jessica demanded calmly.

"You're not wrong."

"Why? I..."

Candace smiled. "You never stopped either," she reminded Jessica. "You kept digging like I knew you would. I had hoped you would not. And, before you start an argument that we spent over six years circling, I want you to hear me out for once."

"I'm listening," Jessica promised.

"I could not have used anything you dug up. Whatever I found out it was through FVI's surrogates, Jess. I didn't pay. I didn't even ask. I just let it be known where I stood. They found me. They always do."

"Candy, it's not as if I have a paid henchman."

"I know," Candace laughed. "But, you will pay. That could compromise everything, Jess. You know that too."

"I wanted to protect you. Believe it or not, I still do."

Candace nodded. "Jessica..."

Jessica held up her hand. "Not like that," she said assuredly. "I will always care about you. We were friends before we were lovers, Candy. Maybe we were better off that way all along."

"I don't regret us," Candace told Jessica.

"Neither do I. I'm not blind. I never was. Maybe you don't need me to help..."

"I did. I do," Candace said. "That's why I called you about Cooper in the first place."

"Why ask what I know if you don't..."

Candace sighed. "Things have changed, Jess. It isn't just me they are coming after. It's my sons—both of them in a way."

"You just said no media mud."

"I did. I won't hurt Cooper that way. If you can't understand that, understand this—if we show that woman talking about Cooper now, we both know it will only open debate about which came first. We both know that. It can't come from me," Candace said.

Jessica understood the unspoken sentiment. "You want to plant some seeds."

"Yes, I do," Candace said.

Jessica rubbed her forehead in thought. "How much do you know?"

"I know Klein's son has been in some trouble. I also know that there have been multiple sexual harassment settlements. And, I am aware that Mr. Klein has been inclined to make some payoffs."

"Sounds more like defectors than surrogates you were talking to," Jessica said.

"Mmm. Surrogates and advocates can become defectors in a heartbeat when you don't deliver on your promises. You're lucky if they turn on you in the light of day," Candace said. "Most of the time it happens behind your back.

Jessica looked down and sighed sadly.

Candace mentally slapped herself for her choice of words. "I didn't mean you," she said honestly. "Jess, you need to let that go. I have.

"You're not the one who made the mistake."

"I made plenty of mistakes in our relationship and we both know it."

"Not the same thing," Jessica returned.

Candace smiled reassuringly. "Maybe it is, or maybe it isn't. Who's to say? I hurt you. You hurt me. In the end, we both were to blame."

"What do you want me to do?" Jessica asked. Candace smirked and shrugged. "Ahhh…. Plausible deniability it is," Jessica laughed. "You know," she turned somber. "I realize that you have never wanted to dig up the past. The fact is, Candy, I am almost positive Lawson Klein's great-grandfather was responsible for that boy's death. I know you think that is…"

Candace shook her head. "Jessica, please…"

"Candy, come on, I thought that you believed in justice?" Jessica challenged Candace.

"I do. Who will get justice? My God, Jess, think about that time. Jeremiah was my grandfather's friend—good friend, in fact. He even wrote about the whole thing in his diary."

"You know more than you've ever said," Jessica surmised.

The smile Candace offered was tinged by sadness. "I do know. I know that Jeremiah Klein lived a secret life, one my grandfather was well aware of. In fact, one my grandfather and other's sought to keep quiet."

"See no evil. Hear no evil. Speak no evil?" Jessica guessed wryly.

"No, not the way that you are thinking. Look what happened when the truth spread?"

"You think they kept it quiet out of friendship? Who let it out?"

"I don't know," Candace admitted. "Based on what my grandfather wrote, Jeremiah was terrified of his father. You know, he and Jeremiah had been friends since childhood. Granddad wrote that Jeremiah always wanted to come play here, even when they got older, Jeremiah tried to distance himself from his father. Ezra ruled by the rod and staff principle."

Jessica groaned. "If you are so sure, why not let it be known now? Candy, Ezra Klein's money founded FVI."

"I know that too."

"I don't..."

"I know that you don't understand. You never have. Lawson Klein is not responsible for what happened back then. That doesn't mean he was never affected by it."

"Candy, you can't seriously feel sorry for..."

"For Lawson Klein? No. I don't like to make wars, Jessica. You know that. I am not afraid to fight them when I need to. This latest move? Attacking my son? That's war. He has no idea whose battlefield he just stepped onto."

"You do know that if these allegations come to light, no matter how we lift it to the surface, it will inevitably lead to the past."

Candace nodded. "It always does."

"What aren't you telling me? What are you afraid people will find out?" Jessica wanted to know.

"I'm not afraid. I'm just aware. In any war, there are always casualties. I'd like to limit those as much as possible—on both sides."

"And, what do you hope to gain?" Jessica asked. "Other than the evisceration of Klein, that is."

"I want FVI sent back to the dark ages where it belongs," Candace replied.

Jessica finally smiled. "How much do you want to know?"

"Only what you feel I need to, when I need to."

"And you?"

"Well, FVI has had several complaints lodged against them here in New York. I think it's time my AG took a look at those a little more closely."

"So, you do it on the record, and I do it off?" Jessica chuckled. Candace shrugged. "There's something a bit Shakespearean in this plan of yours, you know?"

Candace grinned. "Well, occasionally I do enjoy the theater.

Jessica laughed. Candace would never play dirty. Over the years, that had often frustrated Jessica, but it was also one of the reasons Jessica Stearns had fallen in love with Candace Fletcher years ago. Candace would do battle when necessary. Candace would only use ammunition that she believed was warranted and information that she felt confident was accurate. Governor Candace Reid had not changed in that capacity. There were shorter ways to meet an objective, easier ways to win a battle. Candace had once told Jessica that there was only one way to win a war—that required more integrity than manipulation. History had a tendency to repeat itself until it was set right. Candace had always believed that.

"You haven't changed," Jessica said.

Candace let out a slow breath and nodded. "No, I have."

"No, you..."

"No, I have," Candace repeated. "I never had much taste for going after anyone; you know that."

"Candy, you didn't start this," Jessica reminded the governor.

"No, but I could choose to ignore it and take the higher ground. Once upon a time, I would have."

Jessica shook her head. "What did you say to me a little while ago? Maybe and maybe not?" she asked. "If you don't take Klein and FVI on, who will? You and I both know that their work has hurt plenty of people over the years."

"Yes, I do."

"I'll keep you in the loop with what I think you have to know."

"I appreciate it," Candace said.

"Candy?" Jessica began. Candace waited for her to continue. "Cooper *is* your son. Don't forget that. Laureen Cosgrove can't touch your family in any way. That includes Cooper, and neither can Lawson Klein."

Candace smiled wanly. "They already have, Jess. They already have."

CHAPTER TEN

Jonah watched as Laura headed upstairs to put J.J. in the crib that Candace and Jameson kept. "J.D., if this is a bad time," Jonah began.

Jameson narrowed her gaze at the young man. "Why would it be a bad time?"

"I mean, Mom just got home yesterday and I know that you have..."

Jameson stopped Jonah's diatribe. "Your mom is looking forward to seeing all of you."

"Maybe. After we talk? I don't know, J.D., Mom might not be so happy," he mumbled as Jameson walked with him toward the living room.

Candace stepped out into the hallway. "Might not be happy about what?" she asked. Jonah looked up from the floor at his mother. "Jonah?"

"Hi, Mom," Jonah greeted Candace as he leaned in and placed a kiss on her cheek.

"Mmm," Candace smiled knowingly and put her arm around her son. "Just tell me one thing right now?"

"What?" Jonah asked.

"Am I about to become a Nana again?" Candace wondered.

"No," Jonah chuckled.

"Good, because I could use a little time to get used to being Mommy again first," Candace replied good-naturedly.

"How are you feeling?" Jonah asked Candace.

Candace rolled her eyes playfully. "Not you too," she mock-scolded him. "I'm fine. Other than your brother's attempt to paint himself blue like Genie this morning, all is well."

"Coop painted himself?" Jonah laughed.

"Not just himself," Jameson offered. "He also managed to paint part of his floor in the process." Jameson exchanged a smiled with Candace. "It's washable."

"Yeah, that's a loose term," Candace snickered.

Jonah looked at Jameson in confusion. "He got paint everywhere," she said. "Took your mom over half an hour to get it off. You should see the blue ring he left in the tub," she laughed.

"Sounds like an eventful morning," Jonah said.

"Oh, that was only the beginning," Jameson replied just as Laura walked into the room.

Candace watched as Laura smiled half-heartedly at everyone and walked up beside Jonah. Jonah put his arm around Laura as a gesture of comfort. Candace looked at Jameson with concern.

"Why don't you all sit down," Jameson suggested. "I can make some coffee or…"

"No," Jonah said. "Maybe after."

"Okay," Candace agreed. "Whatever it is that's on your minds, let's just get it out into the open," she suggested.

Jonah took a seat on the sofa beside Laura and Jameson led Candace to the loveseat nearby.

"We know that you both," Jonah began to speak when Laura interrupted him.

"I'm sorry about my father," she said regretfully.

Candace smiled at the young woman. "Laura, you are no more responsible for anything your father does than Jonah is for anything that I do. You don't owe anyone any apologies."

"I know," Laura said. "But, I hate what he has said about you and I know that he is behind this interview and this media parade with Coop's grandmother. He has no right…"

"No, he doesn't," Candace agreed. "What he does with FVI is no reflection on you in our eyes—not ever. Neither Jameson nor I ever want you to doubt that."

Laura nodded and Jonah squeezed her hand in reassurance. "When I say he has no right," Laura began and then trailed off nervously.

Jameson looked at Jonah curiously. Jonah shook his head slightly and Jameson understood that whatever Laura wanted to share it was likely going to be painful for her to say and equally difficult for everyone to hear. She reached over and took Candace's hand in preparation.

"Go ahead," Jonah whispered his encouragement to his girlfriend.

Candace looked directly at Laura and softened her gaze. "You don't have to tell us anything, but you can always tell us anything," Candace assured the young woman. Laura nodded. She looked at Candace despairingly, and Candace's heart plummeted in anticipation of what was to come. Candace squeezed Jameson's hand. "Jameson, why don't you and Jonah go and start some coffee out in the kitchen? Let Laura and I talk for a bit."

Jameson stood up and gestured to Jonah. "Come on; you know how it is. They'll end up talking about us anyway," she said lightly.

Jonah looked at Laura. "You okay?" he asked. She nodded and he kissed her on the cheek. "If you need me…"

Candace winked at her son and waited until he had left the room with Jameson to speak. She made her way to the sofa and sat beside Laura. "It's just us."

"I don't know if that is easier or harder," Laura confessed.

Candace smiled. "There is nothing that you could tell me that will change how I feel about you, Laura. Not one thing," Candace said assuredly. "You have the same look on your face that Jonah did the day he told me about you."

"You mean when he told you I was pregnant."

"It was a lot of news to digest," Candace joked. "Listen, I doubt very much that what you want to tell me will surprise me either. I have lived a while," she said with a wink.

Laura finally met Candace's gaze. "He's the last person who should talk about family values," Laura said more harshly than Candace would have expected. Candace listened attentively. Laura shook her head in disgust. "It started when I was about seven, I think. I didn't know. I mean, I knew that it was wrong, but I didn't know I could say anything."

Candace felt the knot in her stomach tighten measurably. She braced herself for the rest of Laura's inevitable story, hoping that she was wrong about the direction it was about to take.

"He was almost thirteen then. I knew if I told anyone he would make it worse, so I didn't."

Candace nodded. She watched as Laura's eyes filled with tears and Laura's posture slumped in despair. "Take your time," Candace encouraged the young woman.

"Mark...I finally told my mother," Laura said. "At first, he just came into my room at night. But...Well, when my mother started going out more, I was about twelve, Mark was seventeen, almost eighteen—then he started...He was in charge, you know? I would get home from school and he would be waiting."

Candace sensed Laura's difficulty in continuing. "I think I can imagine," she told Laura gently.

Laura looked at Candace and the pleading in the young woman's eyes nearly broke Candace in two. Candace reached out and pulled the young woman into her embrace and began to rock her as Laura's tears overflowed. "I'm so sorry, sweetheart," Candace said.

"I told my mother," Laura choked through a sob. "She told him—my father," Laura continued.

Candace sighed and held Laura protectively. "You did the right thing telling her," Candace said.

"No, I didn't. He didn't do anything," Laura wailed. Candace closed her eyes as the waves of pain rolled off of Laura. "I heard them arguing," Laura explained. "He told her that I was exaggerating. He was sure of that. Mark…. Mark was the star," Laura sobbed. When my mother challenged him…"

Candace readied herself. "It's okay if you need to stop."

"No, I want to tell you…I need…"

"Okay," Candace tried to reassure Laura. "Just slow down. I'm not going anywhere."

"He told her that I was like her. She was unreasonable and overly dramatic. She yelled back and he…He hit her or he pushed her—hard. I know he did. I heard her hit the floor and her cries," Laura finally managed to get the words out. "After? It was worse, like he wanted to punish me for telling. The only reason he stopped was that he went away to college," Laura said. "I made sure not to be home when he was."

Candace continued to rock Laura gently. She mentally processed the information. "I'm so sorry," Candace said genuinely. "That you had to go through any of that."

Laura collapsed into Candace gratefully. "I'm so sorry."

"Sorry? Sweetheart, why are you sorry?" Candace asked.

"If it weren't for me, he wouldn't be trying to hurt you so much."

Candace pulled back and directed Laura to look at her. "Laura, what your father does through FVI…When it comes to me and to my family—that started before you were even born, honey. Please, listen to me. You have done nothing wrong, not then and not now."

"I want to tell them," Laura said.

"Tell who, what?" Candace wondered.

"Do an interview, tell someone how he is—who he really is. I want to help you."

Candace sighed. She wiped the tears from Laura's cheeks and shook her head. "No, sweetheart, you don't. Just listen," Candace said when she saw Laura ready to protest.

"Don't put yourself through that. Have you ever talked to anyone about this? What happened with your brother?" Candace wanted to know. Laura shook her head. "Mmm. No one?"

"Just when I told my mother, but we never talked about it. We never really talked much after that. She barely looked at me to tell you the truth."

Candace nodded. She guessed that Laura's mother had been suffering from guilt and fear—guilt that she had been too fearful to protect her daughter. It made Candace wonder what kind of man Lawson Klein truly was. She had always deemed him a bigot and she had long regarded him as arrogant and selfish. Candace knew that Lawson Klein and FVI were willing to play dirty, even resort to violent tactics. While the group had never been directly implicated, FVI had been linked to several violent protests and abortion clinics. More than once, someone equated with FVI had been arrested for an assault on someone affiliated with a women's health clinic, and most recently a man who had beaten a transgender teen in Ohio had been linked to the group. Family Values International always publicly distanced itself from any such incident. Whether or not FVI directly involved itself in the incidents was debatable. It was evident that FVI held influence over many of the people who propagated such attacks and protests.

Lawson Klein was technically the Media Director at Family Value International. It was a well-established fact that the Klein family had bankrolled FVI's beginnings and continued to be one of its most lucrative sources of funding. Lawson Klein's influence went far beyond the scope of press releases and interviews. He was not simply the face of FVI; he provided the fuel for its engine. Laura's revelations did not so much surprise Candace as they did dishearten her further. The idea that any parent would allow their child to suffer to save public face disgusted Candace beyond description.

Candace let Laura continue to cry in her arms. "Listen to me now, okay?" Candace said. "You let me fight this fight.

I've told you before; I know that it is not the same. I do know that, but you are part of this family, and I want you to remember that."

Laura continued to cry uncontrollably. "I'm horrible," she croaked almost inaudibly.

"Why would you say something like that?" Candace asked.

"I wish you were," Laura mumbled. I love my mom," Laura said.

"Of course, you do."

"But, sometimes I wish you really were my mom," Laura confessed.

Candace understood Laura's feeling and the sentiment perfectly. Candace loved her mother but she had never felt the bond to her mother that she had felt instantly with Pearl. And, Candace had seen that in Jonah with Jameson. He loved his father and he had liked Jessica, but Jonah and Jameson shared a bond that went far beyond friendship or step-parent and step-son. He regarded Jameson as his parent and Candace was positive that as strange as it might have seemed to some people, Jameson felt exactly the same way. She kissed Laura on the head as her thoughts turned to Cooper. Candace and Jameson had not given birth to Cooper. They had not been the ones to care for him the first few years of his life, but Cooper was every bit as much their son as The Three Stooges, as Candace affectionately referred to her children. And, Candace had no doubt that in Cooper's mind and heart she and Jameson were his mothers.

"You know," Candace began. "Families are really what we make them," she told Laura. "I understand. I love my mother. She's my mother. But, Pearl? Pearl is truly my mom. Whether I skinned my knee or had a broken heart, Pearl was always the person I sought. She still is."

"But, you've known Pearl forever."

"True," Candace said. "Rick was my son—as much as Jonah or Cooper or Lucas," she said lovingly. "Cooper asked

Marianne if he could have three mommies," Candace told Laura.

"Not really the same," Laura said sadly.

"No?" Candace raised her eyebrow. She smiled at Laura and directed Laura to look at her. "I think it is exactly the same," she said. "In some ways that makes it all the more special. I chose Pearl. Pearl chose me. My kids all got me. Rick and Cooper, they chose me. I chose them. Just like I choose you," Candace said. Laura fell into her again, a new wave of emotion overtaking her. "Love doesn't have limits, Laura. You can love as many people as you choose, and in my experience when you love someone, you will always love them. That doesn't mean that they are beside you forever. Things separate us— our choices, their choices, even death. You don't have to stop loving one person because you find refuge in another."

Laura held onto Candace and Candace let the young woman cry out all of her tears.

"Would it still be okay?" Laura asked hesitantly.

"Would what be okay?" Candace asked.

"You said once that if I wanted to, I could call you Mom," Laura's voice dropped.

Candace felt the warmth of a tear bathe her cheek. "I would be honored."

✕✕✕

"Want to talk about it?" Jameson asked Jonah.

Jonah nodded and accepted a beer from Jameson. "J.D., I don't know how to help her sometimes."

"Laura?"

"Yeah."

"Maybe the best thing you can do is just listen," Jameson offered.

"If I didn't think it'd destroy her, I would beat the shit out of them."

"Her father?"

Jonah nodded again. "And Mark."

"Her brother?" Jameson asked for clarification.

"J.D...."

"What is it, Jonah?"

Jonah shook his head disgustedly. "He touched her, J.D. Not once either. Often. From the time she was small until he left for college."

Jameson's pulse immediately picked up its pace and her ears began to ring. "What do you mean he touched her? Mark? You mean he abused her?" she asked. Jonah sighed and nodded.

Jameson felt her stomach flip and pushed back the urge to be sick. Abuse was something that Jameson understood from a unique perspective. She had been a naïve teenager and had begun dating a young man three years older. He had made the decision for both of them that it was time to be intimate. Jameson had protested but fear forced her into submission. It was an experience that still haunted her at times. She had struggled with intimacy and trust for years. Candace was the only person Jameson had confided in about the experience. And, it was Candace who had gently nurtured and reassured Jameson when memories surfaced. Jameson took a deep breath and let it out slowly.

"J.D.?"

Jameson smiled at Jonah as best she could. "All you can do is listen and keep assuring her that she is safe with you," Jameson said. She saw Jonah's unspoken question and addressed it. "I can't even imagine one of my brothers doing that," Jameson said. "And, I can't.... Well, it's bad enough when you are old enough to understand."

"J.D..."

"I was a teenager, kind of a naïve teenager. He was older. I thought.... Well, what I thought doesn't really matter. He had different ideas."

"He..."

Jameson nodded. "What I can tell you, Jonah is that no matter how many times I've told myself that it wasn't my fault, no matter how many days or weeks pass that I don't think about it. Eventually, something brings it back. It never goes away. You learn to move through it. You learn that it can't define you or conquer you, but it is part of you—part of your life."

"Does Mom know?" Jonah asked.

"Yeah, she knows. And, Jonah, the fact that Laura told you...It means she truly trusts you, not just that she loves you. Your mom is the only person I have ever talked to about what happened to me...Well, until now."

"You didn't have to tell me," Jonah said honestly.

"No, but I trust you, and I think maybe...Maybe I can help you understand how she might be feeling."

"I hate them, J.D. I hate them for hurting her, for what they have said about Mom ...Now, for doing something that might hurt Coop. I hate them."

Jameson nodded. "You're angry and you have a right to be angry. I get it."

"No, J.D., I've never hated anyone. I swear to you, Lawson and Mark Klein? I..."

"Jonah," Jameson gentled her voice. "I understand how you feel. Believe me, when I tell you—I do. You need to let that go. That's not what she needs."

Jonah rubbed his hand over his face in frustration. "When will it end?"

"I don't know," Jameson replied honestly. "You have to trust us now, okay? Let your mom and me handle Lawson Klein."

Jonah looked across the table at Jameson and closed his eyes. "It's not your job to defend..."

"We're your parents. It is our job," Jameson declared without hesitation.

Jonah opened his eyes and finally let the hint of a smile show on his lips. "Weird, huh?"

"A little," Jameson admitted. She laughed. "Never thought I'd be anyone's momma."

"You're pretty good at it, you know?"

Jameson shook her head. "I have no idea what the hell I am doing most of the time," she confessed.

Jonah laughed. "Me neither," he said. "Can I ask you something?"

"Sure."

"Being married...Are you glad you and Mom got married?"

Jameson tried not to laugh. "Caught the bug, huh? First Shell, now you."

Jonah shrugged. "I just worry."

"About?"

"Being a husband. I mean, poor J.J. is stuck with me. Laura gets a choice."

"Seems to me that she has already made it," Jameson reminded Jonah.

"Were you scared? Asking Mom, I mean?"

"Terrified."

"Did you think she would say no?" Jonah wondered.

"No, not really," Jameson answered. "I wanted my proposal to be perfect, you know? Memorable. Your mom is...Well, I wanted it to be perfect."

"It was," Candace's voice replied.

Jameson looked up at Candace, who was smiling in the doorway. Jonah turned in his chair and Candace smiled at him.

"Mom?"

"She's okay," Candace told Jonah. "She needs you right now, though. She went upstairs to wash up," Candace explained.

Jonah nodded and hopped to his feet. He stopped and hugged his mother. "Thanks, Mom." Jonah turned to Jameson. "I don't know what we'd do without you—both of you," Jonah said sincerely.

Jameson smiled. "You'd pay for babysitting," she teased.

Jonah chuckled and nodded as he left the room.

"So? Am I guessing we will be paying for two weddings soon?" Candace asked.

"If I liked to gamble, I'd say the odds were good," Jameson said. She pulled her chair out and Candace moved to sit in Jameson's lap. "Perfect, huh?" Jameson asked.

Candace leaned in and captured Jameson's lips in a tender kiss as her reply. She let her head fall against Jameson's gently as their kiss broke and sighed.

"You're not going to let this one go," Jameson said knowingly.

"I can't this time," Candace said. "They've done too much damage. At least, without FVI, it will be harder for him to be heard."

Jameson sighed. "I don't want you to get hurt."

"I never enter a battle that I can't win, sweetheart."

Jameson kissed Candace sweetly. "You are not in this alone."

"I know. That's why I can do it," Candace said.

"You really think you can take down FVI? Candace, they have a lot of money and a lot..."

"And, more skeletons than a graveyard, Jameson. Trust me on this."

"If you've known that all along, why now?" Jameson asked.

"You think that I haven't been working on this all along?" Candace laughed. "I have. Many people have. It takes time. I've just stepped up the pace. The less airtime Lawson Klein and his hate mongers get, the better. I don't have the luxury of time anymore," Candace said. "Not when he targets my children."

"I know. I just worry about Laura."

"So do I," Candace agreed. "Jameson..."

"I know," Jameson guessed where Candace was turning their conversation. "I told Jonah...About me, I mean. I'll talk to her."

Candace smiled compassionately. "Only if..."

"I'm fine," Jameson promised. "I have you."

"Yes, you do."

"I love you, you know?"

"Yeah? Enough to go get Chinese?"

Jameson rolled her eyes. "Yes."

"Really?" Candace was surprised.

"Yeah, Jonah loves Chinese take-out. I'll get you some soup."

"Soup?" Candace asked indignantly.

"Yep. Soup. If you behave, I'll get extra fortune cookies."

Candace arched an eyebrow? "Why? Hoping your fortune will predict you will get lucky?"

Jameson moved Candace off of her lap. "I don't need Chinese for that," she said as she made her way to retrieve her coat. She opened the back door and looked back at Candace. "Besides, I know where your stash is anyway."

"You do not!"

Jameson shrugged and gloated as she stepped through the door.

"Jameson!" Candace went to the door and called after her wife. Jameson waved without turning around. "She does not," Candace muttered.

"Hey, where is J.D. going?" Marianne asked as she entered the kitchen.

Candace shook her head and started laughing. She turned back to Marianne and smiled. "Lunatics."

"What?" Marianne asked.

"Nothing. Nothing a little Chinese food can't cure."

Marianne was puzzled. "Okay…."

"Come on," Candace gestured to her daughter. "Sneak me a small glass of wine before she gets home."

"Mom!"

Candace waved off her daughter. "I'm over twenty-one."

"And on antibiotics."

"Want that free babysitting to continue?" Candace teased.

Marianne laughed. "One *small* glass."

⚔ ⚔ ⚔

"I really don't think it's a good idea," Michael Weller offered his unsolicited opinion.

Lawson Klein took a sip from his coffee cup and shrugged casually. "What's wrong? Starting to like the governor?"

"I'm more concerned with how some people might perceive this where Laura is concerned."

"I told you, she made her choice."

"Lawson, I am telling you that you are rolling the dice pushing this. Laura is still your daughter. A lot of our donors have expressed some concern in your dismissiveness. She is your daughter. You do remember what FVI stands for?" Weller challenged.

"I ought to. My father funded it."

"Yes, I know," Weller replied. "I know the history, Lawson."

"And, who, Mike is FVI's largest donor?"

"This is not about your influence or your commitment," Weller told Klein. "You have a blind spot where

Candace Reid is concerned. Why is that? People are starting to ask questions—pointed questions. She's hardly the only liberal elected official. And, she's hardly the only lesbian out there. What's the obsession?"

Lawson Klein set down his coffee cup and reclined in his chair. "You think I am obsessed? I would call it focused, focused on the agenda that my father and Dominick Ward set years ago when they began this organization—family values. That means traditional family values, Michael. The Fletcher family has never been traditional. You have no idea."

"Lawson, everyone close to this has heard the old tales about your grandfather and Candace Reid's. It's not..."

"You think this is about some old fossil of a rumor?'

"You tell me," Weller challenged. "What is it about?"

"Have you looked at the governor's approval ratings? Popularity lately?"

"Of course."

Klein nodded and leaned forward. "And, what exactly do you think that means?"

"Lawson..."

"It means that people are sympathetic, Michael. It means that we are losing."

Weller scratched his brow. "It's still an uphill battle for them."

Klein's face grew hot and he pushed his chair back in anger. "Uphill? What channel are you watching? When my daughter lives with that family? In that filth all around her? What the hell do you think that has done to my credibility? To the credibility of this organization? Our collateral is in the toilet!" Klein stood and began to pace the room. "Bad enough she was knocked up before she was married! I should never have let her go away that far to school. Now..."

"Laura is an intelligent young woman," Weller attempted to calm Klein.

Klein spun on his heels and glared at the man a few paces away. "Is that right? Well, intelligence and morality are not synonymous! You want me to reach out to her, why? Because she is biologically my daughter? She's a traitor to her family!"

"Because she fell in love with Candace Reid's son? Lawson, why can't you see reason..."

"Reason? Let me give you reason, Michael..."

"Lawson, please..."

Klein took a few steps forward and placed his face directly in front of Michael Weller's. "She has made it her mission for years to discredit me."

Weller stood his ground and spoke evenly. "I do not agree with Governor Reid. Respectfully, Lawson, it has never been about you. And, Candace Reid is hardly the only person who has FVI in her crosshairs."

Klein stared furiously at the man in front of him. "It has always been personal."

Weller let out a sigh, took a step back and shook his head. "No, Lawson...I fear it will be now."

CHAPTER ELEVEN

ONE WEEK LATER

"Worried?" Marianne asked Jameson.

"About your mom? No," Jameson replied honestly. "She was ready to get back to work."

"Driving you nuts, huh?"

Jameson laughed. "Maybe a little. She must have called Dana and Dan a hundred times over the weekend."

Marianne laughed. She had come into the kitchen late the previous evening and found her mother sitting in front of her laptop with a cup of tea. Candace had been so focused on whatever was in front of her that she had failed to notice Marianne's presence. Marianne had been content to observe her mother for a few moments. Candace had been peering through her glasses intently, her eyes scanning back and forth thoughtfully. Marianne had been enthralled. The moment had taken Marianne back to her childhood. Marianne had never told her mother that she would often sneak downstairs after she had been put to bed to watch Candace as Candace worked quietly in the study or to listen as Candace addressed someone on the phone. Marianne remembered thinking that her mother was the most powerful person in the world. Candace seemed in command of everything. As she had stood watching her mother the previous evening, the same thought passed through Marianne's mind. Now, however, that thought was tempered by an understanding of the depth Candace possessed. Candace had seemed more than commanding. To Marianne, Candace's edges had softened.

"Something you want to share?" Jameson asked Marianne, noting the whimsical expression on Marianne's face.

"I was just thinking about Mom, I guess."

"Who's worried?" Jameson teased.

"No," Marianne said with a smile. "I'm not worried about her either. I think Shell is, though."

"I got that feeling when she called me right after your mother made it to Albany."

"J.D., I'm not worried about Mom. I really am not. I am worried about Coop."

Jameson nodded. "I think we all are."

"He's little, but he is not dumb. He's bound to hear something," Marianne said.

"Yeah. I guess all we can do right now is shelter him as much as we can and remind him that this is his family."

"When are you and Coop headed to Albany?"

"Later this afternoon," Jameson told Marianne. Marianne nodded. "Something wrong?" Jameson asked.

"No," Marianne promised.

"Not very convincing."

Marianne giggled. "Truthfully? I guess I will miss you a bit."

"You know, you can always come to Albany for a few days if you really start missing the chaos," Jameson reminded Marianne.

"Thanks. I was kind of wondering..."

"What?" Jameson wondered. Marianne bit her lip for a minute. She hated to impose on Jameson's generosity. "Marianne, what? Do you need me to take the kids for a day or something?"

"Actually, Scott offered me a chance to lead a new group at the center in Ithaca this Thursday. It's a bereavement group that they are starting for residents," Marianne explained.

"That's great," Jameson said.

"Yeah, well...The thing is, I would have to be there at nine in the morning."

"So? Stay at my mom's Wednesday night. She would love to see you. If you want, I can pick Spence and Maddie up Wednesday afternoon," Jameson offered.

"Well, actually," Marianne began. Jameson's eyes grew wider in anticipation. "I guess Scott already called your mom. She offered to take the kids, but, J.D. I think that's too much."

Jameson's burst of laughter took Marianne slightly off guard. "I'm sorry," Jameson continued to laugh. "You forget she raised three kids," Jameson reminded Marianne. "I don't think it could get to be much more than it was dealing with me, Toby and Doug."

"Maybe so," Marianne conceded, "but, J.D. Maureen is not..."

"Not what?" Jameson asked. "She's my mom and as far as she's concerned that makes you her grandkid. Which, I will grant you is completely weird. Anyway, she loves Spence and Maddie. Please, have you seen her with my nephews and niece?"

"Point taken."

Jameson could tell that Marianne still felt as if she might be imposing. "How about this? I will pick Spence up on Wednesday afternoon. I have a meeting not far from here at noon. I'll be here by about two. That will give you plenty of time to get to my mom's for dinner. And, besides, your mom will be thrilled to have Spencer and so will Coop."

"Oh, I see," Marianne raised a signature Stratton eyebrow. "This is all about Mom and Coop."

Jameson shrugged innocently. She was positive that Marianne could see right through her. Shell and Melanie were headed to Melanie's grandmother's house Tuesday for a visit. Shell had promised Cooper that he could join them. Melanie's grandmother adored Cooper. Jameson was also sure that Shell was looking for an excuse to spend some sister time with the toddler. Shell and Melanie had both been working at a hectic pace. With Candace out of commission for over a week, that had left Jameson also away from the office completely. A great deal of work had fallen to Shell and Melanie in Candace and Jameson's forced absence.

Cooper spent the most time with Marianne. Marianne might have been joking about being the "cool" sister; Jameson understood that Cooper was totally in love with his oldest sibling. When Candace and Jameson were otherwise engaged and even at times when they weren't, Cooper gravitated to Marianne. He had even begun to ask about spending the night with his older sister. Cooper trusted Marianne. Jameson was often amused by the playful sibling rivalry between Shell and Marianne. One thing that Jameson had grown to understand, they competed in every circumstance. It was a loving competition. It was also in the sisters' nature. Jameson was positive that Shell was hoping to score a few points with her little brother. Jameson had intended to use the day to dive into some of the projects at her architectural firm. The opportunity to spend some one on one time with Spencer would always take precedence over work. Everyone knew that.

"J.D., if you have things that you need to do I can ask Grandma."

"What? No. I do have a potential client I want to visit on the way back, but that is only to tour the facility. Spence loves that. He can be my assistant," Jameson offered.

Spencer loved to play Jameson's assistant. He would proudly carry the small tablet Candace and Jameson had given him and mimic everything that his Jay Jay did. Jameson had not had many chances in the last few months to spend alone time with her grandson. She tried. She knew that Spencer missed that time. As much as Jameson loved Cooper, she missed time with Spencer as well. He had captured her heart instantly. Jameson adored all of Candace's children and grandchildren. She had a unique relationship with Spencer. That was something that Jameson desperately wanted to preserve and nurture no matter what changes happened in life.

"Spencer would love that," Marianne let Jameson off the hook.

"Good. Cooper will be home after dinner. I'll let your mom know when I call her later. I'll bet she'll clear the time for the three of us to have dinner."

Marianne smiled knowingly. "As long as you are sure it's not a problem."

"Nope. Not at all," Jameson said as she placed her coffee cup in the sink. "Right now, I need to round up my son and get him ready. Let's just hope he hasn't painted himself again."

Marianne snickered. Not only had Cooper managed to paint himself blue the previous weekend, he and Spencer had also found delight in a mud bath the day before. Jameson had made the offer to clean the offending toddlers. Marianne was fairly certain she had never seen her mother as amused as she had been the day before. The light in Candace's eyes when Jameson had emerged from the task as dirty as Spencer and Cooper had been when Jameson had brought them into the bathroom had warmed Marianne's heart. Marianne tried to push back her laughter as she recalled the scene in the hallway the evening before. Candace loved to tease Jameson. Jameson had turned the tables on Candace in an instant.

Candace stood next to Marianne and watched as two squeaky clean toddlers emerged from the bathroom. She arched her brow when Jameson came into view. Jameson had mud in her hair, on her shirt and jeans—even on the end of her nose.

"What?" Jameson feigned innocence. "I cleaned them up—good as new!"

"Mmm? And, who is going to clean you up, Pig Pen?" Candace asked.

Jameson's gaze narrowed and her eyes twinkled. Candace was back to herself. She had become more playful each day, and she had not indicated any discomfort from her surgery in a couple of days. Jameson pursed her lips and wiggled her eyebrows.

"Don't you even think about it," Candace held up a warning finger.

Jameson's sly smile forced Candace to take a step back. "Jameson..." Jameson closed the short distance between them swiftly and gently threw Candace over her shoulder. "Jameson! Put me down right now!"

"Nope. You're dirty. You need a bath."

Marianne covered her mouth and snickered.

"You're no help!" Candace called back to her daughter.

Marianne shrugged. "She's got a point!"

"She got me that way!" Candace protested.

"Tsk. Tsk," Jameson said as she stepped back through the bathroom door. "Sorry, Marianne...Would you mind..."

Marianne held up both hands. "I'll go watch a movie with the boys. Just keep it down."

"Funny," Candace bit back.

"That's it, Governor. Into the shower with you," Jameson said as she kicked the door shut.

Marianne began to laugh softly.

"Something funny?" Jameson asked Marianne.

"I was just wondering how much of a hard time Mom gave you last night after you threw her into that shower.

Jameson smiled. It was no secret to anyone in their family that Jameson had been terrified when Candace was admitted to the hospital. Jameson had done her best to give Candace the space that she always required and not hover. It had been a challenge at moments for Jameson. Her protective-ness had been kicked into overdrive by Candace's health scare. She had been tentative about touching Candace at all. She held Candace when they slept, but she feared hurting her wife. Candace had attempted to reassure Jameson for days un-successfully. Candace had grown extremely playful, and her mood had improved dramatically as the week wore on. Some-thing in Candace's eyes had told Jameson the evening before that the time for tentativeness had come to an end. Candace needed normalcy. She needed Jameson. And, the plain truth was Jameson needed Candace as well. She smiled as the memory of their impromptu shower flooded her thoughts.

"Jameson, what has gotten into you?" Candace asked as Jameson finally placed her on the floor.

Jameson looked at Candace intensely. Candace could see evidence of a passionate storm brewing in Jameson's irises. Jameson reached out and caressed Candace's face, drawing her closer until their lips finally met in a tantalizing kiss.

Candace traced the outline of Jameson's cheek with her fingertips. "You are filthy," she whispered.

Jameson said nothing. Her hands traveled slowly to the front of Candace's blouse, and one by one Jameson slowly released the buttons. She kept her gaze locked with Candace's as her hands pushed the offending fabric from Candace's shoulders. Her hands lightly traced patterns over Candace's shoulders at the same time Candace's hands wandered and unbuttoned Jameson's denim shirt.

Jameson reached around Candace's back, taking her time to enjoy the softness of Candace's skin as she unhooked Candace's bra and allowed it to fall away. Jameson continued to slowly undress her wife, leaving no part of Candace untouched as she went. She kissed Candace tenderly as Candace freed Jameson from her jeans. Jameson removed the last vestiges of her clothing, reached into the shower and started the flow of water and then took Candace's hand.

Candace smiled at Jameson. She followed Jameson into the stream of hot water, delighting in the passionate haze that colored Jameson's eyes. Candace brushed the water droplets from Jameson's face, rubbing her thumb over a small patch of dirt. She shook her head affectionately. "What am I going to do with you?" she asked Jameson rhetorically.

Jameson made her reply in the form of a possessive kiss.

"Jameson..."

Jameson's touch meandered over Candace's shoulders, up her arms and over the swell of her breasts. She held Candace's gaze firmly and lovingly.

Jameson had not even begun to touch her, and Candace was finding herself breathless. The heat from the steady stream *of water that pelted Candace's skin paled by comparison to the fiery passion lighting Jameson's eyes. Candace sometimes wondered when that might fade—the desire that burned between them. In moments like this, when Jameson looked at her, Candace felt confident that the passion they shared would never diminish. She fought to keep her eyes open when Jameson's fingertips brushed over her nipple.*

Jameson watched as need began to etch the small creases at the corner of Candace's eyes. Jameson ached to touch Candace. She had missed the feel of Candace against her—Candace's softness, the sound of Candace's desperate sighs as she would begin to submit to Jameson's touch. Jameson felt as if she fell in love with Candace over and over again. Each time she felt herself begin to fall, she would begin to crave Candace all over again. And, every time they came together, Jameson found herself lost in the sensations that Candace's closeness provided. It was an intoxicating blend of comfort and eroticism, longing and tenderness. Candace was Jameson's sanctuary, her safe harbor.

Candace watched as Jameson's gaze wandered lower. She heard Jameson suck in a short breath, and she closed her eyes in anticipation. Her hands gently held Jameson's head as Jameson's tongue circled Candace's nipple, tugging lightly.

"God, Jameson..."

Jameson continued her sensual exploration, tasting and teasing Candace's flesh deliberately, knowing each place to linger. She pressed Candace up against the far wall and gripped Candace's hips tightly. Dropping to her knees slowly, Jameson trailed warm kisses over Candace's abdomen. She kissed a small area where one of the incisions for Candace's surgery had been made. Jameson's fingertips gently circled it, and she looked up at Candace. Candace looked at Jameson and smiled lovingly. Jameson sighed, and Candace cupped her cheek.

"I'm all right," Candace promised.

"I don't want to hurt you."

"I told you, loving you could never hurt me."

Jameson's hand drifted sensually lower and then back to Candace's hip. She leaned in and allowed her kisses to cascade over Candace's stomach in time with the spray of the water. She looked up briefly to catch Candace's expression just before Candace's head fell against the wall. Jameson held on more tightly and placed a faint kiss to Candace's center. She heard Candace gasp and swiftly allowed her tongue to tease the woman standing before her.

"Jesus!" Candace cried out.

Jameson intended to take her time as much as she could. That had never been easy. From the first time that they had made love, Jameson had always became lost in Candace. She had missed Candace, missed touching her and making love to her. Jameson was a physical person. She always had been. She had always felt more comfortable expressing her emotions with actions. It might have been a bouquet of flowers, take-out Chinese food, fixing a broken sink or a sweet kiss. Jameson often wished she could write poetry. She frequently felt that words failed her. Candace had a command of words, a way of articulating what she felt and believed. That remained something that Jameson was constantly in awe of. For Jameson, words never seemed enough, and she had never felt any confidence in her talent for exposition. It didn't stop her from leaving Candace notes or taking the time to leave impromptu messages on Candace's voicemail. But, Jameson's creativity was not found in crafting speeches or declarations. She worked with her hands. Making love to Candace afforded her the ability to communicate the depth of her emotions and her devotion.

"Jameson," Candace called through a sigh when she felt Jameson's tongue begin to circle her repeatedly.

Candace attempted to steady her breathing and keep her balance. Jameson's gentleness had always astounded her. Even in the heat of passion, even when their lovemaking became demanding, Jameson's touch remained tender. There had been moments—many of them—that Candace had believed she might die from the connection that pulsed between them when they made love. Candace forced her eyes open and looked down at Jameson. Jameson's hands held her securely, her thumbs continually caressing Candace's skin. Candace closed her eyes again and gave over entirely.

Jameson felt Candace's legs beginning to quiver and pressed herself against Candace firmly to ensure that Candace would remain upright. She looked upward, needing to see Candace when Candace finally let go.

Candace was positive that if Jameson had not been holding her so tightly, she would have fallen. Her body hummed from the myriad of sensations invading it. Jameson was bathing her in a flurry of erotic kisses that sent shivers up and down her spine in spite of the warm sprinkles of water that fell over her skin in a soothing caress. She was struggling to breathe against the waves of pleasure crashing over her. She gasped when she felt Jameson's hand move to the small of her back and pull her what seemed impossibly closer. Immediately, Candace began to fall into Jameson.

Jameson caught her and held her in place, never slowing the pace of her touch.

"Jameson!" Candace cried out as a series of shudders buckled her knees. "God! Oh, my God."

Jameson continued until she felt Candace's shaking subside. She never released her hold on Candace as she trailed kisses back over Candace's middle. Carefully, Jameson made her way back to her feet and came face to face with Candace. She let her fingertips dance over Candace's eyelids, coaxing Candace to look at her again.

Candace opened her eyes and took Jameson's face into her hands. She searched Jameson's eyes, attempting to convey all that she felt without the noise that words sometimes could bring.

"I love you," Jameson said.

Candace smiled. "I love you too."

Jameson kissed Candace lightly and tipped her head in curiosity when Candace's lips twitched with a devious smile.

"What are you grinning about?" Jameson asked.

Candace reached out and rubbed a small area on Jameson's cheek with her thumb. She laughed. "You are adorable."

"Huh?"

Candace reached over Jameson and retrieved a washcloth. She poured a small amount of soap onto it and gently wiped Jameson's cheek. She showed Jameson the mud on the cloth and arched her eyebrow.

"What? Worried I have mud in those hard to reach places?"

Candace shook her head. "On the contrary, I sincerely hope you do."

"I am positive that I do not want to know where you just disappeared to," Marianne commented. Jameson had completely tuned out for a moment, and she was sporting a rosy blush to her cheeks.

Jameson shrugged. "Mud."

"Like I said, I don't need to know," Marianne said.

Jameson wiggled her eyebrows, smirked and started to make her way out of the room.

"She's right, you know?" Marianne called after her.

"Who's right?" Jameson turned around.

"Mom. You really are a lunatic."

Jameson winked.

Marianne laughed. "Oh, Mom…. I hope I find that again someday."

"Happy to have you back," Dana told Candace.

"Happy to be back," Candace returned.

"You seem…"

"I seem what?" Candace asked.

"Frankly, you are in a better mood than I expected," Dana admitted.

Candace nodded. She sat back in her chair and shrugged. "You expected, what? The claws?"

Dana chuckled. "I don't know, Candy. I know how you already felt about Lawson Klein."

Candace sighed. "Well, I don't control Lawson Klein as we both know."

"Uh-huh. What are you up to?" Dana wanted to know.

"I'm not 'up to' anything, as you so eloquently put it. At least, not anything new."

"You're finally going to go after him," Dana surmised.

Candace took a deep breath and let it out slowly. "I'm going to see an end to his influence at FVI. That much I can promise you. I don't have to go after him, Dana."

"Candy, he will not go away silently."

"No, I don't expect he will."

"And, for the record, he seems to have stepped up his campaign against all things you," Dana said.

Candace nodded. "What now?"

"More of the same, but more and more and more. I know that you are reluctant, but I think...Candy, I honestly believe that it would be a wise decision to do an interview with J.D. You don't have to show Coop..."

"Fine. Set it up. No Cooper," Candace told her. Dana was astonished. "Why so surprised? We both knew that I would have to do this eventually."

"Yeah, but you were completely against it just last week," Dana reminded Candace.

"A lot can change in a week."

"Why do I think that there is something you have not told me yet?" Dana asked.

"There's lots of things that I haven't told you," Candace replied. Candace rolled her eyes when Dana folded her arms across her chest. "Oh fine," Candace said. "Shell and Mel got engaged."

"You have got to be shitting me," Dana responded.

Candace laughed. "Not shitting you, no. And, if I am not mistaken, Jonah and Laura are headed in that direction soon."

"You weren't kidding about things changing in a week."

"No, I wasn't," Candace said as the door to her office opened. Candace looked across the room at the face of her Chief of Staff. "Bill?"

Bill DeGrasso stepped in and made his way to Candace's desk. He silently handed her a piece of paper. Candace looked at the note and then at the face of the man before her. She shook her head.

"How many casualties?" she asked.

"I don't know yet," he replied.

"All right. You know who to call. Get it in motion," she told him

Bill DeGrasso nodded. "I would say welcome back..."

Candace nodded. "I would say thanks."

DeGrasso chuckled uncomfortably and left the room swiftly.

"Candy?" Dana asked.

"Train derailment on the red line near Port Chester."

"Shit."

"You know what to do."

Dana immediately reached her feet. "Candy..."

"Go on. Let's find out what we're dealing with so we can deal with it," she said. Candace sighed as Dana left the room. "Welcome back, Governor."

⚒⚒⚒

Jameson opened the door to Candace's office slowly. "Hey, we didn't want to disturb you," she poked her head into the room. "Susan said we should go ahead and come in."

Candace looked up from her desk and smiled gratefully. "Susan's a smart woman," she said.

Jameson pushed the door the rest of the way open and Cooper bolted past her for Candace. Candace pushed back her chair and accepted an excited toddler into her lap. She hugged Cooper tightly and kissed him on the cheek before turning her attention to the three people seated across from her desk. "Keep me in the loop," she instructed them. "I expect hourly updates unless anything of consequence happens. You interrupt me no matter what should that occur. If it seems relevant, assume it is." Dana, Bill DeGrasso, and Dan Moore nodded before beginning to make their way from the room.

"Hell of a first day back," Dana spoke quietly to Jameson.

"I heard," Jameson replied.

"Dana," Candace called over to her press secretary.

"Yeah?"

"Why don't you call Steve and see if he can bring the boys over here for dinner. It's going to be a long night, I think. If he wants, stay the night. God knows there is enough room," Candace commented.

Dana shook her head. "Candy, I can't ask you to do that."

"You didn't ask. Don't make me make it an order," Candace replied.

Dana laughed. "I will call him. I think you just want an excuse to talk about the Mets."

Candace shrugged. "I'd accept the distraction."

Jameson watched Dana leave and then closed the door. "So? Never a dull moment, huh?" Jameson asked lightly.

Candace shook her head. "Cooper," she called for her son's attention. "Why don't you go and find Aunt Shell? She went to the kitchen just before you got here." Cooper smiled and hopped off Candace's lap. He looked back up at her. "Yes, sweetie?"

"Mommy? You work all day?"

Candace sighed. "I do have to work," she told him. "But, I will tell you what—I will try and sit down later and watch a movie with you. Okay?"

Cooper nodded. "Momma says Spence is coming."

Candace looked at Jameson curiously. "Wednesday, Coop," Jameson reminded him. "That's two days from now."

"Yep! And, I get Shell!"

Candace laughed. "That should be a fun day. Go remind her," she suggested.

"Okay!"

Jameson opened the door for Cooper and he sped off to his appointed task. "How are you doing?" she asked Candace.

Candace groaned. "I'm not sure I can answer that." Candace tried to rub the fatigue from her eyes. "Twelve people confirmed, Jameson. That's twelve too many. It's bound to rise. And, injuries? More than sixty."

"Do they know?"

"Specifically? No, not yet. It's a mess from what I have been shown. Disrepair, Jameson. There are so many issues...."

"This is not your fault," Jameson reminded her wife.

"No, but it is my responsibility."

"Candace, you have only been sitting in that chair for a few months."

"Doesn't matter," Candace said. "You know that and I know that. Tragedy does not bring out the rational side of people."

"I saw your statement."

Candace sighed heavily. "There will be closures. There will have to be, I suspect."

"What can I do?"

Candace smiled. "You're doing it."

"Standing helplessly in your office?" Jameson quipped.

Candace laughed. "I don't know about the helpless part."

"I'll keep Coop out of your hair."

Candace shook her head. "No, don't. If I am in a closed meeting, I will let you know. Otherwise, let him come, Jameson."

"He has to learn…"

"Jameson…"

"Okay, I think I get it," she said. "You sure there isn't anything I can do?"

"Turn back the clock twenty-four hours so I am still in bed?" Candace joked.

"Fraid I left the time machine at home," Jameson replied. Candace grinned. "It was nice of you to tell Dana…"

"It's going to be a long night," Candace observed candidly. "She lost a lot of home time over the last week."

"That's not your fault either."

"No, but it…"

Jameson held up a hand. "I know—your responsibility. Candace, Dana knows what her job entails and so does Steve."

"And, I know how quickly time passes," Candace said. "Today is just another reminder…"

"I get it," Jameson interjected. "Any dinner requests?"

"Scotch."

"You're telling me there is none hidden in this cave you call an office?"

"There was."

Jameson laughed. "You call me a lunatic?"

"If the jacket fits."

"Nice."

Candace winked. "Thanks."

"I didn't do anything," Jameson said.

"Yes, you did."

Candace made her way to Cooper's bed and looked down at him sleeping peacefully. She brushed her fingers through the curls of his hair and sighed. She continued to watch him sleeping, feeling tears begin to slip over her cheeks. She needed to see him, to know that he was safe and close. She closed her eyes and tilted her head upward in silent prayer. Candace implored anyone who might be listening to give her strength, to help her face another day—another grieving family. She prided herself on seeing the good in the world, in believing in the possibility of leaving the world a better place than she had found it. Some days tested her beliefs and her resolve. She took a slow, deep breath and crawled into the bed beside her son. Cooper instinctively snuggled against her and Candace accepted him gratefully.

"I love you, Cooper," she whispered to the sleeping toddler. "So much."

✂︎✂︎✂︎

Candace walked into the bedroom a little after two in the morning. Jameson rolled over and flipped on a light.

"Why are you awake?" Candace asked.

"I wasn't."

"I'm sorry," Candace apologized.

Jameson patted the bed and Candace collapsed onto it, Jameson pulling her down instantly. "Want to talk about it?"

Candace held onto Jameson. "Fourteen, Jameson—fourteen people gone."

"Candace, it was an accident."

"No...Yes, but no. It was avoidable."

"Every accident is," Jameson said honestly. "You're doing everything you can and that is all you can ever do."

Candace laid her head on Jameson's chest. "Two children," she spoke softly. "Five mothers...Three grandfathers, a grandmother...Jameson, I," Candace's thoughts trailed off. Jameson held Candace and tried to sooth her by gently caressing her back. "I'll never get used to it," Candace said honestly. "Seeing it. What do you say to these people? There's nothing. 'I'll fix it.' That's an empty promise now."

"No, it isn't."

"Certainly puts things in perspective."

"How so?" Jameson asked.

"All this nonsense with FVI. It doesn't seem all that important when I think about it. It is. I know it is. It hurts people. It has the potential to..."

Jameson kissed Candace on the head. "Rest."

"I was resting. I fell asleep with Cooper for a while."

Jameson pulled Candace closer. "He's okay."

"For now."

"Candace...."

"Jameson, I'm tired of seeing children lose their parents—Parents lose their children. It makes me...It makes Lawson Klein seem so small. What does he hope to gain in hurting these children?"

"Your children," Jameson observed.

Jameson had learned that dealing with the tragedy of others always led Candace home. Candace was strong but she was also immensely sensitive. There was no doubt in Jameson's mind that Candace would reach out to the families who had been affected by the accident earlier that day, and not politically. Jameson had only seen the television coverage. That had been unsettling. Candace would have seen far more graphic images and received details that the public would likely never hear. It was a reminder of the unpredictable nature of life and the inevitability of loss. In her short tenure as governor, Candace had already confronted tragedy more than once. Jameson didn't need Candace to explain her feelings. Lawson Klein's quest to dethrone Candace came with casualties, most notably Laura and Cooper. In the midst of loss, that reality both perplexed and infuriated Candace. Jameson understood.

"It's senseless. Tomorrow is," Candace began. "Your children are the ...Jameson, these two precious little babies today...Five and seven...One minute and..."

"They'll be okay," Jameson said. "Laura and Cooper."

"I hope so."

"They will be. We will make sure they are," Jameson promised. She felt the warmth of Candace's tears through her T-shirt. "Sleep," Jameson said. "They are safe, Candace. We're all safe."

"Not really," Candace admitted the truth.

Jameson sighed and looked down at Candace. Candace's statement was not meant to be despairing, only truthful. Every day there were reminders that safety was an illusion in life. For Candace, there would always be more reminders. Her work ensured that reality. Jameson wondered if anyone could comprehend how profoundly Candace was always impacted emotionally by the pain she saw in the world. One thing that Jameson did know, once Candace's inevitable tears subsided, her resolve to make things better would be strengthened yet again. It was one of the many things about Candace that Jameson not only loved, but admired and respected.

"I love you," Jameson said. She smiled when she realized that Candace had fallen asleep. Jameson closed her eyes and let herself slip away, grateful for the woman in her arms.

CHAPTER TWELVE

"Shell?" Cooper looked up at his big sister.

"Yeah, little man?"

Cooper smiled brightly. "You love Mel?"

Shell laughed. "Well, yeah."

"Like Mommy and Momma?"

"Yep."

Cooper frowned slightly and then looked back at Shell. "Jonah loves Waura?"

"Laura, and yeah he does," Shell answered.

"Coop? Do you have a girlfriend?" she teased. Cooper's confusion was evident. "I mean do you love someone?" she tried a different approach.

"Mommy," he answered thoughtfully. Shell smiled. "And Momma."

"Yeah, well, don't tell them but I love them too," Shell said.

"Who does Marianne love?" Cooper asked.

Shell sighed. Melanie looked at her sympathetically. "I'm going to find my mom and see if I can help her with dinner while you and Coop chat."

"Mel?" Cooper looked at the other woman.

"Yeah, Coop?"

"Mommy says I get another sister."

"I would love to be your sister," Melanie told him.

Cooper smiled. "That's fwee! Fwee sisters like fwee mommies," he observed.

"I guess it is," Melanie agreed. She winked at Shell and headed off to find her mother.

Shell turned her attention to Cooper. "Coop, are you worried about Marianne?"

Cooper nodded. "Evewybody loves somebody."

Shell had to close her eyes for a second to gather her emotion. It had not escaped her notice that Cooper had become emotionally attached to Marianne. At first, Shell had felt a small pang of jealousy watching her older sister with Cooper. Somehow, Shell understood it. At times, Marianne could come across as abrasive, even judgmental. There was no way that Shell could deny the reality that Marianne had softened measurably over the last few years. And, while Shell knew that few people looking in would believe it, she worshiped her older sister. Marianne for all of her bravado at times, for the many squabbles and the incessant teasing between the sisters, Marianne had always been Shell's best friend. When push came to shove as it often did in life, Marianne in many ways was Candace's true kindred spirit. Marianne was a devout protector. She could also be the most nurturing person Shell had ever known. It was a part of her older sister that long had been reserved for private moments. Recently, that had begun to change. Cooper loved everyone in the family. Shell knew that, but like Candace and Jameson, he saw Marianne as his protector. Shell and Jonah were his friends. Shell smiled at her little brother. Looking at Cooper as he looked at her with such deep concern for their older sister, Shell began to realize for the first time who Marianne was in their family. Jonah and Shell had always been close friends, but Shell seldom cried on Jonah's shoulder. Marianne was four years older than Shell and nearly eight years older than Jonah. Marianne was not simply their sister; she was often their caretaker.

"Coop, Marianne loves all of us."

Cooper considered Shell's words. "But everybody has someone."

Shell nodded. It had not escaped her notice that Cooper often quietly observed his new family. She often enjoyed watching him when the family was gathered together. Most evenings when the family sat together, Cooper would sit in Candace's lap and watch and listen quietly, many times until he fell asleep against their mother. Shell had immediately been struck by the four-year-old's intelligence and thoughtfulness.

"Well," Shell began again. "Grandma Pearl doesn't have someone."

"She's Grandma," Cooper gave his explanation.

"Oh? So? Your Grammy has your Grandpa. And, you know, Coop—Mom is a Nana too."

"Yeah. She's Spence's Nana."

"Yes, she is and she even though she is a Nana she is still a mom too, and she has your momma to love," Shell tried to explain. Cooper sighed. "Coop, Marianne loved someone very much for a long time," Shell said. "He was Spencer's daddy. But he is..."

"He's with my other mommy in heaven now. Marianne said."

Shell pushed back her tears and smiled. "I imagine that he is...Watching over all of us with your mommy."

Cooper smiled. "Evewybody should get somebody," he declared.

Shell nodded. "Well, maybe someday Marianne will find someone. Don't worry so much about Marianne, Coop," Shell told him. Cooper looked at her quizzically. "Marianne is happy right now loving all of us, I think," she said. She laughed and pulled Cooper into her lap. "Besides, Mom doesn't need to pay for any more weddings right now."

Cooper did not understand why Shell was laughing, and that made her laugh harder. "Shell?"

"Yeah, bud?"

"How many can you have?"

"How many what?" Shell asked.

"People."

Shell closed her eyes and pulled Cooper closer. His innocence astounded her at times. "As many as you want, Coop. You can love as many people as you want to love."

"You can have five sisters?'

"I sure hope so," Shell said. "I mean; you have Laura too."

"That's four," he giggled.

"I'm not a very good counter am I?"

Melanie walked out onto the porch and smiled at Michelle holding Cooper protectively.

"She's good with him," Melanie's mother commented from over her shoulder.

Melanie nodded. "She'll be a great mom someday."

Melanie's mother smiled. "Get her to the altar first," she laughed.

Melanie chuckled. "After what it took to get this ring? You're not kidding."

Candace collapsed her face into her hands for a moment, feeling emotional and mental exhaustion creeping through every fiber of her being. With a deep breath, she made her way to her feet, grabbed her suit blazer from behind her chair, closed her eyes and took in a deep breath for courage. She looked at the pictures sitting on the corner of her desk and smiled. Seeing the faces of her children and grandchildren always managed to help Candace muster the strength to push forward. Her lips curled into a loving smile as she lifted a small photo that Marianne had recently given her of Marianne holding Spencer and Cooper on her lap. Candace closed her eyes for one final moment.

"God, help me get through this day," she mused as her hand reached for the door.

With one last deep breath, Candace emerged from her office and offered an encouraging smile to the group gathered just a few steps away. She was keenly aware of the stress level that permeated her staff currently. In two days, several major issues came across the governor's desk. The most troubling had been the train derailment of the Metro-North line. The train service enabled millions of people to travel in and out of New York City. People were dependent on the service and companies were reliant on the people who traversed the rail system each day to keep them in business. In the end, even physical tragedies morphed into economic realities. For Candace, that reality shifted in less than a second. She would never be afforded the time to process and grieve the human loss the way most could. She was the public face of possibility and promise. It was Candace's duty as governor to speak with compassion and authority, to instill a sense of confidence in the people she had been elected to serve. There was no other option. And, right now an exterior of assuredness was exactly what her staff needed as well. Times like these required a leader, not a boss. Candace made her way to the staff, their expectant gazes meeting the compassionate and composed gaze of Governor Candace Reid.

"It's a new day," Candace told her team. "Forward. That is the only direction we can go." She nodded to the group, sensing their lingering doubt. "Let's go. Follow me," she directed them. "Officer Evans," Candace greeted the young State Trooper, "we have someplace to be."

Dana watched as Candace followed Drew Evans down the hallway of the State Capital. Lieutenant Governor Dan Moore stepped up to walk beside Dana. "She seems to have it all together this morning."

Dana smiled and turned to Moore. She had known Candace for many years, and she had been granted glimpses of the governor that few in Candace's professional circle ever had. It had taken some time for Dana to understand that her friendship with Candace was a rarity. Candace was friendly toward everyone, even most of her adversaries and detractors. She kept many people in her professional life at arm's length personally. Friendliness and friendship were not the same things. In time, Dana had come to realize that Candace respected Dana as a member of the team, but Candace also thought of Dana in many ways as one of her children. Dana did not share a close relationship with her parents. Dana had struggled when she first began working for Senator Candace Fletcher. Candace had pushed her. Candace had tested her. Candace had also nurtured her. At some point—Dana had yet to be able to pinpoint when—the dynamic between Dana Russo and Candace Fletcher had shifted. Dana had become Candace's confidante both in and out of the office. And, Candace had become far more than a mentor to Dana. She had become the mother figure in Dana's life. Dana shook her head affectionately as she trailed behind the governor.

"She's cried her tears," Dana told Moore knowingly. "Now, she'll dry all of ours."

Dan Moore looked ahead as Drew Evans opened the car door for Candace. "I've never seen her cry. Teary, maybe...but..."

Dana nodded. "That's not a luxury she's ever been afforded out here," Dana said. She turned to Moore. "Tears down your cheek in front of the cameras make you appear sympathetic. For her?" Dana caught Candace's gaze momentarily before Drew Evans closed the door. "For her, it is still seen as weakness," Dana explained. "Doesn't mean that she doesn't cry them. She's probably cried more than all of us put together," she said as she exchanged a smile with Candace in the distance.

"You look up to her," Moore observed.

"Yes," Dana replied. She turned to Moore. "And, I love her."

✂✂✂

"Jay Jay?"

"Yeah, Spence?" Jameson glanced into the rearview mirror.

"Where's Coop?"

"Coop is with Aunt Shell and Aunt Mel. Why? You bored with me already?" she teased him.

"Just me and you?" Spencer asked.

"Yep. Just me and you. I thought you could help me with some work and then we will go someplace special and have dinner."

"Can we find Nana?"

Jameson smiled. "Yes, we can. We'll find Nana and then all three of us will go out for a pizza before Cooper comes home." Jameson glanced in the mirror again and caught Spencer bouncing in his seat sporting a brilliant smile. She chuckled. She had missed these moments.

"I stay all night?" he asked.

"Yep. You and Coop can have a sleepover in his room."

"We can build anudder fort?"

"I guess we could do that," Jameson replied."

"You, me, Coop, and Nana."

Jameson couldn't have wiped the silly grin off of her face if she had wanted too, and she had no desire to.

"Nana builds good forts, Jay Jay."

"Oh? Better than mine?" Jameson tried to ask seriously.

Spencer considered his answer. Jameson looked in the mirror and suppressed a laugh when she saw the looks of consternation on his small face. She was confident that she knew what Spencer's answer would be.

"Nana knows how, Jay Jay."

Jameson finally lost all hope and laughed. "I guess, she does," Jameson agreed. "Maybe I should ask her to teach me, huh?"

"Yep."

Jameson kept laughing as she drove. She'd seen the fort that Marianne and Candace had helped the boys build a week earlier. By the time Jameson made her way into the room the next morning, the makeshift fort was a dilapidated mess of blankets and sheets. To the boys, it was a castle, their very own hide-a-way. Both Spencer and Cooper had prattled on about their adventure with Marianne and Candace the entire morning. Jameson was fairly sure that she could spend the evening constructing an extravagant structure in Cooper's bedroom, and it would still somehow fail to measure up to the lopsided mess of blankets that Marianne and Candace had erected. Spencer and Cooper's joy was not about the fort. Spending that time with Candace and Marianne together had been the best adventure either could have asked for.

Jameson glanced back one more time. Looking at Spencer as he studied the buildings outside the car window, Jameson felt an enormous wave of gratefulness pass through her. She had arrived at the house in Schoharie earlier than she had expected that afternoon. Pearl had taken Spencer with her on a walk with Maddie so that Marianne could pack. It had given Jameson some one on one time with Candace's daughter. Jameson found herself replaying that hour. She and Marianne had begun with a rocky start. It seemed nearly impossible for Jameson to believe the way their relationship had changed—how much Marianne appeared to have changed. More and more, Marianne reminded Jameson of Candace. A few years earlier, Jameson would not have imagined that.

"Jay Jay?"

"Yeah, Spence?"

"Will I get anudder?"

"Another what, buddy?" Jameson inquired.

"Daddy," Spencer explained calmly.

Jameson's heart rose into her throat. Spencer's question was understandable, but it was not a question that Jameson had expected. She sometimes forgot how thoughtful both Spencer and Cooper were. Both boys posed questions that frequently surprised Jameson. Cooper and Spencer were both observant and articulate. She often wondered what conversations the toddlers had when they were alone. Candace had recently commented that the two boys behaved more like curious six or seven-year-old children than small toddlers. Jameson had wondered why. Candace had explained her theory.

"Loss," Candace told Jameson. Jameson sighed. "I think so," Candace continued. "Loss and change. They had both been surrounded by adults more than children until they found each other," Candace pointed out.

Jameson thought for a moment about how she should respond to Spencer's earnest question. There had been lots of discussion about Cooper's ability to have three mothers. It was natural that Spencer would begin to think about the possibility of having another father.

"I don't know, Spence," Jameson finally answered truthfully. "I hope that maybe someday you will," she told him.

"Mads too," he murmured.

"Yes, buddy, Maddie too," Jameson agreed. Her thoughts turned back to the conversation she and Candace had about Spencer and Cooper. Eventually, the topic of conversation had wound its way to Marianne.

"She's different now," Jameson observed.

Candace smiled. "Not really, she just isn't as guarded about showing who she is."

"I don't follow," Jameson confessed.

"Marianne has always tried to be Shell and Jonah's big sister."

"She is their big sister."

Candace laughed. "Yes, but she took that role seriously." Candace turned slightly somber. "She's always sought to be a caretaker. If I think about it, that started after Lucas. She tried to be my caretaker before she was even three."

Jameson took Candace's hand. "Candace..."

"It's okay," Candace said. "That's how life works. Marianne could see my sadness. Some things you can't hide no matter how hard you try, Jameson. Children are intuitive, far more intuitive than their adult counterparts," Candace said. "They haven't unlearned that. They are free to feel and free to think. They don't feel restricted in their curiosity so much."

"And, Marianne?"

Candace shrugged. "I think she watched me more carefully than I gave her credit for," Candace answered honestly. "And, I think she saw my many faces."

"What are you talking about?" Jameson wanted to know.

Candace sighed. "Many faces, Jameson. We all wear at least three, the one we show most of the world, the one we reserve for the few that we trust, and the face we wear when we are alone. Marianne saw all of mine when she was very small. I think she tried to emulate that in some way. She tried to grow up so that she could take care of me, help me take care of the other two. She tried to be in control. Life has a way of teaching you that you are never really in control," Candace explained. "That is only another face you wear."

Jameson replayed those words in her mind. Marianne hadn't changed, Jameson now realized. Candace's oldest daughter still sought to be a protector, to be in control. Jameson could see that clearly. Something had changed—Marianne let Jameson see the face that was reserved for only those Marianne trusted the most. That realization hit Jameson like a ton of bricks falling forcefully onto her. For a split second, she felt breathless. Marianne's ability to accept Jameson into her personal space was a far more precious gift than Jameson would be able to articulate.

"You know, Spence," Jameson began. "Your mom is a pretty special lady."

Spencer beamed. "Yep."

"She loves you a lot and maybe one day she will get a chance to love someone else again like she loved your daddy."

"You loved Daddy too."

Jameson nodded. "I did love your daddy," she said. "He was a good friend, and he made me laugh a lot."

"Daddies are silly."

Jameson agreed. Her father often made her laugh. "If we are lucky," Jameson said as her thoughts momentarily shifted to Laura. "If we are really lucky, Spence, our daddies will be silly."

"I hope my udder is silly too."

"Well, I hope one day your mom finds someone to make her laugh too."

�✗

"Sit down," Candace instructed the group gathered in the large conference room.

Candace's patience was beginning to wear thin, and it was only one o'clock in the afternoon. She had spent two hours visiting with the families who had lost loved ones in the train accident and with some of the injured passengers. She had assured them that she remained committed to her infrastructure plan. The project to strengthen the bridges, pitted roads and declining neighborhoods across the expansive state had been a cornerstone of Candace's campaign for governor. It had not been conceived as political folly. Candace believed passionately that investing in programs and initiatives to improve and rebuild areas and services would reinvigorate the state of New York's economy. She believed that infrastructure in many ways held the key to unlocking the state's full potential.

Candace had not been surprised by the resistance she had confronted from leaders in the state legislature. She was well-acquainted with the realities of governing. Promises and plans inevitably faced a vicious opponent called appropriations. Development required expenditures. Every politician vowed to make improvements. Some wielded the argument of spending to stimulate growth. Others took the opposite approach—cut spending, reduce taxes in the belief that fewer taxes would prompt people and businesses to pour those savings into the economy. In Candace's experience, the truth existed in the middle. No successful business leader Candace had ever met lacked an understanding that making money always required spending money. The trick in achieving success existed in finding avenues that spent money wisely while seeking to conserve extraneous resources. She had argued that case vigorously in the Senate. Now, she would argue it as Governor of New York.

Candace waited until everyone was seated to speak. She scanned the faces one by one. The long table held places for twenty people. Behind those twenty, the room was filled with interns and advisers. Candace loathed the reason for this meeting. She did, however, love these moments. This was a moment for her to teach. She was not only the leader at the table, but she would also assume the role of instructor to each person in the room. That was a role that Candace cherished and thrived on.

"So, ladies and gentleman," Candace began to address the room. "We all know why we are here. Let's talk about what we are going to do about that, shall we?"

"Governor Reid," Majority Leader Gordon Ellis spoke first. "Everyone is deeply concerned about the accident..."

Candace immediately interrupted him, anticipating the 'but' in his statement. She spoke calmly and deliberately. "Concern will not allow any of us to atone for the negligence that led to this tragedy, Gordon."

"You are not suggesting that this accident is our fault?" Ellis replied indignantly.

Candace smiled and paused deliberately to let silence hover for a moment before addressing the question. "Fault? In my experience, blame gets nothing resolved," she said. Ellis nodded. "However, it remains our burden to carry the bulk of the responsibility," she continued. "To sit at this table now, with the information you each have and to claim either ignorance or indifference is both unacceptable and the height of irresponsibility."

"No one wanted this to happen," Ellis bit back sharply.

"No, I don't believe they did," Candace agreed.

"Millions of people travel safely every day," Ellis said assuredly.

"No, Gordon. Millions of people have traveled without major incident for much longer than most experts predicted—not safely. Safely would imply that the likelihood of any incident occurring is minuscule at best. You've seen the analysis. I didn't complete the reviews. In fact, I did not even order that they be conducted. Those facts in front of you are not my political opinion. Those statistics and those concrete observations were recorded by people far more qualified to determine the safety of our railways, bridges and roads than ninety-nine percent of the individuals in this room. That includes me and it includes you."

"There is another set of facts, Governor. And, we can't avoid that," Senator David Conlon interjected.

"No, we cannot," Candace agreed, surprising everyone in the room. "We have a budget to meet. No one understands that better than me," she told the room. "So, we had all better be prepared to make some difficult choices in the coming days and months."

Representative Diane Bachman looked at Gordon Ellis. "You know, one more event like this and none of us will be sitting at this table after the next election," she pointed out.

That was a likelihood that Candace understood. She did not want that to guide the decisions facing this room. She pushed the folder in front of her away slightly. "That's a reality of being an elected official," Candace agreed. "And, if that is the reason that moves you to action, I will take it. I would hope, however, that common sense and a conscience would dictate your commitment to this."

"What are you proposing, Governor Reid? That we move forward with the original plan in its entirety?" Ellis asked.

Candace shrugged. "If you had asked me that on Sunday, I would have said yes," she said. "That was before I sat with a father grieving for his two children while his wife recovers in the hospital. I don't even want to think about what she must be feeling right now. So, no, Gordon, I don't believe that we should move forward with the plan in its entirety. It seems to me that the plan is entirely inadequate."

"It's already incredibly ambitious," another voice chimed.

"Ambitious? I'd say ineffectual," Candace replied calmly.

"Ineffectual? Fifteen billion dollars! Your proposal is just under a billion dollars for the MTA alone," Ellis responded swiftly.

"That it is," Candace agreed. "Over a twelve-year time frame and I might add that the state's commitment is only one-third of that figure."

"That remains to be seen," Ellis rebuffed her.

Candace lifted her eyebrow at the Majority Leader. "I suppose it does," she conceded. "However, the more quickly we appropriate our commitment, the more likely we are to stay within the parameters I have set." Candace could tell that Ellis was ready to pounce again. He reminded her of a dog with a bone. "A rabid dog," she thought silently. Candace softened her expression deliberately. She allowed her eyes to roam over the faces in the room, taking the time to meet with each pair of eyes that represented a potential obstacle.

"This is your personal crusade," Ellis muttered just loud enough that Candace understood. She offered the man a sardonic smile and pursed her lips.

"Uh-oh," Dana whispered to Dan Moore.

"What?" Moore whispered back.

Before Dana could respond to the Lieutenant Governor's question, Candace answered it.

"Crusade," Candace repeated the word. "That's an interesting assertion—a crusade. And, what is it exactly that I would gain from this crusade?"

"You are hell bent on..."

"I am determined to see this state thrive. That is why I am sitting here. That is what I have done for the last twenty-four years of my life," Candace said evenly. She allowed her eyes to pass over the room one final time before meeting Gordon Ellis's nervous gaze intently. "There are times when we all have to make difficult choices." Candace stood up and looked at the room. "You want guarantees? You want a guarantee about budgets, investments and execution?" she asked them rhetorically. "I understand. I can guarantee you that there will be another accident—the railway, a bridge, our water—when it might happen? That I cannot say. How soon and how severe will depend largely on what choice you each make," she said. She took several steps toward the door, stopped and turned back to address the room one final time. "Perhaps this is my crusade," she looked at Gordon Ellis before turning her attention back to the rest of the room's occupants. "Crusades happen throughout history. Figure out which side of history you want to be on," she said. "Dan and Bill will guide you through your questions this afternoon. I have another meeting that I am overdue for," she said. "Dana?" Candace called for Dana's attention.

Dana nodded and made her way to Candace's side. Dana snickered when the entire room stood. She watched as a satisfactory smile graced the governor's lips.

"I appreciate your work on this," Candace told the room. "Dan will bring any concerns he feels I need to address to my attention." Candace nodded and stepped through the large wooden doors. She rolled her eyes when the door closed behind her.

"What do you think they will do?" Dana asked curiously.

"They'll ask for some reductions," Candace replied knowingly. "But, they will pass it."

"You think so?"

"I know so," Candace said.

"It's an aggressive budget," Dana said honestly.

"Yes, it is."

"You're really not worried?"

"I'm always worried, Dana," Candace replied. "I'm just betting that they are worried a little bit more than I am right now, even if it is about different things."

"Candy, who are you meeting this afternoon? I didn't..."

"No one," Candace said. "I have some things to settle before I can leave. I happen to have a dinner date," she offered with a smile. "I don't intend to be late for that."

"Let me guess—J.D."

"And her handsome young protégé."

"I thought Coop was spending the day with Shell?" Dana asked.

"He is. Jameson is picking up Spencer this afternoon."

"Everything okay with Marianne?" Dana wondered.

"I think so," Candace replied.

"Missing them?" Dana guessed. "The kids, I mean."

"That never changes," Candace admitted. "Besides, Spencer gives me an excuse to eat something less than healthy."

"J.D. is still hovering; I take it?"

Candace groaned. "I love her, but I'm not quite ready to be put out to pasture."

"Put out to pasture? It can't be that bad."

"Want to bet? She got up early to make me lunch."

"That's sweet," Dana said.

Candace stopped walking and shook her head. "No, Dana. Chocolate is sweet, ice cream, Riesling, cheesecake maybe...Kale? It's green, Dana. Green like a pasture."

"Movie stars eat kale."

"Dana...Do you know there are programs for children to grow kale for zoo animals?" Candace asked. Dana snickered. "I'm serious. I realize that I live in a three ring circus, but do I look like one of the elephants? Be careful how you answer that," Candace held up a finger.

Dana started laughing. "It's good for you," Dana told Candace.

"What? Living in the circus?"

"No," Dana laughed harder. "Although, I think you like being the ringmaster," she offered. Candace smirked. "Kale. The kale is good for you."

Candace shook her head. "I don't think so. Chicken wings and a glass of Chardonnay—that would be good for me not elephant food."

"You realize kale is classier than chicken wings, don't you?"

"Are you suggesting that I have no taste?" Candace challenged her friend.

Dana shook her head. "Nope. I'm starting to wonder who the lunatic is in your family, though."

Candace laughed. She had desperately needed a moment of levity. "You aren't the only one Dana—trust me. So? Share my kale while we review the morning?"

"Oh, I would, but I ordered delivery while you were dressing down the Majority Leader."

"You did not."

"Yep."

"What kind?" Candace asked.

"Oh no, J.D. will kill me if she finds out I am enabling your junk food habit."

"She won't have to. I'll be dead from starvation."

Dana laughed loudly as Candace opened the door to her office. "Good thing I ordered you lunch too."

Candace's eyes gleamed. "You might just earn that raise yet," Candace said.

"I know where my bread is buttered, Governor."

"I love butter."

Dana laughed again, enjoying the familiar banter. Candace needed a diversion even if it only lasted a moment. Dana had some additional information to share with the governor. Information that pertained to Lawson Klein. Chinese food might have been the only way to make it palatable at all. It might have been a stretch, but Dana was willing to try just about anything. "J.D. might kill me, but at least, I will be alive for her to take her shot," Dana mused.

CHAPTER THIRTEEN

"I hope you don't mind that I invited Scott to dinner," Maureen said.

Marianne shook her head. "Of course not."

Maureen Reid smiled. "You sounded a little...I don't know—apprehensive?"

Marianne shrugged. "I suppose I am—just a little."

"Well, I thought it might give you both a chance to talk before tomorrow—in a social space."

"I really don't know how to thank you," Marianne said.

"Thank me? Thank me for what?" Maureen asked. "I put you to work almost the moment you walked through my door."

Marianne laughed. It was true. Maddie had fallen asleep just before Marianne had pulled into Maureen and Duncan Reid's driveway. That gave Maureen the opportunity to recruit Marianne as kitchen staff. Marianne didn't mind. Maureen had always made her feel comfortable. She had grown to love Jameson's parents. They had been tremendously welcoming of all of Candace's children. Candace and Maureen Reid had become fast friends, and that friendship had blossomed over the years that Candace and Jameson had been together. Maureen Reid was only six years older than her daughter-in-law, the same age difference that separated Marianne and her step-mother. Somehow, that didn't seem to matter anymore, least of all to Marianne. That was a fact that Marianne was sure surprised some people. She was grateful for Jameson's family. They had become hers.

Jameson's father had immediately made himself available to help Rick when Marianne and Rick had first moved back to New York. And, when everything had fallen apart, Duncan and Maureen had swiftly stepped in and helped with caring for Spencer and Maddie during Candace's transition from the Senate to the Governor's Mansion. Marianne had been privy to a few conversations between her mother and Jameson's mom. She always enjoyed listening to the two women, and while she had never told either of them, their willingness to include her had been a lifeline at points for Marianne. Marianne listened far more than she contributed to any dialogue when she was with the two women. Sometimes Pearl would enter the mix, and Marianne would inevitably find herself pulled from the sadness of loss into the humor of life. Candace, Maureen, and Pearl were all mothers with grown children. They spoke freely, many times seeming to forget Marianne was one of those children. They were also all women who had known loss in life. Being with them had given Marianne hope during a time when hope had often been a scarcity in her life.

"I'm a little surprised that he asked *me*, to tell you the truth," Marianne confessed to Maureen.

Maureen nodded her understanding as she placed a pan into the oven. "Sit down," she told Marianne.

Marianne handed Maureen the salad she had completed and took a seat at the kitchen table. "I'm not grounded am I?" Marianne teased. Maureen looked momentarily confused. "Well, you told me to sit. Did I chop something incorrectly?" Marianne joked.

"How much time have you been spending with my daughter?" Maureen asked curiously.

"Why?"

"That's exactly something J.D. would say."

Marianne smiled. "Actually, quite a lot of time lately," she admitted.

Maureen narrowed her gaze. "Interesting."

Marianne shrugged. "That's surprising I take it? Me and J.D. spending time together."

"Not really," Maureen replied, surprising Marianne. "J.D. grows on you," she winked at the younger woman. "So? Why nervous about tomorrow?" Maureen wanted to know.

"I'm not the one who speaks in front of groups of people," Marianne said. "That's Shell and Mom. Me? I never had much interest in that. I'm not sure that I will be particularly good at it. I mean, I am used to talking about things now. I've been doing it for months in group…Talking about Rick, talking about the kids, my family—how I feel. But, leading a discussion like that? I don't know. Who am I to lead people through their grief?"

"I'd say that you are exactly the person to do that," Maureen said. Marianne was stunned. "Why does that surprise you? Look at Spencer. He's adjusted incredibly well to life now, Marianne. That says a lot."

"Maybe, but I didn't do that alone. I had Mom and J.D., my dad, Shell, Jonah, Pearl. Hell, I've had you and Duncan and Scott along the way. It's not like I have had to do it alone."

"And, neither do the people you will meet tomorrow," Maureen observed candidly. "They will have you and Scott to help guide them to find their way back. I can't think of two people more qualified."

"I just hope that I don't let anyone down," Marianne explained.

Maureen smiled. She had instantly felt a connection with Marianne, which had taken Jameson completely off guard. Jameson's mother had managed to cultivate a healthy relationship with Candace's daughter long before Marianne and Jameson had fully turned the corner from acceptance to friendship. Maureen had understood Marianne, it seemed. She had the advantage of being removed just far enough to see what drove Marianne. And, Maureen also realized that Marianne continually sought Candace's approval. It wasn't difficult to see for anyone looking in. Maureen and Pearl had talked about it on several occasions. What people often had failed to see in Marianne was her nurturing nature. That was something that Maureen knew Marianne herself sometimes failed to see.

Anyone who took a moment to observe Marianne with Rick and their children would have immediately noticed her attentiveness to her family. Shortly after Jameson had moved into Candace's home, Jameson had confided in her mother that she was at a loss as to how to reach Marianne. Everything was going fine with Candace's other two children. Marianne had been a tough nut to crack for Jameson. Maureen had offered her daughter a few observations.

"Don't try so hard," Maureen told Jameson.

"I'm not."

"Umm-hm."

"Mom, I'm not. What am I supposed to do? She hates me! I mean, she's civil but she hates me!"

Maureen laughed. "I don't think Marianne hates you, J.D."

"Okay, she hates me with Candace."

"I don't think so."

"Mom! You know what happened at the barbecue. Come on. She thinks I'm going to ruin Candace's life and then run away from the mess."

Maureen took a deep breath. "I don't think so."

"Is that all you can say? 'I don't think so?' Well? Help me out! What do you think?"

"Are you sure you really want to know what I think?" Maureen challenged her daughter gently.

"Yes."

"Okay. I think that you are right about one thing; Marianne is worried about her mother. And, why wouldn't she be, J.D.? She's not here all of the time to see the two of you together like Shell is or I am. Whether or not you like it, the fact that you are only six years older than Marianne is probably a bit unsettling for her."

"What about me?" Jameson asked. "God, Mom, I didn't expect to fall in love with someone who has kids my age, you know?"

"You didn't expect to fall in love at all," Maureen cracked.

Jameson rolled her eyes. "Jonah is in California. He's not here often and he doesn't hate me."

"Marianne doesn't hate you, J.D. She just isn't sure what to make of you if I had to guess. And, I think that maybe, just maybe, there might be a hint of jealousy going on."

"Jealousy? Over what?"

Maureen smiled. "Over the fact that you have such a close relationship with her sister and her mother for one thing. Maybe because she's gotten used to Candace placing her personal attention with the kids and not with you."

"You sound like Pearl," Jameson commented.

"Well, Pearl is a smart lady so I will take that as a compliment. What does Candace say about this?" Maureen asked.

Jameson smirked. "Why do I think you already know that answer?"

Maureen shrugged. "Maybe I do."

"Weird."

"What's that?" Maureen asked.

"You and my partner being besties."

Maureen shrugged again. "I love Candace."

"Yeah, I know," Jameson chuckled. "Mom, what if Marianne never comes around?"

"She will. Give her some time, J.D. Marianne is not as hard as you make her out to be."

"Oh? An hour in Candace's kitchen with Marianne and Candace and you've defanged the demon?"

Maureen laughed. "A bit dramatic? Let's just say that I have watched her. Spend a little less time worrying about what Marianne thinks and a bit more actually watching what she does and listening to what she is really saying. That's my advice. You two aren't so different," she told Jameson.

"You are insane."

"Am I?"

"Yeah. Marianne and I are like oil and water."

"Mmm..."

"Mom, seriously! What do Marianne and I have in common?"

"Well, for one thing, you both love Candace."

"Uh-huh..."

"That's a pretty big thing, J.D. It's your common ground. The sooner you two realize that, the better off everyone will be. You both want to protect her. The big difference is that you are not trying to compete for Candace's affection or for her approval."

"There's no competition," Jameson said flatly. "Candace loves her kids more than anything. You don't even need eyes to see that."

"Mmm."

"What?"

"She doesn't love them more than she loves you," Maureen observed.

Jameson was shell-shocked by her mother's observation. *"No, the kids are ..."*

"Her children, J.D. I love you more than you will ever be able to understand. I do not love you more than I love your father. I love you differently. Part of the reason I love you so much is that you are part of both of us."

"Okay? But, Mom...The kids are not part of me and Candace."

"Not in the same way, no."

"Not at all," Jameson returned.

"Really? And, why is it that you are so concerned about the three of them all of the time? About Spencer?"

Jameson thought for a moment. *"They're Candace's kids,"* she made her reply.

"And? That's it? They come with the package is that it?"

"No," Jameson said. "She loves them."

"And, you love her," Maureen said. "And, they are part of her," she continued knowingly. "You see parts of her in each of them."

Jameson scratched her brow. "I guess."

"You know. Give Marianne some time, J.D."

"Maybe. But, Mom...The kids...They will never be part of me. It's not the same. They have a father."

"You think that being a part of someone is all about biology?" she asked.

"You just said that."

"I said that you were part of your father and me."

"Exactly," Jameson commented.

Maureen smiled. "No two relationships are the same, J.D. There are parents and children who never truly know each other. You know that too. You've seen it with your uncle and Craig. Let me ask you something..."

"What?"

"Do you feel like Candace is part of you?"

Jameson smiled. "Completely."

Maureen nodded. "Being part of someone is not about biology, J.D. It's about love. It's what you feel and what you see when you stop looking so closely. You are looking and listening with your eyes and your ears where Marianne is concerned. You're worried about the relationship."

"Of course, I am worried about our relationship. She's Candace's daughter, Mom. That means that she is part of my life forever."

"Forever, huh?"

Jameson sighed and nodded. "Does that surprise you?" she asked her mother.

"No. I knew the first time you sat in this kitchen and told me about Candace that you had finally found your way home."

"Home?" Jameson was confused.

"Yes, home. Didn't you just say that a person didn't need eyes to see how much Candace loves her kids?"

"Yeah..."

Maureen raised her eyebrow. "I don't think anyone could miss how much you love Candace either," she said. "Or, J.D., how much she loves you. That's home. And, that is why this has you so worried."

"Maybe. I don't want to let anyone down. I just wish I knew what..."

"You are looking for something to do," Maureen said. "Some action you can take to make everything perfect for you and Marianne overnight."

"Not perfect...And, yes...There has to be something I can do. It's..."

"J.D., do you love Marianne?"

"What?"

"It's a simple question, Jameson. You love Shell, don't you? Jonah? Spencer? Rick?"

"Well, yeah...But, I have..."

"So? Do you love Marianne?" Maureen asked knowingly. Jameson sighed. "Mmm. Stop trying so hard and just love her for who she is. Be yourself, not what you think Marianne wants you to be. Love Candace and be honest with her kids. It will work itself out in time."

"I hope so. You have more confidence than I do," Jameson admitted.

"I told you a long time ago that falling in love happens in an instant. What I didn't say is that we fall in love in different ways. You think that means what you and Candace have. It does. We also fall in love with our children, our friends, our parents. That does happen in an instant. Although, sometimes it takes us a while to realize that it has happened at all," Maureen said. "If you recall, I also told you that relationships are by design; they take time. Once you realize that the first part has already happened, it will be easier for you to give it time, sweetheart."

Maureen looked at Marianne whose eyes had drifted to the table. She sighed. "Who are you worried about letting down?" Maureen asked.

Marianne looked up sadly. "Everyone. Scott, the people in this group..."

"And?" Maureen prodded gently.

Marianne sighed. "The kids, Mom...J.D. What if I never get it all together? They've put up with so much already. Sometimes...Sometimes I wonder why they put up with it at all. What if I never get over it?"

Maureen smiled compassionately. "You remind me of J.D. right now," she told Marianne. She saw the confusion in Marianne's eyes. "They love you," Maureen said.

"I know, but Mom and the kids...That's kind of a given, right?"

Maureen nodded. "And, J.D. is not."

"She didn't sign up for all of this."

"All of what? Life?" Maureen asked.

"My life. My issues. Jesus, if I think about it, that's pretty much all I have ever given her."

"I don't think J.D. sees it that way," Maureen said.

"You know, when I said that Scott asked me to lead this group tomorrow, she...She didn't even hesitate to change her schedule to take Spencer."

"She loves Spencer. I don't think J.D. could love the kids more if she had given birth to them."

"I know."

"Mmm. I don't just mean your kids."

"I know. She's a kid magnet," Marianne chuckled. "I'm glad that she and Mom decided to adopt. I think she would have missed a lot."

"So am I," Maureen beamed. She loved her grandchildren. "But, I didn't just mean the little ones," Maureen clarified. Marianne looked at Maureen hopefully. "She loves all of you, Marianne. Maybe more than you sometimes realize. I can't speak for her. I do know that much. I had a similar conversation with her in this kitchen a few years ago about you. I'm going to tell you something that I told her—stop trying so hard. It takes time. She was worried about finding common ground with you back then," Maureen explained.

Marianne put her face in her hands regretfully. "I put her through hell."

Maureen chuckled. "You gave her a good run for her money," she conceded. "It was good for her."

Marianne dropped her hands and looked at Maureen as if Maureen had completely lost her mind.

Maureen laughed. "It was—good for her. It taught her how to let go a little," she said. "You don't think so, but it taught her about being a parent more than anything else, I think."

"Surprised she wanted any kids after that."

"You're too hard on yourself, just like her," Maureen chuckled. "You know; it's always been interesting to me."

"What's that?"

"How much alike you and Jameson really are."

Marianne raised her eyebrow. "You are probably the only person who would ever see or say *that*."

"Oh? I don't think that's true. You might be surprised how many people can see that," Maureen said.

"How so?"

"Well, you both love your mom in a way that I think few people would deny."

"True."

"And, you both share a familiar acquaintance called grief," Maureen said. "Just like you share that with your mother and Scott. All of you have lost someone well before you should have—someone that meant the world to you. You and J.D., you both want to be able to fix everything overnight. You want to be able to control what's happening around you and to you."

"Control freaks, huh?"

"No," Maureen corrected Marianne. "But, sometimes you both have a hard time accepting the fact that some things in life take time. Relationships are one of those things; healing is another. Give yourself a break. Whether or not you think so, J.D. loves you just as much as she does Cooper. It might be different; it's different with every person. But, Marianne, she loved you before there was a Cooper, and I do know this, J.D. would do anything she could for you—for any of you."

"Because she loves Mom."

"Partly, only partly. It might have started that way. Now? I think if you step back, you will realize that your friendship with J.D. can stand on its own. You're not giving her or yourself much credit otherwise."

"I guess. Scott? I mean, he's gone so far out on a limb for me. I'm not sure sometimes I know why. I mean, I know he and Rick were friends, and I know..."

"You know, Scott loves J.D. as much as you love your brother and sisters. Those three were inseparable," Maureen said quietly.

"J.D., Scott and Craig?"

Maureen nodded. "Cousins, best friends, I don't know. They drove us crazy at times," she laughed. "They just...Well, some people are meant to find each other, I think. Sometimes we find them early on, sometimes it takes some time," Maureen observed. "The hardest part is that someday someone has to let go, and you never know when that day is going to come. Some people become a part of you. Losing them is like losing a part of yourself," she said. Maureen took hold of Marianne's hand. "You have a lot of common ground with J.D.—believe me. She understands, Marianne. So does Scott. They lost each other for a long time too in their grief and their guilt. They don't want to see that happen to you."

Marianne nodded. "I just want them to be..."

"Proud of you," Maureen said. "I know. If they weren't, you wouldn't be sitting here right now," she said. "Give yourself the time, Marianne and give them the credit they deserve, all of them. Life deals us some shitty blows. It also gives us some amazing gifts, and you never know when those will land on your doorstep either," Maureen said. Marianne laughed. "That's funny?"

"No," Marianne said. "I was just thinking how much alike you and my mom are. I don't think I would have imagined so many parents in my life a few years ago," she kept chuckling.

Maureen laughed. "Too much motherly advice?"

Marianne shook her head. "No. I just hope I can give it as eloquently someday."

Maureen nodded. "I have no doubt. Now, come on. Let's open some wine before my nephew and my husband get here."

"You really are like Mom," Marianne said playfully.

"I'll take that as a compliment."

"You should."

✖✖✖

"What do you mean?" Candace asked Dana. "Before you answer that, tell me this—do I need to get the bottle of scotch out now?"

Dana laughed. "Candy, I just know that he has made arrangements to go on camera himself."

"And, what does that have to do with me?"

"Directly? From the little I have been able to get out of some of my sources, nothing. Indirectly? It has everything to do with you."

"Dana, Lawson Klein has never even met Jameson or Spencer. And, from what I understand he didn't even bother to speak to Jonah the one time Laura attempted to introduce them. So, what could he say that would affect me?"

Dana groaned softly. "He's going to speak about Laura."

"Excuse me? What about her? About her having a baby out of wedlock? What? How does that serve his cause?"

"No, he is going to talk about the fact that she has long had issues with authority. That's what I am told, that she would do or say anything to hurt her family and has tried in the past. I also understand that he is going to make a claim that illegitimate children are nothing new in the Stratton family."

Candace set the chopsticks in her hand down, wiped her face with a napkin, closed the container of lo mein that sat in front of her and reached for her cell phone.

"Candy?"

Candace ignored Dana. She held the receiver to her ear and waited.

"Candy?"

"We need to talk," Candace replied.

"What's wrong?" Pearl asked. "You sound angry?"

"I'm not sure there is a word for what I am right now," Candace replied.

"Whatever it is..."

"It's more than one whatever. Let's just say I think the skeletons in Granddad's closet are about to see the light of day," Candace explained.

Pearl sighed. "Candy, I have told you again and again that I don't care who knows about my parents. I don't want you to worry about me, if that's what you are worried about. It was bound to happen someday. I'm seventy-seven-years-old. That's a long time to keep a secret."

"I'm afraid it's not just your secret that is going to get some airplay, and that worries me even more."

"What are you talking about?" Pearl wanted to know. "I know you don't have any illegitimate children. Please tell me Shell is not pregnant or something? Or..."

"No," Candace chuckled, appreciative of Pearl's humor. "It's Laura, if I had to guess."

"Everyone knows about little Jameson."

"It's not the baby that's the secret. And, I have a feeling what Lawson Klein plans to tell the world will be a sad spin on the truth. As much as I loathe the man's ideology and be-havior, this is not something I expected."

"You want to explain?" Pearl asked.

"Yes, but not over the phone."

"Do you want me to come up there?"

"Jameson and I are supposed to have dinner with Spen-cer tonight. I don't want to ruin that for either of them," Candace said.

"Do you want me to come up there in the morning?"

"No. I think Jameson and I need to come home for this conversation. I need to do a little more digging. Marianne will be home in the afternoon. I'll see if Maureen is willing to come back with her and watch the boys for a bit."

"Family meeting?" Pearl surmised.

"Somewhat, I'd like Marianne's support."

"What about Shell and Jonah?" Pearl asked.

"Not yet. Not until I have a better handle on things."

"Candy, you just got back to Albany," Pearl reminded Candace.

"Well, one afternoon at home won't be an issue. Trust me on that. I will be here in the morning and then head home for a bit in the afternoon. There are too many ears here."

Pearl understood Candace's concerns. She was having a hard time imagining what anyone could possibly say about Laura that would be driving Candace's obvious concern. The tone of Candace's voice told Pearl that whatever it was, Can-dace was worried. She detected a note of something else in the governor's voice—determination.

"Candy, whatever it is, it can't be that bad."

"I wish that were true," Candace said. "I'll call you when I am on my way tomorrow," Candace said. She turned her attention back to Dana slowly.

"What the hell was that about?" Dana asked.

Candace massaged her eyes and then her forehead. "If I am right, I think Lawson Klein is about to reveal my family's ancient history. That concerns me less than the idea that he is willing to reinvent a piece of his daughter's."

"Why do I not like the sound of this?"

"Dana..."

"Candy, what could he possibly have?"

Candace took a deep breath and let it out forcefully. "My grandfather," she said. "My grandfather was Pearl's father."

Dana's jaw dropped to her knees. She had wondered what Jessica's cryptic dialogue had been pointing her to. "Does Pearl know?"

"Yes, she knows."

"Oh, my God, Candy. I don't know that I can keep Klein from..."

"It's not Pearl I am worried about. She can handle it. Frankly, I think it might be a relief for her."

"If you are worried about the political fallout, I can't see that revelation impacting you or any of the policies we are driving all that much."

"No, maybe not. I suspect he is going to weave a fairytale about Laura. If I am right, he will assert that I am somehow responsible for feeding her delusions with my feminist principles."

"Not following."

"Dana...Laura...Laura was abused by her brother. Lawson knew. You should know, from the little that I do know, it wasn't Mark Klein who was punished or counseled for his behavior."

Dana closed her eyes and shook her head. "Why would he want that out?"

Candace shrugged. "I said that he will tell a fairytale."

"You think he is going to say that Laura made that up and that her view of reality is distorted? That you are now encouraging that path?

"Yes, I do."

"Why would he do that?"

"Well, it's only a guess, but I am betting he is afraid that Laura will come forward," Candace guessed. "And, he wants a chance to tell the story first. Make it *his* story. Paint her as the perpetrator and his family as the victim."

"Again, why? To defame you? That's insane, even for Lawson Klein. Candy, that won't score any points for him with anyone already in your corner. In fact, it will probably strengthen their support. And, honestly, the people who are always on the fence? This is not the kind of message to sway them, particularly not out of an election cycle. The only ones he will gain any clout with are the ones who are already on his bandwagon."

"I know."

"So?" Dana asked again. "I understand the reasoning he has on your grandfather's legacy. I even get how he might benefit from connecting Jonah to that...at least, in some circles. Why expose this? It's a gamble for him."

"I'm not sure. Either he's even more arrogant than we give him credit for or he's afraid he'll be hung out to dry if he doesn't come up with something. I don't care what the motivation is. It will devastate Laura. And, frankly..."

"I think I know what you are going to say. Look, I will try and hold the wolves at bay for a few days. Throw some bones out there that raise fuchsia flags at the press. The red ones don't seem to catch their attention anymore."

Candace smiled wanly and sighed. "Do what you can. Call Jessica. Tell her what I told you."

"Jessica again?"

"Just do it, Dana," Candy said. "I hate to do this to you. Get your team ready and I will have Susan schedule a meeting for tomorrow night here."

"Candy, are you up to all of this yet?"

"Do I have a choice?" Candace returned.

"Why don't you just go home tonight..."

"No, we promised Spencer. And, I have a meeting at eight in the morning with Brett Stein from the city's environmental protection department. It can't wait. Heaven knows the last thing we need is an issue with New York City's water. I want to review the risks and concerns he has. I will head back after that. I had planned to spend the rest of the afternoon reviewing the budget proposal with Dan. It's fine. Dan prefers evenings. Actually, more like late nights." Candace chuckled. "I can meet with him late."

"And, what about you?"

"Dana, I don't have the luxury of me right now. We both know that."

"I do, but..."

"Stop worrying about me. Worry about stalling this Klein debacle so that I don't have to."

Dana got up from her seat and nodded. "I can..."

"And, greasy food be damned. Make sure there are chicken wings at tomorrow's meeting," Candace tried to lighten the mood.

"I'll see what I can do."

"Good."

CHAPTER FOURTEEN

Scott sat quietly in a chair observing Marianne as she tried to comfort a cranky Maddie. He was grateful to be sitting in his aunt's living room with Jameson's step-daughter. Scott had no illusions about what had been the catalyst to healing the long rift that had separated him from Jameson—Candace. He had missed his cousin and his best friend for years. When their cousin Craig had died from an overdose, Jameson had pulled away deliberately from Scott. He had understood. That had not changed the fact that the separation had served as another heartbreak in his young life. He had felt incredibly alone in his guilt and his grief. Ultimately, he had turned his pain and his frustration into determination—determination to help anyone he could heal from the devastation that addiction caused in people's lives.

Scott also understood that addiction came in many forms. Most people thought of addiction in terms of alcohol and drugs. People could become addicted to nearly anything, so much so that it became detrimental to their quality of life. He had counseled men and women with addictions to bad relationships, food, work, sex, even to grief itself. Marianne had impressed him. That was something that he had not shared with her. He was not sure that she was ready to hear that, and he was positive she would be unable to accept that as the truth. Marianne still lingered in doubt, seeing her inevitable moments of emotional struggle as weakness. Scott was aware of that. Marianne did not see the strength that she possessed. In less than six months' time, she had learned to cope with her grief far better than Scott would have expected, and with grace. He believed that giving Marianne the opportunity to help lead others through that grief would likely serve as another stepping stone in her healing process. He smiled as she cooed to the baby on her shoulder. Maddie rubbed her eyes, stopped fussing and put her head on Marianne's shoulder.

"See? You are great at reassuring people," Scott told Marianne.

Marianne looked across the room at Scott. "Not quite the same thing."

"Oh, I don't know. I don't have any kids, but I'd have to imagine that keeping calm with two of them is a lot more difficult than what I do."

"Only when they are teething," she winked at him.

"I am so glad none of us can remember that," Scott said absently, looking into his coffee cup.

Marianne tried to keep her laughter to a dull roar. The serious expression on Scott's face amused her. "That *would* be terrible," she offered.

Scott looked back up at Marianne. She lifted her eyebrow at him. "It's got to hurt," he said thoughtfully. "Something poking through your gums," he shuddered at the thought.

"Try childbirth," Marianne deadpanned.

Scott shuddered again. "There's a reason we don't do that," he said. Marianne was curious, and Scott continued. "Men, I mean. No way," he gave his assessment. "We were not built for pain."

Marianne laughed, and Maddie fussed. "Sorry," she whispered into Maddie's ear, patting her daughter's back while she continued to chuckle. She looked back at Scott quizzically. "Not that I mean to pry, but I'm surprised you aren't married with your own brood. You and J.D. are kid magnets."

Scott shrugged. "I don't know. Me and J.D. are big kids," he joked. Marianne looked at him expectantly. Scott sighed. "I guess I just haven't found the right person."

"Have you even looked?" Marianne teased.

"No," Scott laughed.

"That's what I thought."

"Did you? Look?" he wondered.

"Maybe. To tell you the truth, I don't remember. One day Rick was just there and he never left."

Scott nodded. "Yeah, that hasn't happened to me."

"It will."

Scott offered Marianne a doubtful smile and changed the subject. "I get the feeling that you are a little worried about the group."

"I guess I am still not sure what makes you think I am the right person for this."

Scott knew that nothing he could tell Marianne would reassure her. Her confidence would grow as she worked with the group. He had learned over the years to recognize the best people to lead, and in almost every case, those individuals entered their new roles with skepticism. It was not skepticism born of fear or self-doubt. It was humility. Scott recognized that Marianne's loss had humbled her. That is precisely what he knew would make her successful. He smiled at her and nodded. "Nothing I say will change how you feel walking into that room."

Marianne was surprised. "Not what I expected you to say."

"I know. I also know it's true."

"So, no advice?"

"Be yourself," he said.

"That's it?"

"Yep, pretty much. We'll see how you feel tomorrow afternoon," he said with a smile.

"A little confident?"

"Only about the things I know."

Marianne narrowed her gaze. "You must be seeing something that I don't."

Scott nodded but said nothing. "Yes, I do," he thought silently.

✖✖✖

"Nana?" Spencer called into the door of the Governor's Mansion. He looked up to Jameson. "Where is Nana?" he asked.

"I don't know, Spence," Jameson answered. "I guess we will have to try and find her."

Spencer beamed with excitement. The familiar game of hide and seek was not one that he was able to play most days at "the big red house" as Spencer called it. Jameson was positive that Candace would have welcomed Spencer's game anytime. But, Jameson also knew that both Spencer and Cooper needed to learn that there were boundaries. She had spoken briefly with Candace earlier in the afternoon, and Jameson thought that some playfulness with Spencer might be exactly what Governor Candace Reid was in need of.

"Well?" Jameson encouraged Spencer. "Let's get going. I'm getting hungry. We need to find Nana soon."

"Nana!" Spencer called as he moved through the hallway. "Nana!"

✖✖✖

Jonah walked into the bedroom he shared with Laura and stopped abruptly. Laura was sitting on the edge of the bed, her phone in her left hand while her face rested in her right.

"Laura? Who were you talking to?" he asked.

Laura picked up her head slowly and shook it despairingly. She sighed and closed her eyes. "My mother."

Jonah was stunned into silence for a moment. "You called your mother?"

"No, she called me."

Jonah took a deep breath and made his way to Laura's side. He gently stroked her back in reassurance. "Do you want to talk about it?"

Laura shook her head again. Most times, she was unsure how to talk about her family. She loved her mother. And, Laura could recall a time when she had laughed with her mother and cried in her mother's embrace. Distance had crept between them long before Laura Klein had left for college. It had left a hole in Laura's heart that she had yet to find a way to explain to anyone. When little Jameson had been born, Laura had found her despair over her mother's lack of support and affection had turned to palpable anger. As a mother, Laura simply could not fathom treating a child that way.

"I don't know that there is anything to say," Laura told Jonah.

"What did she want?"

"I really don't know," she confessed. "She asked me to consider coming home. It would be easier for everyone, she said." Laura let out a caustic chuckle. "Easier? Easier for them? I'm supposed to leave my family? I mean, honestly? Like she would have ever done that. Certainly not for me."

Jonah's emotions floated between sadness and fury. He leaned in and kissed Laura on her temple, pulling her closer. "It is; you know? Your family? Us, I mean."

Laura pulled back slightly. She caressed Jonah's cheek and smiled genuinely. "I hope so."

Jonah nodded and sucked in a nervous breath.

Laura felt Jonah tremble slightly next to her. "Jonah? Something wrong?"

"No," Jonah replied. He looked at Laura. "I suck at romance."

"What?" Laura giggled.

Jonah sighed. "Thing is, I've been thinking..."

"About?" Laura prodded.

"About our family," he said.

"In what way?" Laura wondered.

"Well...In the way that would make it official. I mean, would make you officially part of my family. Not that you aren't as far as everyone is concerned. I mean, you know...You know Mom and J.D., they think of you as..."

"Jonah?"

"And, I mean you and me...Well, I already think of us as..."

"Jonah!" Laura called for Jonah's attention. Jonah snapped to attention and looked at Laura. Laura smiled sweetly. "What on earth are you waffling on about?" she teased.

"Making it official. Getting married."

"Are you asking me to marry you?" she asked him curiously.

"Yeah, I guess I am."

"Really?"

"What do you mean—really? That's surprising?" he asked.

Laura kept smiling. "Yes."

"Why is it surprising? We have a son. We love each other. I want to be with you. I mean, I don't know what that..."

Laura giggled. "Yes, I will marry you...If you are asking," she teased. Jonah tipped his head in confusion. "Jonah? Are you?" she asked lightly.

"Will you?" he asked again.

"I already said yes," she pointed out.

"You did?"

"Yes, about two seconds ago," Laura reminded him.

"Are you sure?" Jonah asked.

"Are you?" she returned playfully.

"Completely."

Laura nodded. "Jonah, you do realize that my father and..."

"I don't give a shit what your father or brother says about me."

"Good," Laura told him.

"They'd better not hurt you ever again," Jonah said flatly.

"I'm okay," Laura said.

"I'm telling you," Jonah began. "I mean it. They had better leave you out of it."

Laura smiled at Jonah, but with evident sadness. "Honey, that is not going to happen. At least, not for a long time. I love you for wanting to protect me. You can't. Not from them. Only I can do that."

"Laura..."

"It's true. As long as I have you and J.J. I will be all right."

Jonah leaned in and kissed Laura softly. "Not the most romantic proposal, huh? I'd hoped to do something more traditional."

Laura's eyes lit up, and she winked at Jonah. "Nothing about our relationship has been traditional," she reminded him. "I'm not sure I would want to change that now."

Jonah laughed. "I do love you, you know?"

"I hope so. You're going to be stuck with me now."

"Nah, you're the one getting the short end of the stick," he quipped. "You get stuck with my crazy family."

Laura shook her head. "For that, I will never be able to thank you enough," she said honestly. "But, I can try," she told him, placing a playful kiss on his neck.

"Uhhh...Uhh...Laura?" Jonah whimpered as she teased him.

"Hum?"

"Uhh...Ummm...Uhhh...It's one o'clock in the afternoon," he pointed out when Laura's hand began unbuttoning his dress shirt.

"So? As I recall, J.J. was conceived in the afternoon."

"Uhhh...Mmm...Yeah, but that was before we...Oh, Jesus! Before we had..."

"If you are not quiet, you'll wake him up from his nap, and I won't get to finish what I am starting," Laura whispered.

"Oh...Yeah...I mean...Oh, God!"

"And, my father worries that I lost religion. He doesn't know this family at all," Laura giggled as she continued.

"Sweet Jesus!"

Laura laughed. "If only he knew," she thought.

✗✗✗

"Nana?" Spencer asked as Candace lifted the covers to tuck him in.

"Yes, Spencer?"

"Coop gets twee mommies?"

Candace smiled at her grandson. "Yes, he does," she agreed. Spencer frowned. "Spencer?"

Spencer looked up at Candace pensively. "Jay Jay gots one mommy and one daddy."

"Well, I guess that's true. Some people only get one of each."

Spencer scratched his head. "Mommy gots one mommy too."

"Well, that's true, Spencer. Your mommy has me as her mommy. Is there something you are worried about?" Candace wondered.

"Can evewybody have that?"

Candace nodded and took a seat on the edge of Spencer's bed. "Can anyone have more than one mommy or daddy?" she asked him. Spencer nodded. "Sure they can."

"I have lots of grandmas," Spencer observed.

"Yes, I guess you do."

"More den Coop, cause Coop's got you and Jay Jay as mommies."

"That's true."

"So...I gets more grandmas and he gets more mommies."

Candace grinned. She had grown accustomed to the loving rivalry that existed between siblings. In many ways, Spencer and Cooper existed like siblings. They spent a great deal of time together and were continually cared for by the same adults. She also suspected that Spencer was curious about his father; could he have another daddy someday? Candace was aware that he had already asked Marianne that question. Marianne had told Spencer that maybe one day he would, but that she could not promise him that. Candace brushed Spencer's bangs aside gently.

"You know, Spencer you can love as many people as you want to. Sometimes you might call them Mom or Dad or Nana. Sometimes you just call them by their name but you still love them as if they were your mom or your dad or maybe your brother or sister. Like Grandma Pearl, that's a good example. She isn't really my mother and most of the time I call her Pearl, but in my heart?" Candace looked at him. Spencer looked at her curiously. "Right in here," Candace pointed to her heart. "Pearl will always be my mom."

Spencer pursed his lips in consideration and then looked back at Candace. "Like Jay Jay and me," he said. Candace waited for his explanation. "Jay Jay is my Nana too," he said. "But, I just call her Jay Jay."

Candace smiled broadly. "Yes, Spencer, just like that."

"Nana?" he began again. "Does everybody get a person?"

Candace was puzzled by his question. "What do you mean, sweetheart?"

"Mommy doesn't have nobody," he observed honestly.

Candace kissed Spencer's forehead lovingly. "Well, sweetheart...Your mommy had your daddy for a long time."

"Yeah, but he's in heaven, Nana. He can't be here too."

"Oh, Spencer...No, Daddy can't be here like he used to be, but I am sure he is watching over you all of the time and over your mommy too," Candace said honestly.

"Yeah, I know. But...Mommy's sad," he said.

Candace choked back her tears. Marianne had traveled miles in her healing process, but healing would never mean forgetting. Some part of Marianne would always carry sadness. That was part of loss. A person learned to live with grief, to laugh again, to live again, and hopefully to love again. Children were not afraid to offer frank assessments of what they saw and felt, at least, not children who felt secure and cared for. Candace was grateful for Spencer's openness. It served as a reminder that he felt safe and loved. She often found herself wondering if the adults that surrounded her could benefit more by listening to the children in their lives. Children had not installed all the filters that adults had been instructed were necessary for survival. Candace frequently mused that her children and grandchildren had taught her more about life and people than any history or psychology class had ever been able to. Innocence equated to honesty. Spencer's words were tainted with sadness—not for himself, but for his mother.

"Mommy misses your daddy," Candace replied. "We all do."

"She can have a person, Nana. Right?"

Candace smiled earnestly. "Yes, Spencer. I hope one day that your mommy does find a person that makes her happy again."

"She cries, Nana."

"I know," Candace said. "And, that is okay. I still cry sometimes when I think of my Granddad and Grandma or my father. Sometimes I laugh when I remember them and sometimes I miss them so much I still cry. That's okay. It's okay for you to cry too," she told him. Spencer's smile piqued Candace's curiosity. "Why the big smile?" she asked lightly.

"Daddy says I don't have to cry," he told her. Candace's gaze narrowed as she listened. "He tells me that all the time," Spencer said flatly.

"Does he?" she asked.

"Yep. He can't be here too. Daddy wants to be silly."

Candace bit her lip to quell its quivering. The bright happiness in Spencer's eyes told her that Spencer spent time talking to his father. While she had never been one to place much stock in the notion that those who had passed on could speak back, it was clear that Spencer believed his father was speaking to him. She would never take that away from her grandson.

"He does?" Candace asked.

"Yep. He says Mommy can be silly too."

"Yes, she can," Candace agreed.

"Yep. And Jay Jay and Mommy is fwends now."

Candace nodded. "That they are."

"Daddy likes that."

Candace breathed in slowly. "Does he?"

"Yep. Cause Jay Jay was his best fwend. Like me and Coop," he said.

"I guess in a lot of ways she was."

"Yep."

"Hey," Jameson called into the room as Cooper bolted in and toward Spencer's bed.

"Coop!" Spencer bellowed. Cooper vaulted onto Spencer's bed, smiling broadly.

Jameson noted Candace's glassy eyes and tipped her head slightly in question. Candace mouthed the word "later" in response.

"So, Coop was hoping he could sleep in here with you, Spence," Jameson explained.

Spencer nodded his approval.

"That means sleep," Jameson said as firmly as she could manage. She suspected that sleep would only claim the pair of toddlers who were bouncing on their bottoms, shaking the bed beneath them after they had giggled themselves into exhaustion.

"Okay," Cooper answered.

Candace leaned in and kissed both boys.

"Mommy?" Cooper looked at Candace quizzically.

Candace smiled at him. She was certain he had sensed the emotional storm brewing within her. Cooper was an extremely sensitive little boy; particularly it seemed where Candace was concerned. He was able to read her in ways that Candace was sure would surprise most people.

"Did you have fun with Shell today?" Candace asked him.

"Yep! Shell and me got ice cweam!"

"Oh, you did, huh?" Candace asked.

"Yep.

"Shell loves ice cream," Candace noted. "You two get some sleep," she said, placing another kiss on each boy's forehead.

"Good night," Jameson called from the doorway just as Candace stepped up beside her. She gently shut the door and looked at Candace. "Want to tell me what you and Spence were talking about that got you upset."

"Not upset," Candace said. "They just never cease to amaze me."

"The kids?" Jameson guessed. Candace nodded and looked back at the closed door when she heard Spencer's voice. "You are not seriously eavesdropping on our son and our grandson?" Jameson teased.

Candace poked Jameson lightly. "Rank has its privileges. Yes, I am," Candace said.

Jameson snickered and leaned closer to the door with Candace.

"You asked?" Spencer's voice carried through the door.

Jameson chuckled. "I can't believe Marianne and Shell haven't taught them how to whisper," she joked.

Candace laughed. "The girls were never particularly good at that either. Still aren't," she reminded Jameson before turning her attention back to the boys behind the door.

"Yep. Shell says evewybody can get somebody," Cooper said.

"Yep. Nana said I can love lots of people," Spencer told Cooper.

"Yep," Cooper agreed. "I got Mommy and Momma. You'll get one, Spence."

"I don't need one," Spencer said. "Mommy does."

"She can get one too," Cooper said assuredly.

Jameson looked at Candace. "Spence asked me if he could get another Daddy today," she told Candace. Candace grinned. "Oh...He asked you the same thing, huh?" Jameson chuckled realizing Spencer had traversed the same topic with Candace.

Candace nodded. "Sort of. I think he's more worried about Marianne finding someone to make her happy again."

"Sounds like Coop is too," Jameson replied.

"Sounds like they wanted to test all of our theories on the subject," Candace laughed. She took Jameson's hand and began to lead her away.

"Done snooping, Mom?" Jameson teased.

"Cute," Candace said.

"They might be waiting a while for cupid," Jameson said.

"Maybe. A friend would be good for her. I mean, a friend other than you or me," she told Jameson.

"Well, maybe this new group will help with that," Jameson offered. "I think that's why Scott asked her to lead it, at least, I think that is part of the reason."

"You talked to her, didn't you?" Candace asked.

Jameson smiled. "Yeah. I called her while Coop was in the tub."

Candace nodded. "How is my daughter?"

"You know Marianne," Jameson replied. "But, actually? I thought she sounded good. Nervous, I think, but also looking forward to it. What about you? What's new in the wild west?"

Candace laughed. Jameson had begun referring to the Governor's Office as the Wild West. It had been meant in jest.

Lately, Candace found the comparison eerily accurate. "Oh, you know…Preparing for a showdown."

"He can't win," Jameson said frankly. Candace shook her head. "Candace, what are you going to do?"

"About Lawson Klein?" Candace asked. Jameson nodded. Candace grimaced.

"Fight fire with fire?" Jameson guessed.

Candace shook her head. "No. That never works. It just burns everything in its wake."

"You're going to ignore him?"

"No, I'm going to douse the flames of his ignorance," Candace replied. "And let him drown in the pool of public perception that it leaves."

Jameson groaned. "Jessica found something," she guessed.

"Jessica always finds something," Candace replied. "This time, it just all happens to be true."

"And Laura?"

"I don't know, Jameson. I wish I could protect her. Even if I could shut down his mouth, I can't shield her from his intentions. In a way, that is the worst of it."

"I'd like to…"

"Me too," Candace confessed. She sighed when her pocket vibrated and she lifted her phone. "Dana?" Candace answered. She closed her eyes as she listened to Dana and rubbed her forehead. "Send it to me. Yes, now. Dana, it's not your fault. We both knew this was inevitable. I just had hoped we could stall a while longer to get our ducks in a row…No, I'll call Pearl. You call Shell. It's all right, Dana. It's not your fault. No, don't issue anything. I'm sure. I will deal with a statement after I talk to the family tomorrow. I know you are. I am too. I'll speak to you in the morning. Get some rest."

"Candace?"

Candace shook her head. "Well, Granddad's skeletons are tomorrow's front page in *The Post*."

Jameson groaned. "I'm sorry, Candace."

Candace shrugged and let go of a heavy sigh. "So am I."

"You seem to be taking this pretty well," Jameson observed.

"It was inevitable, Jameson. Some people think that the truth lies in perception. There is truth to that on many fronts. But, it is also true that concealing the truth never works forever. The fact is, the deeper you bury it and the longer it takes to unearth, the more blinding it is when it eventually sees the light of day. It always sees the light of day."

"Are we still talking about your grandfather and Pearl?" Jameson asked.

"Only partly," Candace replied.

"Worried about Laura's story?" Jameson guessed.

"I'm worried about a lot of things," Candace admitted. "Truth can be twisted, Jameson, like tangled roots. Those roots can choke the life out of the garden they were meant to feed if you don't tend to them. That's why keeping the truth out of the light of day is such a dangerous business. Just like roots, truth tends to curve and bend in the darkness. It forgets where it started, what it was meant to serve in the first place."

Jameson nodded. Even in the midst of upheaval, she loved listening to Candace's analogies and metaphors. "What are you going to do?"

"Give it the light it has been deprived of for far too long," Candace replied.

"Are you sure?" Jameson asked.

Candace pulled Jameson into their bedroom. "I am," she said. "You can't tend a garden in the darkness," she observed. "If you want it to blossom, you have to give it light."

"Yes, but the heat of the truth can be destructive too," Jameson reminded her.

"Yes, it can," Candace agreed. She leaned in and kissed Jameson on the cheek. "And, that is why we need the rain. That's where you come in."

"Me?" Jameson asked with surprise.

"Yes, you," Candace said.

"I'm not following," Jameson confessed.

"I know," Candace said. "That's what makes you the rain, love." Jameson was still confused. "Just trust me," Candace said.

"I do. I just don't know what I can do," Jameson replied helplessly.

Candace smiled lovingly. "Trust me, Jameson. You'll know what to do when it's time."

"If you say so."

"I do."

"I'm sorry," Jameson told Candace. "I know this whole thing is..."

Candace kissed Jameson's lips softly. "This was inevitable—all of it. I need to call Pearl."

"Do you want me to..."

"Just be ready to hold me when I come back."

Jameson nodded her understanding. "Always."

CHAPTER FIFTEEN

"Is he determined?"

Michael Weller nodded. He had spent several hours with Lawson Klein privately trying to convince the man to step back where Candace Reid was concerned. "I believe so."

"He's jeopardizing us unnecessarily," Grant Hill replied.

Weller nodded again. Grant Hill had been heading Family Values International for three years. The organization had blossomed under his guidance. He seemed to intrinsically understand how to leverage the court of public opinion without completely alienating FVI's adversaries. He had deliberately dialed back the inflammatory rhetoric, choosing to implement a softer tone toward oppositional forces, maintaining the group's core message without employing hardline tactics or decidedly bigoted remarks. In the process, FVI had attracted the support of more moderates than ever before. The group maintained a pro-life stance, but Hill had pointedly made statements regarding the abuse of women and the need to discuss openly the valid concerns that reality posed in the abortion debate. He had been a clear opponent of same gender marriage, but had made the decision to keep the issue to a dull roar in FVI's public platform. Weller sometimes wondered if Hill was truly a conservative.

"He won't listen to me," Michael Weller said.

Hill reclined in his chair and thought for a moment. He looked across the room at Weller and bit his lip. "Let him go."

"Excuse me?" Weller asked. "I thought the board wanted him reeled in?"

"Can you? Reel him in, Michael?" Hill challenged.

"I don't know."

"Then cast him away," Weller said.

"What are you saying?"

Weller took a deep breath and let it our deliberately. "He has a right to speak however he chooses."

"But..."

"But not on behalf of FVI. If he invokes our name, then he will leave me no choice but to make it clear that his position does not reflect that of our organization," Hill continued.

Michael Weller shook his head. "Grant," he said through a cautious breath. "Lawson Klein has been the centerpiece of FVI for his entire adult life. He's not going to go quietly."

"Michael, I cannot abide this. His actions depart from what the board's mission is."

"Not as Lawson sees it," Weller interjected.

Hill nodded. "I'm not sure what Lawson sees these days. I do know that attacking his daughter publicly does not align with our values. As I recall, the name is still Family Values International."

"I've pointed that out a few times," Weller said.

"I'm sure you have," he said. "Lawson has been teetering on the line for several years, Michael. Surely you know that. If we want to have a real voice in the congress or anywhere else, we have to accept that we need the help of those people walking a tightrope. Politicians have to temper their rhetoric if they want to hold office. That's true of FVI. His actions have already raised eyebrows. No one here is Candace Reid's advocate. You might be surprised that we have several board members who recognize her ability to derail us if we are not careful."

"You think Governor Reid has that much power?"

"On her own? No," Hill replied. "With her family? Possibly, yes. Scandal always has two ways to play out. You throw a scandal into the public and you accept that coin toss, Michael. Lawson is taking a big gamble making Governor Stratton's personal tale known. He's blind for some reason where Reid is concerned."

"Stratton was considered a moral beacon, Grant. I would think that his affair and his concealment of it would raise a few eyebrows morally speaking."

Hill smiled. "Perhaps. But, when you raise someone else's morals into question, there is inevitably questions about your own. And, Michael I think we both know that the concept of morality differs in many people's eyes. That is why FVI exists."

"You sound oddly pragmatic about all of this," Weller observed candidly.

"My job is to grow FVI in every conceivable way. That is what will increase our sphere of influence."

"Maybe if you talked to him…"

Hill shook his head. "He's on his own. The piece in *The Post* this morning put another nail in his coffin. And, as I understand it, Lawson has Giselle Brace visiting him at the ranch this afternoon," he said. Hill noted the evident surprise reflecting in Michael Weller's eyes. "Didn't share that with you I take it?"

"No, he did not. How did you know?" Weller inquired.

"Ah, Michael…Everyone loves a great story. Everyone also loves to create a villain and see a hero prevail. You and me? We are few people's hero in the media, might I remind you. Those who do hold us in higher regard do not want to see us back in the villain's saddle. Many of our supporters—financially speaking—support us quietly. That does not mean that they are unconcerned about their investments."

Weller groaned. "And, Lawson?"

Hill shrugged. "The next few days will tell his tale."

"And, us?"

Hill smiled silently in response to Michael Weller's question. Weller nodded his understanding. Lawson Klein was on his own.

✖✖✖

"Mom!" Shell called into her mother's office.

Candace looked up from her desk and over the rim of her glasses. "Good morning, Shell."

"Good morning? Mom…Have you seen *The Post*?"

"I saw it."

"That's all you have to say? Is that what this family meeting is about this afternoon?" Shell asked.

"In part," Candace replied, returning her attention to the papers on her desk.

"In part? Mom…"

Candace remained focused on the information in front of her. "Where is Bill?" she asked Shell.

"Where is Bill? Right behind me. Mom…When are…"

Candace looked up just as Bill DeGrasso stepped into the room. "Bill, I hope you had plenty of coffee."

DeGrasso grinned. "I'm awake."

Candace smiled at her Chief of Staff. "So, are we ready for Brett?" Candace asked.

"Mom," Shell broke into the conversation. "Don't you think that he will have heard about the story in *The Post* by the time he gets here?"

"I would expect so," Candace answered evenly.

"And, that doesn't concern you?" Shell challenged her mother. DeGrasso grimaced when Candace looked up at her daughter and slowly removed her glasses.

"Why should my grandfather's dalliances concern the New York City EPA?" she asked her daughter.

"I'm just saying…"

"Don't make something out of nothing, Michelle," Candace warned gently. "What the press prints about my life has zero bearing on my agenda."

"You know that's not true," Shell replied cautiously. "You still need the support of the public to get that budget passed if you want this plan…"

"Thank you for your concern. We will discuss your concerns on the way home after this meeting," Candace told Shell. "So?" she turned her attention back to DeGrasso. "Should we head down to the conference room?" she suggested as she reached her feet.

"Mom," Michelle leaned into Candace.

Candace stopped and steadied her breathing in an attempt to press down her frustration. She loved Shell and respected Shell's views and opinions, but one thing that her daughter still had difficulty grasping at times was that when Candace said later, she meant that Shell should drop it now. Candace smiled at her Chief of Staff. "Bill, why don't you head down and give me just a moment with Shell?" DeGrasso nodded his understanding. Candace turned back to her daughter and shook her head. "I appreciate your concern, Shell."

"Mom…I just…"

Candace held up her hand. "I do appreciate it. I also understand that you are worried about me. I told you when you took the position in my campaign that you would need to be prepared to hear and see things in ways that you never had before."

"It's not that. I've heard it all; I mean we all have…"

"No, you have not," Candace rebuffed Shell's assessment. "There's a great deal that you kids have never had to encounter because I have been able to shield you from it over the years. God willing, I will be able to continue to do that as much as possible."

"For Cooper," Shell guessed.

"For all of you," Candace corrected her. "But, you? You will inevitably hear more than your sister and brothers. You will see more, both the allegations that have merit and the cheap shots that people take. I can't shield you from that if you want to be part of this administration in any capacity. There are perks to working here. There are also drawbacks and pot-holes, Shell. This is one of them. You need to be able to separate yourself from that in this office. That is part of the deal and one of my expectations. Dana has her job and she does it incredibly well. You let her worry about the press. You support Bill and me on policy."

"Can you really dismiss one from the other?" Shell asked honestly.

Candace smiled. "No, you can't at the end of the day. But, you have to appear to believe that you can. When we are heading into a meeting, I expect you to anticipate anything that might arise. And yes, that includes things that are said about me or this administration that *could* derail us. I also ex-pect that you trust me to handle them as I see fit. And, I expect that you understand my intention is to keep everyone on the topic at hand. That includes you."

Shell sighed. "Are you okay?" she asked. "Grandma Pearl?"

Candace reached over and hugged her daughter. "We are both okay," she promised. "Now, let's get this meeting over with and address the EPA's concerns. Then we can worry about what is troubling you."

Shell walked beside her mother as they traversed the corridor that adjoined Candace's offices and the large confer-ence room that would play host to the meeting. "I just worry about you," Shell admitted quietly.

Candace kept walking and smiling. "I know that you do, and I love you for it. Try not to forget who is the mom and who is the governor," she said lightly as she walked into the con-ference room.

Shell watched as the occupants of the room rose to greet her mother. Candace greeted the room in good humor, extending her hand to each person at the table and making the usual pleasantries, thanking each for agreeing to an early meeting. Shell smiled proudly as she watched her mother work the room effortlessly. Candace carried herself with a quiet confidence. Nonetheless, Candace Reid's presence filled any room the moment she entered it. Candace's mood would directly set the tone for any meeting. Shell bit the inside of her cheek to quell a chuckle. It occurred to her watching her mother as she moved toward her seat, that Candace had the same presence in a conference room, on a campaign stage, or in the kitchen. The moment Candace entered any room, all eyes went to her. It would be impossible to forget who the leader was of their family or The State of New York.

"No way could anyone forget that," Shell muttered.

"Forget what?" DeGrasso leaned in and whispered.

"Who's in charge," Shell replied.

DeGrasso nodded. "Not likely, no."

"Are you sure you don't mind?" Marianne asked Scott as she buckled Maddie into her car seat.

"Why would I mind? Gives me a chance to see J.D."

"Uh-huh, and babysit two toddlers for a couple of hours," Marianne reminded him.

"What is it? Think I can handle a group of teenage addicts but not two little boys?" he countered.

Marianne closed the car door and pursed her lips. "Should I answer that honestly?"

"Hey! If J.D. can manage, I'm sure I can."

Marianne nodded and opened her car door. "I have every faith in you," she said, keeping her face forward to hide the smirk gracing her lips.

Scott started the engine and turned to her. "Do you at least trust me to drive us there?"

"I don't know," Marianne quipped. "Do you drive like J.D.?"

"Why? Is J.D. a bad driver?" he asked. Marianne shrugged. "I see. Well, you'll just have to trust me on both counts."

Marianne smiled as Scott pulled out of the driveway. "I guess so."

✄✄✄

Pearl was sitting at the kitchen table sipping a cup of tea when Jameson entered. "Hey," Jameson called over.

"Jameson," Pearl greeted the younger woman with a smile. "Oh, now…Don't you look at me with those puppy dog eyes of yours," Pearl warned. "I am fine."

"Yeah, I am sure that is true. But, I wish…"

"What? That I could keep my past corked up in a bottle forever? I don't." Pearl said honestly. "I told Candy when she ran for governor; I have no qualms about anyone knowing who I am. I know who I am and who my family is to me." Jameson nodded. "Where are the boys?" Pearl asked.

Jameson chuckled. "In the backyard," she explained.

"Trying to get them filthy in time for Scott to get here?" Pearl guessed. Jameson gloated. "That's what I thought."

"Hey, he can use the practice," Jameson replied.

"Why? Is he expecting?" Pearl quipped.

"No, but he needs to get broken in," Jameson began to explain her theory. "You know Scott," she said.

Pearl nodded. She had gotten to know Jameson's cousin Scott quite well, and it pleased her to no end to see the bond between Jameson and Scott strengthen. They often reminded her of Candace's children. Squabbles and teasing aside, the affection between Scott and Jameson was evident. Pearl was certain that Scott would find any excuse he could to see Jameson. She also suspected that he might have welcomed an opportunity to spend more time with another member of the family. She wondered if anyone, even Jameson, had picked up on Scott's interest in Marianne.

"Oh no...What are you grinning about?" Jameson asked Pearl.

"I'm not grinning," Pearl denied the accusation.

"Yes, you are," Jameson countered. "You are up to something."

"I am not 'up to' anything as you put it," Pearl replied.

"Yeah, right," Jameson said. "Nice try."

Pearl shrugged just as the back door opened with a thud.

"Jay Jay!" Spencer ran into the kitchen. Jameson looked over at him. "Coop's hurt."

Jameson sprung from her chair and flew out of the back door with Pearl following behind. Spencer looked up at Pearl helplessly. Pearl looked over to where Cooper was lying on the ground in a ball. "It's okay, Spencer," she tried to reassure the little boy.

"Coop," Jameson knelt beside her son. "Cooper."

Cooper turned and looked at Jameson with watery eyes as he held onto his right arm with his left hand. "Momma," he cried.

"What hurts?" Jameson asked him. "Your arm?" Cooper nodded.

"He crashed," Spencer tried to explain.

Jameson sighed and looked at Cooper. "Did you fall off the swing?" she asked. Cooper shook his head. "No? Where did you fall from?" Jameson asked. Cooper looked over Jameson's head. Jameson threw her head back and groaned. "She is going to kill me," Jameson thought to herself. "Cooper," Jameson called to him softly. "Are you telling me you were in the tree?" she asked. Cooper nodded. Jameson took a deep breath and scooped Cooper up into her arms. "Can you show me where it hurts?" she asked. Cooper pointed to his forearm. Jameson smiled at him. "Okay, let's get you in the house and take a look, okay?"

Pearl shook her head at Jameson and smiled. "He's definitely yours," she whispered. Jameson groaned again as she walked back toward the house.

"Grandma?" Spencer looked up at Pearl, meeting Pearl's compassionate and slightly amused eyes. "Is Coop okay?"

Pearl put her arm around Spencer's small shoulders as a gesture of reassurance. "Cooper will be fine, Spencer."

"But, he's hurt."

Pearl nodded. "He'll be okay," she repeated, leading a sheepish Spencer back toward the kitchen.

"Oww," Cooper cried out.

Jameson grimaced at the sound of Cooper's cry. She smiled at him gently. "I think we need to get that arm looked at, buddy."

"No!" Cooper cried.

Jameson sensed Cooper's fear. Her cousin Craig had broken his arm after falling off the garage roof when Jameson was nine. She couldn't be sure, but she guessed Cooper might be headed for a cast and a sling. Jameson smiled at her son and kissed his forehead. "Sometimes, monkeys fall out of trees," she teased him. Cooper looked at her apprehensively. "It'll be okay, I promise." Jameson kissed his head again and stood to face Pearl. "I need to call Candace."

Pearl pursed her lips and nodded. "I'll keep the monkeys grounded."

"Am I in twouble?" Cooper called to Jameson.

"No," Jameson assured him. She took a deep breath as she walked toward the living room. "But, I might be."

✖✖✖

"Thank you for taking the time," Candace shook Brett Stein's hand.

"I appreciate your work on this, Governor," he told Candace sincerely. "It's been an uphill battle to get anyone in authority to hear our concerns. I know it's not just the city."

"No, it isn't." Candace agreed, "The best way to deal with a crisis is to avoid it," she said. "So, let's make sure we do that."

"Mom," Shell leaned into Candace's ear and whispered with some urgency.

"Excuse me," Candace smiled at Brett Stein.

"Of course," he answered.

"What is it, Shell?"

Shell sighed. "Jameson texted me while you were in the meeting. You need to call her."

"Why?" Candace asked hesitantly.

"She just said that she tried to call your phone and that you needed to call as soon as you were free."

"Why do I not like the sound of that?" Candace asked rhetorically. She stepped away and into the far corner of the room before lifting her cell phone from her jacket. Candace took a deep breath and waited for Jameson to answer.

"Hi."

"Jameson? What's wrong?" Candace wanted to know immediately.

"What makes you think anything is wrong?"

"Jameson."

Jameson groaned. "Cooper fell."

"Cooper fell? Running? What do you mean he fell? How did he fall? On the stairs?"

"Not exactly," Jameson replied.

"Uh-huh. Is he okay?"

"Not exactly, no. I mean, yes…I think he might have broken his arm. Pearl's driving us to the emergency room right now."

Candace closed her eyes and rubbed them gently. "Jameson, is…"

"He's okay, honey. I swear. He just didn't land well."

"I am almost positive that I do not want to know. I'll meet you there."

"What about the family meeting? You have to be back in Albany…"

"We'll deal with that after we deal with Cooper. I'll be there as soon as I can. Just keep me posted."

"I will. At least, there won't be a long wait like in Albany," Jameson offered.

"Thank God for small favors," Candace said. "Can I talk to him?"

Jameson looked at Cooper, who was leaning into her in the back seat. "Mommy wants to talk to you," she explained, holding the phone to his ear while he held ice on his arm.

"Hi, Mommy."

"Hi, sweetheart. I hear you've had some excitement."

"I falled."

"You fell, huh?"

"Yeah, on my arm."

"I'm sorry, sweetie, Momma will take good care of you," Candace said.

"Yep. It hurts."

"I'll bet it does."

"Yep. Momma says trees are for monkeys," Cooper offered.

Candace tried not to laugh. She instantly pictured Jameson's expression in her mind—a deer caught in head-lights. "Momma has a point," Candace said. "I'll see you as soon as I can, okay?"

"Okay."

"Let me talk to Momma."

"Okay. I love you," Cooper said.

"I love you too," Candace told him. She heard Jameson sigh on the other end of the phone. "Monkeys, huh?"

"Something like that," Jameson replied.

"I'll be there soon. Keep me posted," Candace said. Jameson sighed again. "Try to relax. It's part of being the zookeeper," Candace joked. She had been through enough emergency room visits, cuts, scrapes, bruises and broken bones with The Three Stooges over the years to have learned that children were quite resilient, and in the end, proud of their war wounds. After talking to Cooper, she was positive this event would end up in that category. "Relax, Jameson."

"I'm trying."

"I'll see you soon," Candace promised. She discon-nected the call and chuckled.

"Everything okay?" Shell asked.

"Depends on what you mean by that," Candace an-swered. She saw the unspoken question in Shell's eyes and continued. "Looks like your little brother might have broken his arm."

"What?!"

"He's okay. Playing monkey," Candace chuckled. "I need to get to the hospital to meet Jameson. Can you follow and drive Pearl and Spencer back to the house?"

"Yeah, of course," Shell replied. "You seem pretty calm."

Candace shrugged. Her stomach was actively fluttering with nervousness. One thing that Candace always hated was seeing her children in pain. She was sure that Cooper would recover fully and likely long before Jameson if she was reading everything correctly. "He's okay, Shell."

"What about the family meeting? You could be there for hours."

"I doubt it will take that long in Cobbleskill," Candace observed. "See if Bill and Dan would be willing to come out to the house tonight to review the budget. I'll bet you can entice them with a promise of Pearl's lasagna."

"I'm sure. What are you going to entice Grandma with?" Shell teased her mother.

Candace laughed. "Sympathy," she explained. Shell opened her eyes in astonishment. "What? You think you and Marianne invented that ploy?"

Shell laughed. "I'll meet you in your office. Another hospital visit," Shell muttered.

"I have to say, I'd hoped to avoid them for a while," Candace confessed.

"Me too," Shell admitted solemnly.

Candace smiled at her daughter. "I need to find Drew."

"I'll have Susan let him know on my way to Dan," Shell promised.

Candace nodded. "It never ends."

"Why?"

Lawson Klein admonished his wife for her question with a glance.

"I just don't understand," she said softly.

"You don't need to understand," he told Mary Klein. "If Laura makes this public, we will be on the defensive. You want crosshairs on our son's back?" Klein questioned his wife.

"I'd rather no one got hurt," she replied under her breath.

"Well, it's too late for that," he surmised.

"But...Here? In our home? Lawson..."

"Here in our home is best. I have been doing this a long time," he said.

"What about Laura?" she tried to reach him.

"Laura has no care about her family," he spat.

Mary Klein hung her head as her husband headed to answer the front door of their home. "Oh, Lawson."

Candace made her way through a set of doors and up a small corridor with Drew Evans at her side. "I'll bet he looks better than she does," Sergeant Evans said lightly when he caught sight of Jameson leaning against a wall.

Candace chuckled. Jameson looked utterly defeated. "Do me a favor, Drew?" she began. "Go see if you can find Pearl and let her know that Shell is outside on a call and will be right in." She winked at the young trooper as he headed off to follow her direction and turned her attention back to Jameson. Candace approached quietly. "Hey," she reached out for Jameson's hands, which were covering Jameson's eyes.

Jameson lowered her hands and looked at Candace apologetically. "I'm sorry."

Candace raised her eyebrow. "Why? Did you push him off the branch?"

"What? No!"

Candace leaned in and kissed Jameson on the cheek. "It's not your fault, Jameson."

"I left them in the yard alone. They were playing with Cooper's car when I..."

Candace smiled. "Jameson, they play outside all of the time."

"Yeah, but if I had been…"

"Maybe. You could be three feet away, and one of them could fall and get hurt."

"Not out of a tree!" Jameson argued.

Candace chuckled. "He is your son," she reminded Jameson. Jameson huffed. "Where is he?" Candace wondered.

"They are taking another x-ray. He seemed okay to go without me, and I can't go in with him…I just…"

"Stop beating yourself up," Candace told Jameson.

"You're not mad?"

"At you?" Candace asked. "No."

Jameson breathed a sigh of relief. "I feel awful."

"First one is always the hardest," Candace said.

"First kid?"

"Why? Want another one? Candace teased.

"Not really, no," Jameson replied. "I already broke the first one."

Candace laughed. "I meant the first real injury. It's always the worst."

"What were they thinking, climbing that tree?" Jameson wondered aloud. Candace raised her brow again in response. "Okay, I like to climb, I admit it. They are three and four! How did they even get up to that branch?"

"Who knows?" Candace answered with her own question. "They are kids, Jameson. Kids who want to do everything they see you do," she reminded her wife.

"Great."

Candace kissed Jameson on the cheek again just as she caught sight of Cooper smiling in a wheelchair headed straight for them. "Don't look now, but here comes the silly monkey."

"Mommy!" Cooper called out to Candace. Candace leaned down and kissed Cooper's head. "I get a cast!" he exclaimed proudly.

Jameson tried to smile. Candace took her hand in reassurance. "You do?" Candace asked.

"Yep! Blue!" he told his parents.

"I explained that he could pick a couple of different colors," the nurse told them.

Candace nodded. "How does it feel?" she asked Cooper. He grimaced. "Still hurts, I'll bet," she surmised. Cooper nodded.

"Did you ever have a cast?" he asked Candace.

"No, but Jonah and Marianne both did," she told him. Candace snickered at the wide-eyed response she received from both her son and her wife. "In fact," she told them. "Marianne fell out of that same tree when she was about a year older than you are now." Jameson's jaw dropped open. "Close your mouth, honey," Candace whispered. "You'll catch something for sure, and then we'll be stuck in here with you," Candace said.

"She bwoke her arm too?" Cooper asked.

"No, she broke her ankle," Candace explained.

"Ouch," Jameson muttered. She followed alongside Candace back into the small examination room.

"Someone will come take you down to the casting room in a few minutes," the nurse said just as a doctor stepped into the room behind them.

"Well, Governor," he spoke.

Candace turned to the sound of a familiar voice. "Fred," she greeted him with a hug.

"Long time, no visits," he teased Candace. "I had thought you'd given up on repeat performances after Jonah went to college."

Candace laughed. "Jameson, this is Dr. Fred Braddock."

Jameson accepted the hand of the gray-haired doctor. He offered her a gentle smile of understanding. "She looks like you did that time Marianne fell out of the tree."

"I looked that bad?" Candace challenged him.

Fred Braddock shrugged. "First one's always the worst," he told Jameson before turning his attention to Cooper. "So, young man...Seems you and your sister Marianne have a few things in common."

Cooper beamed at what he perceived as a compliment. He worshiped Marianne, and Dr. Braddock's words filled his innocent heart with pride.

"The good news is that it was a clean break. Young bones mend quickly," he said. "But, you will have a cast for about four weeks," he said. "And, I'm afraid swinging from trees will be off limits for a while."

"More like forever," Jameson muttered. Both Candace and the doctor chuckled.

"So, I thought I would steer you down to see my good friend Jeremy. He'll get that cast on for you. I'm headed that way myself. I just wanted to stop by and say hello to your mom."

"Blue!" Cooper exclaimed.

"Ah, yes...A good choice," Dr. Braddock agreed. "You know, back when your sister made her visits, it was only plain, old, boring white that you could get."

"She's bigger," Cooper explained.

Candace smiled. "God, that was almost twenty-eight years ago," she mused.

"The first time," Dr. Braddock reminded Candace.

"There was more than one?" Jameson asked.

Candace shuddered. "Later," she told Jameson.

"Do you want your parents to go with you?" Dr. Braddock leaned in and whispered the question to Cooper.

"Did Mawianne?" Cooper whispered back. Dr. Braddock shook his head. Marianne had been a proud little girl.

"By myself!" Cooper declared.

"Are you sure?" Jameson asked Cooper. Cooper nodded. "Coop..."

Candace took hold of Jameson's arm and stroked it lightly with her fingertips as she addressed Cooper. "Okay, Cooper. We'll wait for you here." Cooper smiled.

"He'll be back shortly. You have time to grab a coffee or," Dr. Braddock began.

"We'll wait here just in case," Jameson said.

Dr. Braddock grinned. "Nice to have your support again," he teased Candace.

"Does it earn me your vote when I need it?" she asked.

"Never a doubt," he promised as he left.

"Don't you think we should..." Jameson started.

"No," Candace cut off Jameson's thought midstream. "He needs to do this. And, you need to let him."

"What if he..."

"Jameson," Candace said. "What did you tell me when Cooper was sick, and I wanted to stay home?"

"That's not the same thing."

"Yes, it is," Candace said.

"This is my fault."

"No," Candace put the thought to rest. "No, it was not. It was a mishap. And, knowing my kids—all of them–knowing Cooper is *our* son? It will not be the last," she surmised.

Jameson willingly let Candace wrap her in an embrace. "I feel horrible."

"I know," Candace said. "Me too."

"You do? You seem so calm."

"Jameson, you of all people should know that how I seem and what I feel are not always congruent."

Jameson stepped back. "I know. I didn't mean to break him—literally."

Candace laughed. "You really are a lunatic," she joked.

"I'm serious. And, I've screwed up your day."

"No, just made it more interesting."

"Breaking our son?" Jameson asked.

"Stop," Candace laughed. "Besides, it gives me an excuse to work from home tonight."

"You're not going back to Albany?"

"And, leave you with Humpty Dumpty? I think not," Candace quipped.

Jameson pursed her lips. "You're enjoying this, aren't you?"

"No," Candace promised. "But, you do make me laugh—most of all when I need to. It's one of the reasons I love you so much."

"I am sorry," Jameson said regretfully.

"I know you are," Candace replied. "You can make it up to Cooper with pizza."

"And you?"

"I'll think of something."

CHAPTER SIXTEEN

"Think he's okay in there?" Jameson asked Marianne.

Marianne grinned. Scott had settled in with Cooper and Spencer to watch a movie. "Coop saved his butt with that broken arm," she joked. "He gets off easy with Aladdin."

Jameson huffed. "No kidding. I break my kid and he gets to help pick up the pieces."

"You didn't break him," Marianne laughed. "That tree is evil."

"So I have heard," Jameson replied.

"Yeah. All of us have fallen out of it at some point. To tell you the truth, I'm surprised Mom never had it taken down," Marianne told Jameson. Jameson nodded. "J.D., seriously, it is not your fault. Give yourself a break."

Jameson shook her head. "I think there has been enough breaking for one day."

"So? What is this meeting about?" Marianne asked as they made their way down the hallway. Jameson sighed. "That bad?" Marianne inquired.

"Yes and no," Jameson said. "It just pisses me off, I guess."

"What's that?"

"The way people come at her," Jameson replied.

"I know. You do know that she can handle it, right?"

"I do, but when they drag other people into it? She doesn't deal with that as well," Jameson pointed out the obvious.

"No, she does not," Marianne agreed. She pulled Jameson to a stop just shy of the living room. Jameson looked at Marianne curiously. "Whatever you need, J.D. I hope you know that I am here."

Jameson smiled at her step-daughter. "Thanks. You know that goes both ways, right?"

Marianne nodded. "J.D., I mean it. She might be protective of all of us, she sometimes forgets that goes both ways too."

"I know."

"I don't just mean Mom. I mean both of you," Marianne clarified.

Jameson nodded her understanding. "Let's get this over with."

"There you two are," Candace looked at Jameson and Marianne as they entered the room.

"Here we are," Jameson agreed, taking a seat beside Candace on the sofa.

"Okay, Mom. We are all accounted for," Shell piped up.

"Thank God for small favors," Candace said. "I will assume that you all know about the article in *The Post* by now?"

Jonah snickered. "Shell has *The Post* beat be a New York mile."

"Ha-ha," Shell replied giving Jonah a dirty look. Candace rolled her eyes.

"How are you doing, Grandma?" Marianne looked over at Pearl.

Pearl smiled genuinely. "Me? Well, sooner or later the cat always gets out of the bag," she said. "Don't worry about me," she said.

"So, it's true?" Jonah asked hesitantly.

Candace smiled at Pearl and Pearl answered. "Yes, it's true, Jonah. All of it, in fact."

"Wow," Jonah mumbled.

Pearl laughed surprising everyone. "What?" Pearl asked the room. "Goodness, it's not war, kids. To tell you the truth, it feels good to just have it out in the open and not have to think about it so much."

"What does it mean, Mom?" Marianne asked. "I mean, what does it mean for you?"

Candace shrugged. "Very little, I suspect. Another distraction."

"Okay?" Jonah asked cautiously. "So, if it's just a distraction, why the big family meeting?"

Candace felt Jameson's hand slip into hers. She took a deep breath and looked directly at Jonah and Laura. "Because I do not think it will be the last stone cast in my path. The story about Cooper still has some legs, although it has not played the way people had hoped. And, they are expecting me to retaliate."

"What does that mean?" Jonah asked.

Laura sighed. "Me. He's going to drag me into it," she guessed. Candace offered Laura a sympathetic gaze, confirming the young woman's suspicions.

"You?" Jonah looked at Laura. "Why? Your father has already tried that. What can he possibly..."

"It's why she wanted me to come home," Laura surmised.

"Who?" Jameson asked Laura.

"My mother," Laura responded.

Candace inhaled deeply to calm herself. "She asked you to come home?" Candace asked Laura. Laura nodded. Candace looked at Jameson and shook her head.

"You think he's going to say something, don't you?" Laura guessed.

"I think it is possible, yes," Candace confessed. "I'm sorry, Laura," she said sincerely. Laura smiled as best she could.

"Say what?" Jonah demanded.

Candace spoke softly. "Laura, you don't have to share anything..."

Laura smiled again. "It's okay," she said. Laura turned to Jonah and took his hand. "About Mark abusing me," she said flatly.

Jonah's jaw fell open and he turned to his mother. "Mom?"

"I don't know, Jonah," Candace said. "I think that is a possibility, yes."

"Why would he do that?" Jonah wanted to know.

"Because he thinks I will first," Laura said plainly, keeping her eyes locked with Candace's.

"That son of a bitch! I'll kill him!" Jonah popped out of his seat in anger.

"Jonah," Jameson called across the room calmly. Johan swallowed hard.

Shell shook her head. "I don't mean to..."

"It's okay," Laura said.

"You don't have to," Jonah started to whisper in Laura's ear.

"It's okay," Laura repeated. "It was a long time ago," she explained. "My older brother...He took some liberties..."

"He molested you," Shell mumbled in disbelief. Laura nodded.

Marianne looked at her mother and then closed her eyes. "Jesus," she whispered.

"Why would he want that out in the press? That's not aligned with his questionable morals," Shell observed sarcastically.

Candace groaned. "I don't think he *wants* it out there, Shell. I think he is betting that we will put it out there first."

"So? It's indefensible!" Shell argued. Candace sighed.

"He'll say I made it all up," Laura offered her assessment. "That's what he's always said."

"Mom, can't you stop this?" Jonah asked urgently. Candace shook her head regretfully. "There has to be something you can do!" he demanded angrily.

Laura clasped Jonah's hand. "Jonah," she called to him. "This is not your mother's fault."

Candace fought the urge to be sick. She knew that she could not control the likes of Lawson Klein. Still, Candace felt indirectly responsible for his actions. His energy was ultimately directed at her, fueled by some deep-seeded hatred he had always held toward Candace. Candace had never managed to grasp Lawson Klein's campaign against her. That he sought to fight against her politically, she could understand. He had taken a decidedly personal path on more than one occasion. That tactic completely perplexed Candace. For a long time, Candace had wondered if the ancient rumors about Lawson Klein's great-grandfather and grandfather served as his motivation. It might have provided a basis for his dislike of all things Stratton related, but Candace doubted that ancient history could be the sole motivator in Klein's continuous crusade to conquer her. No matter her rational understanding, she felt responsible for Laura.

"I wish I could stop him," Candace said honestly.

"No one can stop him," Laura commented bluntly.

Candace regarded the younger woman thoughtfully for a moment before addressing the statement. "No one can stop him from speaking—no," she agreed.

"But?" Jonah sensed his mother had more to say.

Candace sighed audibly. "But, perhaps we can make it less enticing for him to speak and even less likely that anyone will be willing to pass him the microphone."

"Do you have something to use against him?" Shell wanted to know.

Candace nodded. "There are inconsistencies in many of his dealings—yes—among other things. I would prefer to leave that aside."

Laura spoke up immediately. "Don't worry about me if that is what is stopping you."

"I will always worry about you," Candace told Laura.

"If you don't call him out then what?" Jonah asked.

Candace looked briefly at Jameson. Jameson smiled at her and turned to face the room. "Your mother and I want to know if you will all agree to participating in a human interest story about the family."

"That's what this is about?" Shell asked. "Why wouldn't we?"

"Because," Candace said. "Because this will not be a fifteen-minute interview on an evening news program. It will be in depth and there will be pointed questions if we agree to it. I can request that certain topics be left off the table. I cannot guarantee that," she explained honestly.

"I'm in," Shell said.

Laura smiled at Jonah and nodded. "Count us in that equation," Jonah said.

Candace looked at her eldest daughter. Marianne took a deep breath and nodded her agreement.

"Marianne," Jameson called for Marianne's attention. "You do not have to do this. If you aren't ready, we will all respect that. All of us."

Marianne nodded. "I'm not sure I will ever be ready, J.D. The truth is, that doesn't matter right now. Yesterday it was Cooper. Today it's Pearl. Tomorrow it might be Laura. They did this to Mom with Jessica. They tried with you when you visited Scott at the clinic. They are always trying something. They don't care who gets hurt in the process."

"No, they don't," Candace said. "But," she took the time to look at each face in the room. "The truth is, there will always be a Lawson Klein. Maybe not as hurtful, maybe not as directly, but there will always be someone looking for some way to undermine me. And, that puts every one of you in the line of fire. For that, I am sorry."

"No," Marianne stopped her mother. Candace looked at Marianne in amazement. "No way. You have nothing to feel sorry for," Marianne said emphatically. "You have stood behind all of us at every turn, Mom. I know if Rick were here, he would say the same thing. No way. They take a shot at any one of us, they are firing at all of us. Anyone who comes at you or you and J.D. has to deal with all of us. It goes both ways."

Jameson smiled at Marianne gratefully.

"Exactly!" Shell said. "I'm sick of this asshole," she said. Shell groaned when all eyes turned to her. "I'm sorry, Laura."

Laura shook her head. "Don't be," she told Shell. "I know that I am not really part of the..."

"You are as much a part of this family as anyone in this room," Pearl said.

Candace looked directly at Laura. "Pearl is right. You don't have to do this," she said.

"Yes, I do," Laura said. Jonah winked at her. "I have a family to think about too. I have a son to consider. This is his family. No matter what, it always will be. I'll do whatever you need me to."

"You really think that an interview with the family can turn this around?" Shell asked.

"I think that Mr. Klein's clout is wearing thin in ways that he does not seem to want to acknowledge. He's fanning flames that are inevitably going to consume him in their wake. That doesn't mean no one else will get burned in the meantime. So, no, to answer your question, I do not believe that agreeing to this will turn it all miraculously around. It will not quell chatter among those who choose to jump on his bandwagon. What it will do is offer an honest, forthright, human response. This offer has been on the table since we announced Cooper's adoption."

"Mom, you didn't want to expose Coop," Marianne reminded her.

"No, and I still don't. But, the truth is, that is inevitable too. Better that I have some control on the when and the who."

"What if he talks about Laura?" Jonah asked.

Candace smiled sadly. "That has to be up to Laura," she said.

"What do you think we should do?" Laura asked.

"I think that you and Jonah should stay tonight and sit down with Dana when she gets here. She's the best to advise you in this case. Afterward, we can all sit down together," Candace suggested.

"When do we do this?" Shell asked.

Jameson answered. "Your mom and I were thinking that we should do it before the Fourth of July festivities—at least, in part."

"We'll allow a glimpse of the barbeque to be included," Candace explained. "The Fletcher-Reid clan unmasked."

"That's still four weeks away," Shell said.

"Yes, and that gives us time," Candace replied.

"What about in the meantime?" Melanie asked sheepishly.

"We go about life like we always do as much as we can," Candace said.

"Mom?" Shell looked at Candace.

"Yes?"

"Can we do something about FVI?" Shell asked hopefully.

Candace's only reply was a smile. Pearl noted the mischievous sparkle in Candace's eyes. "Oh, she's up to something," Pearl whispered to Marianne.

"Is Grandma going to be part of this?" Jonah asked his mother.

Candace smiled and looked at Pearl. "I hope so."

Pearl winked. "Fine by me as long as you pay for the hairdresser."

"It's not a glamour shoot," Shell laughed.

"It is to me," Pearl replied.

Candace laughed. "God help them; I hope they know what can of worms they are opening."

�✂✂

"Lawson, please," Mary Klein practically begged her husband. "Don't do this. Please. You don't even know that Laura will say anything."

"You talked to her, didn't you?" he asked. Mary Klein hung her head. "Why? Why would you betray me like that?"

"She's my daughter!" Mary's head snapped up.

"You're my wife!" he screamed before storming out of the room.

Mary Klein closed her eyes and shook her head sadly. "I can't do this anymore," she muttered.

✗✗✗

"J.D.?" Jonah grabbed hold of Jameson's arm. "Can I talk to you for a minute?"

Jameson nodded and led Jonah to Candace's study. She closed the door and directed him to sit. "You okay?" she asked.

Jonah shook his head. "I hate this," he said. "I feel like such an asshole."

"Come again?"

"It's my fault, you know?" he said.

"No, I don't know. What are we talking about?" Jameson asked.

"Laura. Think about it. If it...Well, it's because of me that he is doing this to her."

"No, Jonah. It's because of him—not because of Laura or you or your mom. It's because of him. Don't put that on yourself or on anyone else. Put the blame where it belongs."

"But, J.D..."

"No," Jameson dismissed Jonah's thought flatly. "Don't," she told him. "I understand. I do. I've had that thought so many times. Have I made it harder for your mom, for all of you? Maybe if she hadn't married me," Jameson shook her head. "She reminds me all of the time that if it wasn't me, if it wasn't her sexuality, it would be something else. Lawson Klein is an angry, bitter man, Jonah. I don't know why. I don't care why," Jameson said. "Laura loves you. She needs you. And, that means you need to let this idea that any of this is your fault go. Let it go now."

Jonah sighed. "I asked her to marry me."

Jameson smiled. "She said yes, I take it?" she asked. Jonah nodded. "So, why the long face?"

"I didn't plan it. I mean, I planned on doing it, but then we were talking and it just felt like the right time. I didn't even get her a ring. I suck."

Jameson laughed. "Did she seem concerned about that?"

"No."

"I didn't think so."

"I still feel horrible. Look how you planned to ask Mom."

Jameson laughed. "Yeah, well, I chickened out so many times it isn't even funny."

"Why?"

Jameson shrugged. "I worried about making it perfect, I guess."

"See what I mean?" Jonah pointed out.

"Yeah, I do. But, it would have been perfect no matter what as long as she said yes."

"That's what Laura says."

Jameson smiled. It had not escaped Jameson's notice that Laura had placed Candace on a high pedestal. Candace had stepped in to nurture Laura. Laura was attached to Candace and she respected Candace's ideas and opinions on every topic. Candace had not told Jameson about Jonah and Laura's formal engagement. Jameson suspected that Candace already knew, and that Laura had sworn her to secrecy.

"Laura's a smart girl," Jameson complimented.

"Thing is," Jonah started. He looked at Jameson and sighed.

"What?"

"We don't want a wedding."

"Okay? Kind of hard to get married then," Jameson joked.

"No," Jonah chuckled. "I mean we don't want any fanfare."

"I can understand that," Jameson said. She and Candace had felt the same way.

"I was sort of wondering," Jonah started again before trailing off. Jameson smiled at him. "Well, we were kind of hoping it could just be you and Mom…. Coop too…and J.J. That's it," he said. Jameson nodded. "I mean, you don't have to, But, well, J.D. the truth is that's really what I want. Just you and Mom to stand with us."

"I'd be honored. So would your mom, I am sure."

"Shell and Marianne will be pissed."

Jameson laughed. "Marianne will understand," she surmised.

Jonah looked up hopefully. "It's not that I don't love them. I just…"

"Jonah, you don't owe anyone an explanation."

"Maybe we could just do dinner after?" he suggested sheepishly.

"Well, why don't we see what your bride to be thinks," Jameson suggested. "When do you want to do this?"

Jonah bit his lip. "Next week sometime."

Jameson nodded. "Just let us know when and where."

"That easy?"

"Yep," Jameson said. "I'm sure your mom will clear her schedule."

"It's hard for her," Jonah said. "I mean, not having any of her family even want to be there. That's why. I mean, I know she loves Shell and Marianne, Mel too… But, the thing is sometimes so much family—I think it makes her a little sad, you know? Missing her family, even if they are assholes. They are still her family."

"I get it," Jameson told Jonah. "So will your sisters. They aren't as dense as you think."

"J.D.?"

'Yeah?"

"Just… I have to, well, I want to get her a ring. I was kind of wondering if you would help me."

Jameson laughed. "I'm not laughing at you," she promised. "I just would have thought your mom would be better suited to that task."

"Why? Mom's never bought anyone a ring."

"Good point," Jameson agreed.

"How did you know what to get?" he asked Jameson.

Jameson shrugged. "I know your mom."

"Yeah, but Laura doesn't wear lots of jewelry."

"Neither does your mom, unless she has the occasion."

"So, what do I do? I want it to mean something."

"It will mean something because it is from you and it's a promise," Jameson said honestly. "Think of something that she likes—something that has meaning to her."

"That's easy. J.J. or well, Mom," Jonah laughed.

Jameson nodded. "I have an idea."

Candace listened attentively as her Lieutenant Governor listed off numbers. She hated budgetary reviews. Budgets were a necessary evil in governing. A necessity that few could ever agree on. It was always an uphill battle to balance a budget, at least any budget that managed to accomplish anything bold. Candace had often thought that government would work better if it had the ability to make the money it needed to spend like every other business. That was less than practical. Candace laughed inwardly wondering how many laws would change overnight if policy makers had to actually find a way to make money from the services they sought to provide. Taxes never seemed enough, yet they presented a burden for many and seldom seemed fair or balanced. No one wanted to pay more taxes than they had to, even if people expected everything should be provided for them as a result of what they did pay. Candace wondered why it was that people could not grasp the fact that it cost money to build things. It cost money to maintain things. It even cost money to collect the money to try and build and maintain things. The entire thing made Candace dizzy most days.

Candace moved her glasses up and down on the bridge of her nose, feeling the first twinges of a headache mounting. It had been an extremely long day, one that still had no end in sight. Dana had joined the small group in Candace's study after spending a little over an hour with Jonah and Laura. She had attempted to advise them both on how best to handle anything Lawson Klein might feel compelled to offer the press. Candace had been deeply engaged in the budget conversation when Dana had finally made her way into the study. She was curious to know what had transpired and how her son and Laura had reacted to Dana's advice. She had found her thoughts drifting to the subject on and off all night. She wished that she had been able to sit with her children during that discussion. Jameson had stepped in willingly and assumed that role. For that, Candace was grateful.

The conversation around her seemed to drone on and Candace's thoughts began to spiral again. When she had left her family earlier that evening, Jameson had headed into the kitchen with Laura, Jonah and Dana. Candace had deposited Cooper in the capable care of Marianne and Scott in the family room. Cooper had seemed in good spirits after his adventure to the emergency room that morning. Candace anticipated that as the evening wore on, Cooper's mood would likely shift.

Three hours into an arduous meeting, she was finding that her ability to concentrate on numbers was steadily waning.

Dana regarded the governor from across the room thoughtfully. She watched as Candace finally removed her glasses and massaged her temples. Dana privately wondered if most people took the time to honestly get to know Candace, if they ever thought to look below the surface. Candace had mastered presenting a controlled exterior in difficult situations. Dana admired Candace's ability to keep everyone around her calm and focused. But, Dana had spent long hours in the company of Candace Reid over the years. Over time, their professional relationship had evolved into a close friendship. Dana had been allowed to see the subtle vulnerabilities in Candace that only those closest to her ever caught glimpses of. Numerous concerns were weighing on the governor's mind and heart. Dana knew that. The state budget was, without any question, one of those things. However, Dana knew better than anyone that the greatest concerns plaguing Candace's mind involved the people just down the hall from the study. Dana was just about to suggest that the group take a break when a soft knock fell on the door, followed by the tired face of a four-year-old peering into the room sheepishly.

"Mommy," Cooper called over to Candace. He rubbed his eyes with his left hand.

Candace looked over and called Cooper to her. "Come here, sweetheart," she directed him, placing the papers in her lap on the table in front of her and opening her arms to her son.

Cooper staggered sleepily to his mother and climbed into her lap. He laid his head on Candace's chest and Candace kissed the top of his head.

"Can't sleep?" she guessed. Cooper nodded. "Is your arm hurting?" she asked him. He nodded again. "Where's Momma?" Candace asked him.

"She went outside with Jonah."

Candace held Cooper securely and rocked him gently. "Do you want me to take you upstairs?" she asked him. Cooper shook his head. "No? What would you like, sweetheart?" she asked.

"Stay with you," he mumbled and nestled closer to her.

Candace sighed softly and kissed Cooper's head again. "You don't want to go to bed? Isn't Spencer upstairs now?"

Cooper shook his head again and yawned. "He's sleeping with Mawianne in the big room."

"Where's Uncle Scott?" she asked him.

"He sleeping too. They all falled asleep on Genie," Cooper explained.

Candace smiled. "Did you just wake up?"

"Uh-huh," he mumbled. "Addlin is over."

Candace tried not to laugh at Cooper's sluggish speech. He was clearly exhausted. She also noticed that he kept jostling himself to get comfortable. "How about I get you something to make your arm feel better and then you can lay down," she suggested.

Cooper shook his head dramatically. "I want to stay with you," he whispered.

"You can stay with me," she promised him. "We'll go get you something and gran a pillow and blanket, okay? Then you can lay right here while I work," she told him. "How does that sound?" Candace asked knowingly. Cooper smiled. "Good," she said. Candace looked at the other occupants in the room. "I think we could all use a breather. Dana knows where everything is," she commented. "Let me get Coop settled and we can finish up."

"Candy, if you need to call it a night," Dan Moore began to suggest.

"No," Candace stopped him. "I appreciate that, but there is always going to be something that divides my attention," she said honestly. "We need to wrap this up and we all know that."

"We are all tired," Bill DeGrasso said honestly. "Dan's right. One more day won't matter. We've accomplished a lot already. And, Candy it's been a crazy day for you."

Candace smiled gratefully at her Chief of Staff and then at her Lieutenant Governor. "Yes, it has," she agreed. "But, we are in the homestretch. Another two hours and we can officially put this to bed for the time being. We'll know where we can stand firm and where we need to be prepared to bend. Who knows what might get thrown in our path tomorrow? Go grab a coffee in the kitchen with Dana. Stretch for a few minutes. Tomorrow we can all sleep in a little longer," she told them with a wink.

"Are you sure?" Dan asked.

Candace smiled. She lifted Cooper, who wrapped his legs tightly around her waist. "I'm positive," she assured the group. "I'll see you back here in about twenty minutes."

Dan Moore waited until Candace had left the room to speak. "Dana," he addressed Candace's press secretary.

"Yeah?"

"She looks tired," he observed candidly.

"We are all tried," Dana replied honestly. "She's okay, Dan. And, she's right. A million things could happen tomorrow and probably will," she chuckled.

"You still think FVI is going to exploit Laura Klein?" Bill asked Dana.

Dana shrugged. "It's a possibility. Candy thinks that is what he will do. She's usually right—unfortunately."

"Dana," Dan began cautiously. "Do you think it will work? His tactic, I mean? Do you think it will chip away at her enough over time to keep her from making a run?"

Dana shrugged. "Publicly speaking? No, I don't," she said. Dana heard Dan's deep sigh of relief. "Personally?" she went on. "I don't know that answer," Dana confessed. "Sometimes I think we all want her to keep climbing far more than she wants to."

"That's why they wanted her here," Dan observed. "To position her. If we pass this budget. Barring any major catastrophe that she somehow mismanages—Dana, she is almost a given to be the nominee in three years."

Dana nodded. "Three years is a long time, Dan."

"You're starting to sound like her," Dan chuckled.

"I can think of worse things," Dana replied.

✖✖✖

"Quiet," Jameson said as she and Jonah walked back into the kitchen from outside.

"J.D., thanks for tonight. I mean just for listening."

"No need to thank me," Jameson said. "You'd better go up. We were out there a lot longer than I realized."

"By the sounds of it everyone went to bed," Jonah laughed.

"Mmm. I need to go extricate Cooper from Marianne and Scott," she said. "I wonder if they are still stuck watching Disney movies," she mused. Jameson laughed. "I'll bet Scott had a blast," she said playfully.

"Yeah, well, I he was with Marianne he probably did," Jonah offered his assessment.

"You think Scoot is interested in Marianne?" Jameson asked Jonah.

"Don't you?"

Jameson sighed. She knew Jonah was right, but she wanted to avoid the reality as long as possible. She and Scott had worked hard to mend the long rift that had separated them. She loved him like a brother, but she was not in love with the idea of her cousin pursuing her step-daughter.

"J.D.? Is that a bad thing?" Jonah asked.

"I don't know," Jameson answered truthfully. "I don't think Marianne is ready for dating," she continued. "And, Scott?" Jameson sighed again. "I just…"

"Well, if it is going to happen, it's going to happen. She could do a lot worse," Jonah said.

Jameson smiled. That was the truth. Scott was a compassionate, intelligent man who had built a solid career and life for himself. Marianne had been through hell, but in a way she had also blossomed. Jameson loved them both and the idea that anything could ever threaten her relationship with either her cousin or step-daughter concerned her.

"Don't worry about it J.D.," Jonah reassured Jameson. "They're just friends. Anyway, you worry too much about all of us," he said.

Jameson nodded as the pair walked toward the large family room. Jameson stepped in and shook her head in amusement. Spencer was sprawled out in front of Marianne, who was curled up on the couch. Scott was sitting on the far end, his head back on the cushion and Maddie sound asleep on his chest.

"Is that drool on his chin?" she whispered to Jonah.

"Whose? Spencer's?"

"No, Scott's," Jameson snickered. She pulled her camera from her pocket and snapped a picture. "Paybacks, Scottie."

"What do you owe him paybacks for?" Joan asked quietly.

"Nothing right now, but something always come up," Jameson said deviously.

"Shit. I'm glad you're my parent and not my sister," Jonah said.

Marianne stirred at the sound of familiar voices. She opened one eye and caught sight of Jameson. "What time is it?" she asked.

"Late," Jameson replied. "Where's Coop?"

Marianne sat up with a start. "What do you mean? He was sleeping in between us."

"Not now," Jameson noted. She saw the slight panic in Marianne's eyes. "Relax, I am sure I know where he is," Jameson said.

One thing Jameson was certain of was that Cooper would never wander far from the family. Cooper sought security actively. If he had woken up, he would have immediately set out to find either Jameson or Candace. If he was not with Jameson, Jameson was confident she would find him with his mommy.

"I'm sure he is with your mom," Jameson said. "You need some help getting Spence upstairs?" Jameson offered.

Marianne looked over at Scott, and Jameson caught the twinkle in her eye. "No," Marianne said. "They are content. We're fine here until someone decides otherwise," she said.

Jameson nodded. "He drools more than Maddie," Jameson joked, pointing to Scott.

"Must run in your family," Marianne teased Jameson.

"I don't think so," Jameson responded.

"Yeah, well, you can't see yourself when you fall asleep in the recliner," Marianne said with a yawn.

"I do not drool," Jameson defended herself.

"You do—a little," a voice whispered from behind Jameson.

Jameson spun to face Candace ready to bite back with a clever retort. The sight of Cooper clinging to Candace stopped her. "Is he okay?" Jameson asked with concern.

"Sore," Candace replied.

"I'll take him up," Jameson reached for the toddler. She extricated Cooper from Candace's arms, smiled at Candace and made her way out of the room.

"I'll see you guys in the morning," Jonah said, placing a kiss on his mother's cheek. "Night, Mom." Candace smiled.

"Is Coop okay?" Marianne asked Candace.

"He's fine," Candace said. "His arm woke him up, I think. He just wanted..."

"His mom," Marianne finished her mother's thought. "Yeah, I get that."

Candace scanned the scene in front of her and bit her lip to quell a suspicious smirk. "He is going to be miserable tomorrow if you let him stay like that," Candace nodded to Scott.

Marianne smiled. "Yeah, but he looks so cute."

Candace nodded. "Can't argue with that," she said. "See you in the morning."

"Are you and J.D. headed back to Albany tomorrow?" Marianne asked.

"Unfortunately, yes," Candace replied.

"If you need me to take Coop or..."

"I know," Candace said. "Goodnight."

Candace shook her head and laughed quietly as she left the room. She was looking forward to sleeping late. Late would likely mean eight in the morning—is she was lucky. It was already after one. Six hours might have seemed a short night of rest to most people, Candace would welcome it. She stepped into Cooper's room and found Jameson sitting on the edge of Cooper's bed silently.

"You okay?" Candace asked. Jameson made no reply. Candace made her way behind Jameson and grasped her shoulder. "Jameson, come to bed. He's all right."

"This time," Jameson commented.

Candace squeezed Jameson's shoulder in reassurance. She had thought that the day's activities had helped to ease Jameson's guilt. The day had definitely served as a distraction. The distraction had apparently not managed to reassure Jameson.

"Come on," Candace urged Jameson gently.

"How do you do it?" Jameson asked.

"Do what?"

"All these years... How do you keep them safe?" Jameson asked without turning to face Candace.

"I wish I could claim that," Candace said. "We both know that I can't."

Jameson closed her eyes for a moment. Cooper had been on her mind all day, even when she had been sitting alone with Jonah, even when she had been listening to Dana impart advice. Nothing had served to take her mind off of Cooper's accident. Jameson felt responsible. No matter what Candace said, no matter what Jameson logically knew, she could not seem to help feeling guilty.

"Jameson, come to bed," Candace urged her wife.

Jameson stood and reluctantly followed Candace across the hall. Candace closed their bedroom door and swiftly made her way to Jameson.

"I want you to listen to me," Candace said. "Cooper is fine. Cooper is going to have lots of falls, Jameson. Sometimes you won't be able to see what is broken right away. Those are often the hardest ones of all."

"If I had been..."

"Maybe. Maybe not," Candace dismissed Jameson's argument before it began. "You can't protect him from everything."

"God, I want to," Jameson said.

Candace smiled. "I know, so do I."

"It's not just Cooper," Jameson told Candace.

"What is it?"

"Jonah and Laura," Jameson replied. Candace nodded. "I'd like to kick his ass," she said. "And, I know that would only make it worse," Jameson admitted. "But, Candace? After everything he's said about you? Cooper? Pearl? Now? His daughter? What kind of person does that?"

"I don't know," Candace confessed. "An unhappy one." Jameson groaned. "All right, out with it," Candace said. "That's not all of it. Let's have it."

Jameson closed her eyes in resignation. "Marianne. Well, and Scott."

"Um-hum. What about them?"

"Candace, come on! You saw that scene downstairs."

Candace nodded. "I did, yes."

"And, you are okay with that?"

"I'm not sure there is anything to be okay with," Candace said. "And, Jameson if there is or if there will be, that is between Rick and Marianne."

"I know. It doesn't worry you?"

"Of course, it worries me," Candace said. "But, I am guessing not for the same reasons that it worries you."

"I don't want to see anyone get hurt. And, what if they did? What..."

"Whose side would you take?" Candace guessed. She moved closer to Jameson and kissed her gently. "Stop worrying about what ifs."

"Why? You worry about them all of the time,"

Candace laughed. "Touché. I just meant that you can't live their lives. Right now, I think Marianne needs a friend. Maybe that's all it will ever be."

"And, maybe not."

Candace shrugged. "Stranger things have happened."

"Yeah, you married me," Jameson lightened measurably.

"What was I thinking?" Candace teased.

"That I am cute."

Candace laughed. "You are certifiable."

"And cute."

Candace shook her head. "You've got me there," she said. "Come on, we both need some sleep."

"Candace," Jameson stopped her wife. "Is there anything we can do? I mean to sop Lawson Klein? I just..."

Candace kissed Jameson on the cheek. "People like Lawson Klein spend so much time dwelling on what other people are doing that they forget someone is paying attention to them," she told Jameson.

"What does that mean?" Jameson wondered.

"It means exactly what I said. You know that old saying about people in glass houses casting stones?"

"Yeah?"

"Lawson Klein might live in a mansion, Jameson. It is one with very thin panes of glass."

"Like karma, huh?" Jameson said.

Candace smiled. "Something like that."

"I hope you are right," Jameson muttered.

"It pays to know your enemies, Jameson. It's just as important to notice the people you think are you allies."

"Speaking from experience?"

Candace crawled into bed. "You could say that, yes."

"And, what am I?" Jameson teased. "Your enemy or your ally?" she flirted.

"You," Candace said placing a kiss on Jameson's lips. "Are," she pulled back and then kissed Jameson again. Candace pulled back and gloated at the excitement in Jameson's eye. "My pillow," she finished playfully and rested her head on Candace's chest.

Jameson groaned. "How come I have to be the pillow?"

Candace snuggled closer. "I'm not the one who drools."

"I don't drool," Jameson argued. Candace laughed softly and kissed Jameson's chest. "Candace? I don't..."

"Go to sleep," Candace said.

"Well, you snore."

"And you're a lunatic."

"Yeah, well...it's a survival technique," Jameson defended herself against Candace's gentle teasing.

"And, you certainly have mastered it. Now, go to sleep."

Jameson groaned and then kissed Candace's head. "Do I really drool."

"Go to sleep."

"Candace? You still..."

"I love you, you lunatic, drool and all. Go to sleep."

CHAPTER SEVENTEEN

"**W**ell, that went well," Candace said as she walked through the door to the executive offices at the capital.

"It did," Dana agreed. "Must be a relief for you," she said.

"Relief is an interesting word," Candace replied. "But, accurate, I suppose. If this budget passes, it will go a long way to getting things accomplished."

"Well, it's out of your hands now," Dana said.

"That it is," Candace agreed.

"How is Laura?" Dana asked.

Candace smiled. "Nervous."

"I didn't mean about that. I meant about the interview her father gave."

Candace shook her head. "Quiet. Taking your advice and remaining quiet. I just hope Jonah doesn't cross paths with him. I'm not sure he will be able to hold back."

"Can't say that I blame him."

"Neither do I," Candace said honestly.

"So? Tomorrow is the big day, huh? Still haven't told the girls?" Dana wondered.

Candace grinned. Jonah and Laura were planning to take their vows the next day in Candace and Jameson's backyard. In fact, they were planning to do it on the very spot Candace and Jameson had taken theirs. Candace had understood the couple's desire for something extremely private and small. Jonah had wanted to keep it a secret, even from his sisters. Candace had thought that course unwise.

"They know," Candace told Dana.

"How did they take it? Not being invited to their brother's wedding?"

"Oh, you know Shell," Candace laughed. "She flew into a bit of a spin for a minute."

"And, Marianne?"

Candace shrugged. "Marianne pulled Shell out of the room. I imagine she had some fairly pointed words for her younger sister."

"How things change, huh?"

"That's the truth," Candace said with a smile. "I think they both understand. Jonathan? I'm not certain he will be as understanding when Jonah tells him that he got married."

"He hasn't told his father?" Dana was surprised.

Candace shook her head and sighed. "I debated calling him," she confessed. "I wish he would talk to his father. They just...I don't know, Dana. Jonathan has always been hard on Jonah. He doesn't mean it. That doesn't change how it has always made Jonah feel."

"It bothers you," Dana observed.

Candace smiled. "Jonathan is a good man, Dana. He wasn't good for me and I certainly was not the right person for him. We were together a long time. We've been through death and children together. He loves all three of them. He's just never been particularly good at letting them know that," she explained. "To him, the trust funds, paying for college and weddings—that is how he sees his role."

"Kind of cold," Dana said.

Candace sighed. "It's who he is, Dana."

"Cold?"

Candace laughed. "No, he isn't cold," she said. "He just never had anyone love him the way I did. We learn a great deal from what we're shown," she told Dana. "His parents were a lot like my mother. In fact, he spent very little time with his parents. He tries. He really does."

"Sounds like you two have mended your fences."

"I'm not sure there were that many to mend," Candace said. "We were given each other. It wasn't our choice, at least, it never felt like a choice to either of us. We both did the best we could and neither of us did very well, I am afraid—not by each other."

"You think he will be angry?" Dana wondered.

"Jonathan? No. Hurt. I hope I can convince Jonah to call him tonight."

"Candace, Jonah and J.D...."

Candace smiled broadly. "Jonah loves Jameson. I can't say that I envisioned that. Not what it has become. He looks to her more than he looks to me. She worries about him more than the other two, I think," Candace laughed.

"He's like you," Dana said. Candace's surprise was evident. "He is," Dana repeated her observation.

"Maybe."

"No, maybe. I mean, all of them are like you in certain ways. I see it more now than ever before, Candy. Jonah is so much like you. He even looks like you."

Candace laughed. That fact was undeniable. The older Jonah got, the more and more he resembled his mother. "Poor thing," Candace joked.

"I'm just saying that it makes sense that he would be drawn to J.D. and that J.D. would worry so much about him," Dana said. Candace nodded. "Can I tell you something?"

"I don't know," Candace teased. "Can I stop you?"

"Probably not," Dana admitted. "I just hope that Steve and I have that kind of relationship with our boys and whoever they choose. I worry about that."

Candace laughed. "Dana, the boys aren't even teenagers yet."

"Yeah, but what if I hate their partners?"

Candace shook her head. "I doubt that will happen. But, the truth is I have been lucky and I know it. My kids have good taste," she winked just as the intercom in her office beeped.

"Governor?"

"Yes, Susan?"

"There is someone here to see you," Susan said.

"Who is it?" Candace asked. Silence lingered. "Susan?"

Susan whispered on the line. "I think you might want to see for yourself."

Candace and Dana exchanged a weary glance. "I'll be right there," Candace said. She took a deep breath. "This should be interesting," she commented to Dana as she made her way to the door.

Candace opened the door and froze. She looked across the reception area to a sofa and lost her breath at the sight of a woman sitting with her face in her hands. The woman looked up slowly at Candace with misty eyes. Candace took a deep breath and offered her a sad smile.

"I didn't know what else to do."

Candace nodded. "Hold my calls, Susan," she said. "Come in."

"Governor Reid, I..."

Candace sighed. "It's Candace, Mrs. Klein," she said. "Dana?" Candace whispered to her friend. "Do me a favor and call Jameson. Let her know that I will be later than expected."

✳ ✳ ✳

"Thanks, J.D.," Jonah said as he and Jameson made their way to the car from the jewelry store.

"Don't thank me," Jameson said. "Thank your mom."

Jonah nodded. "I can't believe that she gave it to me."

Jameson smiled. "Why not?" she wondered. "I'm not sure that she thought you would want it," Jameson said.

After Jonah had asked Jameson to help him find a ring for Laura, Jameson had approached Candace about her engagement ring from Jonathan. Candace had always intended to give it to Jonah. Jonah's sometime ambivalent feelings toward his father had led Candace to think that Jonah might prefer something new. Jameson had suggested that perhaps Jonah could have it reset and make it his own in that way.

"She always wanted you to have it, Jonah."

"I know, she told me. It's just... Well, they didn't really have the best marriage, J.D."

Jameson smiled. "Maybe not. They had you. I think that made it worthwhile to both of them."

"You sound like you almost like my father," Jonah said.

"I don't dislike him. Why would I?" Jameson wondered.

"I don't know. Isn't it weird for you?" Jonah asked.

"Not really," Jameson replied honestly. "Your mom is who she is partly because of him. I get that."

Jonah chuckled. "You're a better person than me, I think."

"No."

"Yeah. You have dinner with Mom's exes," he laughed.

Jameson laughed. "Doesn't mean that I always enjoy it," she confessed.

"So, why do it?"

"Well, he is your dad," Jameson pointed out. "He's an okay guy, Jonah."

"He's nicer to you than he is to me," Jonah mumbled.

Jameson took a deep breath. "That's not true. And, I'm not his kid."

"And, I am not your kid," Jonah muttered.

Jameson shook her head. "Well, considering I would have been about fourteen, no," she laughed. "But, that isn't how I feel, Jonah."

Jonah looked at Jameson hopefully. She smiled at him reassuringly. Heart to heart conversations with Candace's children sometimes still challenged Jameson. No matter how much their relationships had grown, Jameson always feared overstepping her boundaries. They had two parents who loved them. And, while Jameson understood that Jonathan

Fletcher often seemed distant, she was also certain that he loved all three of his children. He might have been quiet, even stern, but Jameson had seen the evidence of how much he cared for Jonah and his sisters. In fact, she had often wondered at the genuine affection the man still held for Candace. She had never told anyone about the conversation she and Jonathan Fletcher had engaged in after Rick's death, not even Candace. Now, Jameson felt it was time to share that story, at least, in part. She opened the car door and hopped in. She looked across the seat at Jonah as she turned the key in the ignition.

"Your dad is an interesting guy," she told Jonah as her eyes turned to the road.

"That's not a glowing endorsement," Jonah chuckled.

Jameson laughed. "Actually, it is."

"Really?"

Jameson sighed lightly. "He cares about you—all of you," she said. "Your mom too—more than you realize."

"Guilt will do that."

"Maybe. I don't think it's guilt," Jameson said honestly.

"J.D., Dad cheated on Mom like a thousand times."

"I know."

Jonah shook his head in disgust. "And, he barely saw us even when he lived with her."

"I know that too."

"See?" Jonah said. "Guilt. What else would you call it?"

"Regret, maybe," Jameson admitted. "We all have regrets, Jonah. Sometimes, you don't realize what you have until you don't have it anymore."

"That's just shitty."

Jameson laughed. "I guess it is."

"I don't even know how she can stand to be near him or Jessica for that matter," Jonah said honestly.

"Have you ever asked her that?" Jameson wondered.

"What? Ask Mom why she's nice to them? She'd just say that the past is the past."

"I think what she'd say is that she still cares about both of them. And, they both care about her in their own way," Jameson told him.

Jonah shook his head again. "Funny way of showing it. And, they never cared all that much about us," he said plainly.

"I think you know that is not true," Jameson said. "Maybe you should give them another chance, Jonah."

"Why?"

"Because, you want to."

"Not really," he said.

"You know, your dad told me once that every time he looks at one of you he can see your mom."

"Thank God," Jonah said sharply.

Jameson sighed. "He basically said the same thing," she told Jonah. Jonah looked over at Jameson expectantly. "That surprises you, I take it?" she asked.

"A little."

"Well, like I said, sometimes you have to step away to see things clearly."

"He never loved her," Jonah said.

Jameson nodded. "I think he's always loved her, just not the way he needed to," she said honestly. "And, he loves you. That much I do know."

"Nice that he would tell you," Jonah bit sharply.

Jameson found it fascinating the way that parents could bring out the inner child in their adult children. She hated to admit that she was positive her parents would have noted the same thing in her. Jameson had witnessed the child-like emotional response in all three of Candace's grown children at times. It often made her wonder what she and Candace would confront with Cooper as he got older. No matter how much they loved and nurtured their son, the reality remained that Cooper had biological parents who had in some way let him down. Listening to Jonah now, she desperately hoped that she and Candace would be able to reach and reassure Cooper. Jonah seemed to be the most hurt by his father.

Candace had told Jameson that Jonathan had always been hardest on Jonah. Candace had suspected that it was in part because Jonah had so many physical issues as a toddler. Jonathan had wanted Jonah to push. Candace guessed that Jonathan's pressure had shaped Jonah in many ways. But, she also recognized that it had hurt Jonah deeply as well.

"Maybe he just doesn't know how to say it, Jonah. You do know if you ever needed anything, he would be there for you?"

"Yeah, with money."

Jameson shook her head. "Not just that," she said. "You don't have to take my word for it. Ask him yourself. Ask your mom."

Jonah grew quiet for a moment. He looked over at Jameson who was concentrating on the road. "I know that it's not the same for you," he said tacitly. "It has to be weird."

Jameson smiled, understanding what Jonah was referring to. She decided on the spot that blatant honesty was best. "I love you, Jonah. If that is what you are worried about. And, I love your crazy sisters too. Sometimes I wish I could have known you from the beginning. *That* would have been even stranger," she cracked.

Jonah finally chuckled. "That's hard for you, huh? Saying it?"

Jameson nodded. "Sometimes it is."

"How come?"

"I don't know. I don't have a lot of practice," Jameson admitted. "I never thought I would have kids, Jonah. Certainly not ones who are almost my age," she laughed. "To tell you the truth, I never thought I would be married."

Jonah was genuinely surprised. "Really? How come?"

"Not sure really. Maybe it was just all the things that happened when I was younger."

"You mean what happened with that guy?" Jonah asked.

Jameson let out a ragged breath. She hated talking about her rape. She had only ever truly traversed the subject with Candace and a bit with Laura as a means of support.

"You don't have to answer that," Jonah said regretfully.

Jameson turned and offered him a smile. "It's okay. Yeah, that. That and what happened with Craig. And, really? Jonah, not everyone in my family is all that crazy about who I am, you know?"

"What do you mean? You mean being gay?"

"That's exactly what I mean. Now, I am married to one of the most prominent, liberal lesbians on the planet," Jameson laughed.

"Yeah, but everyone in your family has been so great to all of us."

"Mmm. You haven't met them all," Jameson said. "My parents are not indicative of everyone in our family, Jonah. Trust me on that. But, we all try. We don't always agree, but we try."

"You think I should call Dad," he surmised.

"I think that one day you might wish you had."

"What about you?" Jonah asked with concern.

"What about me?"

"J.D., I am closer to you than I ever have been to Dad," Jonah said honestly. "I know that might seem weird, but I want it to be you with me."

"It's not weird. And, I will be there no matter whether your dad is or not," she reminded him.

"If I call, I will have to ask him," Jonah said. "If he comes... I don't want that to change anything."

"Tell him that," Jameson suggested.

"You won't be..."

"Jonah, whatever you want to do I will support, okay?"

"J.D.?"

"Yeah?"

"Thanks."

✖✖✖

"Can I get you a coffee or something?" Candace asked Laura Klein's mother.

"No. I know I have no right to..."

"Have a seat," Candace directed the woman. "Look, Mrs..."

"Mary."

Candace smiled genuinely. "Mary, I'm not entirely clear on what has brought you here, although I think I can wager a guess."

Mary Klein hung her head in regret. "I never thought he'd go so far," she mumbled.

Candace listened silently, feeling the waves of pain and guilt that emanated from the woman a few feet away. She was torn between a desire to rip into the woman for the pain she had caused Laura and reaching out with sincere empathy as a mother. Silence seemed her ally at the moment and so Candace waited patiently for Mary Klein to continue.

"When she told me what Mark had done, I went to him. I thought he would be furious. He was. It just wasn't with Mark," Mary Klein said. "First it was with Laura. Then, it was with me for even raising such an issue," she explained. "I preferred his anger stayed with me, and it did for a long time," she said.

Candace bit her lip gently, wishing there were some words that she could muster that could magically heal the situation she was now confronting. She watched as tears streamed down Mary Klein's cheeks. "Why leave now?" Candace asked as gently as she could manage.

"He can't hurt her that way now," Mary Klein answered honestly. "He can still hurt her. My staying didn't stop that."

"You thought that it would?" Candace asked.

"I don't know what I thought," Mary Klein replied. "I wasn't thinking clearly. I just wanted to keep her safe. I thought...If I took the blame, if I just kept her away from them both as much..."

Candace sighed heavily. Laura had confided in Candace that her mother had worked hard to convince her father to let Laura study at Stanford. Candace was beginning to fit the pieces of a dark puzzle together and she did not like the picture it revealed. "Did he hit you?" she asked.

"From time to time," Mary Klein answered. "That was not the worst. I just...If I had tried to leave then. His arm is long, Governor..."

"Candace," Candace reminded Mary Klein. "I am aware," she said.

"I have never even held my grandson," Mary said.

Candace smiled. "He is a beautiful little boy," she said proudly. "Mary," she began cautiously. "I can't promise you that Laura will want to talk to you."

"I know. I wanted to know that she was all right. I didn't want to show up on her doorstep. And, well, there aren't many places..."

"Where are you staying?" Candace asked.

"Downtown at the Marriott."

Candace nodded. "Does he know? Where you are?"

"No."

Candace nodded again. "All right. I actually have a short day today. You do realize that I have to tell her that we have spoken?"

"I know."

"Laura is...Well, she is a compassionate young woman," Candace said honestly. "I'll have someone take you back over to the hotel. Leave me your contact information and I will be in touch later this afternoon."

"Candace...I..."

"I can't pretend to understand," Candace said honestly. "But then, I have never been in your position."

"I should never have..."

"Should never gets any of us anywhere," Candace interjected.

"I just..."

"Let me talk to Laura," Candace said.

"Is she? All right?"

"She's hurt," Candace answered truthfully. Mary Klein hung her head again. "But, she is strong," Candace continued affectionately. "And, intelligent. She has Jonah and J.J. I think that has helped a great deal."

Mary Klein nodded. "And, she has you."

Candace smiled. She would not deny the remark. "She has our family, yes. Let me talk to her," Candace said. "One step at a time. I have to ask... Do you think there is any chance that he will look to find you?"

Mary Klein shook her head. "I never know what he is going to do, not anymore."

Candace groaned inwardly at the information. That revelation concerned Candace. Lawson Klein's world was beginning to crumble under his feet. That often made people more unpredictable and volatile. She smiled as best she could at the woman before her. "I promise that I will be in touch later today."

Mary Klein nodded her thanks. Candace made her way to her desk and pressed the intercom.

"Susan?"

"Yes, Governor?"

"Could you ask Dana to come back? I have a favor to ask of her."

"Of course. Anything else?" Susan asked.

"No, not right now. Oh, let Drew know that I will be later than I expected."

"I'll take care of it," Susan promised.

Candace looked at Mary Klein. "Thank you," Mary said. "For even agreeing to see me."

"I didn't do it for you," Candace said honestly. Mary nodded. "But, I sincerely hope that it works out for both you and Laura."

✗✗✗

Jameson walked into Candace's office with Cooper on her heels. "Hey."

Candace looked up from her desk and smiled. "Hey, you and you," she smiled at Cooper. Cooper accepted the silent invitation and ran to Candace. "Well, did you miss me?" she asked him.

"Yep! Mawianne took me and Spence for ice cweam."

"She did, huh?" Candace asked.

"Yep. She says she will see me tomorrow."

"That she will," Candace agreed.

"I get to go with Shell now?" he asked.

"Yes, you do," Candace said. "She will be here any minute."

"Mommy?" Cooper asked Candace.

"What?"

"Momma says I gots to wear a tie tomorrow."

Candace snickered. "Yes, you do." Cooper frowned a bit. "Don't you like the tie, Cooper?" Candace wondered. Cooper shook his head. Jameson rolled her eyes when Candace looked at her curiously. Candace looked back at Cooper. "Is it too tight?" she asked him. Cooper shook his head again. "No?" she was truly curious and looked back at Jameson.

"He doesn't like the color," Jameson raised her brow.

Candace suppressed her laughter. Cooper had certain colors that he loved and certain colors he seemed to dislike. She and Jameson had noticed it first in his crayon box. One side was filled with worn, broken, and short crayons. The other side had carefully lined, pristine sticks that had never been touched. Jonah had chosen a dark red color. Cooper never used the red crayons in his box. He preferred blues and greens. When something should have been red, he always seemed to substitute orange.

Candace kissed Cooper on the head and chuckled. "You don't like the red, sweetheart?" Cooper shook his head. "How come?" she asked. He looked up at her and shook his head again. Candace instantly saw fear in his eyes. She looked over at Jameson and then back at Cooper. "Cooper?"

"Dats what the lights are."

Candace sighed. Jameson was confused. "Ambulance," Candace mouthed the word over Cooper's head.

Jameson closed her eyes and groaned. "Coop," Jameson called for his attention. "I will talk to Jonah, okay?" Copper nodded just as Shell walked into the room.

"Hey, little man," Shell called to her brother.

Cooper brightened immediately. He looked at Candace for permission and Candace smiled at him lovingly. "Go on," she encouraged him.

Cooper ran to Shell excitedly. "Easy there, buddy!" Shell laughed. "Don't want to fall on that arm," she told him. He looked at her apologetically. "Aww, it's cool, Coop. I'm just teasing you," she said, giving him a hug. "So, you are stuck with me for a few hours, huh?" she asked him. Cooper grinned and nodded. "Whatya' wanna do?" Shell asked.

Cooper beckoned Shell to him and whispered into her ear. Candace watched in amusement as Shell rolled her eyes and then laughed.

"I'm sure Mel would love that," Shell said. "You know, your momma has her working hard," Shell looked at Jameson.

"Hey! I pay her well," Jameson replied.

"Mm-hm," Shell said. "Well, Coop, ask Momma if Mel can leave work early."

Jameson laughed. "She doesn't need my permission anymore," Jameson reminded Shell. "Take it up with your fiancée," she told Shell. Shell wrinkled her nose at Jameson and stuck out her tongue. "Real mature, Shell," Jameson said. "Don't teach your brother that one, okay?"

Cooper looked back at Shell quizzically. "You in twouble, Shell?" he asked in concern.

Candace put her face in her hands as she shook with laughter.

"No, buddy," Shell promised. "Come on, you and me will go get my stuff and we'll head over to surprise Mel. She's always up for pizza."

Cooper smiled and then looked back at his parents. Jameson winked at him. He loved spending time with all of his siblings and he adored both Pearl and Jameson's parents. Still, Cooper remained reluctant to leave Jameson and Candace unless he received their approval. In some ways, that pleased Jameson. She didn't fear Cooper would ever run off with a stranger for one thing. But, she and Candace had agreed that they needed to continue to encourage Cooper to feel safe leaving them, that they would be there when he returned from his adventure.

"Have fun with your sister," Jameson told Cooper.

Shell watched as Cooper looked at Candace. She pulled Cooper closer to her. "Don't worry, Coop. We'll catch up with Mom after dinner, okay?"

Cooper nodded. "Bye," he waved to his parents.

"We'll see you in a bit," Candace promised. "Not too much sugar, Shell," Candace reminded her daughter.

"Yeah, yeah."

"I mean it," Candace warned.

"Geesh! I got it!" Shell said. She bent over and whispered in Cooper's ear. "We'll still get ice cream."

Candace rolled her eyes when she heard Cooper giggle.

"You know he's going to be high on more than life when he gets back," Jameson chuckled.

"Um-hum. I think he enables Shell's sweet tooth," Candace said.

"So?" Jameson began. "You talked to Laura."

"I did," Candace replied.

"And?"

"She and Jonah should be here shortly."

"She wants to see her mother?" Jameson asked.

Candace nodded. "She needs to, Jameson."

"Mmm."

"Jameson..."

"Oh, come on. You can't tell me this doesn't raise red flags for you," Jameson said.

"It does. Lots of them," Candace admitted. "But, it is her mother."

"You think she's sincere?" Jameson wanted to know. Candace did not answer immediately. "Candace?"

"I want to think so."

"You have some doubts?" Jameson prodded.

"Not really. Just concerns for both of them," Candace replied.

"Did he hurt her?" Jameson asked reluctantly.

Candace shook her head. "I don't know. I think so, yes. At some point, yes, I think so. I think in some strange way that's why she stayed."

Jameson rubbed her forehead. "Fucking asshole." Candace's eyes widened. "Well, he is!" Jameson said.

"I can't argue with that," Candace admitted. "I just am not used to you using that word." Candace tended to swear far more often than Jameson, something she was certain would have surprised many people in their life.

Jameson shrugged. "I reserve it for special occasions and special assholes," she explained. Candace laughed. "Speaking of fathers..."

"What?" Candace sensed some impending doom. "Oh, I don't like this already."

"What?" Jameson asked.

"You have that look on your face like you expect me to implode."

Jameson laughed. "Not at all, actually."

"Okay? Then what is it?"

Jameson smiled at her wife. "I had a talk with Jonah today."

"About?"

"He called Jonathan."

Candace's shock was immediate. "He called his father?"

Jameson nodded.

"When?"

"When we got back to their apartment. Just before you called me."

Candace reclined in her chair. "Huh. What did he say?"

"Jonah?"

"No, Jonathan," Candace clarified.

"Guess we will be having one more tomorrow," Jameson replied.

Candace folded her arms across her chest and pursed her lips. "What exactly did you say to get him to call?"

"Just the truth," Jameson answered. Candace waited for a more detailed explanation. "I just told him that his father loves him. That's all."

"I've told him that a million times."

"Yeah, but you're you," Jameson pointed out.

"What does that mean?"

"It means that Jonah loves you, Candace. I mean, he really loves you. I don't think you realize sometimes just how much those kids look to you," Jameson said. "All four of them."

"They look to you too," Candace pointed out. "Jonah as much as Cooper, I think."

"Yeah, I know," Jameson admitted, surprising Candace a bit. "But, Candace...You are Mom. Like Pearl is Mom. I'm, J.D. It's not the same. And, the thing is a lot of their issues with Jonathan are about you."

Candace closed her eyes and shook her head. "I wish they would let that go."

"They can't. They love you."

"It wasn't all his doing, Jameson," Candace said flatly. "I wasn't the most attentive wife in a lot of ways. I wasn't happy either."

"I know that," Jameson said. "But, you have to understand that you have always been their protector. They want to protect you just as much."

"That's not their job."

"Yeah, it is whether or not you like it," Jameson said. Candace lifted her brow. "Well, it is. It goes both ways when you love someone. You tell me that all of the time."

"I guess I do. So, how did Jonah seem after the conversation?" Candace asked.

"Relieved. Worried. Kind of a little bit of everything."

Candace nodded. "He's worried about you, Jameson— more than me this time."

"He's worried about hurting anyone's feelings," Jameson said.

"And, you? How do you feel about it?"

"I'm glad he's coming."

"Really?"

"Jonah would have regretted that," Jameson said. "Sooner or later he would have."

"You think he is going to cave in and ask his sisters, don't you?" Candace guessed.

Jameson shrugged. "I think that might depend on what happens tonight."

"You mean with Laura and her mother," Candace guessed.

"Yep. Do you think Laura will tell her? About tomorrow?"

"I honestly don't know, Jameson. I just know that she asked if I would go with her to see her mother."

"How are you doing with that?" Jameson wondered.

"I don't know."

Jameson nodded. "Never easy, is it?"

Candace laughed. "Never boring, that's for sure."

"I love you, you know?" Jameson said.

Candace was caught off guard by the declaration. Jameson had turned emotional in an instant. "Of course, I know. What brought that on?"

"All this chaos lately. I guess I feel like I haven't said that enough," Jameson explained. "Talking to Jonah today. I don't know, watching Cooper run to you. I just... I get how lucky I am, even if it's never easy."

Candace smiled. "Not what you expected a few years ago when you showed up on my doorstep, is it?"

Jameson shook her head. "Nope."

"Regrets?"

"Nope."

"You sure?" Candace asked.

"Completely," Jameson replied.

Candace pulled her gaze away from Jameson when the door opened. "Sorry if we are late," Jonah said.

"You're not late," Jameson said.

Candace smiled at Laura. "You sure this is what you want to do?"

Laura nodded. "I have to. Just," she looked at Jonah. Jonah nodded. "You're sure you don't mind? Coming with me, I mean?"

"Not at all," Candace promised.

"Just call us when you want us to meet you," Jameson said.

"Where are you two off to?" Candace asked her wife and her son.

"That's between us. Last night as a bachelor and all," Jameson said.

"Uh-huh. How many singles do you need?" Candace teased. Laura laughed.

"Singles?" Jonah asked.

Jameson shook her head. "Come on, Jonah. Your mother has lost her mind. Any place worth tipping requires something a lot larger than a one-dollar bill."

Candace laughed as the pair left her office.

"You don't think they are really..." Laura watched the door close.

"Not if they know what's good for them," Candace replied evenly.

� � �

Candace sat on the small love seat in the hotel room with Laura who had reached for Candace's hand in support. Mary Klein sat facing them in a wingback chair. Candace felt Laura's grip tighten on and off, and she would gently squeeze back in reassurance. It had not escaped Candace's notice that Mary Klein's gaze frequently drifted to her daughter's hand as it held onto Candace.

"I wish I could take it all back," Mary told Laura.

Laura swallowed hard. "You can't."

"I know you won't believe me, but I thought I was doing the right thing. I thought it would keep you safe, if I was there."

"But, you weren't there," Laura said softly. "After I told you about Mark, you pulled away. Do you have any idea how alone I felt? Mark would torment me, threaten me constantly. It was almost worse than him touching me," Laura said as her tears began to fall swiftly.

Candace let go of Laura's hand and moved it to Laura's back. She pulled Laura closer to her. "It's okay, sweetheart," Candace whispered.

Laura shook her head and looked at her mother. "I needed you. I needed you to do this. To just tell me it would be all right," she cried.

Mary Klein began to cry. "I wanted to," she said. "I just—it was my fault. I should have known. I didn't know."

Candace offered Mary Klein a compassionate glance. It remained difficult for Candace to fathom how Mary Klein had allowed Laura to feel so alone. Abuse had a unique way of distorting thought. It wore people down over time. Candace did understand that. She felt Laura collapse against her. "It's all right," she reassured Laura again. "Let it go."

Laura finally looked directly at her mother. "The thing is, I miss you, Mom."

"I miss you too," Mary Klein said.

Laura wiped her eyes. She looked at Candace and Candace nodded her encouragement.

"Jonah and I," Laura started. "Tomorrow, we're getting married," she told her mother.

Mary Klein nodded. "I'm happy for you," she choked back her tears.

"Thanks," Laura said. "If you wanted to be, I would like you to be there. It's small."

"I would love to be," Mary said.

"One thing, though," Laura said.

"Yes?" Mary asked.

"The thing is, Mom," Laura looked at Candace. "I…"

"Go ahead, Laura," Mary Klein encouraged her daughter. "Whatever it is, I will understand."

"I do want you there. The truth is, you and me? We haven't been close in a very long time. I don't think you really know me at all," Laura said sadly. Mary nodded. "I never really thought we'd be sitting here."

"I understand," Mary said sadly.

"But, you're still my mother. I'd like you to know me."

"I would like that."

"I'm not saying this to hurt you," Laura said. "I'm really not."

"It's all right," Mary repeated.

"Candace has really been my mother for more than a year. Not just because of Jonah either," she said honestly. "I love her. I asked her to stand with me tomorrow, and I hope you can respect that."

Candace held her tears in check when Mary Klein looked at her. "I can see that you mean a great deal to each other," Mary Klein replied.

"I need to get to know you again. Away from him," Laura said with a shiver.

"I would be honored to come," Mary said.

Laura nodded and looked at Candace, who smiled. Candace turned to Mary. "I'm not sure how you would feel about this, but Pearl has offered to let you stay at her home for a bit until you decide what you would like to do," Candace said. Laura looked at Candace in complete shock. Candace winked. "Mothers are like that," she said.

"When did you talk to Grandma?" Laura asked Candace.

"After I spoke with you. Call it instinct," Candace said.

"Pearl was your housekeeper," Mary began.

"Pearl is my mother," Candace corrected her. "In every way that matters. Technically, she is my aunt," Candace laughed.

"Well, anyone who has seen you two together would think you were hers," Laura giggled.

Mary Klein regarded the interaction between her daughter and Candace thoughtfully. Candace stood and Laura followed. "If you feel inclined to accept the offer, my wife will swing by to pick you up later this evening," Candace told Mary.

"I don't want to put anyone out," Mary said sincerely.

"Grandma Pearl wouldn't offer if she didn't mean it," Laura said.

"She's right," Candace agreed.

"And, your wife...I mean, I don't..."

"You'll like J.D.," Laura said. "Everybody does."

"Whatever you do, don't tell her that," Candace joked. "I have to live with her."

CHAPTER EIGHTEEN

"**A**s of this morning, Family Values International has severed its ties with Lawson Klein and The Klein-Bordner Trust," Grant Hill said.

"There is a report that just released claiming that the trust has been accepting funds from pharmaceutical companies implicated in sales to abortion clinics here and overseas. That's in direct conflict with FVI's value statement. What do you have to say about that?" someone called out a question.

"As I said, we have ended our relationship with The Klein-Bordner Trust. I am certain that those allegations will be handled by their board directly."

"Did you know?"

Grant Hill shook his head. "We are not in the habit of patrolling our investors, Nathan. We work on a premise of integrity."

"Mr. Hill?" a reporter called out.

"Yes, Jarred?"

"Is this decision the result of the story regarding Klein's daughter?"

Grant Hill smiled professionally. "Mr. Klein and FVI have taken different directions," he said.

"Do you believe his accusations about his daughter?" the reporter pushed. "Lying about her abuse?"

Hill nodded. "I have three children," he began. "I have no idea what the Klein family has been through. I do know that I believe in the value of family. That is why our organization is called Family Values International," he explained. "My children's interest would always be at the heart of any decision I made as would be my desire to protect them."

"What does Mr. Klein think about your decision?" another voice shouted.

"I suppose that is a question for Mr. Klein."

✂ ✂ ✂

"Almost ready?" Candace stepped up behind Jameson.

Jameson leaned into Candace and sighed. "Brings back memories."

Candace held Jameson close for a moment. "That was a good day."

"The best," Jameson said.

"The best, huh?" Candace teased. Jameson turned to face her and Candace wiped a tear from the corner of Jameson's eye. "You really are a big softie," she said, placing a kiss on Jameson's cheek. "You okay?" Candace asked.

"Yeah," Jameson said. "I am. You'll think it's silly."

"I doubt that," Candace said.

Jameson turned and took a seat on their bed. She looked up at Candace. "Sometimes, I look around me, Candace and I can't believe this is my life."

"Is that a good thing?"

Jameson smiled. "What I mean is, I don't know what I did to deserve all of it."

"I think I understand."

"You do?" Jameson asked hopefully.

"Jameson," Candace sat down beside her wife and took Jameson's hands. "I've been so fortunate. I have terrific kids. I had a father who loved me and grandparents who nurtured me. I have Pearl. I have a career that for all its problems and stresses, I love. But, until there was you? None of it fit to-gether. It was all parts spinning away from each other," she told Jameson. "Now, somehow as fast as those parts can turn, and as bumpy as the road gets, they all seem to spin in the same direction," Candace explained. Jameson smiled at Candace and stroked Candace's cheek. "What?" Candace whispered.

"I wish I could explain things the way that you do," Jameson said. "Thank you."

"What are you thanking me for?" Candace wondered.

"For reminding me all of the time why I love you so much."

Candace leaned in and kissed Jameson tenderly.

"A-aaahemmm," Shell cleared her throat from the doorway.

"He had to cave and invite them," Jameson mumbled against Candace's lips.

Candace chuckled. "We'll be right there, Shell."

"Good. Leave the Bible in the drawer," Shell cracked as she left.

Jameson shook her head and Candace kissed her again.

"I love you, Jameson," Candace promised.

"I love you too. Now, let's go marry off Jonah."

"Mommy!" Cooper called into the room.

"Nana!" Spencer called.

Candace laughed. "Yes, boys?" she looked over at the pair of toddlers.

Jameson smiled at the two boys. They both had on jackets that were slightly too big for them. Finding a suit coat for a toddler was no easy feat. Jonah and Jameson had taken the boys early that morning and bought them each a black tie. The two boys looked adorable. Jameson found herself making an effort to imprint the moment on her mind.

"Uncle is waiting," Spencer made his way to Jameson and pulled on her hand.

Jameson laughed. "I'm coming. Just let me say goodbye to Nana."

"Momma!" Cooper looked at Jameson sternly. "Jonah needs you."

Candace laughed. "You'd better get moving," she said.

Jameson rolled her eyes, kissed Candace sweetly and put her hand out to the boys just as Laura stepped into view. "You look amazing," Jameson complimented her as she left.

"She's right," Candace said. "You look stunning."

Laura sighed nervously. "I hope he thinks so."

Candace smiled. "I promise you, you are the only thing he will notice," Candace said. She made her way to a small table at the corner of the room and opened the drawer. Candace pulled out a small box and handed it to Laura.

"What's this?" Laura asked.

"Open it," Candace said.

Laura complied. She lifted the lid and covered her mouth with her hand. "Candace, this is…"

"They were Pearl's. Marianne got my mother's when she married Rick. I saved my grandmother's for Shell," Candace explained.

Laura lifted the string of pearls from the box. "I can't…"

"Yes, you can," Candace said. "Someday, you can pass them to one of your children," she told Laura. "That's how it works."

"Can you help me?" Laura asked. Candace nodded and fastened the pearls around Laura's neck. "Candace?"

"Hum?"

Laura turned to face Candace. "I…I just wanted you to know that I never thought I would have my Mom to be with me today. Now, I have two."

Candace smiled. "I am glad you feel that way," she said, taking Laura into a hug. "Jonah is a lucky man."

"I think I am the lucky one," Laura said honestly.

Candace pulled back from their embrace and took Laura's hand. "Well? You ready to become part of this asylum of ours officially?" she teased. Laura nodded happily. "Good. Let's go get you admitted."

THE NEXT DAY

"Lawson."

"You did this," Lawson Klein accused the man sitting before him.

"That depends on how you look at it," Grant Hill replied calmly.

"Why?" Klein asked.

Hill leaned back in his chair and took a deep breath, exhaling it slowly. "Someone wise once told me that politics is a great deal like fairytales."

"Really?" Klein challenged the man in disgust.

"Yes," Hill answered. "I had the same reaction as you initially. Ridiculous, I thought. It's true, though. There are kings and queens, pawns, three headed beasts, dragons to be slain, and knights who set out to slay them."

"You've lost your mind," Klein surmised.

"Have I? I don't think so."

"This is no fairytale, Grant."

Grant Hill smiled. "Isn't it? That person gave me a piece of advice that I have never forgotten," Hill continued. "When you face a beast as your opponent, you had better attack with accuracy and make certain that the beast never sees it coming. Otherwise, you risk simply striking a nerve. That, Lawson? That is when the beast becomes the most dangerous."

"Fairytales," Lawson scoffed at the notion. "It's war, Grant. It always has been."

"Perhaps. The same analogy would apply. There is nothing more dangerous than an injured opponent who can see you coming," he said.

"You just set Candace Reid on her throne. I hope you are happy," Klein spat.

Hill shrugged. "Did I? I think it could be argued that you are the one who secured that place for the governor without any help from me."

"I've been fighting this battle…"

"You have done nothing more than strike a nerve. And, not just with Governor Reid," Hill replied.

"FVI is nothing without the Klein endowment."

Hill smiled. "It's only money."

"Hardly. You have no idea who you are dealing with."

"Is that a threat?" Hill asked pointedly.

"It's a reality," Klein returned.

"Be careful, Lawson," Hill cautioned. "You are acting like the king when you are nothing more than a pawn. Knowing your place is half the battle."

Lawson Klein's face grew hot and red. He pinned the younger man with a fierce stare. Hill remained unflinching and unfazed. "I warned you," Klein hummed.

Hill nodded. "Thank you for your service, Mr. Klein."

Lawson Klein stared at Hill for another moment, his eyes boring into the man. Hill continued to regard Klein impassively until Klein turned on his heels and headed out of the office.

Grant Hill exhaled slowly and shook his head. He lifted his cell phone from the top of his desk and promptly made what he was certain would become one of the most important calls in his life. He steadied his breathing as he waited for an answer, aware that he had chosen his side and dubbed himself a knight in the middle of an epic battle.

"No turning back now," he muttered as he waited on the line.

"Good Lord," Candace looked out of the back door into the yard where Jameson was setting up chairs. "How did this turn into a huge affair?"

Pearl laughed. "In this family?" she waved Candace off. "Small never stays small. Besides, you love it."

"I have to do it again in a few weeks—with a reporter in tow, I might remind you," Candace said.

"Look at it this way, it's all practice," Pearl said.

"For?"

"Well, you've got at least two more to marry off, maybe three," Pearl observed. "That doesn't count the grandkids. God knows, how many of those you'll send down the aisle before you're done."

"Oh, dear God," Candace sighed dramatically. "Let's hope they don't all want to get married here and have a barbecue."

"Hey, you started the trend," Pearl reminded her.

"Simple, it was supposed to be simple," Candace replied.

Pearl laughed. "No offense, Candy. Simple has never really fit in this family. And, this family isn't getting any smaller."

Candace laughed. "Truer words," she agreed.

"Mom?" Michelle poked her head into the kitchen. "There's a call on the house phone for you."

"Who is it?"

Michelle shrugged. "He said to tell you that it was Beanie? Who is Beanie?" she asked. Candace smiled. "I take it you know him?"

"I do," Candace replied. "Shell, I'll take it in the study. I'm sorry," she turned to Maureen and Pearl. "I hate to ask..."

"I can finish a salad," Maureen Reid replied. "I can finish your glass of wine too while I am at it," she teased Candace.

Candace chuckled. "Feel free. I have at least two more bottles," she quipped as she left the room. Candace went into her study and closed the door. She lifted the receiver of her phone. "I've got it, Shell."

"Okay, Mom. I'll leave you to Beanie," Shell cracked. "Whoever that is," she said as she hung up the phone.

"Governor," a man's voice spoke respectfully.

"Beanie, huh?"

"That is what you used to call me, isn't it?"

"I remember," Candace said.

"It's done—for now."

Candace took a deep breath and let it out slowly. "You're taking a big risk."

"I wish I could tell you that it's dead, Candace," he said.

Candace nodded silently as she gathered her thoughts. "It's not easy to kill an ideology."

"No," he agreed. "You can sever its limbs. Cutting out its heart? Not so simple."

"Be careful, Grant."

"Worried about me?"

"I will always worry about you," Candace said honestly.

"And, I will always have your back," he said. "Do you remember when you told me to think of politics like fairytales?"

"I remember."

"It doesn't feel much like a Disney movie," he said bluntly.

"Ah, you forget, Grant. Fairytales seldom have happy endings, at least, not for everyone," Candace reminded him.

"He'll be back, Candace."

"I know."

"We'll be ready," he promised her.

"We will have to be," she said. "Be careful," she repeated.

"You too."

Candace hung up the call. She sensed a presence in the doorway and looked up. Jameson met Candace's gaze.

"Problems?" Jameson asked.

Candace shook her head. "More like risks," she replied.

"Anything I can help with?" Jameson inquired.

"I promise, you will be the first to know when there is," Candace said honestly.

"Candace," Jameson called to her wife suspiciously.

"Jameson, there are some things that are best left as they are. Please trust me on that."

"What aren't you telling me?"

Candace slowly made her way to Jameson and cupped Jameson's face in her hands. "Please, trust me."

"I trust you with my life. I know when you are keeping something from me."

"It's not my story to tell," Candace said honestly. "At least, not entirely."

Jameson nodded. "You know that you can tell me anything, don't you?"

"Yes, I do," Candace said.

Jameson closed her eyes. There were times when Candace held back information from Jameson. Whenever Candace became reserved, it always equated to Candace's work. Inevitably, that had ties to their family. It frustrated Jameson at times. Jameson wanted to protect Candace and their family as much as Candace felt inclined to protect everyone. One thing Jameson had to remind herself frequently was the fact that Candace had many people beyond their immediate family whom she sought to protect. Sometimes, that compromised Candace's safety—emotionally, mentally, financially, and politically.

"I wish you would let me help you," Jameson whispered.

Candace kissed Jameson softly and smiled. "You do," she told Jameson. "Now, come on. This house is going to be filled over capacity in a few hours."

Jameson caught the gleam in Candace's eyes and smirked. "And?"

"And your mother is finishing my salad, and my wine if I am not mistaken."

"Uh-huh," Jameson smirked.

"And, Marianne and Scott have the kids in the pool," Candace lifted her eyebrow.

"Yes?"

"And, I still need to take a shower," Candace explained.

"So?"

Candace tugged on Jameson's shirt. "And, so do you."

Jameson smirked. "Are you calling me dirty?"

Candace looked Jameson up and down. Jameson had been planting some flowers with the boys that morning and she was still sporting dirt on her neck, her shirt, and her pants. Candace raised her brow at Jameson and shook her head. "You are worse than the boys. How is it that you manage to wash your hands and nothing else?" she asked Jameson playfully.

Jameson licked her lips and smirked.

"Jameson..."

Jameson grinned evilly and wiggled her eyebrows.

"Oh, no," Candace warned.

Jameson took a step closer.

"Jameson, don't you dare!"

Jameson swept Candace up and over her shoulder. "You need to cool off, honey."

"Jameson! Put me down!" Candace demanded.

"Nope," Jameson answered as she marched down the hallway and into the kitchen.

"Jameson Reid!" Candace demanded again. "Put me down, you lunatic!"

Maureen and Pearl looked up as Jameson swung open the back door.

"Do something!" Candace implored her mother-in-law and Pearl.

Pearl looked at Maureen and shrugged.

"Pearl!" Candace called back from her position over Jameson's shoulder.

"What does she expect me to do?" Pearl looked at Maureen. Maureen laughed. "Those two are worse than the kids sometimes, I swear it."

Jameson kept moving toward the pool while Candace pounded lightly on Jameson's back.

"Don't you dare," Candace warned as Jameson stepped to the side of the pool.

"You said I needed to clean up," Jameson said.

"I said a shower!"

Jameson loved teasing Candace, and she also knew that Candace loved the game just as much, no matter how much Candace protested.

"Nana!" Spencer laughed.

"Mommy!" Cooper called over from the edge of the pool.

"Mommy wants to go swimming," Jameson said.

"I do not!"

Scott leaned over and whispered to Marianne. "I don't think most people would believe that."

Marianne grinned. "What? Their governor getting tossed into a pool?" she laughed.

"Mommy!" Cooper yelled.

Jameson lowered Candace when she heard a tinge of fear in Cooper's voice. Candace stood on the edge of the pool and grinned at Jameson. "I win," she leaned in and whispered, swiftly spinning them about and pulling Jameson down into the pool with her.

Spencer and Cooper started laughing hysterically when Jameson surfaced with Candace clinging to her.

"Very funny," Jameson said as the boys kept laughing.

Candace pulled Jameson to face her and kissed her soundly. "I win," Candace whispered again.

Jameson nodded. "That's debatable, Governor," Jameson replied, placing another kiss on Candace's lips.

"Good Lord!" Shell called out as she made her way toward the pool. "There are children present!"

Candace and Jameson broke apart and both shrugged. Spencer paddled his way to the pair.

"This family is nuts," Scott laughed.

Marianne turned to him and smiled. "Want out of the asylum?" she asked him.

Scott looked at her and took a deep breath. "No."

"Think they know it?" Pearl asked Maureen as they looked out the back door.

"Scott and Marianne?" Maureen guessed. Pearl nodded. "They know."

"Mmm."

"What are you thinking?" Maureen asked.

"I'm just wondering if Jameson will need to add another addition to this house soon," Pearl chuckled. Maureen looked at Pearl curiously. "Seems we add a kid or two every few months," Pearl explained.

Maureen laughed. "Well, if things go the way I am betting, they will be in a different big white house in a few years."

Pearl nodded. She watched the display unfolding in the yard. Candace looked twenty years younger to Pearl as she played with Jameson and the two boys in the pool. But, Pearl knew Candace better than anyone. She could see the faint lines of strain on Candace's face even in the distance. Their family had grown exponentially. And, there were many people in Candace Reid's life that Candace considered family. Pearl knew that too. It wore on Candace at times. Pearl exchanged a momentary glance with the woman she had always considered a daughter. For the moment, all was calm. The storms had passed for the time being. Laughter filled the air around them. There was a wedding being planned, children growing in their midst, new friendships blossoming. But, behind it all, Pearl could see the clouds in Candace's eyes. The life Candace Reid had chosen meant she was called to lead not only a family, but something far greater. That calling came with a price tag. At times, a high price tag.

"Pearl?" Maureen tried to discern the older woman's expression. "Do you think she will? Make a run for the presidency?"

Pearl smiled and nodded. "She won't want to, but she will."

"She won't want to?" Maureen questioned.

Pearl turned to Jameson's mother. "There are things she loves more," Pearl gave her explanation. "Ironically, it is those very things that will convince her to do it."

Maureen looked back out the window. Jameson was helping Candace out of the pool. "Think they'll make it through that?" she asked honestly.

"That is the only thing I am sure of at all."

THE END

TO BE CONTINUED IN

ROAD BLOCKS

www.ingramcontent.com/pod-product-compliance
Lightning Source LLC
Chambersburg PA
CBHW060519180626
46817CB00002B/406